TO BEDEVIL A DUKE

Lords of London, Book 1

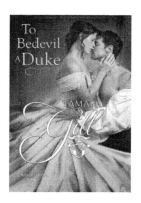

A Duke of many rules. A Lady of independence.

Since her cheating husband created a scandal by dying beneath his whore, Darcy de Merle is determined to enjoy widowhood, and refuses to mourn a man she grew to loathe. Setting the ton ablaze, Darcy holds a ball to re-launch herself into Society on the anniversary of his death.

Cameron, the Duke of Athelby plays by the rules. Always. He's lived through the terrible consequences of what revelry, carelessness, and lack of respect for one's social position can have on a family. So, when he sees Darcy de Merle skirting the boundaries of respectability, it is only right that he should remind her of the proper etiquette that she should adhere to.

Darcy refuses to allow another man to tell her what to do. When the Duke of Athelby chastises her at every turn, reminding her of her social failures, well, there is only one thing to be done about it… seduce the duke and show him there is more to life than the proper conventions set by the ton.

A battle of wills ensues where all bets are off, numerous rules are broken and love becomes the ultimate reward.

CHAPTER 1

London, 1805

Lady Darcy de Merle was foxed. A most scandalous and terrible way to be at her own ball, but the ratafia was quite delicious this evening, and surely she could be excused for imbibing more than she ought when celebrating the one-year anniversary of her husband's death and her relaunch into London Society.

Darcy looked down at her golden silk gown with small puffed sleeves. The empire cut accentuated her small waist and ample bosom enough to garner many admiring glances from the opposite sex. Her dark locks were pulled up into an intricate motif atop her head, and small loose curls fell about her face, softening the look. The pairing of golden gown and dark hair complemented her, and for the first time in years, she felt attractive.

Her departed husband, the Earl of Terrance, had never made her feel so. He was not missed, and it had taken all of Darcy's good breeding to wait out the twelve months required for mourning. Especially when she would never mourn such a man. On his death, he'd left her nothing, which she had expected. Not that it impacted her very much. Her grandfather, having loved her most out of all his female grandchildren, had left her the London townhouse along with a very tidy sum should she ever require it. Darcy had been named for her grandfather, and had chosen to once again be known by his name from the day she'd placed her husband into the cold earth. Her father, the Earl de Merle, had supported her in her choice. Having been witness to her husband's indiscretions, his vile temper and cutting tongue, he was happy she reverted to the name she was born with, not the one given to her upon marriage.

It wasn't to be borne for a de Merle to be treated so shabbily, and as such, Darcy had clasped her freedom upon his death and would not look back. Life was to be lived, and she would never exist again under the atrocious circumstances she'd endured with Terrance.

The Viscountess Oliver and Darcy's dearest friend, came to stand with her. "You look positively decadent in that golden gown Darcy, and you know it. Your husband would have a seizure if he knew you were holding one of London's biggest balls in honor of the anniversary of his death, and your debut back into Society."

Darcy smiled in welcome. Fran was a tall, lithe woman with the most beautiful auburn hair, a trait from her Scottish roots. It amused Darcy that her husband, a man she should never have married in the first place, would be insulted by her actions. Oh, how she'd love to see his fat, ruddy cheeks blossom in annoyance and anger at her defiance of him. "How wonderful that sounds. But you know, as a woman renowned for scandal, I could not allow such an opportunity to pass. One must keep up the standard to which they intend to live. If I did not, that would be a scandal in itself."

Fran linked their arms and walked them along the outer edge of the ballroom floor. "You smell of wine. How much have you had this evening?"

"Enough that I know I should have no more, and I promise I will not." Although Darcy loved nothing more than scandalizing the ton, she would only ever go so far, and never crossed the invisible line that even her family's name could not redeem her from. Two years into her marriage she'd decided that she would no longer live as a doormat to her husband, and had begun attending parties again, dancing and flirting her way about London. Her husband did not approve, would bellow and break furniture and valuables, but Darcy had had enough. If she could not divorce the man, she would at least live her own life, just as he did.

"The last thing you want is to be compromised by a money-hungry rake, looking to catch you at your most vulnerable," Fran said. "Unless of course you wish to be married again."

Darcy gasped. "Not in a million years, Lady Oliver. The last thing that I want is another husband. Although now that I'm free from Terrance, I may look for a lover."

It was her friend's turn to gasp before she grinned, just as she used to when they were young women at Mrs. Dew's Finishing School for Young Ladies in Bath, before they were about to sneak off and have some fun that the teachers were never aware of.

"There are many gentlemen here this evening who'd be only too happy to oblige you, I'm sure."

Darcy looked about. There were a few gentlemen looking her way, some nodding slightly, others giving the best smouldering look they knew how to perform. And maybe one of these men would do. Certainly, Mr. Ambrose could prove useful. That he was a wealthy American and would not be staying long could be a point in his favour. A lover this Season was paramount for her happiness and sanity, if she were honest.

Not that her friend Fran knew, but Darcy had attended a masked ball one evening that opened her eyes to the pleasures women could have. She hadn't participated, merely skulked about drinking champagne, but many others were more than happy to explore, and become better acquainted with the opposite sex within only a matter of hours.

As Darcy was fetching her cloak, ready to leave, she overheard a woman that sounded to be behind the cloak rooms' door, making sounds unlike anything she'd ever heard before. It had been one of ecstasy, of begging and gasping, and she'd wanted to know what it was that the woman adored so. How did a man make a woman react in such a way? Her late husband had never fulfilled her needs, and by the time he passed away they'd not shared a bed for a year or more.

"What do you think of Mr. Ambrose?" Darcy asked, taking two glasses of champagne from a passing footman, ignoring the fact she wasn't supposed to be having any more to drink.

"Delicious," Fran said, giggling. "Although please do not tell Lord Oliver I said such a thing. You know how he can be."

Only too well. Viscount Oliver, Fran's husband of two years, was devoted to her, and at times could be quite the jealous husband. Not that Fran would ever wish to leave him. They were, in Darcy's estimation, quite a lovable couple. Perfectly made for each other.

"I would never tease his lordship, so even if I wanted to

manner. The duke was a towering terror that made most debutantes shudder in their silk slippers, and gentlemen walk with care.

Not Darcy though.

She'd merely dismissed him as a man who thought too much of himself, as he always had. Not a feature that was at all redeeming. That Darcy's godmother—his grandmother and only surviving relative—thought he held qualities that would suit her and other women was an absurd notion. He might be a gentleman, a duke even, but his manners—his lack of knowing when to speak and when to hold one's tongue—made it debatable. Women did not want to be chastised over what they wore, or how they ate, or who their friends were. The duke was only too willing to point out any little flaws if he deemed them so. Darcy shook her head. His grandmother seemed to think Athelby had a heart. How wrong she was.

It was really quite unfortunate that the woman was so completely blind.

"The duke is a no, I can promise you that. He's a young, handsome man until he opens his mouth, and then a grumpy, middle-aged man appears. It is no surprise to me he's not married, for who'd put up with such a displeasing creature?" Although he wasn't displeasing to the eye, her words were not as true as she'd wanted them to sound. Sometimes when he laughed, which wasn't often, she glimpsed the boy he'd once been in the man he'd become, and she longed to have him back.

"Creature may be too harsh a term, Darcy. Maybe his grandmother is right, and he's merely misunderstood."

Darcy shook her head, smiling at Fran. "You've always wanted to see the best of people, but sometimes it just isn't there. And I for one did not escape a marriage, a husband who treated me like a piece of dirt beneath his hessian boots, to merely marry another who would do the same. God forbid that my gown be a little too low cut, or that if I sat before a fire my ankles showed. The duke would have an apoplectic fit! I couldn't stand it, and you know papa would never survive seeing me married to another uptight prig."

Fran laughed just as her husband walked toward them, the grin on his face foretelling that he was here to claim his wife for the waltz that was due to start.

He bowed to Darcy and then Fran, taking his wife's hand before kissing it softly. "I believe the next dance is mine to claim, my dear."

Fran blushed. "I do believe you're right, my lord." Fran grinned over her shoulder as she walked away. "I will be back soon, my dear."

They walked off and joined the other couples that were congregating on the dance floor. Darcy watched them, and the others, as they started to glide through the graceful movements of the waltz. It was a dance she herself loved, but in her current situation, it was probably best that she hadn't been asked to engage in it. No one wanted to see a woman fall over due to her decidedly unstable foxed feet.

"I see you've consumed too much wine this evening," the Duke of Athelby said, startling her.

She smiled up at him, knowing just how well that would annoy him. "I have, and how liberating it is. And you should probably consider yourself fortunate that I am a little foxed."

"And why is that, Lady de Merle…if that is what you're calling yourself these days."

"Why yes, it is. And you do know, Duke, that you're standing next to a widowed woman, someone who has been used, and is not as perfect as we all know you're fond of. Maybe it wouldn't be wise for a man with such stellar manners and an impeccable reputation to be doing such a scandalous thing."

"I'm sure I shall survive, even though your vulgar ball, which is being held exactly twelve months to the day since your husband's funeral, is far from appropriate. I fear such a move will limit the time my grandmother may spend with you in the foreseeable future. I cannot have her reputation tarnished in such a way."

Darcy narrowed her eyes. "Tarnished? You are trying to make me laugh, yes? How absurd that a woman of your grandmother's age would even be worried about her reputation. Are you sure that the real reason you don't want her around me is due to your narrowed views on life?"

The muscle in his jaw worked, always a sign he was fighting to remain civil. Keeping his temper was not something the Duke of Athelby was famous for. Darcy studied his profile, his strong jaw and straight nose. The man was devastatingly handsome, his features severe and powerful. There was a time, when they were both still children, that she had been determined to marry him. He'd been carefree then, as wild and boisterous as herself, and for the month-long house party that their parents had attended, to which they had been brought along, they had been inseparable. It was years before they met again, and by then Cameron had come into his title and the fun-loving, incorrigible, laughing boy that she'd known was gone.

"It is my wish for the connection to be severed somewhat. It is for the best. You must see that," he said with an arrogant lift of his head.

Darcy spotted his grandmother strolling their way and smiled in welcome. "Ah, I see Lady Ainsworth is here. Maybe we can ask her about your new rules."

Athelby sputtered but didn't have time to divert his grandmother before Darcy took the older woman's arm and led her over to a settee near an unlit hearth. The duke followed, and Darcy did her best to ignore his black scowl. The viscountess kissed Darcy on the cheek and kept her hands firmly clasped in her own.

"How is my dear, dear goddaughter? I hope you're enjoying yourself this evening?"

"I am, my lady, very much so, but I've just had the most distressing news." Darcy looked up at Athelby, his steely gaze locked on her. It did odd things to her stomach having his attention in such a way. She turned her attention back to Lady Ainsworth to escape it.

"Your grandson has just informed me tonight that our association must come to an end."

"Now, those were not my exact words—"

Her ladyship held up her hand, halting her grandson's explanation. "What did he say, my dear? You have my full attention," she said, casting an irritated glance at Athelby.

"Due to my husband's death, and holding this ball twelve months to the day since we laid Terrance to rest, the duke believes that I would only bring shame and ruination to your family should we be seen together. This ball is a garish act and one that casts me in the light of a woman who did not love her husband." Not that she had at all, but her ladyship didn't need to know that. "And so, we must part from this night on. Never to be seen together again, I'm afraid."

"Your sarcasm is not lost on me, Lady de Merle," the duke said, glaring to the point that his brows almost joined, and not caring who in the upper ten-thousand saw it.

Darcy wanted him to be aware of her annoyance, and although she smiled sweetly at Lady Ainsworth, what the duke had said earlier was not to be borne. How dare he make her feel like she was the one who'd done something wrong. That her conduct was somehow worse than her husband's whoring and gambling, most of which was with her money. Another little prickle in her soul was that she'd had to walk away from Terrance's London home, a house she'd rightfully saved from being taken back by the bank upon his death. How could she not celebrate being rid of a complete fool? She would not pretend to have a broken heart, or to be a sad little widow.

"Well, that is absurd, and I can assure you, my dear," Lady Ainsworth said, her jowls shaking a little in wrath, "I will be spending just as much time with you as I always have. Your mama was one of my closest friends, no matter the twenty-year difference between us. I promised her that I would care for you until the day I died, and I will not, no matter what my grandson has to say about it, deviate from the honor."

"Thank you, Your Ladyship."

"Grandmother, see sense. If I'm to find a wife of similar standards to my own, surely you can see that our family being associated with a renowned hellion, a woman who flaunts her freedom from the marriage state with little care for her reputation, would not show us in a favourable light," he said, beyond frustrated.

Lady Ainsworth sighed, looking down her nose at her grandson. Not the easiest of feats considering his grace was standing, and both Darcy and her ladyship were sitting. "I will not hear of such stupidity again. Really, Cameron, do step off that high horse you seem so acquainted with these days and return to our level."

Darcy's lips twitched, and she fought not to giggle at the reddening of his grace's cheeks. Really, he was being silly looking down on her so. "What if I promise that whenever I'm around her ladyship, and yourself for that matter, I will be on my best behavior?" she said, taking pity on the man. If it meant she could continue socializing with

Lady Ainsworth, she would take care. When she decided to enjoy her Season and all the opportunities this and others might bring, she never meant to inadvertently hurt others. If his association with her would hurt his chances of making a match, then she would behave herself while around him.

"You're around us tonight, and yet you're foxed. Not that my grandmother has noticed such a thing."

"Oh, for pity's sake, it is a ball, and one that is being hosted by me. I may drink if I wish, and I'll not have even a duke tell me what to do."

"That is enough, both of you," her ladyship said, casting them both a dark glance. "Anyone listening would think you're a bickering married couple already, like so many around us. Your Grace, you do not have the right to be so opinionated about someone who has been a family friend for many years. You need to remember that if you cannot say anything nice, you do not say anything at all."

"I think, Grandmother, that is the first logical thing you've said this evening. It is also my cue to leave." He bowed. "Good evening, ladies," he said, heading in the direction of the ballroom doors.

Darcy growled, throwing daggers at his back as he made his way through the ton. Argh, the man was infuriating and so high and mighty. She had equally good breeding—she was a de Merle. How dare he look down his nose at her.

"Darcy, my dear. I know your mind is no doubt coming up with multiple ways of getting back at my grandson, but please let him be. I'm hoping that when he gets a wife, his emotional wall and his rather cutting opinions may abate a little."

"I doubt that they will, but I promise I shall not cause trouble for him," Darcy said. "We differ in opinions, and no doubt will again. I will not stop inviting him to events or talking to him should our paths cross."

"Thank you, my dear."

Her ladyship paused, a small frown line between her brows the only indication that she was concerned about the duke. Otherwise Lady Ainsworth was a very attractive woman for her age. Of course she had smile lines, and her hair was grey, but otherwise, time had been very kind to her.

"I think my grandson is lonely. And I do believe that is why he's so angry at the world. He spent his formative years with no one to argue, play, and share secrets with. The brothers had an age gap of over ten years, they hardly knew one another. He's grown so used to his own company that I think he finds it hard to socialize. As was demonstrated this evening."

A pang of sadness tweaked inside Darcy at the memory of the carriage accident that had taken the life of the duke's elder brother. But remembering his ungentlemanly words, she tried to push aside any inclination to feel sorry for the duke. Not very successfully, however. "I'm sure you're right, Lady Ainsworth. A happy union is just what his grace needs, and maybe this will be the Season that he finds a woman to warm his bed."

"Sometimes I think you're the perfect person for Cameron. You both certainly have a wicked tongue," her ladyship said, a calculating twinkle in her blue orbs.

Darcy chuckled, waving a footman over to bring them champagne. "We would not suit, and I'm not looking to marry anyone. Marriage to Lord Terrance was quite enough for one lifetime."

Her ladyship sighed, taking a small sip of her champagne. "Well, that is a shame, for I would love to have you as a granddaughter as well as my goddaughter. But," she said, a sad tilt to her lips, "one cannot have everything that they wish. I often fret that I shall never see the two people I care for most happy and settled in the world."

Darcy took her ladyship's hand and squeezed. She was not immune to her words, that often sparked guilt within her. And knowing it was completely on purpose on her ladyship's behalf made her smile. "Do behave, Godmother. I know what game you're playing, and once again, his grace and myself do not suit. My only connection to the gentleman is through you, and that is where it shall stay. As stated previously tonight, and many times at previous events, if you recall."

"One must try to make you understand, my dear. It never hurts to plant a suggestion in someone's mind, for it to germinate and possibly make them wonder if it has merit."

"You're incorrigible," Darcy said, laughing.

"I know," her ladyship replied, no remorse whatsoever in her tone.

Darcy looked back at the duke and tried to imagine him in her bed. He was certainly one of the most striking, powerful men in London. In the throes of passion, wild and wicked, maybe he would look even more so. He turned and looked down at Miss Watson, whom he was currently conversing with, frowning and looking as though he was chastising the poor woman. Darcy shook her head. No, he would never do.

His grace looked up and their gazes smashed together. The pit of her stomach clenched and her cheeks flushed from the inspection he bestowed on her. What a shame she disliked him so much. Or was he like his grandmother said —merely misunderstood?

CHAPTER 2

C ameron, Duke of Athelby strolled down Bond Street, his cane tapping a beat on the cobbled foot-path as he went. People moved out of his way, a common occurrence for him and a helpful one. A few debutants that he'd seen the previous evening at Almacks tittered as their mama bade him a good day. Without stopping and only giving the slightest bow, Athelby continued. Weston's, his tailor, was not much further, and he didn't have time to stop. The new cravats he had ordered last week were not to his standard and became limp halfway through events, and it was not to be borne. He would need to speak with Weston himself, to have the situation remedied. His clothes, along with his reputation, must always be of the highest standard.

No one would ever describe the Duke of Athelby as a man without respect for himself or his name. Never would he allow scandal to tarnish his title again. If his late brother had taught him anything, it was that the family name and what the ducal title meant to people must never be taken for granted. Never used or abused for a life of reckless follies.

His step faltered and he almost dropped his cane when Lady Darcy de Merle, as she was calling herself these days, stepped out of a fabric emporium laughing at something her ladies' maid said. He frowned. Who laughed with their servants? Really, the woman had no shame.

He studied her as she continued her conversation. Darcy was striking, with ebony locks and the darkest, longest lashes he'd ever seen on a woman. Her lips were full, but not overly so. On her coming out she'd been married before the Season's end, and his one regret was never having danced with her. They had been friends once, a long time ago, but a lot had happened since then.

She caught sight of him, and her features shuttered. He ignored the pang of regret that darted through him. It was such a pity to see the smile that had lit her beautiful face fall from view. She curtsied—the shallowest he'd ever seen—as he bowed.

"Your Grace," she said. Or spat more like, as if the word was toxic on her tongue.

"Lady de Merle. I see you're quite recovered from your exertions last evening."

She stared at him a moment, and he had the oddest urge to shift on his feet. An absurd notion, since he'd done nothing wrong. He'd merely pointed out that it was she who had been foxed last evening and made a fool of herself. And after such inebriation, it was quite common for the person inflicted to be ill the following day. Or so he'd heard. He never partook in such pastimes. On top of being morally well-behaved, he also did not drink. Just the thought of having to cast up his accounts was enough to halt any such thoughts, if he had any. Which he had not.

"I am, and what wonderful exertions they were, Your

Grace. But I'm sure, with your stoic way of life, you would not know what I'm talking about."

He clamped his jaw as annoyance tinged her tone, trying to curb his irritation that she'd made a total fool of herself the previous evening. Women should not be foxed —it wasn't becoming, and certainly not for an earl's daughter. She would never fit his mould of duchess. No wife of his would indulge to excess, gossip, or act without decorum. No matter how beautiful she may be, even now looking up at him with eyes that could bewitch the strongest man, Darcy de Merle would not do. Ever.

"I do not, no." He glanced toward the shop from which Darcy had exited and quickly looked away when he spied a woman inside twirling before mirrors and her admirers. They really ought to put up curtains to stop the passing public from seeing such a thing.

"What a shame, Your Grace," Darcy said, waving down a hackney cab like a commoner. "For if you tried a little fun, you might just have some. Good day."

Athelby gaped at her but shut his mouth with a snap when he realized Darcy and her maid were laughing at him.

He walked on, not bothering to wait for her hackney to pull away. To think that his grandmother would like that piece of muslin to be his wife was an absurd notion. And she'd had many absurd notions over the years when trying to matchmake him with some preening miss new to town.

No one so far had met his exacting standards, and in all honesty, it was becoming a problem. He was no longer the young man he had been—within a few months he would turn nine and twenty. He was well due to settle down and beget some heirs.

He didn't want to lower his expectations, and yet...a wife was proving hard to acquire. His brother, God rest his soul, never had trouble with women, and it was a carriage race over a woman, his betrothed no less, that had taken his life. Although Athelby had only been young when his brother had passed away, the pain of his death had wrecked his mother and father, which was something he would never have inflicted on them.

There were women who'd turned their gazes his way, but he'd simply directed his in the opposite direction. None of them had been suitable. The ones he had courted always proved, eventually, that they would not suit. Their laughs were grating, or they were too skittish around a duke, or not skittish enough. They gossiped too much or hung about him with an air of desperation he could never abide.

He wanted a woman similar to him. One who played by the rules, spoke only when required, and did not enter into the games of the ton. Surely such a woman was not impossible to find.

The image of Darcy laughing at him, her mischievous nature that had once been the sole focus of his life—at least for the month-long house party they had attended as children—taunted him. He'd thought her perfect, and fun, not something he thought a girl could be. She'd not lost that love of life, but instead of admiring her for such a view, all it did was vex him.

Disregarding his cravats entirely, he went to White's and was soon ensconced in the first-floor sitting room. He accepted a copy of the *Times* from a footman and started to read the latest political dramas to keep his mind from wandering to the vexing Darcy who aggravated him to no end.

The leather chair across from him groaned as someone sat down, and Athelby wanted to growl at the interruption. He was not of the mind to have another conversation that would probably be as annoying as the last one he'd had on Bond Street.

"Your Grace," a deep, familiar voice said from behind his paper.

Hunter, or the Marquess of Aaron as the ton knew him, was probably the only gentleman in the ton Athelby called a friend. "Aaron, I did not think Thursday was your day for White's."

"It is not, but there is a thousand pounds up for grabs due to a bet which I could not pass up."

Aaron loved gambling, and no matter how many times Athelby lectured his friend on the pitfalls, the stupidity and dangers of gambling, he chose not to listen and continued to squander his family's fortune. Not that the man didn't have more than enough to last him ten lifetimes. However any such waste was really not appropriate.

"Are you not going to ask me what the bet is about?"

Athelby lowered his paper and gave his friend his full attention. "Even though I do not care, I'm sure you're going to tell me in any case."

"I thought the bet would interest you since it involves your family."

"My family!" Athelby sat up, closed his paper, and placed it on the table before him. "What on earth could a bet here at White's have to do with us?" His mind raced as to what it could possibly be about.

Aaron laughed, sitting back in his chair as if it was a lark to see him so addled.

"Well, not really your family, but certainly a close friend of yours and your grandmother's goddaughter," he grinned.

Darcy. "What are they betting on her ladyship this time?" Not that he wanted to know, but still, with the knowledge of what was happening here, he had reason to speak to Lady de Merle and try to correct her manners so that not one of these gentlemen would win such a sum. It was not to be borne.

"They're betting that sweet piece of muslin will be married before the end of the Season. Or have a lover. I should say there are two bets, five hundred pounds apiece —one for marriage, one for a lover."

The notion of Darcy taking a lover made him want to be physically ill. He blinked to clear his vision of her enjoying a man using the carnal knowledge she had gained from marriage. He'd never admit it to anyone, but the day she'd announced her betrothal to the Earl of Terrance something had died within Athelby, curled up and rotted away. Not that she had ever been meant for him. It had never been that way between them. Friends yes, lovers never. It was simply irritation that she had managed to accomplish something that he had not.

That was all it was. Nothing more.

The little devil now sitting on his shoulder snickered and whispered *liar* in his ear, and he flicked a piece of lint from his coat.

"And you're going to add your name to this bet?" Athelby met his friend's amused glance with a narrowed gaze.

"I am and so should you. You know her better than most. I bet should you ask her she may even tell you her choice. For it is rumored she's looking for a lover, and it would be a fool indeed who turned down that little fox."

Athelby clenched his fists and reminded himself that Lord Aaron was his friend. "If she asks you to be her lover, I would hope *you* would turn her down."

Ire flashed in his eyes before he crossed his long legs before the table between them. "Absolutely not! I'm not a simpleton."

The words hit Athelby, another blow to his gut or possibly a little higher. What was wrong with him? It was certainly not jealousy, although the emotion he was experiencing was eerily similar to it. Whatever it was, he would mention it to his doctor at his next appointment, which occurred weekly. One should not ignore their health, and being a duke without an heir, keeping healthy was paramount.

The thought of being jealous of who took Darcy de Merle to her bed was a ridiculous notion and not something any sane man would consider.

"As she's my grandmother's goddaughter, I would hope because of our friendship you would indeed say no to an affair with the lady, and help prevent any trouble she could find herself in should she sleep with a man not her husband."

Aaron sighed, nodding slowly. "I see your predicament, and it's to your credit that you're worried about her. But men of our ilk know how to ensure no unexpected gift is bestowed and delivered several months later."

"You cannot guarantee that, and she would indeed be ruined if that befell her. I ask again, as your friend, do not try to seduce Darcy. She is not for you."

"Who is she for then, shall I ask?" His friend steepled his fingers before his chin and watched him with eyes that could read a blank page, Athelby was certain. "You, by chance?"

"Certainly not," he protested with a laugh, but the sound came out hollow, and that little devil again whispered *liar* in his ear. "I cannot tolerate her wayward manners or flagrant disregard for rules and manners within our society. Sometimes I despair that she is even of noble blood."

"Oh, but you forget who her family is and their strong-willed, proud heritage. The de Merles are not people who can be told what to do. They make the rules that the rest of us should follow. If we don't, we're left out in the cold and soon forgotten."

How very true. It had always surprised Athelby that Darcy seemed to be able to do and say whatever she pleased without ever receiving censure from society. It was almost as if the family were immune to the repercussions of their scandalous pursuits.

"Well, I would be quite happy to be left behind if it meant not living the life that Darcy de Merle seems determined to inhabit." Athelby stood, and straightened his jacket. "I bid you good day."

"Shall I see you at my sister's ball this evening? You know it's her first since marrying the Earl of Glenn, and Sara has always been fond of you."

"I sent my response directly after receiving the invitation. I shall be in attendance."

Aaron grinned. "Very good. See you this evening then, Your Grace."

Athelby left White's. Thankfully his coachman had followed him on his jaunt and was parked out front, so he was able to leave directly. He tapped on the roof with his cane and stared sightlessly out the window. Why did the thought of Darcy moving on with her life, loving someone else and possibly marrying another gentleman, annoy him so much?

He called out the window for his coachman to take him to the residence of Dr. Duncan, his physician. He needed to see his doctor posthaste. There wasn't a moment to lose, for there was certainly something wrong with him. And the name of this disease was Darcy de Merle.

DARCY, and her friend Lady Oliver, had enjoyed their evening so far at the Earl and Countess of Glenn's first official ball since being married at the end of last Season. Darcy had always been fond of Sara and was delighted she'd made a love match with Lord Glenn, who'd always been kind and amiable to others.

One person Darcy didn't particularly wish to see was unfortunately across the room, although tonight he seemed a little out of sorts.

She studied the Duke of Athelby as he spoke to the hosts and the countess' brother, the Marquess of Aaron. The duke held a tumbler of what looked to be brandy, and the notion he would consume such a beverage gave her pause.

"I can see who you're looking at, and I can also see the clock within your mind ticking over as to why he's drinking," Fran said.

"Do you think it's whisky he's drinking?" Darcy had to admit that seeing him throw it back and ask for a refill left her positively astounded.

"It is a little odd, to say the least. Maybe he's trying to be more like his peers, although I doubt that would be the case. Everyone knows how much he detests gambling, drunkenness, and inappropriate behavior."

Hmm. Darcy watched him for a little while longer before a throng of beaux bowed before her during the next few hours and she was swept away into waltzing and cotillions, and all thoughts of the duke were forgotten.

That was until some hours later, when she walked out onto the terrace to find the Duke of Athelby bent over the balustrade, groaning.

"Athelby, can I be of assistance? You do not look very well, your grace."

He cringed noting her presence. "I'm mortified to say

that you've come across me, Lady de Merle, in a state of inebriation. What a hypocrite you must think me."

Darcy smiled, and even though she was certainly thinking it, she wouldn't tease him about the fact right now. He really did seem quite ill. "It's actually a relief to see you such. I had thought for some time that you weren't human."

He barked out a laugh and then groaned. "I'm human, I promise you." His words were slurred, and the duke looked anything but ducal right at this moment. "I know you think I'm a pompous fool. A man who thinks too highly of himself."

Darcy met his gaze. "I won't lie to you since we were friends as children, but yes, I do think that sometimes. But I also wonder why. You never used to be like that, Cameron."

It seemed that her use of his given name wasn't missed by him, even in his foxed condition. Surprisingly he took her hand, idly playing with her fingers. "If anyone saw me now they'd think I was my brother. The drunken fool who couldn't hold his liquor."

"You don't talk of Marcus very often. And you do yourself a discredit, Your Grace. You're nothing like your brother."

He sighed, running his other hand through his hair. "I fear that with only the smallest coaxing I could turn into him. And where would that leave the title, my home, and tenants who rely on me?"

"You are foxed. That will not make you your brother. And anyway," she said, placing her hand over his that continued to clasp hers. "What was so wrong with being like your sibling? I only vaguely remember him, but the times we did meet I never thought him an ogre."

"He was my brother, and I loved him, but I refuse to

follow him into an early grave." Cameron groaned and, turning toward the gardens, retched all over Lady Glenn's roses.

He waved her away, but instead of leaving, Darcy pulled his white handkerchief out of his coat pocket and handed it to him.

The duke took it and wiped his mouth before groaning and dropping his head as he sat on the stone balustrade.

"When I'm better I will kill the Marquess. Aaron stated it was merely a new punch that Lady Glenn's cook had created. I will not forgive the man his duplicity."

Darcy rubbed along his grace's shoulders and ignored the fact that beneath her hand was a very firm, muscular man, more so than she'd thought. She pushed aside the thought of what he'd look like without his shirt and instead said, "I shall fetch you some water. I will be right back." After hearing his fears of turning out like his brother, she couldn't help but feel for the man. In his quest to be the perfect duke, he'd become a man who never relaxed, who no longer knew how to live, even in moderation.

She did as she promised and within a few minutes returned to where she had left his grace, only to find him missing.

"I am here," he said, the slurred voice sounding from behind her.

She looked about then went and sat next to him in the small alcove that was situated between two windows. The rooms were not lit, and not in use this evening, so they were kept hidden. Probably a fortunate thing considering his grace was not very well. Should anyone catch him in such a state, the gossip that would befall him would not be easy for the man to take. Such a stickler for proper manners, he could not bear to be seen as anything other than what he preached. And after tonight, she understood a little as to why that was. His grandmother had tried to tell her in her way, but it wasn't until Cameron had explained that Darcy understood him better.

"Drink this, but only in sips. It should make you feel better."

He took the glass and did as she bade, not saying a word, merely sitting there like a lost little boy. Although he didn't look like a boy at all. In fact, the disarray Darcy now saw him in—untied cravat, messy hair that was no longer suitably combed, and slightly bloodshot eyes—made him look wild, untamed, and nothing like she'd ever seen him before.

In fact, the duke in this unkempt state was exceptionally handsome.

"Please do not tell anyone of my state. I know we're not friends, but please, if you can do this one thing for me I'll be forever grateful."

Darcy turned her attention toward the garden, seemingly thinking over his grace's question, though she knew she would never tell of his shame. She might be a woman who enjoyed parties, dancing, and revelry, but she was not a snitch or a gossiper. And she could never make fun of a man who'd had a cruel joke played upon him.

She turned to look at him and a shiver stole over her when she found him staring at her. In this dark alcove, his grace seemed predatory, nothing like he normally was. It left her a little unsure and wary. Maybe it was she who'd had too much wine this evening.

"I will not tell a soul, ever. You have my word."

His grace sighed and leaned back against the house. "I feel dreadful. Is this normal? If so, I wonder why so many people indulge in such pastimes."

"You drank quite a few glasses, Your Grace, and in quick succession. It is no wonder that you do not feel well."

Darcy stood, holding out her hand to him. He took it and stood.

"Walk to the front of the house, and I shall have your carriage called at the same time as mine. Return home, keep drinking water, and get some sleep. You may have a megrim tomorrow, but you should start to feel better by the afternoon."

The duke took her hand, bending over it and kissing her gloved fingers lightly. "Thank you, Darcy."

It wasn't often he used her name. In fact, she couldn't remember the last time—maybe it was when they were thrown together as children. Again a shiver of awareness flowed through her, and she stepped back to break whatever absurdness was taking over her body.

"You're welcome, but go. Wait in the shadows and you will see your carriage soon enough. And may I suggest in future not to listen to Lord Aaron. You know how much he loves to have a laugh at others' expense."

"I do, and his lordship will have his comeuppance if it's the last thing I do."

Darcy smiled and left, doing what she promised. While waiting for her own carriage, she watched as his grace came from beside the house and stepped up into his vehicle. Again, she was reminded of how tall he was, his athletic form that she'd not noticed until tonight.

She sighed, wrapped her cloak tighter about her, stepped down the three steps from the house and climbed up into her own carriage, calling out the address for Sir Richard Walton's card party that she'd also been invited to. With her good deed done for this evening, it was still early, and more fun was to be had. And maybe, just maybe, luck would be on her side tonight and she would win a few hands instead of always donating her funds to others' deep pockets.

CHAPTER 3

Darcy did not see his grace at any events over the next several days. She put it down to the duke being embarrassed over what she'd seen him doing and the state of his dress and appearance. Not to mention what he'd told her of his brother, which in his inebriated state may not have been on purpose.

Now, after too long a time, Darcy wanted to see him—something she'd never thought to imagine—if only to see for herself that he had survived his night of drunkenness and was well again. Back to his normal self, insulting matrons and scaring the breeches off young bucks who acted without decorum. This evening she'd not even seen her godmother, whom she'd been told had returned to the family's country estate after coming down with a cold. Darcy would have to write her well on the morrow and wish for her speedy return.

Darcy's heart thumped when the master of ceremonies called out the Duke of Athelby. She turned to see his grace making his address to their hosts.

He searched the crowd as he walked through the

gathered throng before his gaze caught hers and did not shift. Darcy smiled at him, nodding slightly, and he in turn came toward her, the sea of people seemingly moving out of his way so his progress was swift and without incident.

Darcy curtsied, holding out her hand as he bowed, kissing her fingers slightly. "Lady de Merle. I hope I find you well this evening?"

"And I you, Your Grace."

Understanding dawned in his eyes and he laughed. Darcy stood mute for a moment. The duke had a wonderful, rich laugh. A laugh that lit up his eyes and changed his stoic look to one of animated delight.

Damn it all to hell.

"I am very well, and I promise to only drink non-spiked punch this evening."

She smiled. "You know, there is no crime in having whisky, champagne, or wine, Your Grace. As long as it is in moderation."

"And this from a woman who not a week ago was in her cups."

Disappointment stabbed at her that his grace's attitude had not changed. Here he was, back to his cutting jibes within five minutes of arriving at the ball.

"I may have been foxed, but I did not have the pleasure of regurgitating it like others are wont to do."

His jaw clenched. "Touché. I cede your point."

"I should think so."

Lord Aaron joined them and bowed before Darcy.

"I believe this next set is mine, Lady de Merle."

Darcy dipped into a curtsy before the duke, not missing his flash of annoyance that the marquess had asked her to dance. It sparked a little devil inside of her to play up to his lordship and irritate Athelby more than she ought.

"It is, my lord." Darcy took his hand and let him lead her to the dance floor as others set up to join in a quadrille.

The dance gave Darcy the opportunity to find out why the marquess had played such a trick on his friend. "Did you know that the punch you gave his grace last week was anything but punch, and was, in fact, some sort of beverage that made him foxed?"

The marquess grinned, laughter in his eyes. "I did know, but my sister's cook is very clever indeed, and anyone drinking the brew had no idea that too much of it would leave you in your cups."

"I thought you and the duke were friends. How could you let him get into such a state knowing he is against those sorts of vices?"

"Because," the marquess said, growing serious, "if he does not loosen up a little, see life for what it is, that it is to be lived and enjoyed, it will end with him a lonely, bitter old man. I do not want to see that for him. He deserves better."

"That, my lord, is something we at least agree on, but I would ask that you do not trick him in such a way again. It was not becoming of you."

The marquess seemed suitably chastised. "I promise I shall not. But what of you and your concern for him? I did not think you even liked Athelby."

What the marquess said was certainly true. They were not close, nor was she very fond of him up until the night she found him vomiting onto roses. But she had been associated with his family as a young girl and owed it to his grandmother to look out for him if she had to. "My love for his grandmother and our friendship as children make me say these things. Do not read anything further into that concern, my lord."

The dance took them from each other for a few steps

before they were reunited. "Well, you may not be attentive toward the duke, but he's certainly taking notice of you," the marquess said. "Even now, he's watching, probably trying to find fault with both our steps."

Darcy frowned. It was not very becoming of his lordship to laugh at his friend so. Having had enough of him, she stepped out of his hold and dipped a quick curtsy. "If you'll excuse me. I find I do not wish to dance with you, my lord."

He raised his brows, clearly shocked. "You do not?"

"No," she said. "I think you're a dolt."

The few people about them gasped and some of the gentlemen laughed before she walked over to the duke and took his hand, pulling him onto the dance floor. "Shall we?" she asked.

With elegance and ease, Athelby guided her back into the steps. They were silent for a time before he said, "You seem displeased. Is anything the matter?"

"Only that you have very strange friends, Your Grace. If I were you, I would watch what you say around the marquess. He does not seem true to me."

"If what has your feathers ruffled is solely due on my behalf—for my honor—do not tax yourself. Aaron is just as honest as I am, if not a little less cutting. If he teased me before you, and said something that seems beneath our friendship, you should not worry about it. For I shall not."

"He said that you have a concern in me, beyond that of a friend."

The duke looked down at her, and she was shocked to recognize desire in his grey orbs. Who would've thought the too-proper duke even had such emotions in his indifferent body and mind?

"He is mistaken."

Really... Darcy narrowed her eyes, not believing that for a moment. "I'm relieved to hear it."

ATHELBY COULD SEE by the disbelieving lift of Darcy's brows that she did not agree with his statement, and she would be right. After her help the other evening, and the lack of rumors concerning his embarrassing slip of etiquette, she'd proven to him that she was trustworthy. More so probably than his oldest friend Lord Aaron.

"Do you know that there are two bets on me at White's as to who I'll take as a lover or even a husband?"

He pulled her closer than he ought, blaming it on the crush of dancers around them. "I do, and I have stated to those who have placed a bet that they are vulgar and not gentlemanly in the least."

She smiled up at him, and the breath in his lungs seized. Blast it, she was so beautiful, so kissable, that it hurt to deny himself. But she was not for him. The de Merles were too wild, non-manageable, and certainly did not play by the rules by which he set his life.

But to taste her, if only once, would surely sate him for the rest of his days.

"How do you know of this bet in any case?"

This time she laughed, a rich, intoxicating sound that almost undid his years of strict decorum and made him seize her here and now. Kiss those smiling lips until they were both lost to each other and noted nothing and no one else around them. He ripped his gaze from hers and stared steadfastly over her shoulder. Anywhere but at the temptation that was in his arms, which would lead him to ruination just like his brother.

"I know everything that happens in your secret little

White's, and I may have at first been a little put out about the bet, but I now find it quite amusing."

He couldn't see anything remotely comical about the bet. It was belittling to her and to anyone who partook in such scandalous behavior. Darcy did not deserve to be the butt of jokes and games of his fellow man. "I do not."

"I can tell by your face that you do not. But should I play the little game that all the gentlemen at White's are betting on? Who would you suggest that I marry? Or, alternatively, who should I make my lover?"

He stuttered, unable to respond straight away. "I wouldn't know how to give such advice."

She harrumphed, and he refused to look at her. How could he when he didn't want her thinking of any of the gentlemen of the ton in that way? Not that she was for him either, he reminded himself. He simply thought it best for Darcy to remain a spinster for the remainder of her days. Perhaps travel the continent and become an expert in embroidery. Anything but to marry again where he would have to watch her from afar.

"So you're not able to tell me which men I should consider and those I should keep well away from? You're around the gentlemen when they're ensconced in their little club. I should think you'd hear everything they really think and mean, certainly more than any woman would ever know."

"Even if I did know of a few gentlemen who'd be suitable, I could not in good conscience tell you of such things. It's against my moral judgement." He lost contact with her for a few steps before he pulled her out of the dance to stand beside a partially open window.

"Tell me, Your Grace, do you think your high moral judgement will keep you warm in bed? Do you not yearn for the comfort of a woman, to have her love you in all ways that a man and woman should?"

Athelby swallowed. This conversation was well beyond his knowledge. He tugged at his cravat that was suddenly too tight. "You should not say such things."

Darcy moved closer than she ought now that they were no longer dancing and yet, to his dismay and pleasure, he did not pull back or move away to where he was safe. Damn it, he was turning into his brother. A man who could not say no to a woman.

"Would you, do you think Your Grace, be suitable as my lover?"

He turned and looked at her, and blast, he could not hide what he'd tried to for so many months. To tell her that she was all that he thought of when alone. That when she'd been married to that coxcomb the Earl of Terrance, the thought of her with him in his bed, lying with him night after night, had tormented him. The stoic, cold man that he was could not wholly be blamed on his reckless sibling. A lot had to do with his jealousy of the earl and who he had as his wife.

But as much as he longed to have Darcy, he would never succumb to the baser elements that haunted many fellow men, not just him. He was not a rake, a rogue who would have any woman he wished, only to discard her when he no longer had use for her. Or engage in stupid carriage races where you ended up dead.

The woman he married would be an upstanding, well-connected virgin. A woman of impeccable manners. Not the bedevilling minx staring up at him right at this moment, daring him with her crystal blue eyes to bend down and kiss her before all the ton.

"Never, Lady de Merle. We would not suit." His words were cutting, and he tore his attention away to the gathered throng so as to ignore the flash of hurt and despair that had entered her eyes.

"What about your friend the Marquess of Aaron? Maybe I should take him to my bed."

He clasped her arm, pulling her to look at him. "You will not, and nor will he."

She raised one brow in disbelief. "And you know this how?"

"Because I told him to keep his filthy hands off you." He turned on his heel and strode toward the supper room doors just as a footman announced the short repast was ready. He did not turn back, yet the burn of Darcy's gaze at his back scolded him and did not abate for the remainder of the evening.

***

Darcy found it hard to sleep that night, and many nights after, for thinking about what the Duke of Athelby had said to her before he scuttled off like an injured wolf.

It wasn't to be borne. He could not just say something like that and then leave! And no matter how much they might dislike one another, there was an odd attraction between them that they both needed to admit to.

Act on...

She lay back in her bath, splashing water onto the floor. *What am I to do with this absurd attraction?* Athelby was not the kind of man who indulged in liaisons. Something tugged inside of her. Had he ever been with a woman at all, in any way? Not just intimately, but even a simple kiss?

After what he'd told her of his brother, she doubted he would've allowed himself the slightest slip in giving into the base desires of man.

Tonight was the Foxes' masquerade ball, a sought-after event that marked the middle of the season. She had not attended when married since Terrance had forbidden it.

Of course, his denying of her own entertainments did not stop him from taking part, and often returning home with ripped clothing, a missing mask, and numerous love bites over his neck and body.

The door to her room opened then closed just as quickly before the light footsteps of her maid pattered across the Aubusson rug. "Your gown is ready, my lady. Would you like me to help you out of the bath?"

"Yes, thank you," Darcy said, standing, and took her maid's hand as she stepped out. The gown of royal blue with a second skirt of embroidered gold thread would suit her dark colouring and golden mask. "I'll wear my hair half down this evening, Jane."

"Yes, my lady."

Within a couple of hours, Darcy found herself in the ballroom for the masked ball. The terrace doors were open, allowing the hundreds of revellers to walk the lawns and gain some air should they wish it.

The abundance of candles, the patterned gowns, and the beautiful masks would make finding anyone she knew difficult, and yet there was only one person that she really wanted to find.

She danced a couple of reels and the first waltz with a gentleman who played as coy and secretive as she did. For her first masquerade, she found she was enjoying it very much. To be incognito was liberating, and she was pleased to find her flirting abilities had not died along with her husband.

It was while dancing a jig, where many a partner was changed during the movement of the dance, that a shiver of awareness ran down her spine. Her new partner clasped her hands and moved her along with the dance.

She looked up and recognised Athelby's grin. "We meet again, Your Grace."

"I see my mask has not fooled you." He did not sound pleased, but Darcy paid no heed to his tone. Tonight, she would kiss this man if it were the last thing she did. Once and for all, she would see if this absurd attraction she had to him was warranted or some figment of her warped imagination.

"I would know you anywhere, Athelby." And if she did not recognize him by sight, her body alerted her to his presence. Just as it had this evening, and if she were honest, for many years before.

ATHELBY FROWNED DOWN AT DARCY. Anything but let the little minx know that having her in his arms again left him reeling, warring with his morals on what he desired to do and what he ought to do.

The biggest conundrum he had, and one he hated to admit to, was that Darcy made him nervous. Each and every time he was around her he fought not to babble like a fool. And after their discussion about who would suit her best as a lover or future husband, something told him that his nervousness would only increase.

"I find that hard to believe, Lady de Merle." He used her title, not her given name. The less intimacy between them the better. Or so he told himself. Even though the dance commanded he change partners, he kept her in his arms.

"Do you? I simply have to look for the angriest-looking gentleman, the one who's scowling at everyone, and I know I've found you. Even behind your mask you ooze annoyance. You're like an elephant trying to hide behind a stick."

"Really, what an absurd analogy." Athelby tried to take offence, and yet he found his lips twitching to smile. He would again discuss this maddening attraction to a woman who wasn't suitable to be his duchess at his next visit to Dr. Duncan. Surely there was a pill of sorts one could take to cure themselves of feelings.

The dance ended, and he walked her toward the terrace doors. "Would you care for a stroll? You seem a little flushed."

"As long as you do not try to seduce me, Duke." Darcy grinned up at him and slid her arm about his, leading him outdoors. The air was chill, but refreshing after the stifling ballroom.

"Your reputation is safe with me. I should say, you're probably the safest woman in England right about now." Not exactly true... Out of the corner of his eye, he watched her looking up at the stars, and his gut clenched at how very pretty she was, the mask no impediment to her beauty.

They strolled toward the back of the garden, the sound of running water and some whispered voices all that could be heard. With the Foxes' estate backing onto Hyde Park, the gardens were quite extensive, and there were many places people could disappear to for a tryst or stroll.

Athelby would not be one of them.

A marble bench glowed under the moonlight, and he led Darcy toward it to sit for a time. Taking the opportunity, he pulled off his mask, and was glad to see Darcy did the same.

"Have you ever kissed a woman, Your Grace?"

The question caught him by surprise and he spluttered before answering, "Of course." He'd kissed his grandmother hello and goodbye, and other family members too. So, in all truth, what he stated was not a lie. Not really. But he understood her question, and the truth was, no. He'd never kissed a woman with passion. To make them both yearn for and crave what kisses were wont to lead to. His brother kissed too many women in his younger years, and his foolish actions all in the name of women led to his early demise. He would not make the same mistake. He was the last surviving Athelby heir. If he died, the ducal title would die with him.

He could feel Darcy regarding him, and as much as he wanted to not look at her, he couldn't help himself. He turned, and the pit of his stomach clenched in the most intoxicating way. A feeling he'd never suffered before, but wanted to again and again.

"Would you like to kiss me, Athelby?"

God damn it yes, he did. "No."

CHAPTER 4

Damn him to Hades and back. After such a question, the last thing Darcy thought any sane man would do was stand upright as if he'd been poked by a scalding fire iron and take ten paces. She remained on the seat, watching him, not yet ready to give up her quest for the evening.

Athelby needed to be kissed, to be shown that just because his brother may have passed away after a very reckless life, it did not mean that one kiss with her would lead him down the same road. The man needed to be shown that life could be passionate without peril, disaster, and death. Not everyone was like his late sibling.

"No, I would not. I do not know what game you're playing, my lady, but I do not find it amusing in the least."

She shrugged. "I want to kiss you, so I asked if the feeling was reciprocated. You have stated it is not. There are no hurt feelings or broken hearts, I merely wanted to show you that by kissing me, the ducal line shall not fall. It'll be there tomorrow just as it is today. That is all."

"You wanted to use me?"

She barked out a laugh, not the most ladylike thing to do, and yet for the first time ever, his grace didn't scold her about it. "No, I wanted to kiss you. Simply a man and a woman enjoying each other." She stood and sauntered over to him, amused when he retreated away from her until his back came up against a large oak tree.

"I do not want to kiss you, Lady de Merle."

"No? Well, that is a shame." She ran her hand down the lapels of his coat, the accelerated breathing and heart rate telling her more about what the duke was feeling than what he was saying. "Aren't you the least bit curious about what it would be like? We've rarely got along, but maybe we would get along grandly in this regard."

The more she spoke about kissing the man, the more she wanted to reach up and do it. Take his lips, that looked perfectly in proportion to the rest of his face, and see if they were as soft as she suspected they were.

"We would not," he said, his attention snapping to her mouth.

Darcy bit her bottom lip, and didn't miss the clench of his jaw. Oh yes, the duke wanted to kiss her. And if she were a woman of the world, which she was in a way, he wanted to do it with a desperation that she herself admitted.

"Just a little one. You wouldn't deny a lady that small request, would you?"

He frowned, and she clasped the lapels of his jacket, going up on her toes so as to reach him better. "Do not deny me, Duke," she whispered.

"Damn you, Darcy."

She gasped as the little control she'd had just a moment ago vanished and she was seized by the duke, wrenched against his chest, his mouth coming down hard against hers, his tongue thrusting against her own.

She moaned, shocked and delighted at the pleasure that coursed through her. She had not anticipated wanting to do a hell of a lot more with the duke than kiss, but she certainly did now.

This would never be enough. She wanted more, so much more, and the hard part would be how she could get what she wanted. How to convince the duke that they could be together like this, without his fear of becoming a debauched rake like his brother impeding his decision.

He held her firm, his hands slipping further around her back where one thumb brushed against her bare shoulders. Darcy tried to keep up, but her mind was spinning. The duke could kiss, very well, considering he'd not kissed anyone like this before.

He may say otherwise, but knowing him and his ways, Darcy was sure she was the first.

Leaning up further on her toes, her breasts brushed him as she slid her hands through his hair, keeping him exactly where she wanted him. The kiss turned molten, and she grappled not to lose the little control she still held.

ATHELBY SLID his hand over her delectable body, barely hidden by her silk gown, and clasped her thigh, lifting it a little against his own. His breath came out in a rush and his heart threatened to burst. Darcy kissed him with a desire that ignited him to flame. His cock hardened, painfully so, and her pleading whimper when she rubbed against him almost made him lose himself in his breeches.

He ought to be ashamed of himself. This was not what he should be doing with her. His moral compass had completely deserted him. He tried to think of his brother —his death and the woman behind it. Remind himself that his sibling's recklessness over a woman—a woman the family would never have allowed him to marry in any case —was the reason he participated in the stupid carriage race that killed him.

But when Darcy slowed the kiss, her tongue coaxing his, all Athelby wanted to do was ravish her. Take everything and all that she would give. Her kiss was all that he thought it would be, and it would never be enough. Not for him.

"Let me court you, my dear. I need more than just this one night," he said, taking her lips again as if his life depended on it.

DARCY'S MIND whirred at the mention of courting. She'd already married a man who was controlling, mean, and vindictive. Not that the duke was vindictive, but he could certainly be cutting, and he liked control most of all. She might wish to take him as a lover, but never as a husband. She did not escape by chance one terrible marriage, only to enter another of very similar particulars.

She wrenched herself out of his arms, and he stepped toward her, his gaze unfocused and mad with desire. "What are you doing?" he asked, breathless.

"Saving us from a mistake." She righted her gown and fixed her hair, holding up a hand when he reached for her. "No more, Your Grace. I shouldn't have teased you so into kissing me, and I apologize."

He stood there, shock and annoyance settling on his features. Then he took a calming breath and ran a hand through his hair, looking about to see if anyone had been watching their blatant fondling session in the garden.

"It is I who should ask forgiveness. I was carried away with unexpected emotion." He bowed. "Good evening, Lady de Merle."

Darcy placed a hand across her lips to stop herself from asking him to stay, to finish what she'd feared for some weeks now was between them. Desire—a scorching, intoxicating need for each other—that she feared she had sparked to life tonight with her teasing and their kiss.

He collected his mask, and she watched him disappear up the garden path. She sat back down on the bench. There was only one way forward from tonight. She would have to keep well away from the duke, not attend any events that he might also attend, and try to keep herself from doing exactly what she wanted to again.

Take the Duke of Athelby to her bed.

ATHELBY HAD, up to tonight, been successful in avoiding Darcy de Merle. But upon entering the musical loo hosted by Earl Musgrove and his wife, which was to be followed by a light supper repast, his days of avoidance were over.

He stood at the front of the music room, where Lady Musgrove had set up chairs before a makeshift stage where fellow guests would perform, and a small orchestra would play to complement the singers.

In the past, he had enjoyed these types of events very much. He did not have to converse too much with those attending, and with supper served just afterward, most were eating, and therefore conversation was again not overly required.

His location gave him the perfect opportunity to watch others as they arrived. He nodded as the Marquess of Aaron talked to him about the latest Crown Lands Act in Parliament, but his mind was otherwise engaged. In fact, his mind and body had not been his own for the past fort-night. It belonged to another.

Endless hours of reliving the kiss he'd shared with Darcy haunted his mind. His body ached as it never had before. He'd lost count of how many times he'd woken in the middle of the night, his cock as hard as a rock. Sometimes, at his lowest ebb, he'd found his hand had been clasped about it, stroking it, teasing it as he wished she had.

It was utterly mortifying and inappropriate, and he would quite literally die of shame should anyone know what he'd been thinking. What he'd been longing to do with the little minx who stood laughing at something her friend Lady Oliver was saying. The way he was going, he would be as debauched as his brother before the Season's end.

"If you keep staring at de Merle the way you are, you'll be made to marry the chit. What have you done with the lady that's made you so possessed with her person?" Aaron asked, taking a sip of his wine.

Not as much as I'd like to have done.

Damn it. He wrenched his gaze down to the floor and studied the parquetry for a moment. "I've not done anything with her ladyship. She merely annoys me."

Torments me...

"The betting book at White's now states that Lord Thomas and Sir Fraser are front-runners in contention as her lovers. They've been quite attentive to her, and she's certainly allowed them to show their affection, if you understand me."

"She's allowed them to kiss her?" He shut his mouth with a snap and stood tall, lifting his chin so as not to show that the mention of Darcy kissing another hurt. Hurt like bloody hell.

"I understand Sir Fraser has had the pleasure, but then, you know with these young bucks, they often tell tales just to boost their own self-importance."

"They should not be associating their scandalous behavior with Lady de Merle if it isn't true. Her reputation could be tarnished by such rumors."

"She is striking, I must admit. And I've meant to apologize for my behavior the other week. My teasing of you was not warranted, and I'm sorry I spoke of you in such a way to Lady de Merle."

Athelby nodded once. "Apology accepted. But you should not concern yourself. I never take any notice of your nonsense when you're in your cups."

The marquess snorted, lifting his wine glass up in salute. "As you should." He paused for a moment. "Lady de Merle does seem to take an interest in you though, Athelby. Are you sure you're telling me the truth that there is nothing between the two of you?"

There was a lot between them, but nothing he would ever admit verbally. Not even to his closest friend. He raised his attention to where he knew Darcy was located and their gazes locked. Again, his stomach somersaulted in the most dizzying, intoxicating way and he clenched his jaw.

Damn it. He'd hoped after being away from her these past weeks such a reaction would not occur. How wrong he'd been. If anything, it was worse.

Denial, it would seem, made the bond grow stronger.

"You've kissed. I can see it between the two of you as clear as air. And you want to do it again. Admit it, man, you've had a tryst with de Merle."

"No tryst, just a kiss." Blast, he had not intended to say a thing about it. He wrenched his attention away from Darcy and frowned at his friend. "Do not tell anyone of what you know, and do not put my name down as a contender for her ladyship's hand, either in marriage or as a lover."

"I think you could be a contender for both, for the way she's looking at you right now, I would say you're more likely to be her lover before anything else."

The thought of having Darcy beneath him in his bed made his blood beat at a crescendo that even the instruments about to play could not reach. "I will not sleep with her. Ever." To do so went against all his morals, the way in which he'd lived his life. Fleeting liaisons were not who he was or ever would be. He was a respectable, upstanding duke. Not a rake.

"Oh well, from the looks of Sir Fraser you've missed your chance. And Lady de Merle seems quite pleased by his attentions, if I'm any judge of character."

"I do not care." Athelby sat and steadfastly refused to move his attention from the stage, even though the singing was yet to commence. Aaron sat beside him, shaking his head, but apparently deciding not to voice whatever it was he was thinking.

Athelby thought that was for the best, considering his mood was decidedly soured. Whether it was due to Darcy fawning over another gentleman, acting inappropriately yet again, or because it was not he himself that she was acting inappropriately with, he couldn't be sure.

THE MUSICAL NIGHT hosted by the Earl and Countess Musgrove was something Darcy had been looking forward to, up until the point when she saw Athelby in all his elegance standing beside the Marquess of Aaron, his dark, intense inspection of her rattling her more than she'd like to admit and leaving her flushed.

She had resolved to keep her distance from him, and had done quite well until now. Their set was wide and varied, and it hadn't been hard to avoid him at the balls and parties they were both invited to. If she heard from his grandmother when he was to attend an event, she simply ensured that she attended at a different time.

It had all worked out splendidly, until this evening. A musical loo was not something she'd thought the duke would be interested in, and yet here he was, as handsome as ever, cold and aloof as he'd always been.

She shook her head as she ate a crab cake during the supper repast. After the music he'd seemed to disappear, and she assumed he'd returned home or moved on to attend another event. The fact that his absence left her a little bored and forlorn was not to be considered. She was determined never to marry again, no matter how enticing being courted by the Duke of Athelby might be. She could not risk another bad marriage like the one she'd had to endure with Terrance.

"Fran, darling, I'm going to use the ladies' retiring room, and then I think I shall leave. I wish to go for a ride tomorrow morning, and I'll never rise should I not head home soon."

Her friend handed her glass to her husband, who was standing with them. "Would you like me to accompany you?"

Darcy waved her suggestion away. "No, I shall be fine, and my maid is waiting for me there. You stay here and enjoy this delicious repast."

She exited through the door she'd seen other ladies slip through. A footman explained where the retiring room was and pointed her in the right direction. She walked past a bank of windows, some of which were bay in design. Red velvet drapes hung down on all of them, allowing privacy to anyone who sat upon the seat overlooking the gardens if they so wished. Walking past one that was drawn closed, she stifled a scream when a large hand came out and pulled her into the secretive alcove.

"You!" The wild, ravenous look on Athelby's face gave her pause, and she didn't say another word.

"Yes, me," he said, pushing her against the wall and taking her lips in a searing kiss. Against her better judgement and rules, her past mistakes and wishes for the future, Darcy clung to him, all but climbed up against his person and made herself as close as she possibly could while the kiss carried on.

It was too much. This need, the all-consuming obsession with him, could not be possible. "Touch me, Cameron," she gasped as he tried to lift her up to get them as close as achievable.

Failing that, he moaned and rocked against her instead. One hand fiddled with the base of her gown, before the cool night air kissed her ankle, calf and then thankfully, finally, her thigh. Athelby paused, pulling back a little to stare at her. "I don't know what to do."

Darcy fought to understand what he was saying through her desire-consumed mind before understanding dawned. Taking his hand, she guided him to where she wanted him to touch her most.

He didn't pull away and stop what she was showing him, and the fact that this man, a duke no less, was not skilled in the ways of what a woman wanted suited her. He was hers to mould. To teach touches, kisses, and whatever else they did together. To know no one else had been with Athelby like this was a powerful elixir that was hard to deny.

At first, his touch was hesitant, too careful, as if he was scared to hurt her. This kind of endless teasing was almost enough to send pleasure ricocheting through her. "Slide your hand against me, explore and learn me, Cameron."

• • •

CAMERON HAD NEVER, ever wanted to take a woman as much as he fought not to take Darcy. She stood before him, his to take, her legs spread as the wall supported her while he teased and touched the most private of parts of a woman.

When he'd pulled her into the curtained space, he'd not thought this would happen. He'd meant to chastise her for teasing Sir Fraser and leading the poor fellow on. But the moment she'd entered the space, all he'd wanted to do was kiss her. Taste her one more time.

The woman's anatomy was not as he'd expected it to be, and touching Darcy like this allowed him to learn what she liked, what made her gasp and cling to him like he was the only other living soul on earth.

"Athelby," she gasped when his finger found a peculiar, small entrance. Seeing if his touching of her there was something she enjoyed, he slid one finger a little way inside.

Darcy kissed him hard, her tongue meshing with his, and emboldened, he slid his finger fully in. It was then he realized she was riding his hand, just as he imagined a woman would ride a man's phallus.

His balls ached and were tighter than he'd ever known them to be. Other than the times he'd woken up in bed, panting and as hard as hell after dreaming of the woman who currently resided in his arms.

"I'm going to come," she whispered against his lips.

Her lips parted, her head tilting back as she continued to ride him. Athelby nibbled and kissed her while she peaked, her bottom lip clasped tight in her teeth to stop any notifying sound. In time she regained her composure, and already he longed to have her in such a state again.

He'd never slept with a woman before, probably a fact that Darcy now knew, and the pleasure she seemed to experience made him yearn to know if it would be the same for him. He'd gained so much enjoyment from watching her, to be more involved, finding his own release... would it be as addictive as he imagined it would be.

Just the thought had him wishing she'd undo his front falls, sit him on the bench at the window, and ride him until they both found release.

Their gazes locked, and instead of pulling away, Darcy wrapped her arms around his shoulders, kissing him lightly before she said words that were never truer. "We have a problem, Athelby."

And they did. A big one.

CHAPTER 5

Darcy sat astride her grey mare, Montclair, and galloped as fast as the horse would carry her down Rotten Row. The park was deserted, bar her groom Peter who sat atop his own horse under a copse of trees not too far away.

The sensation of flying always invigorated Darcy, and she patted her mare as they trotted to a stop, then turned her back toward her groom. They had been out for some time already, and soon the park would have the early morning riders who would not take well the sight of a woman, astride and galloping down the row. All faux pas according to the ton, and rules that Darcy always enjoyed ignoring.

She trotted back to Peter and smiled. "Time to return I think."

"Right ye are, my lady."

Darcy rode ahead, and as they walked the horses across the park toward the northern gate, a group of men entered on beautiful, well-bred mounts that Darcy couldn't help but appreciate. But one man stood out more than the rest.

Athelby.

They stopped and dipped their hats and Darcy in turn smiled but didn't slow. "Good morning, gentlemen," she said, liking the fact that all of them threw her admiring glances. Today she had worn her newly purchased silk jockey bonnet, which went perfectly with her navy-blue riding suit with gold buttons, and she looked almost regimental. Not to mention the colouring always complemented her blue eyes.

The men moved on—all but one.

"Go ahead, Peter," she said, stopping now that Athelby had. "I wish to have a word with the duke."

"Yes, my lady," he said, doing as she bid.

Athelby turned his horse to come up alongside hers. Darcy raised one brow but didn't say a word. After they had left each other two nights past, she'd not seen him at any events. Was he avoiding her again? More than likely, and it wasn't to be borne. He could not raise such deliciousness within her and then disappear. Her husband had never given her such pleasure in the short amount of time they were married, and other than giving herself release a few small times, with Athelby it was the first time a man had raised such emotions.

She wouldn't allow it. The Duke of Athelby was going to be her lover if it were the last thing she did this Season.

"Are you well, my lady?" he asked, his tone distant, and yet his eyes were the window to his soul, and she could see he was struggling. What that struggle was exactly, she couldn't be sure. Wanting her while fighting the emotion, or her ineligibility due to his standards, she would assume. He'd always been such a stickler for rules, so to disregard them after finding pleasure in her arms would go against all that he believed in.

He wanted her, of that she had no doubt. But would he

act on it, really act on it, and make her fully his? That, she wasn't certain of.

"I am very well, thank you. And you?" If he was going to be all formal and absurd, then so was she.

"I am well." His jaw clenched, and he looked away, adjusting his seat a little. The action made her attention snap to his thighs, and she bit her bottom lip seeing that he had very muscular legs and that the tan breeches he had on were very much accentuating his fine form.

It was crass of her to ogle the man in such a way, but really, what was one to do when she found him absurdly attractive, and if she had her way, she'd help him out of those breeches and not let him get back into them again until she was fully satisfied?

"I want to kiss you." His words sounded torn, a deep rumble that tumbled her common sense into dangerous ground.

Ignoring all sense of decorum, and considering they were a little way from the gates of Hyde Park, Darcy tempted fate. She leaned toward the duke and caught his gaze. "Then kiss me, Athelby."

His attention slid to her lips and for a moment she actually believed he would do as she asked, before he thought better of it and straightened his spine. "I cannot kiss you here."

She shrugged, knowing that was too true, but wanting to tease him a little about it in any case. "Pity, for I so dearly would love you to." Darcy pulled her horse to come around the back of his and took the opportunity to slide one finger across his bottom and down one leg as she went. "Are you attending the Leeders' ball this evening?"

"Yes," he said, pushing her hand off his thigh.

She grinned. "Maybe we can continue to further our acquaintance there?" Her words finally and triumphantly brought out a small grin from the duke, and Darcy chuckled. How handsome and approachable he was when he wasn't scowling at everyone, growling like a lion with a prickle in its paw.

"Well then," she said, moving off. "I shall see you there, Your Grace." She trotted away and didn't turn back to look at the duke, but she knew he would be watching her, more than likely debating all the pros and cons of doing what they both wanted.

Each other.

By MIDNIGHT, Darcy had all but given up hope that the duke would attend the Leeders' annual ball. She stood beside a grouping of house plants and swallowed down the last of the numerous glasses of champagne she'd already had this evening.

Damn him. If he thought to avoid her again, run away like a little man-child, he could think again. She wouldn't allow it. Even though tonight there was little she could do.

This late in the evening, the guests were well in their cups, and the dancing was still the focal point, although some of the gentlemen had wandered into the card room and commenced gambling.

Darcy sighed and placed her glass on a passing footman's tray, and debated taking another or going home. Even her friend Fran had left some hours ago, and Darcy had only stayed due to the possibility Athelby would arrive.

He would pay for this deception.

She took another glass and sipped. She would give him until the end of this drink to arrive and then she was going home. Distracted by her annoyance at the duke, she didn't notice the gentleman who came to stand beside her until a warm finger touched the nape of her neck and slid down the full length of her spine, all the way down to her bottom.

Darcy grinned as hope bloomed in her chest. She took another sip. "How very inappropriate of you, Duke."

He leaned close to her ear, his whispered words igniting fire in her blood. "I want to be inappropriate with you. Only you."

The breath in her lungs seized and she swallowed. She wasn't used to the duke turning the tables on her and being the one to seduce. It was normally she who goaded and taunted. Even so, it was refreshing and so very arousing to have him do it instead.

"Dance with me, Darcy."

This time she did place her glass down on a passing footman's tray, and let the duke lead her onto the dance floor for a waltz. She went into his arms willingly, needing to be close to him, to smell his freshly laundered clothes, his sandalwood cologne, and something else that was just Athelby.

A little alarm went off in her mind that she was getting herself too involved with him, seeing possibility where no possibility should be seen. "You're a very good dancer for a man who doesn't often take to the floor."

He moved them with grace and ease about the room. Considering his height and her own, they fit perfectly, and their dance was effortless.

"I had a very good teacher, and of course I was the most avid student."

"Why is that so easy to believe?" Darcy chuckled, and he frowned.

"You should not mock people merely because they take an interest in all that they learn. I have never done things by halves and I should not start now."

"And yet," she said, wanting to harass him a little more,

"you've teased me, only completed half of what I want you to do with me, so who is the bad student now?"

Desire burned in his gaze and she shuffled closer still. "I want you in my bed, Athelby. And I want it soon."

He tripped a little, but righted them quickly enough that no other dancers about them noticed. "Lady de Merle, while I—"

"Don't you dare, Your Grace. You will finish what we both started. What we both want."

For a time he was silent, and Darcy fought not to lose her temper with him. It was not at all gentlemanly, if this was a gentlemanly act at all, to cry off and leave her wanting him fiercely, while he pushed down his own desires and refused her. Right at this moment, she damned his brother to the pits of hell for scaring his younger sibling into being a prude.

"Darcy, I…" Again, he stumbled over his words, and she took pity on him. Maybe he wasn't going to cry off. Run away like she thought he would.

"What, Athelby? What say you?"

The little frown line was back between his brows, and she wanted to reach up and smooth it away with her finger. But here and now was not the time.

"I'm…I'm… God damn it all to hell," he swore. "I've never been with a woman in that way before," he whispered, looking about to ensure no one was listening.

Darcy didn't react, for she knew that already. Had suspected when he'd not known how to touch her. The kissing he had taken to very well and quickly indeed, but the touching of her at the musical loo had only occurred because she'd told him what to do, where to touch.

To know no one had had the man in her arms before was more exciting than anything she'd ever known in her life. To have it confirmed was doubly so. Maybe that was why husbands found gaining brides who were untouched so arousing. She could certainly agree with the notion a lot more now that she had Athelby in much the same way.

"I know," she said, playing with the little bit of hair at the base of his neck. "And if anything, knowing this only makes me want you all the more."

Their dance had slowed and they stood scandalously close, but for the first time ever, it seemed the Duke of Athelby was not concerned with proper etiquette and correct behavior.

"I will not have you at a ball," he whispered, pulling her into a tight spin as they came to the end of the room. "I want you in my bed. Not in a window alcove."

"I found our last rendezvous in the window alcove very rewarding indeed. I could make the same a possibility for you. There are ways, you know, for a woman to pleasure a man in much the same way."

He sucked in a breath and closed his eyes for a moment. "The thought of us, of you doing such things to me...please do not say it here. No one wants to see the Duke of Athelby hobbling off the dance floor with his cock pushing out the front of his breeches."

Darcy laughed, taking a quick glance downwards just for fun. "Take me back to your home. Let me show you all that there can be between a man and a woman."

"No. I do not wish to rush this with you."

Although disappointed, she could understand his caution. "Very well, we shall take it slow. But promise me that after this dance we will leave, together and in your carriage. If I do not kiss you soon, I shall expire."

Thankfully the dance came to an end, and they were able to make their goodbyes to their hosts for the evening. Darcy called for her carriage and spoke to her maid, notifying her that she had other transport to return home.

Using the shield of her own carriage, she walked two steps and jumped up into the duke's. No sooner had she sat on the squabs than did the horses move on and they were on their way.

"I told the coachman to drive around until advised otherwise."

Darcy went about untying the rolled-up blinds and pulling them down over the windows.

"What are you doing?" he asked, not moving from the seat opposite her, simply watching her with amusement.

"Making this little abode private so no one can see in."

"In that case…" Leaning forward, he snipped the locks on the doors and now they were fully alone and unable to be disturbed.

Settling back on her seat, Darcy watched him for a moment.

"What now, de Merle?" he asked, grinning a little.

She bit her lip, desire curling throughout her body. "What indeed, Athelby."

LATER THAT EVENING Athelby would wonder how the hell he'd not known a carriage could be a vessel of pure, unadulterated pleasure. For years he'd travelled within such an abode, seen couples alight from their vehicles and often deliberated why the women looked starry-eyed and the men most pleased.

His brother had certainly looked that way often enough.

Now he knew the reasons behind all that. For Darcy de Merle had shown him what they could have between them if he chose.

Darcy moved from the other seat and came to sit beside him. Hell's blood, she smelt good enough to eat. As sweet as a rose and just as pretty. Unable to deny himself, he cupped her jaw and kissed the side of her mouth. Small little kisses across her neck toward the base of her ear. His attempt to seduce her seemed to work, if her soft sighs were any indication.

"I'm going to pleasure you, Duke. Now sit back," she said, pushing him against the squabs. "And enjoy."

Damn it, he bit back a groan at her lascivious promise. As it was his cock sat rigid in his pants, ready and waiting for her to do whatever it was she had planned.

"Promise me that whatever I do, you'll not try to stop me. Know that what I'm doing is because I want to, that it's acceptable and will be enjoyable."

"Very well," he said, not willing to deny her anything.

He shifted his legs further apart as slowly, delicately she undid his front falls. He tried not to cringe when his cock sprang forward, eager for her touch. She ran her finger along the top of his cock, taking the little bead of moisture that sat there and sliding it between her lips, licking it.

"Fuck," he gasped, having never used such a word or imagined such an action was possible, or that anyone would want to do such a thing for that matter. But seeing Darcy do so had his heart beating a million times too fast, his body not his own. For right now, at this very moment, Darcy owned him. All of him.

And damn it all to hell, he wanted to do the same to her. Lie her back on the squabs, part her lovely long legs and lick her from ankle to core. The thought of what she'd taste like there, the crude naughtiness of it, left his cock more rigid and he fought not to clasp Darcy's cheeks and guide her over him.

Kneeling in front of him, her gaze captured his and her perfect pink tongue came out and licked him from base to tip. He fought not to pass out from the wonderful sensation of having her lick his cock.

He'd missed out on so much, and the thought maddened him before she stroked her tongue over his throbbing length again and he lost all thought.

"You're teasing me," he said breathlessly.

She grinned, licking him a third time. "Good things come to those who wait." But she didn't make him wait too much longer. Fascinated, he watched her lips circle the top of his cock and slide down, taking a good third of his phallus before she started the opposite way. He did clasp her face then, if only to anchor himself to reality. Darcy's sucking, licking, teasing of him was relentless, an endless torture that made his stomach clench and his balls ache. Her tongue was soft against his skin, pushing against his pulsating veins.

Dear heaven, he was lost...

For what was probably only minutes, but felt like hours of pleasure, she sucked him, used her small hand about the base of his cock and stroked while her mouth entwined magic about his soul.

Never did he ever have any idea such a thing was possible. That a woman would take a man so, and seemingly enjoy it, if Darcy's aroused moans and breathy sighs were any indication.

The carriage turned a corner and he caught her arm and braced them both by pushing against the window. Darcy adjusted and took him deeper, clasping his balls after each glide of her hand and mouth. The action, a little different than before but more determined, had stars form before his eyes.

He found himself pushing into her mouth—such an ungentlemanly thing to do, but he could not help himself. The need to reach the pinnacle that he'd long denied himself was too much to ignore. He wanted to fuck her mouth, hard, do base things with her and make her come against his own face.

All these thoughts bombarded his mind, and crying out, he climaxed. He tried to pull away, to save some dignity for himself, and her too, but Darcy wouldn't have it. She stayed fixed upon his cock, licking him, sucking and swallowing all that she pulled forth from his release.

His breath ragged, he stared at her as with a little wipe of the corner of her mouth, she sat back on her haunches and grinned. "How do you feel, Your Grace?"

How did he feel? By God, he felt lethargic, hungry for more, intoxicated, drunk on her and what she did to him. "I did not know that it could… That a woman could do such an act to a man. I never listened to the bawdy talk that sometimes occurs at my club."

She came to sit beside him, kissing him gently, slowly, in a way that only aroused him to want more of her. He could taste himself on her, and his cock twitched. "There are lots of things we can do, if you're willing."

He warred with himself. He wanted her, knew that he'd go mad if he didn't have her soon, but to engage in a liaison wasn't something he considered respectable. Darcy needed to be his wife, and perhaps, should he play by her rules for a time, she would come to see the same. He could not just sleep with a woman and then leave her to the wolves, something his brother often did.

He tapped on the roof, signalling the driver to return Darcy home. "Will I see you at the Duncannons' ball two nights from now? I will give you my answer then."

Darcy righted her gown and sat back against the squabs, tidying her hair and ensuring it was similar to how she'd had it set before going out for the night. "Very well, I shall wait to hear what you choose."

"Thank you," he said, frowning at the fact she was annoyed by his hesitation in having an affair with her. Not that he didn't want her—he did. Desperately so.

But by having her, losing himself to her, did that mean he also lost who he was, what he believed to be right? At this time, he couldn't see any other way forward but that path, and he wasn't sure anything, even Darcy, was worth losing his values over.

CHAPTER 6

Darcy sat alone under a large oak at her friend Fran's garden party and covertly watched the Duke of Athelby. He hadn't noticed that she was present, as her chair sat in a lovely shady spot, with some of the branches of the tree hanging down and partially hiding her from view.

She shifted her attention to her friend Fran, and for the first time she noticed a small bump in her friend's otherwise small waistline. She narrowed her eyes on the little mound. When was Fran going to tell her about that little bundle? She smiled at the thought of her best friend not only marrying for love, but starting a family, something she'd wanted to do ever since they were at Mrs. Dew's Finishing School for Young Ladies.

Today the duke wore tan breeches and knee-high boots that were so polished one was sure to see their reflection in them. His bottle-green coat hugged him like a second skin, and she flushed, remembering how she'd managed to delve beneath those fine clothes and give him pleasure. Have his large hands entwine in her hair, pulling her, holding her against his member as she pleasured him. Make the demanding, righteous Duke of Athelby crumble and come apart in her arms. And how delicious it was having him react so.

She crossed her legs, squeezing her thighs a little in expectation. Should they get an opportunity today she would steal him away, lock him up in a room somewhere in the sprawling mansion behind them and have her way with him.

Maybe even make love to him this time. If he wished it.

A footman came by and offered her ices and she took one gratefully. After her less than garden party thoughts, she needed to cool off a little.

The duke continued to stroll through the guests, talking to those who were game enough to speak to the fierce-looking man, before he stopped and quite obviously searched the party. Was he looking for her, maybe?

When their gazes locked, his shoulders slumped just a little. Whether it was in relief at seeing her present, Darcy wasn't sure, but his determined steps toward her certainly implied he'd captured his quarry.

He came to stand at the end of her chair, towering over her, and oh, how she wished he could crawl up the seat to lie atop her, lift her gown and settle between her thighs and take her.

She swallowed, again shifting on her seat as the thought of having him left her needy, a greedy little minx desperate for his touch.

He looked about, not that anyone was nearby. She was the only one lying on the chairs put under the tree to shade guests who wanted to rest for a time. She raised her brow, but didn't say a word, and neither did he. He simply stared at her, his gaze raking her body and leaving her shivering from the raw need that shimmered in his eyes.

His jaw clamped, and he frowned. "Where can we go?"

Oh my... His words made her gasp a little and her heart skip a beat. "Do you wish to be alone, Your Grace?" she asked, playing coy and not simply saying, "me too" as she so wished to.

"I've thought of nothing else but what you did to me the other evening, and it's past time that I returned the favour. It is only right as a gentleman that I do."

"Of course. And as a man who believes manners are a pinnacle we all must strive toward, I would think less of you should you not have offered," Darcy said, coming to stand toe to toe with the duke, "to taste me with your mouth as I tasted you. Enjoyed you, Your Grace." She ran her finger across his bottom lip.

His nose flared as he seemed to struggle with his emotions. Seeing the duke mad for her left her longing for him again. It was the most intoxicating thing she'd ever seen, and her heart did a little flip of rejoicing.

"Somewhere close by. The house is too far away."

Darcy chuckled. The house wasn't all that far, although they would have to cross the lawns and weave their way through the multitude of guests who congregated there, only too ready to stop a duke and try to catch his eye for their daughters.

"There is a summer house hidden in the gardens. If you follow the path until it comes to an end and turn left, you'll see it a little way along. It overlooks the park beyond and the small lake this estate has itself."

"Perfect." The duke strode off in the direction she stated.

Amused, Darcy watched him, then went to talk to a nearby group of women before she too strolled to where they would meet.

Trepidation and expectation made her heart thump

and her stomach clench in excitement. Would the duke enjoy touching a woman so, kissing her in the most intimate of places? Her husband had only ever performed it on her once, and upon awakening the next morning, he'd proceeded to tell her he'd been so far into his cups that he'd thought her one of his mistresses, and that he regretted the action. That he would never do such a thing again.

Before Terrance said that, Darcy had thought that perhaps their marriage could work, that he did find her attractive and wished to only be with her. How wrong she'd been. Such an immature, green fool.

She raised her chin and determinedly continued toward the summer house. The duke was not her deceased spouse. He was a man who desired her, wanted to do all that she wished to do with him. Was passionate and eager to please her, in a sexual regard at least, which was more than her husband had ever been.

She pushed open a small gate on the path, and going through it stopped to admire the summer house. It was a rectangular stone structure, with two large windows and steps leading up to a double glass door. For decoration, the roof had a small castle-style balustrade running about its edges. Darcy had always loved this building, and during the time her friend Fran was being courted by the viscount, they had often spent afternoons here, swimming and enjoying each other's company, while her friend fell further and further in love.

It had been the best of times, and now, hopefully, she would make more delightful memories.

The duke stood in the doorway of their abode, his cravat, coat, and waistcoat nowhere to be seen. Lounging against the wood, he looked casual and so delectably handsome that heat pooled between her legs.

How she wanted him, all of him.

"Waiting for someone, Your Grace?"

He laughed a deep rumble that echoed with determination and need. Shivers slid down her spine and she rushed toward him, eager to have him kiss her, touch her, be with her in any way he was willing.

The moment they touched, a spark lit a flame within her and she kissed him deep and long. The duke did not hold back and, only too willing, met each stroke of her tongue, each clasp of her wandering hands, with that of his own.

Her hair tumbled down about her shoulders as his fingers spiked through it. She pulled his shirt from his breeches and ripped it over his head, leaving his heaving, muscular chest hers to admire.

She stood back a little and admired the view, running her finger over each ripple of muscle. His skin was sunkissed, making her wonder what he did that he was able to have such a skin tone. The thought of him working shirtless left her mouth dry.

Instead of asking, not wanting to delay what she longed for him to do to her, she leaned forward and kissed where his heart beat fast. Her hands went about his back as she kissed her way up his neck and found his more than willing mouth.

This time the kiss was slow, languorous, an unhurried seduction that made her ache to have him.

"I want you, Athelby." Her voice was breathless and full of need, but she did not care that he would hear that. She could no longer pretend that their little liaison was merely that, a temporary fling. For it was not, not for her at least. Not anymore.

He picked her up, kicking the door closed, and carried her over to a day bed in the middle of the room. For a moment she hoped that he would strip himself of his breeches, but instead, watching her, he slid her dress up over her legs to pool about her waist. Warm air fragranced with roses kissed her skin and she bit her lip as he placed large hands on each of her knees and slowly spread them apart.

Oh, dear lord...

His fingers played with the silk stockings still tied against her thighs before his lips skimmed their way up toward her aching mons. For a man that had never done such a thing before, he certainly seemed to know what he was about.

"You're so beautiful, Darcy." He paused, placing a small kiss to her very core and making her gasp. "Tell me if I'm not doing this right, or you want more or less of what I do."

She could only nod, and watch entranced as he lowered his head again, and this time, slid his tongue against her sex. She moaned, clasping his head lightly and lying back on the cushions to enjoy his wicked, delightful lips.

His touch was unsure at first, tentative, and yet with that, it only made her more frantic. The need coursing through her grew, ebbed and slowed with each of his kisses, each slide of his tongue, until she could not hold back her need any longer.

"Cameron," she gasped. "Touch me with your fingers as well as your mouth. Please," she moaned as he flicked the little nubbin that gave her pleasure with expert authority.

"Like this?" he asked, his words muffled slightly.

She sighed as he slid one finger into her heat, his tongue flicking her toward madness. It was too much and not enough. Unable to help herself, she clutched him between her thighs and rode his mouth as he brought her to climax.

She shouted his name as wave upon wave coursed through her body. The pleasure left her lethargic and sated, and she lay there spent for a moment as he came to lie beside her, pulling her into the crook of his arm.

"I fear I shall never grow tired of having you in such a way, Darcy."

She looked across at him, running her hand over his stubbled jaw. "I fear that I shall never grow tired of you having me in such a way either."

He came to lie on her and kissed her long and slow, her heart doing a silly little flip, one that could only mean one thing. That not only did Darcy de Merle care for the man in her arms, but that she'd possibly grown to love the complicated, opinionated Duke of Athelby.

CHAPTER 7

There was only one explanation for the emotion that was coursing through Athelby's veins right at this moment. Jealousy.

The woman who had pushed his morals to one side and conquered him was waltzing about the floor, more than happy by the looks of her smile and sparkling eyes to be swung about by the blasted Sir Fraser again. Athelby never thought he would have such a reaction to seeing Darcy dancing with another, but now, after all they'd shared these past weeks, she wasn't meant for anyone else. She was his, and he was hers.

He clenched his jaw. A proposal was all that was required of him. Not a small task considering as much as he longed for her, thought of nothing but the minx and enjoyed her company, she was not the most suitable of women to be his duchess.

Darcy de Merle was almost as opinionated as himself. She was a widow and not a woman who allowed anyone to take advantage—certainly not a husband. When she'd married the Earl of Terrance there may have been a time she was green, vulnerable, and eager to please, but not anymore. Now Darcy was hard, wearing her armor like a shell that protected her from harm, and be-damned to anyone who tried to tell her what to do or how to think.

Athelby admired her for it, but when she became his wife, she would have to concede to the rules of his household and society in general. There were expectations and standards that she would need to meet, which he hoped would not be long in coming to fruition.

He just needed to get her to say yes.

The dance was exceedingly long, and by the time Darcy was deposited back with her friend Lady Oliver, Athelby's disposition had gone from cool to glacier.

Darcy took a flute of champagne and commenced an animated discussion over something or other. She was utterly beautiful when enthusiastic in such a way, and he could only hope he could make her as happy once married.

Another gentleman he wasn't familiar with bowed before her and soon she was dancing a reel. Was she ignoring his presence? He'd certainly not been able to catch her eye this past hour. What was she about not looking at him, or even noting his presence, just as he had noted hers upon arrival?

His annoyance spiked and he left the ballroom, heading toward the card room instead. At least there he would not have to watch her flirting, see her happiness when in another man's arms.

The thought brought him up short. Why did he care so much as to what she did with the other gentlemen? They were not engaged, had no understanding. As a widow, Darcy was free to do whatever she wished as long as it was done with discretion.

He slumped into a chair, not heeding who he was

seated across from, and joined in on a game of chance. That he was even in this room, a gambling den where gentlemen threw their living away without a care, was telling indeed. He was not himself, had not been thinking clearly for some weeks now, and it was all due to the little dark-haired minx waltzing about in the ballroom.

Never did he gamble, or drink, and yet tonight he'd found himself doing both. Wilfully ignoring his morals, all because Darcy was not paying any attention to him. He was, in one word, pathetic.

He played several rounds before quitting the game, down a tidy sum due to his distraction. He poured himself a tumbler of whisky, left the room, and wandered the deserted corridors just beyond before finding a billiards room.

The cold, dark, empty space suited his disposition well.

The door shut behind him and he heard the lock snip. Spinning about, he glared at Darcy as she walked toward him. Seeing the slight grin on her lips in the moonlight ignited his ire.

"What are you doing here, my lady?" he asked, his tone cold.

"I've been waiting for you to end your silly card game. I had thought you'd come back to the ball, but when you did not, I followed you here. Why are you avoiding me, Your Grace?"

That she used his title was telling. So she'd picked up on his displeasure perhaps, or she was playing off against him when he too had used her title instead of her given name.

"I'm simply finishing my drink before calling my carriage. The ball has bored me, and I find I no longer wish to be here."

Hurt flickered in her gaze and he cringed that he'd

possibly upset her somewhat with his words. Did he wish to injure her? Maybe, and he hated the fact that it was solely due to jealously. Having to share Darcy with others, when he wanted her only for himself, was not something he handled well, it would seem.

"So you weren't going to come dance with me? You were going to scuttle away instead?"

"I do not scuttle, madam." He pushed one of the red balls across the table, completely missing the other balls set out at the opposite end.

Darcy came toward him, running her hand along the side of the billiards table. "We haven't seen each other since the summer house. Are you angry with me?"

Yes, damn it, he was angry. Angry that he wanted her so much. Angry that she seemed immune to him. Angry that others claimed her time. He frowned. "It has been a busy couple of days."

"Of course," she said, coming closer still. "I'm sure being the Duke of Athelby is very demanding."

Was she teasing him now? "Let me escort you back to the ball, Lady de Merle. I'm certain there are many other gentlemen who are only biting at the bit to dance with you and wondering where you are."

"I think not." Darcy came to stand in front of him, and this time her finger ran across the front of his coat, up his lapels, then slid about his neck, playing with the hair at the nape of his neck. "I do not care to dance with anyone else but you, Duke."

"That did not look to be the case earlier, my lady."

She pouted and then chuckled, a seductive sound that went straight to his nether regions. "You are displeased with me, and it's because you're jealous. Well, well, well, I had not thought I'd ever see the day that the Duke of

Athelby would be so telling. And in front of a woman as well."

"I'm not jealous." *Liar.* Damn it, he was so jealous he could hardly see straight. The thought of her returning to the ball, dancing with others, had him clasping her hips and holding her firmly before him. "I'm not jealous," he repeated, in the hopes it would be true.

"I do not enjoy seeing you dance with others either, Cameron." She leaned up and kissed him, and unable to deny her anything, he returned in kind and gave himself up to the de Merle.

Darcy steadied her heart as Athelby took control of the kiss and turned it from a chaste peck to something so much more. A kiss that was molten, full of need and ownership, his of her and hers of him. Through the embrace she came to realize that there was no turning back from the feelings that they both raised in each other. And nor did she wish to.

For weeks now they'd teased, kissed and danced with each other in this game of seduction, but no more. Tonight, right at this moment, Darcy wanted Athelby with her whole body and soul, and blast it, she would have him.

He walked her backwards until her bottom hit the edge of the billiards table. Without hesitation, he picked her up and deposited her onto the green, velvety top. The kiss continued, demanding and hot, and she fumbled with his front falls, wanting to feel him, touch and stroke him, not have any article of clothing impeding her desire.

He gasped through the kiss when finally she freed his member, and with a long, slow caress left heat to pool between her thighs.

"I want you, Darcy. I cannot breathe for want of you."

He fumbled with her dress, any care long gone as they frantically tried to rid themselves of their clothes so they could both end this torturous game they played.

"I too." She wrapped her legs around his hips and pulled him against her. His hard member jutted out, and using her hand, she guided him into her, a delicious impalement that left her full, heady with need and completeness.

For a moment Athelby didn't move. His hot breath rasped against her neck, making her shiver.

"Ah, Christ, Darcy. You feel like heaven."

He was heaven as well, a torturous, exciting gentleman she couldn't get enough of. He didn't move, just remained still, and Darcy couldn't stand a moment longer of the inaction. "Rock into me, Cameron. Please."

The duke swallowed and meeting her eye he did as she asked, his thrusts slow at first, before becoming long and deep, meaningful and controlled. For a man who'd never had a woman before, he was certainly exceeding all her expectations.

Not only that, but he didn't seem to be slowing, or showing signs of not being able to last, as her husband was wont to do when they had shared a bed. No, Athelby clasped her bottom, pulled her more solidly into him and took her, pushing her toward a climax that she'd only ever reached by herself, or with this man over the last few weeks.

She clutched at his shoulders, and the mural on the ceiling caught her eye. It was of a woman and a man, lying on a bed of clouds and entwined much like she and the duke were right now. How fitting that they were in a room with such artwork and creating their own masterpiece. He slowed, placing small, delicate kisses up her neck before taking her mouth. "Show me what else we can do. I'm certain this is not the only way."

She chuckled and disengaged herself from him before sliding off the table. "Lie down on the settee, and I'll show you another way."

He threw her a devilish grin, and strode pant-less with not one iota of care to the settee. She caught glimpses of his tight derriere as his shirt moved as he walked. Possessiveness shot through her that the man before her was hers, no one else's to ever see in this way, no one else's to kiss and love.

Cameron was hers.

On the settee, his jutting cock stood upright, ready and willing for more lovemaking. Darcy came to stand beside him, taking in all his glory and wanting to prolong their night for as long as she could.

"Wrap your hand around yourself and stroke. I want to see you do it."

His eyes widened, but he didn't deny her request, merely did as she asked, and touched himself.

"Tell me, have you ever done this before?"

"No." He sucked in a breath, his other hand reaching out to wrap about one of her legs, pulling her gently toward him. "But since I've had you, from the moment we first kissed, I've woken up hard and longing to be with you every day. I've wanted to take myself in my hand and pump myself to completion if only to imagine it was you I was losing myself within."

"You don't have to imagine any longer." She leaned down and kissed the tip of his penis. He mumbled something unintelligible and just to tease him further, she took him in her mouth, sliding her tongue down his rigid length and tasting them both on her lips.

"You're killing me," he said, his hand coming to clasp her hair, making it further unravel.

Not that Darcy cared. She was long past caring if anyone saw or knew what they were about. So long as she had Athelby, the ton could go hang, and after tonight there was no doubt in her mind that he would agree to make her his mistress. For them to have a liaison without any strictures or rules on the other.

The thought of the Duke of Athelby being her lover sent a shiver of delight down her spine and unable to deny herself a moment longer, she gathered up her dress about her waist and straddled him.

His gaze turned molten as she lifted herself a little and then took him within her. With each delectable inch, the urge to moan, to cry out with the wonderfulness of it all, was hard to deny, and she bit her lip to stop herself.

"Fuck, Darcy. I had no idea of what I denied myself."

She rode him, supporting herself on his chest as she became the one in control of the speed, the depth, and angle of their lovemaking. It was wholly satisfying and increasingly hard to stop herself from riding him like a wanton. "Had I known the Duke of Athelby was a man of many hidden talents, I would have seduced you years ago."

THE PAIN WAS REAL, torturous, and so fucking good he wanted to cry out. Having Darcy atop him, riding him, pulling him toward climax while he was fully embedded in her, her hot heat licking his cock and dragging him along, was the best thing he'd ever experienced in his life. All the years he'd denied himself a woman. What had he been thinking? What sort of man lived a half-life due to such a choice?

He'd been bitter for so long, angry and alone, but now,

with Darcy, she'd shown him that there was more to life than duty, rules, and regulations. Not that he would allow them to stay as they were for much longer.

Oh no. Darcy de Merle would be his wife before the Season's end. She would be safely stowed in his life and bed and no one would ever touch her, mistreat her, or dance with her again. She was his, and he was hers.

Wholeheartedly.

I love you.

Never had he ever seen anyone so beautiful, so free, and giving themselves with abandonment to him. Wanting to look upon more of her he slipped her bodice down and freed her breasts. They rocked with the force of their love-making, and he clasped one, circling her nipple with his finger until it puckered.

"Yes. Touch me," she begged, laying her hand atop his, clasping her breast.

She leaned back a little and the movement pushed him toward climax. Oh, dear god, he wouldn't be able to hold himself back for much longer.

"Cameron. Yes!" she panted, a light flush crossing her cheeks. Her pleasure brought his forth, and it shot through him like a bullet. He moaned her name, leaning up and kissing her hard as he spilled his seed within her hot, wet core.

His breath was ragged, and he watched as slowly they regained their composure, although he was unwilling to move. If he had a choice, he'd never move again, so perfect was their current location.

"I fear, Lady de Merle, that I'm unable to live unless you're in my life."

Darcy clasped his cheeks, kissing him slowly and with such perfection that his cock twitched, wanting more of the same. More of her, a delicious morsel that he'd never tire of.

"I fear the very same thing, Duke."

Relief swam in his blood at her words. Tomorrow, first thing, he would gain a special marriage licence and make Darcy his bride. There wasn't a moment to lose.

CHAPTER 8

The following morning Darcy sat in her room and asked her butler to allow the Duke of Athelby to wait in the library while she finished her morning routine. He was unfashionably early, and she'd not thought to see him again until tonight at Lord Boulder's dinner.

She frowned as she came down the stairs. What was he about being here at this time? Did he regret last night? Maybe now that he'd had her and some hours had passed since she'd taken his virginity, he was rethinking his future with her.

She paused at the library door, swallowing the sickness that threatened to rise up. She did not wish for them to part, and she so hoped he would be open to being her lover. They did make quite a good pair, and after last evening, were more than compatible with each other.

The butler opened the door and she strode in, coming to a halt when she spied him beside the unlit hearth. Today he was the Duke of Athelby, regal, authoritative, serious, his clothing immaculate. His hair was combed back and in order. Not even his cravat would dare to be out of place today, it would seem.

His appearance was formal, and it gave her pause.

"Good morning, Your Grace. I hope I have not kept you long."

He shook his head, a flicker of trepidation passing through his eyes before he blinked and it was gone. "Not at all. And I apologize for coming so early, but what I have to say could not wait until the suitable at-home time."

"Of course," she said, coming to sit before him on the settee.

He started to pace before stopping and clasping his hands behind his back. "I'm sure you know why I have come here today?"

She smiled up at him, wanting to untie his cravat and ruffle his hair. He looked so severe and cross, nothing like the man who'd come apart in her arms the evening before. Not willing to let him stand before her in such a way, Darcy went over to him and wrapped her arms around his waist. "I believe I know why you're here, and it was something I was going to talk to you about this evening. When we had some time alone."

"You were?" he asked, clearly shocked but not pulling away from her impromptu hug.

"Yes, you wish to discuss the formalities of us becoming lovers, do you not? And I do not mean only when we're together at balls and parties, although those times are wicked fun, but here and at your residence as well. We will be discreet, I promise."

The duke stumbled back and clasped the mantle for support. "Clearly you jest."

"Jest? Why would I joke about such a thing? I mean, I do not know the rules of having a lover, of being some-one's mistress, but I do believe it requires us to not show open displays of affection, while being together quite often when alone. To partake in house parties and trips with our mutual friends so we can be alone."

The duke placed his arms behind his back, lifting his chin in a determined set. "I did not come here to ask you to be my mistress."

Despair made her knees weak, and she sank back onto the settee. "Then why did you come?"

"I came, Lady de Merle, to ask for your hand in marriage."

For a moment words failed Darcy and realizing she was gaping at him, she shut her mouth with a snap. "To be your wife!"

"Yes." The cold, determined word left her reeling.

"No." Her response wasn't at all filtered, and she cringed when hurt flickered through his eyes.

"May I ask why, madam, that me asking for your hand in marriage is so abhorrent to you?"

She clasped her hands in her lap and took a calming breath. "It's not abhorrent, but marriage is not an institution that I wish to be a part of again. My first marriage was a disaster and only diverted when his lordship decided to have a heart seizure beneath his whore. I do not want to be beholden to anyone, but I do wish to have a man in my life. To make love to him whenever I wish without having to promise to obey and honor him before God, when it is most likely, as I well know, that it's only the woman who has to abide by the rules."

"I am not Lord Terrance, Darcy. I would never dishonor you in such a way as to have a mistress."

"I have heard such declarations before, you know, and it did not make one ounce of difference when Terrance saw someone he wanted."

Athelby started to pace, and she steeled herself to be strong.

"Cameron, we can have a life together, be lovers and enjoy ourselves without marriage getting in the way. You said yourself only a few weeks ago that I was not suitable to be a duchess, and you are right. Nor do I wish to be."

The muscle at his temple jumped.

"Please don't be angry with me." Fear seized her that she may lose him. "I do want you, just not marriage."

"I cannot have a mistress, Darcy. It is bad enough that I have slept with you without taking vows before God. Over the last few weeks I have fallen under your spell, and I cannot remove myself from it. You know I am a man of rules and for doing what's right. Do not ask to be my mistress. I could not dishonour you so. I want you as my duchess. I'd like a wife. Children."

Tears pricked her eyes that she would hurt him. "I cannot be your wife. I will not be any man's wife ever again." She stood and went over to a decanter of whisky and poured herself a dram. "My marriage was horrible, truly awful, and Terrance has cured me of the ill wish."

Cameron stormed over to her, taking the glass from her hand and making her look at him. "I am not the earl, damn it."

She took the glass out of his hand and drank it down in one gulp. She would need all the alcohol she could get to tumble through denying her duke. "What you just did is why I'll never have another man think they own me. You do not get to choose what I want. You do not get a voice in what I'll do. If I wish to drink whisky at nine twenty in the morning, I damn well shall. And if I want to say no to your proposal, I shall do that as well." She hated hurting him, but the fear of marriage, of being owned, was too great, and she couldn't help herself. "I wish to be your lover, but that is all. Do not ask any more of me than that."

Athelby glowered at her, any pretence of not being angry with her long gone. In fact, she would easily surmise that he was furious.

"You could be carrying my child. Are you going to make an innocent babe a bastard simply because you do not wish to be a wife?"

The statement made her start. She'd not thought of such a possibility. "If I am increasing, which we shall know soon enough, I will marry you, without hesitation. I would never do that to a child, but we don't know that yet, and so as of this time, my answer is no."

"You stubborn woman." He stalked to the door and ripped it open. "Let me know via correspondence what the outcome of that possibility is, and we'll deal with it then. Until such time, good day to you, my lady."

"Cameron," she said, following him into the foyer. "Please try to understand my reasons. They were never put in place to hurt you. I would not wish to do that."

"And yet you have." He bowed. "Good day to you, madam."

She swiped at a wayward tear as the duke slammed the door in her face. She went to the window and watched him enter his carriage, that door too being slammed even though the coachman had been trying to close it with dignity.

His carriage pulled away, and the severing made her clasp her chest. Was it wrong of her to never marry again? Was she being selfish and cruel to a man who did not deserve to be tarnished with the same dark cloud as her husband?

Yes, the duke was opinionated, a nuisance when it

came to rules, but he was also passionate, caring, and wanted her to be his wife. Was she wrong in saying no?

She walked back into the library and sat before the unlit fire. That conversation had not gone at all as she'd planned upon seeing him here this morning. Never had she thought the duke ever wanted her, especially as a wife. So many times, he'd said she was too opinionated, too wild, like her family. Not to mention she was not a virgin, pure and sweet like so many gentlemen wanted to marry. She had been married to a man who cared not the briefest bit about her, who ruled her and made her obey him at every turn while living his life in the exact opposite way.

She rubbed her temples as a headache threatened. Not that Athelby was like that, but being so rule-abiding, how long before he turned into a mirror image of Terrance? Made her toe his line and not put a foot wrong. The wife of a duke had a lot more responsibility than an earl's countess, and Darcy did not care for it. No matter how much she cared for Cameron, as far as she was concerned the title could go hang.

For a time, she sat in the room before a maid entered and she requested tea. Pain tore through her that she'd pushed away the one man that she'd ever longed for, loved even, if she were honest. They were opposites, there was no doubt, but that opposition suited each other perfectly.

She thought over his brother's death and could understand his need to marry her. His brother had cared little for the fairer sex, had bedded many women, and had died in a reckless carriage race over his current lover, leaving many broken-hearted women in his wake.

Athelby's determination to not be like his sibling made him honourable and made her love him more than she thought possible. He'd stated he was not Terrance, and he'd proven that many times since they had been together.

He cared for her, loved her, and instead of asking her to be his mistress, he'd wanted her as his wife.

She swiped at another tear. What had she done? Her fear of rules had ensured she'd pushed away the man she loved. Maybe forever. Whatever would she do now?

IN THE WEEK since Darcy had denied him, Athelby had become a complete and utter dunce, and even he knew it. And yet he found it hard to alter his course. All too easily, he had reverted to the prim and proper duke, as so many called him—glowering at any person who dared to look happy, partook in a dance, or slipped even the slightest with etiquette.

He was an ogre, and he hated it.

After her denial of him, he'd spent the next few days in a haze of despair. Had even contemplated having her as his mistress and be damned to a wife. The life she asked for, where both were free to do as they pleased while coming together for pleasure, was appealing, and one night he'd almost knocked on her front door to beg her to do just that. Forget his proposal and have him in just the way she wished.

But the pain his brother had inflicted on the family, the scandal that had rocked a ducal line that had been a pinnacle of grace and dignity, could not be repeated again, and certainly not in his time. He could not do it.

The Marquess of Aaron came to stand beside him, throwing him an amused glance. "There are rumors afoot that you've won the bet at White's. Some are even saying you were seen in a highly scandalous embrace with Lady de Merle at Leeder's ball."

Athelby glowered at Hunter, if only to keep up the appearance that the notion he was the source of gossip did not rattle him to his core. Oh, dear god, had anyone seen them in the billiards room? He cringed and downed the last of his whisky, one of the vices he'd taken up that he did not wish to give up now that he'd started.

"As I said before, the betting book at White's can go hang."

Hunter chuckled, clapping him on his shoulder. "The source was a reliable one, and I'm sorry my friend, but he's a gentleman who's married to one of London's most gossiping tongues."

Sir Walton's wife.

Damn it. Athelby looked across the sea of dancers and met Darcy's troubled gaze. So she too was aware of what was being said about the ton.

"What are you going to do about the situation, my friend? You cannot leave de Merle to the wolves. After her previous marriage, she does not deserve to be ruined simply because you could not keep your hands off her."

The steely tone of Hunter's words fired his ire. "I asked her to marry me, if you must know."

Hunter choked on his wine, apologizing to a nearby matron who looked at him with distaste. "Well, I never thought I'd see the day."

"And nor will you, for she said no."

His friend had the good grace to look appalled before he laughed. In fact, the bastard threw back his head and bellowed over his misfortune. Athelby clenched his fists at his side lest one of them connected with the Marquess' jaw.

"I cannot believe it. The delectable Darcy de Merle turned down the Duke of Athelby. Whatever are you going to do about it?"

What could he do about it, save kidnap the lady and force her to marry him? Which of course was an absurd notion and not one that sat well with him. Kidnapping, no matter if you loved the person or not, was out of the question.

Too scandalous for starters.

"There is nothing to be done. I asked, she said no. Duke or not, I cannot force her hand."

"Do you want to marry her still?"

"Of course I do," he said without question or pause. He would marry her tomorrow if she would only say yes. But she did not want him in that fashion. Darcy wanted a lover, a temporary bedmate to pass the time. Not an annoying husband who curbed her freedom. Or so she thought.

"Will you share as to why she rejected your offer?"

Athelby met his friend's gaze. "She simply does not wish to marry again, and who could blame her after marriage with the Earl of Terrance? Never was there such a disgusting piece of flesh as he and his many whores."

Hunter whistled. "I gather you did not like the chap."

In truth, he'd always hated the man, the one reason more than any other being the simple fact he'd married Darcy. His grandmother was right about her. She was perfect for him simply because they were complete opposites.

He sighed. "I asked her to be my wife, and she asked me to be her lover. And you know Darcy's temperament, there will be no changing her mind."

"Show her you're willing to change. Maybe even be her lover for a time and win her that way. At least you'll be together."

Hunter made a good point and Athelby thought about it a moment. "I don't want a mistress, and I certainly know better than to make a de Merle one. I'd have her family down on my head and demanding retribution at dawn."

"True," Hunter said, pursing his lips. "They would not care for it on second thoughts."

He had that right, and as much as he wanted Darcy, he wasn't willing to make her his whore. It was certainly what being a mistress, in a liaison such as she suggested they have, would make her. And he did not want such an outcome. He wanted her to be his wife, his duchess. His everything.

"I will talk to her again. With the whispers about town over our indiscretion, it may make her open to negotiation and discussing the marriage option once more."

"I wish you well, my friend."

"Thank you," he said, and watched Hunter disappear into the crowd before heading toward Darcy. Coming up to her, he was pleased that the small group of women who had congregated about her dispersed.

She curtsied. He bowed. "Lady de Merle, please would you care to dance?"

Darcy raised one brow and watched him for a moment. He couldn't discern what she was thinking or even if she'd say yes. In fact, when she continued to remain silent he couldn't help but look about and see if others were watching their exchange.

He sighed, noting they were. "Please dance with me."

She shrugged and placed her hand atop his own and he led her onto the floor as the first strains of the waltz sounded. He pulled her against him. Her warmth and scent of roses intoxicated his soul and he fought not to clasp her too tightly, beg her to be his bride so they might never be apart again. Tell her that he'd never curb her exuberance for life.

She wouldn't meet his eye, simply stared over his shoulder. "I gather you wish to discuss something, Your Grace."

"I do. I'm sure you've heard the rumors that are circulating London about us."

"I have."

She said nothing more, and he wanted to shake some sense into her. Did she not know such a scandal could ruin her? As a man, a duke, there was no risk to him. Oh yes, some of the matrons of the ton might look down their noses at him for his indiscretion, but they would not dare cut him in society. Darcy faced the complete opposite, widow or no.

"And with the knowledge that if this story about us continues to gain momentum your reputation could be tarnished, ruined in this set, will you think on my offer some more? I know I'm not the easiest of men—I certainly have my opinions on matters pertaining to etiquette and rules—but I promise I shall try and make you happy, be a better husband than your last one. Give you all that you want and more." He was begging now, but he didn't care.

Darcy did look at him then, her paleness giving him pause. "Are you well?" he asked.

She shook her head. "I'm sorry, Athelby, but I cannot marry you. I do not wish to be bound by rules, marriage, and man. I want to be on my own, to do as I please whenever I please."

"You can still do that with me," he said, desperate to make her his. "You can do whatever you want, just be my wife."

"I may have seduced you, Duke, shown you another side of life, but who you are is ingrained in every ounce of yourself. I do not want anyone to change who they are just to please me. If you're not willing to be my lover, in a union such as where we promise fidelity for however long that may be, then after tonight we cannot meet like this again."

"So you'll cut me from your life should I not agree to make you my mistress?" Athelby's stomach clenched. "Be reasonable, Darcy. The rumor about us is true, you know that very well, not to mention the woman telling all and sundry is one of the ton's biggest gossipers. You'll be ruined."

"And if I am I'll return to my home in Devon, retire to a country life and travel. I do not need society, and I will not do what I'm told merely to save my reputation. I will not be owned by any man again. The last one was quite enough."

"I am not Terrance, surely you must see that." He pulled her to the side of the room, heedless of whoever noticed their hasty departure from the dance. "Marry me, please."

"Why are you so determined? I don't understand you."

He frowned. "Damn it all to hell," he said, ignoring the gasps about him. "I'm determined, Darcy de Merle, because I damn well love you—I think I have always loved you—and I want you. I want to shower you with everything that I am and own. I want to give you freedom if only you'll promise to return to me each night."

DARCY STOOD before the Duke of Athelby and could not form words even though hundreds of them bounced about in her brain, begging to come out. He loved her?

Butterflies took flight in her belly, and she clasped her abdomen. Had Cameron really just uttered those words, and before the ton?

Yes. Yes, he had.

It was certainly the most scandalous thing he'd ever done, in public at least, and it warmed her heart knowing that he'd declared himself so all could hear. To make her see how much he wanted her as his wife and not care who was about them.

How very rule-breaking that was.

Not that she was willing to let him persuade her so easily. The Duke of Athelby was against public displays of affection, against allowing couples to dance more than once when at balls and parties, and against many other things too numerous to mention. She laughed to herself. Athelby could've given her deportment teacher Miss Rivers a lesson or two, and Darcy had never thought to know someone as strict as that old biddy.

"You love me. Why?"

Athelby stood tall, placing his hands behind his back as if facing a set down from his peers, and yet he remained calm, his beautiful sharp features cajoling her to change her mind.

"I have always loved you, I believe, and yet it wasn't until you said 'I do' with Lord Terrance that I realized what I'd lost due to inaction. I may not have always loved your opinionated manners, your love of life, your honesty and loyalty to your friends, but I do now, so very much. I think your laugh is the sweetest sound on earth and your kisses the most wicked. I adore that when I'm with you, I forget myself, my rules and regulations, and just live." He stepped toward her, cupping her cheek. "Be mine and let me be yours. Please, Darcy."

Oh dear… Darcy swallowed and hoped her heart didn't pump out of her chest. People had stopped dancing and not a whisper could be heard as everyone in attendance watched the Duke of Athelby declare himself in the most public manner.

"If…and I have not agreed to anything as yet, Your Grace, but if I do, will you promise not to tell me what I can and cannot do? Will you promise me that if I wish to travel, visit friends abroad, that I shall be allowed to? That I will not be made to sit at home, alone night after night, while you while away your time at houses of ill repute? That you will love me, stay true to me from this day forward?"

He nodded, stepping closer still. "We shall put all those promises in our wedding vows."

Darcy smiled, hope making her eyes well up with tears. "Then yes, I shall be your wife."

Athelby laughed, his shoulders slumping in relief before he pulled her against him and kissed her. Devoured her would be a better term. Surprisingly, their public display of affection had the guests cheering and shouting congratulations while he kissed her still, held her steadfast against him and wouldn't let her go.

"Your Grace, I do believe you've forgotten yourself and where you are," the Marquess of Aaron whispered to them both.

Darcy chuckled and pulled away from the kiss but not Athelby's embrace.

"And what if he has? We're to be married, so what does it matter?"

Athelby went to speak, but Darcy placed her fingers over his lips, not willing to hear all the silly little tonnish rules they were breaking and who would be quite put out with them over the next few weeks and months. If anyone chose to be insulted by two people agreeing to love and marry one another then that was their problem and not hers to worry about.

"Shall we leave, Your Grace?" Darcy grinned, thoughts of them being alone in the carriage, of having Athelby in her bed for the rest of the evening, making her impatient to depart.

He tucked her arm into the crook of his and they made

their way across the ballroom floor. They stopped by Darcy's godmother and Athelby's grandmother, Lady Ainsworth, who was wiping away tears with her handkerchief.

"Oh, my dears, I'm so happy." Her ladyship kissed them both and clasped her hands before her. "I knew you were perfect for one another and I knew it was only a matter of time before you saw it yourselves."

Darcy looked up at Athelby and smiled. "How wise you were, Godmother. If only we were quicker to realize ourselves."

Others congratulated them on their way to the entrance hall. Darcy wrapped her cloak about her as they waited for Athelby's carriage to come around front.

"Is the Duke of Athelby's rule-breaking going to continue this evening?"

"What did you have in mind?" he asked, leaning down to whisper the words against her ear, causing a shiver to run down her spine.

"That you come home with me and warm my bed."

The duke's gaze burned with hunger and it spiked her own need. He stormed from the entrance hall and yelled for his vehicle to hurry up. Darcy grinned and followed. Oh yes, maybe the Duke of Athelby was up for some mischief after all.

CHAPTER 9

A thelby snapped the door to the carriage shut and wrenched Darcy onto his lap, taking her lips with a hunger that was as foreign and welcome to him as ever.

She kissed him back with passion, and his cock hardened, straining against his breeches. Darcy wiggled against him, and he could not wait to take her. He had to have her now.

Desperate to feel her, he ripped at her gown, pulling it out of the way as she came to straddle his legs. She was wet, so deliciously wet for him that he groaned as he ran his hand over her core, teasing, flicking, before slipping two fingers inside.

She moaned, her own hands busy untying his front falls. His phallus sprang into her hand, hard and heavy, and she teased him, wrapping her beautifully clever fingers around his member and sliding up and down.

"Fuck, Darcy," he gasped, pulling her atop him and impaling into her hot core. The carriage rocked along as he pitched into her. Their lovemaking was frantic, the carriage full of gasps, moans, and declarations for more, harder, faster, deeper…

Mine. Mine. The words reverberated in his mind. The woman in his arms was going to be his wife, his duchess. How the knowledge warmed his soul.

She rode him, took her pleasure, coming apart in his arms, and he soon followed her into bliss. To imagine endless nights and days to come, years of her beside him, attending events, balls, family obligations, while knowing always she was his made his eyes well. He blinked, not believing the Duke of Athelby would succumb to such emotions.

Darcy watched him, wiped a small tear that ran down his cheek and met his gaze. "I love you, Cameron, so very much. I'm so glad of that night where you finally kissed me. You said earlier that you believe you've always loved me. Well, I may have stated that I disliked your ways, your rules, but I've never disliked you. Deep down I've always wanted to know what you'd be like if I peeled off your layers, got to know you again, and then debauched you as I so longed to do."

He chuckled. "Debauched? I suppose yes, you've totally ruined me as I've ruined you. I love you, Darcy, so very much that I cannot see my way forward without you beside me."

"And you will not have to, for I'm going to be your wife, and will corrupt you even more and maybe even spoil you so you'll never be able to live without me again."

"Shall we put those declarations in our wedding vows as well? Best to start as we mean to go on."

Darcy smiled, kissing him with a sweetness that made him ache. "We shall."

EPILOGUE

Four years later

Darcy strolled toward the duke, who sat sprawled on the lawn of their London estate, their two children giggling and running about him every time he made a lunge to grab and tickle them until they couldn't take it any longer.

Their birth had not been easy, and she thanked God every day that even though they could not have any more, they were blessed with two delightful, happy, healthy children.

Darcy came up to them and clasped Henry from behind, whisking him into the air and making him squeal. "I've got you," she said, kissing him multiple times on his neck and cheek before putting him back down, where he resumed his game with his father. Darcy sat and pulled Henrietta onto her lap, cuddling her and giving her too her fair share of kisses.

"Are you having fun with Papa? I wanted to tell you that Cook has made up some ices for you in the kitchen, if you wish to have some."

The children squealed and ran off as if the devil himself was on their heels, their nursemaid not far behind.

"You scared the children away," Cameron said, leaning over and pulling her down to lie beside him.

Darcy lay over his chest, looking up at him. "I did, didn't I?" she chuckled. "Is it terrible of me that I don't feel the least guilt about that?"

"You're a minx, but then, I would not have it any other way." He pulled her up toward him and kissed her.

Darcy deepened the embrace, having been away all afternoon at house calls.

"Let's leave for Ruxdon early, and get out of London. I'm tired of the Season and all that we're obligated to do during it. If we go home, we can do as we please, and with summer not far away, maybe we could even take the children boating for a day."

Cameron rolled her onto her back, pinning her to the ground with one leg scandalously between her own. She gasped, clutching at his hair and kissing him again.

"We'll leave the day after tomorrow, but you're aware Grandmother will wish to come? You know she never likes to be separated from the children. She adores them so."

"I do not mind, and with her at Ruxdon it'll give us some time to be alone..." This time Cameron shifted fully on top of her and she gasped. "You cannot lie on me like this here. Someone may see us."

He was unmoved, except for one part of his person that was moving and growing at a very rapid pace. "What do you expect? The Duke of Athelby has been corrupted by a de Merle. There is no saving me now or halting my desires. You did say you wanted to know what it would be like married to a debauched duke."

"I did say that, didn't I?" She sighed and gave herself

up to kissing him, teasing him just as he liked. There were many things she now knew the duke loved, and in turn, she adored that she was the woman to give him love and pleasure. That he loved her in return and gave her the freedom that she'd so longed for.

He groaned, the kiss turning from sweet to molten when Darcy shifted beneath him, placing him directly at her core and not in the least backing away from his need.

"Upstairs, Duchess. Now." Cameron stood, pulling her to follow him.

She did, only too willingly. Marriage to a debauched gentleman did make for enjoyable afternoons. And an enjoyable life, actually.

TO MADDEN A MARQUESS

Lords of London, Book 2

She saved his life, but can she save him from himself?

Hunter, Marquess of Aaron, has the ton fooled. Outwardly he's a gentleman of position, with good contacts, wealth and charm. Inwardly, he's a mess. His vice—drinking himself into a stupor most days—almost kills him when he steps in front of a hackney cab. His saviour, a most unlikely person, is an angel to gaze at, but with a tongue sharper than his sword cane.

Cecilia Smith dislikes idleness and waste. Had she been born male, she would already be working for her father's law firm. So, on a day when she was late for an important meeting at one of her many charities, she was not impressed by having to step in and save a foxed gentleman rogue from being run over.

When their social spheres collide, Hunter is both surprised and awed by the capable, beautiful Miss Smith. Cecilia, on the other hand, is left confused and not a little worried by her assumptions about the Marquess and his demons. It is anyone's guess whether these two people from different worlds can form one of their own...

CHAPTER 1

Cecilia Smith stood on Curzon Street and tried to hail a Hackney cab. The streets were busy with coal carts, people walking along the cobbled footpath and gentlemen with their ladies out for an afternoon stroll. Cecilia pulled her spencer closed as a light breeze chilled the air, and waved to another Hackney that too, trotted past without a backward glance.

What was going on? Did they not see her? The thought was probably closer to the truth than she liked to admit. Here in Mayfair, in the drab, working-class gown that she was wearing, it was any wonder no one bothered to stop to pick her up. The working populace that was her sphere wasn't well-to-do enough for this locale, and it had not passed her notice that a lot of those out and about had thrown her curious, if not annoyed glances her way that she'd dared enter their esteemed realm.

From the corner of her eye, a flash of black arrested her attention. Turning to look, she observed as a gentleman stumbled toward a street lamp, leaning up against it as if it were the only thing keeping him upright.

He was a tall gentleman, his clothing was cut to perfection, and fit his tall, muscular frame well, but his eyes that she could see even from across the road were blood-shot with dark rings beneath them.

Was he ill, suffering apoplexy or merely drunk?

A hackney cab barrelled down the road and showed no signs of slowing. Cecilia turned her attention back to the gentleman and horrifyingly watched as he started across the busy thoroughfare.

Without a moment's hesitation she started toward him, and looking toward the hackney cab wasn't sure if even she would make it out of its way before it was too late. What an absurd, stupid man for putting himself and now her also in danger. Did these Mayfair dandies have no sense?

He stumbled just as she made his side, and heaving him with all of her might thumped him hard in the chest, sending him to fly backward and toward the safety of the side of the road. Unfortunately, he reached out at that very moment and brought her down with him. The man's head made a loud crack as it hit the cobbled pavement.

The hackney cab rattled past without so much as a by-your-leave and Cecilia scrambled to her feet and stood next to the man, peering down at him. The scent of spirits wafted from him, almost as if he'd bathed in the stuff and his uncertain footing and stupid attempt to cross the road without care was all too clear. Nevertheless, she couldn't just leave him there, even if she really wanted to. How lovely it would be to be able to prance about town at midday, drunk and without a care, as this fellow seemed to do. He must be one of those rich nobs that waltzed at balls and believed everything that was said or written about them was true.

If only they knew that her class laughed and mocked them at every turn. If it weren't for her kind, London would screech to a halt, no matter what the upper ten-thousand thought. They might make the laws, employ many, but it was her lot in life that kept the city running, and the country counties too when she thought about it.

He moaned, and she kneeled beside him, tapping his cheek lightly. His clothing smelt of stale wine, his breath reeked of spirits and a hard night, not to mention there was a slight odor of sweat that permeated the air. When he didn't respond to another gentle prod, she gave him a good whack. His eyes opened, his dark blue orbs wide in shock before narrowing in annoyance. This close to him, Cecilia noticed his sharp cheekbones, strong jaw and his too perfectly shaped nose was probably prettier than her own.

"What do you think you're about hitting me like that? Have care, miss, miss, miss."

She stood and held out her hand. He gazed at it in confusion before she sighed and leaning down again, took his hand in hers. "Stand, before you're nearly run over again by another carriage. And do be quick about it. I'm late for my meeting already."

He moaned as he allowed her to help him up. Cecilia led him onto the footpath and ensured he was well off the road before she let go of his hand. "Is your home nearby? Can I escort you there to ensure your arrival is to a satis-fying end, unlike the one you almost had on the road just now?"

He frowned, rubbing his forehead. "I was on the road?"

"Yes, you were. Just how foxed are you sir?"

"I'm not a sir," He replied with an arrogant tilt of his head.

Cecilia took a calming breath to prevent herself from pushing the imbecile back onto the road. Really. Wasn't a sir? "Pray tell me, what are you then? I'm sure it's important that I must know to correct my silly ways?"

"Are you being sarcastic?" A small quirk turned his lips. Cecilia found her attention riveted on the spot and she vexed herself that she would be so pathetic as to look at his mouth at such a time.

"You are a smart one, sir."

"I would have you know, I'm the Marquess of Aaron, Hunter to my friends. Hunt for those of even closer acquaintance."

"Well, aren't we vulgar." Cecilia stepped away from him, dusting down her gown after their collision. "If you're safe and well enough to manage to get yourself home before you're struck by another vehicle I shall leave you now." Cecilia turned and started down the pavement. She left the marquess standing behind her, his agape mouth the last memory she'd have of him. She smiled a little, imagining he'd not been talked to so abruptly before. Not that he didn't deserve to be brought down a level or two.

"Wait!" he demanded, his footsteps hastened as he came up beside her. "You didn't tell me your name."

Since his lordship was so particular about titles, Cecilia decided to play a little trick on him. "I am the Duke of Ormond's daughter. Heir to a massive fortune and looking for a husband."

He started. "Really?"

"No. Not really. I'm Miss Cecilia Smith. My father owns and runs J Smith & Sons, Lawyers and I reside in Cheapside if you must know. I am also late for a charity meeting. So if you do not mind, I shall leave you to your stupor and go."

She moved on and ignored the light chuckle she heard behind her. He didn't follow, but she felt the heat of his gaze on her back. It was a pleasant feeling knowing he was watching her, not that she would ever see him again. Their social spheres were eons apart and he would only look to her Society for mistresses. Never marriage, unless it was absolutely necessary due to financial woes or some other such reason.

And as much as she hated to admit it, Cecilia had heard of the Marquess of Aaron and the wild and naughty antics the rich toff was known for around London. If what they wrote in the papers about him was accurate, he was a man who lived life fast and hard and left a bevy of young women pining for him to marry them. It was rumored that if he asked for a dance, they were instantly in love with him.

Cecilia rolled her eyes, not impressed by her first encounter with the gentleman. Waving again to a Hackney coming toward her, she sighed in relief when it pulled up, and she was able to travel the few blocks to her destination. The carriage rocked to a halt on the corner of Fleet Street and St Bride's Avenue. Cecilia stepped down from the carriage, paid the driver before turning her attention to the meeting at Old Bell Tavern where she wanted to press her idea for another orphanage and school on Pilgrim Street in Ludgate where a large, unoccupied building currently sat. Her father had promised her the funds, and now all she had to do was get the women at her meeting to agree and then all her plans would come to fruition. It was the right thing to do, and she was sure she wouldn't have any trouble getting them to agree.

If she managed to be instrumental in making just one of the orphaned children of London have a good stable job that enabled them to live a full and happy life, then her work at the charity was worth it. It was the best day in the world when children who'd arrived, sick and poor left and became house and ladies' maids, cooks even, if their inclination leaned them in that direction. The boys becoming footmen, stable hands and those who were mathematically inclined, stewards even. If one wanted to change, one had to work toward the goal and not believe everything would just fall in your lap.

With invigorated stride, Cecilia pushed open the doors at the Bell Tavern and headed for the private parlor where they always had their meetings. Life was excellent, and she was about to make it even better, especially for those who lived on the streets that had no life at all. Not yet at least.

CHAPTER 2

Hunter watched the hellcat disappear down the street. She produced a lovely view for him from behind, the cut of her gown, no matter how plain and dull, didn't take from the small waist, plentiful bosom and delectable bottom that swayed a little with each step. Miss Smith was a tall woman, and it brought forth the image of how lovely and long her legs would be, how far about his waist they would go during certain physical exercise…

He blinked as a bout of dizziness assailed him, and he clasped the oil lamp on the footpath to steady his stance. Hell, he needed a drink. His mouth was as dry as the Egyptian desert. A matron walked by and looked down her nose in distaste. Bowing, Hunter went to tip his hat, and his hand met with thin air.

What the devil happened to his hat! He'd left Whites late and tumbling into a carriage, remembered meeting a good friend for some late night gambling near St James Park. He'd meant to end the night at his mistress's boudoir, but apparently, he'd not made it there at all. Hunter frowned, rubbing a hand over his jaw. In truth, he had no idea what the night had entailed or how much he'd lost at the tables.

Walking on, he looked back to where Miss Cecilia Smith had disappeared. She was long gone, and a pang of regret pierced him that he wouldn't see her again. Not many women would openly show their distaste for his current appearance including the fact he was still as foxed as he was last evening.

She had a certain spunk about her that he couldn't help but admire. He supposed finding a woman who was so blunt, crass almost was more prominent in the middle class, since so many ladies had to work alongside their husbands and fathers. And here in London, there were many such women.

Hunter made the curb and hailed down a Hackney Cab. No more walking, his stomach churned, and it was probably best that he didn't cast up his accounts all over the street. The cab pulled up and flicking the driver a coin, Hunter settled onto the squabs. He would go home, bathe and retire to bed. Tonight Lord Stone was hosting a men's only evening that included exotic dancers from…. Hunter grimaced, not able to remember, but knowing they would be as beautiful as they were favourable with their affections.

He smiled and shut his eyes, resting for a moment. What a wonderful, decadent, indulging life he led. May his life never end.

CECILIA STOOD before the members of the London Relief Society and glowered. "What do you mean we cannot open a new orphanage and school on Pilgrim Street? The building is there, vacant and derelict. We simply need to find out who owns it and then purchase the damn place."

"Ladies, please. Allow Miss Smith to explain before we all dismiss this latest idea," the Duchess of Athelby said, staring down the few women who'd argued with Cecilia over the last ten minutes. "Cecilia deserves to have her say."

The duchess, a woman of high importance in the *ton*, was a welcome addition to their members, and she'd joined not long after she'd married the duke. Over the past year, they had become good friends. The duchess was a woman genuinely willing to help those less fortunate.

Her friend, Katherine Martin whose father was a well-known and respected builder in London raised her hand, capturing everyone's attention. "All Miss Smith is trying to say is that we should not give up so easily. Those of us here from working-class families know when things get tough we simply pull up our sleeves and get the work done. There is no difference here. We can and will do this. We must."

Cecilia smiled at her friend who always supported her. They had grown up together, had lived next door to each other in Cheapside for as long as Cecilia could remember.

"The building is too broken down to house children, and I still think we should direct funds to the schools we already have," Miss Tapscott said, her prude little mouth mottling up and reminding Cecilia of the back end of a dog.

Cecilia fought not to roll her eyes. "Miss Tapscott, we cannot simply turn a blind eye to the need that is prevalent in Ludgate, why, a lot of London's boroughs in fact. I agree the building does need work, but we have family, parents even who own and run varied trades in London and beyond. If any women are suitable to get this building transformed into a school and home for those less fortunate, to turn around their lives and give them some chance, then it is us."

"She's right, and Miss Tapscott," Katherine said, standing, "your father owns a mill. Surely you could persuade him to donate some lumber to rebuild the parts of the building that are in need of repair."

"I'm sure I could persuade my father to help with the supply of wood. He has many men working beneath him you know. He's quite successful even if he doesn't get up to London much," Miss Tapscott said, giving a pointed glance at Cecilia.

"Very good and I'll instruct my father to find out who owns the building and we'll commence with the purchase of it. I'm sure if we find the owner, who obviously does not use or wish to use the building of concern, we'll be able to persuade them to sell." Cecilia slipped her notes into her little leather carry bag, announcing the end of the meeting. "We'll regather here next week at the same time. Our duties are to find out what help and assistance our families and friends can be toward this new school and home for underprivileged children. Are we all in agreement?"

The seven ladies present concurred, and within a few minutes, Cecilia and Katherine started toward the tavern's door.

"Good meeting today and I'm so pleased we were able to talk the ladies around to see the benefits of having the new school built. The number of children who require our help are growing daily, and in Ludgate, there isn't a facility like ours, and it's sorely needed."

"I agree," Cecilia said, opening the door for her friend before going to the curb and hailing a hackney. "Father will help me track down the people who own the building and then we'll be able to move forward with our plans." A hackney arrived after much waving was had.

Katherine climbed up and slammed closed the carriage door. "We're to attend the Opera tonight. I wonder if Mr. Elton will be present."

"I'm sure he will be, and you'll be swooning all over him again. Not that you should. He's a little old for you."

"He is only thirty, Cecilia." Katherine grinned and looked out the window. "But I do like him. What a shame he's courting Miss Tapscott."

"Emily has nothing on you." Cecilia sighed thinking about her own run in this afternoon with the obnoxious Marquess of Aaron. "Did I tell you who I had the unfortunate event of saving today?" A little shiver ran over her skin at the thought of him. Of how close he'd been to being hit by the hackney. What a drunk fool he was and what a shame that was the case. For should the marquess be appropriately attired, not dishevelled from the night before and the revelry he so obviously took part in, he'd be very handsome indeed.

Oh, who was she fooling? He was handsome in any way he was presented.

Katherine turned her full attention toward Cecilia. "Who? You never mentioned running into anyone before the meeting."

"I was late if you remember, and the reason for that was the very handsome, very rakish Marquess of Aaron. I was walking down Fleet Street when I noticed the man stumbling along, and then the fool thought to walk out in the middle of the road and try and be hit by a cab. What else was I to do but save the prig."

Her friend's eyes widened. "And did you?"

"Did I what?" Cecilia asked, frowning.

"Save him!"

She laughed. "Oh yes, I got him off the road without any harm done to his absurdly beautiful bone structure.

But I really ought to have let him be hit. No man should ever be that perfect."

Katherine laughed. "You bantered with a marquess. Oh, what a story to tell your grandchildren one day. He's famous about London. Everyone wants to be his friend and be part of his set. He is known to be vastly naughty and flirts with even the old matrons in the *ton*. And you saved his life. He owes you."

"He doesn't owe me anything. In all honesty, I was glad I was there to help him for he was as foxed as they come."

"In the middle of the day, his lordship was drunk?" Katherine sighed, sitting back in the squabs. "This shouldn't surprise me as I've heard other rumors about his lordship."

"What rumors are they?" Cecilia tore her gaze away from the streets outside their carriage that slowly started to meander their way into their neighbourhood, a much less savoury one than the one the marquess would hail from.

"That he's always inebriated. That there hasn't been an outing he's attended this year where he hasn't been foxed or in such a state by the time he leaves. It really is a great shame that he isn't able to attend balls and parties without being so drunk. His lordship might find that he enjoys himself more if he wasn't in such a state, but so far not many have seen him otherwise. I suppose his wayward life could be blamed on his parents."

Cecilia didn't like the idea of the Marquess having such demons. Indeed today when she'd saved him it had been in the middle of the afternoon. Most people of his set were sleeping the day away, gaining their strength for the next night's entertainments. But his lordship had not been. He'd still been returning home from who knows where. The smell of him certainly wasn't pleasant as one would expect a nob to be. Was what Katherine saying true? How terrible if it was so.

"His parents? What do you mean?" Cecilia asked.

Katherine met her gaze. "His parents before they passed away were famous for their public arguments, their lively love-hate relationship." She shrugged. "Although I've not heard Lord Aaron has acted in such a way in public with a woman, he's certainly as wild as his sire was behind doors."

"How do you know all this about the marquess? I've never heard you mention his name before today."

"I read the paper, but also, my ladies' maid has a sister who works for the marquess, just as a scullery maid. Even so, the stories that she's been told about his lordship, the parties that take place at his townhouse, the company he keeps and what they get up to is beyond anything we've ever imagined. There will be stories told about his lordship for years to come I'm sure, even after his death."

Which would be sooner rather than later if he kept up such antics. Walking out in front of carriages indeed. Stupid, handsome fool.

LATE THAT AFTERNOON, Hunter lay back in his bath and groaned when his servant knocked on his bathroom door.

"My lord, your steward would like a word with you downstairs in the library when you're ready. He's willing to wait."

"Tell him to come up here and speak. I'll not have my bathing rushed." He'd only just got into the damn tub for crying out loud, and with any luck, the pounding headache he currently suffered with would abate a little in the warm, soothing water that smelt of lavender.

Hunter rested his head back on the tub and looked up at his ornate ceiling that had cherubs floating about in clouds. Really, the image was absurd, but a reoccurring effect upon the ceilings throughout his home.

The thought of another who had a rounded ass just like the cherubs above him floated into his mind. Miss Cecilia Smith. A very plain name for a woman who was completely the opposite of that. She was extremely attractive for a woman of the middle class, untitled, located in a different part of London and their social circles couldn't be more different. But she was extraordinarily beautiful.

Her ethereal golden locks had sat tied on the top of her head, little wisps floating about her face with the most striking, intelligent blue eyes he'd ever beheld. She'd saved his life, and for the life of him, he couldn't remember if he'd thanked her.

And nor would he get the chance now, since it was unlikely he'd ever see her again. A shame for he'd love to get to know her better. He was in need of setting up a new mistress, his current one was too needy, had become a whiny little thing who was no longer fun. Maybe a woman of Miss Smith's class would accept such a proposition from him. He dismissed the idea as soon as he had it, she had a father who was in law, would have family and friends who expected her to marry well, she would not be looking to be his lover, no matter how rich he'd make her.

He started when a loud knock sounded on his bathroom door. "Come in," he said, sighing as his thoughts and ideas for the delectable Miss Smith vanished from his mind.

"My lord, apologies for interrupting you, but I have some urgent business matters which must be discussed."

"And they are?" he asked, flicking a glance at his man of business Mr. Marsh. His steward was a tall gentleman, but too thin by far, looked as if a good meal would kill him. His hair was washed and kept pulled back from his face, that had an overly broad forehead. He was smart man and hence why he was working for Hunter. Probably a good thing that his forehead was so broad, if only to hold in his massive mind.

"The property on Pilgrim Street that is empty has had an offer of purchase against it." He ruffled through his papers. "Ah, the charity by the name of London Relief Society wish to meet and negotiate a price."

Hunter sat up in the bath. "That property is marked for development for a gentleman's club for the middle class as it were. Building for it was to commence next year. Why is anyone offering on it? The property was taken off the market months ago." He had the idea for a gentleman's club for the middle class, to give those who were bankers, lawyers or barristers a place to go and enjoy good wine, food and intelligent company. It had been one of his best ideas, and it was now in the final stages of planning and design.

"I believe, my lord that they wish to open up a school for the children who need it, an orphanage of some kind."

The location made sense, as in that part of town there were hundreds of kids running about, their parents either working or unfortunately dead and unable to keep track of them. In this part of London, the seedier side of the city was kept at bay, not spoken about and relatively ignored. Hunter had wanted to revamp the area a little, offer it a little luxury to those who lived and worked there. Putting an orphanage and school did not suit that plan at all.

"How much did they bid for the building in its current state?" Hunter asked, having not thought he'd ever have anyone interested in the site.

"Two hundred and fifty pounds, my lord."

An excellent sum, but still no gentleman's club. "And when does this charity wish to meet?"

His steward ruffled through his papers once again. "The meeting is set for tomorrow at four in my offices on Regent Street. The charity will attend and make their formal offer."

What was he doing tomorrow evening…. Ah, there was a card game at Whites he'd wanted to attend. Many a gentleman would be present who didn't play as well as they ought, and Hunter often left with a much more massive purse than the one he arrived with.

"Do we know who will be in attendance from this charity?" Hunter asked, his voice bored even to his own ears.

Again Mr. Marsh ruffled through his paperwork. "A Mr. John Smith and his daughter, Miss Cecilia Smith. Mr. Smith is the owner and barrister from J Smith and Sons."

Hunter sat up in the tub. *Miss Cecilia Smith.* Could it be the very one who'd saved and chastised him not hours ago? "I think I shall attend and hear what they have to offer. Although I have no intentions of selling, I have other business on Regent street and will be in the area. It is only right that I attend and notify this charity of my plans for the site."

"Very good, my lord. I will see you at four tomorrow," Mr. Marsh said, bowing and leaving him in peace.

Hunter shut his eyes, revelling in the warm, fragrant water. Tomorrow he would purchase a new phaeton carriage. Baron Abram had started to race them from London to his estate in Kent and Hunter wanted to take part. Now he would be able to and enjoy himself at the gambling parties that were hosted after such sport.

A capital idea if ever he had one.

CHAPTER 3

Cecilia Smith shut her mouth with a snap when the Marquess of Aaron sat down across from her in Mr. Marsh's office on Regent Street. Her breath hitched, and she swallowed the nerves that took flight in her belly. This could not be happening. Only days before their paths had crossed and now, again, here he was, staring at her with amusement that made her hackles rise, and her cheeks to heat.

To be sure nothing was out of place, Cecilia checked her attire and satisfied all was well, met his gaze. He didn't need to know she'd eaten a pastry prior to coming here, and it would have been just her luck that the crumbs were sitting upon her bottle green day dress.

The Marquess's steward started to discuss the plans for the building, and it was enough to bring Cecilia out of her musings on his lordship and concentrate at the job at hand.

"A gentleman's club! That is preposterous," she said, raising her chin. "The location is not Mayfair or Knightsbridge, it is Ludgate. We do not want your gentleman's clubs here. What is needed is more homes for those who are less fortunate than yourself."

Mr. Marsh's mouth pinched, and Cecilia smiled at him. She would not play this high and mighty lord's game. He would not make the London Relief Society start from scratch and find some other place to purchase. As the building stood, two-hundred and fifty pounds was probably more than they ought to offer, but it was paramount in their plans for the future, the children's future in this area and so they had offered a little more to make the deal tempting to the vendor. In this case, though, she had not thought the vendor would've been the marquess and a money hungry vulture one at that.

"The property, even in its current condition is valued more than what you've offered. But as I stated before, my client will be remodelling the building for a gentleman's club, not an orphanage."

Cecilia placed her hand on her father's arm when he went to speak, and instead caught the Marquess's eye. "Maybe his lordship, considering the fact that I saved his life only days ago, will rethink his plans with the building. Had I not stopped your foxed self from walking out in front of that hackney, you wouldn't even be here today to accept or reject our offer of purchase. Nor would you be able to make it a gentleman's club like you're so set to do."

He leaned back in his chair, smirking and Cecilia's stomach fluttered at his absurdly appealing visage. "Touché, Miss Smith, but I still will not sell you the building. I thought I would do right by your charity and meet with you, explain my plans, not negotiate another option."

Anger and disappointment surged through her veins. "Children are relying on us, children who'll never have a roof over their heads unless I supply that cover. Your belittling of their circumstances by wanting to make a frivolous, and boring gentleman's club, promoting affluent lifestyles that help no one, makes you look like an ass."

The steward gasped, and her father clasped her hand, shaking his head. "Cecilia, apologize to his lordship at once."

She ignored them all. "And while we're at it, let me remind you your building may be the most suitable, but it is not the only one available in that area. We can look elsewhere if need be, you may want to remember that." Even though it was suited best of all they'd viewed and would be the cheapest option available to them at this stage. But he didn't need to know that if he was playing hard for a higher offer.

The marquess leaned back in his chair and folded his arms across his chest. The action made his arms seem a lot larger than what she remembered them from the day before. In fact, today his lordship looked practically normal. Certainly he wasn't foxed, or sleep deprived as he had been. If anything, he had an air of intelligence that she hadn't thought he possessed.

"Had you offered twelve months past, I might have thought on the offer, but since then I have put in place plans for the remodelling and structuring of the building's usage. So now, unfortunately, Miss Smith you are out of luck."

"So it would seem," she said, standing and putting her notepad back in the leather case she carried to all her business dealings. "Come, father, this meeting is finished."

The marquess stood and held out his hand to her. Cecilia looked at it for a moment debating whether she really wanted to shake this man's hand or for that matter touch him at all. The last time she had, it left her feeling a little lost and not herself. It wasn't to be borne.

With a sigh she shook it, tightening her hand to the

point that he narrowed his eyes. Good, she wanted him to know she was no pathetic, whimpering miss that he could pull the wool over. She was an educated, worldly woman who could read this marquess like a book. He may be laughing at her now, thinking her a silly fool for trying to do business with a lord, but she would show him. Their dealings would not end here. And he would not win this war. Not today, or ever.

He arched a brow, a slightly sardonic smile slanting his lips. "What a strong handshake you have, Miss Smith. Almost masculine in fact."

She laughed, pulling him closer to her so that only they could be heard. "I will not play your game, nor will I allow you to build your gentleman's club. I think you should take some time and think over our final offer. I do not wish to, my lord, but the class I hail from is the very one you're trying to market to, and my father is well known. Your club will need members, yes? If you do not sell to me, I shall ensure no one of my set ever sets foot in your building."

He grinned, holding her tight and not letting her remove her hand from his grasp. "How very delightful you are, Miss Smith. Do tell me what else you have planned for my future. I am quite enraptured."

Cecilia wrenched her hand free. "Nothing more, my lord. I think what I stated is enough."

Taking a fortifying breath, she helped her father to stand as sitting for long periods tended to make him seize up a little. Walking outside, they were soon in the family carriage, heading back to the offices. Cecilia tugged her gloves off, slapping them against her skirts. "That man is the most vexing, arrogant, too high in the instep man I've ever met in my life. Not to mention one of the dumbest. A gentleman's club, for men like you, papa. How absurd."

"You were extremely blunt with the marquess. He could make your life, even in the small Society we grace hard for you to make a good match in marriage. You should watch how you speak to people, my dear. It is not becoming of you."

"Pfft. I don't care a fig if it's not becoming of me, he is a fool."

Her father frowned and studied her for a moment. "What did you mean when you said you saved his life two days past. Have you met the marquess before?"

Cecilia nodded and looked out the carriage window, the streets busy with shoppers and people out for strolls or calls. Not her though, at three and twenty she was a fortified spinster and solidly on the shelf just as she wished it to be. With her friends and her charity, she was never lonely or sad about her circumstances. If anything it enabled her to spend more time with the unfortunates of the world. And she'd much rather be with them, than tending to a husband, locked up at home day in and day out with nothing else to do but sew and host parties.

"I was running late for a meeting at the London Relief Society, and I spotted this man wandering, stumbling really onto the street. No one seemed to be taking any notice of the danger he was in, and I intervened. Stopped him from being hit by a passing carriage. I should've let him be flattened. I would've got my building then for two-hundred and fifty pounds. His estate would've sold it off right smart, just to be rid of it."

Her father scowled. "Cecilia you should not speak so vulgar. You're better than that. I know you have a good heart, and there will be other buildings. His loss and stubbornness will be your gain, mark my words."

The carriage pulled up in front of J Smith and Sons,

her father's offices. Cecilia glanced at the building's glass doors with her father's name which included 'and sons' on it. Not that she had any brothers, a point he never brought up, but the disappointment he felt was sometimes palpable in their home. If only women could be lawyers, bankers and stewards, and then 'and sons' could be replaced with the wording 'and daughter'. But it was not to be. Her father had chosen who would take over the firm after his death, and it was not her.

"Did you wish to come inside and see Mr. White? I know he'd like to see you again."

The man her father intended for her was Mr. Justin White, a pompous lawyer who had trained under her father and now helped run the firm. Cecilia couldn't stand the man, he was demanding and had not an ounce of empathy in his body, certainly not for her or her charities. As much as her father wished it, she would never marry the man. Even if he did end up inheriting her father's company.

If she ever married, and that was a very big if, she wanted a man who cared for those who were born less fortunate. Give time and money to her causes and try and make some change to these people's circumstances. A husband who would not expect her to be a wife, cossetted at home, seen but never heard. And certainly not a husband who did nothing but idle his life away in folly and meaningless pursuits. Like a certain marquess she could think of.

"I'll excuse myself this time, thank you, father. After today, I wish to return home in any case and have a long, hot bath. I need to wash off the autocratic, obstinate stench of Lord Aaron."

Her father chuckled and left her alone in the carriage. The remainder of the trip she stared sightlessly outside thinking about the marquess. How dare he deny her with little thought for the fortunes of others. Was he so unfeeling to so easily ignore what was needed for her charity, the children and families relying on them?

She wrung her gloves in her hands. No matter what she said to the gentleman's steward or her father for that matter, the building was really their only option. At this time there wasn't anything else on the market, and their limited refurbishment budget only went so far. The building next door to their preferred, although for sale, needed a lot more work, so unless they could get more funding, which was highly doubtful, his lordship's property was their only alternative. They simply must gain it in some way. If only she had kept check of her temper and not concluded the meeting prematurely. Sometimes her irritation really did get in the way of progress.

There simply must be a way to change his mind. Maybe she could ask him again, bring some unfortunate children with her so he could see why his building was so important to them. Make him see the struggles going on outside of his precious Mayfair.

Cecilia pursed her lips as an idea so delicious popped into her head. Oh yes, the marquess should she pull off this idea would sell to her, and quickly, especially with what she had in store for him. She called out to the driver, directing him to their Spitalfields orphanage and school. She needed a little help from her friends there. Poor Lord Aaron would be banging down her door to sell, and more than likely with her friends help, before the week's end.

HUNTER STROLLED down St James's Street, his cane a regular crescendo against the cobbled footpath as he headed for Whites. After his meeting with Miss Smith the previous week, he'd found he had no stomach to attend his allotted entertainments planned and had missed two balls and a picnic in Richmond Park. Most odd and unlike him. The vexing chit had annoyed him greatly, and not a little of what she said pricked his conscience. Never did he flaunt his wealth, his ability to spend whatever he wished, whenever he wished without a care to anyone else. Did he?

Surely he did not. It was merely his way of life. How he'd grown up. It was certainly how most of his set lived.

Hunter paused and turned about, sure he was being followed. Two, male, children's voices sounded behind him, and he turned again, this time catching the two little rascals who stopped and made an obvious attempt at looking at the sky.

"Do you have something you wish to ask me, boys?" he asked, walking up to them.

Their faces were not the cleanest, nor were their clothes well kept. Patches dotted the garments, obvious they'd been repaired many times over. One of the boys pant leg sat way too high on the lad's ankles. Certainly in this part of London they looked out of place.

This week he'd had several such episodes of children begging him for funds. Out the front of his home he was ambushed by a group of young boys, no more than eight years if a day, begging him for money, their grimy little faces and beseeching eyes ensuring he reached into his coat pocket to give them what they wanted.

He'd thought such an incident was unique, but he'd been wrong. On his return home from a ride in Hyde Park, he'd been accosted by a young woman, her gown was tidy, but she had an air of poverty that dulled her cheeks and eyes. She'd begged him for money to help pay for food for the children she had in her care. Again, he'd reached into his pocket and with nothing but a sovereign, had handed over the coin, granting her a boon she'd likely never see again.

The next few days had passed without incident, but now again, here he was being asked for charity. Never in his life had he been such a target and it truly was becoming absurd. One did not see beggars in Mayfair and St. James.

"Well, boys? What is it that you want?" Although he could guess easily enough.

They stared at him before flicking each other a glance. "We're looking for donations, my lord. To help with our school."

"Your school?" It hadn't been a word he'd heard so far with the other children looking for cash and the word *school* caught his attention. "You are being taught someplace." Hunter narrowed his eyes, curious and starting to see a pattern to all this accosting.

"Spitalfields Orphanage and School. We're raising funds so we can purchase a new building for children in the Ludgate area of the city. Us kids need a lot of help to make a go of it, sir. Help from men like you."

"You certainly do speak as though you've been taught reasonably well." A knowing feeling lodged in the pit of his stomach. "Tell me, who is your patron of the school. So I know where to send a donation."

"Miss Cecilia Smith, my lord."

The older boy whacked the younger one in the stomach, glaring at him. "Ye weren't meant to tell the toff anything, just to get a donation."

Why did it not surprise him... Hunter fought not to roll his eyes. The woman was a minx, a busybody who was now sending her students to ask for funds from a gentleman in Mayfair. He pulled out of his pocket a gold coin and tossed it in the air. As quick as a flash the elder boy's hand reached out and snatched it.

"Make sure Miss Smith receives the donation. And pray tell her, it is all she'll be receiving from me so she can stop sending her charges to do her dirty work."

The boys ran off, laughing and smiling, no doubt at their good fortune at gaining some funds just as their patron had said.

Hunter turned about and headed to Whites. The betting book always had good juicy wagers to lay some funds on, and he wouldn't get the opportunity again to check the log as he was headed to his good friends, Hamish Doherty, Earl Leighton's this evening for a ball.

His steps slowed as he walked along St James Street, the thought of Miss Smith bombarding his mind. What would she think of how he had managed her tricks? Would she be infuriated, challenged? Would her cheeks flush a becoming pink and her eyes sparkled with righteous fire at once again being denied? Suddenly, inexplicably, he could imagine how beautiful she would look in the latest cut and style of gown. A gown that would hug her breasts, and float about her long, thin legs hinting and teasing at what lay beneath. Her hair pulled high, showcasing her elegant neck and perfect profile. Any colour other than the drab grey he'd seen her wearing to date would set off her creamy complexion that looked un-kissed by the sun. A part of him hoped he would see her again. Even if he had to endure another set down, no matter how nicely worded she put them.

I want her. He faltered momentarily at the awareness. Should he wish her to be his mistress, maybe he ought to gain favour by visiting her charity, seeing for himself how she helped and what she did for these unfortunates of London.

Turning about, he looked to where the boys had scurried off to, but they were long gone. Where was it they said they were from again? Hunter started back the way he came and hailed a hackney.

"To Spitalfields Orphanage and school, and quickly."

CHAPTER 4

"I cannot find the box with the new chalkboards, Darcy, do you know where Katherine placed them?" Cecilia asked, wiping a loose strand of hair from her face. All day they'd searched for the missing chalkboards for the children who had just started at the school this week. And with Katherine out with her father in the country regarding a building job, Cecilia had not been able to ask where she'd placed them.

"Lord Aaron, what brings you here?"

Cecilia stopped looking through the cupboard that sat behind a large, reception desk that Darcy, the Duchess of Athelby was too standing behind. The marquess was here? Oh dear lord, that means he'd found out she was behind the children who she'd sent to pester him for funds for their charity. *Damn it.*

She stood, and made her presence known. The Marquess's attention snapped to her, but this time there was no amusement in his gaze, merely indifference. How changeable the man was.

"You know Miss Smith, Duchess?" he asked, not taking his gaze off Cecilia.

Darcy came over and took Cecilia's hand, pulling her over to where his lordship stood. "We've been friends these past twelve months. Our friendship was formed when I joined the London Relief Society, which of course Cecilia runs. I will do anything, as you well know, to help those less fortunate."

Cecilia bobbed a small curtsy. "Can we help you with anything, Lord Aaron?"

He gestured to a room off the side of the front office in which they stood. "I was accosted in the street by two little scamps who hail from this location. Asking for funds on St James Street mind you. This I believe was the fourth instance this week. I've come to suggest you keep a closer eye on those who explain they're under your care and charge."

Darcy grinned and patted Cecilia on the arm. "I think I'll leave you to deal with our delightful friend." She came around the desk and kissed the Marquess's cheek. "Come for dinner this week. We'd love to see you."

Cecilia ignored the stab of jealousy at seeing Darcy kiss a man who she had started to think about more than she ought. The past week she'd been endlessly thinking whether she'd see him again. Wondering if he'd figure out she was the one behind the children begging him for help and come to seek her out, just as he had done now. Cecilia had initially hoped he'd be so annoyed he would want to be rid of her, sell her the property and never see her again, but the thought gave her pause. To think she wouldn't get to verbally spar with Lord Aaron again left her feeling a little lost and disappointed.

She came and stood before him, and again was reminded of how very tall he was. She wasn't a short woman, and normally towered over men, so it was nice, in an exasperating kind of way that he peered down at her.

"Will you not answer my charge, Miss Smith."

"I don't know what you mean," she said, feigning any knowledge of his accusation. "None of our students would dare interrupt or intrude on a very busy and important marquess's affairs. Certainly not on St James's street where the famous Whites' Club is located. How very rude of two young boys to stop you from having your cigars and brandy with men of your ilk, where you'll discuss horses, money and what else is it that you discuss?" she said, forcing the most interested visage she could manage considering she had, in a roundabout way, just insulted the lord.

He stared at her a moment before his eyes narrowed just the slightest. She smiled.

"The boys said they were from this establishment and after our meeting yesterday I can only assume you mean to annoy me with your students until I gave way and sell you my building."

"You could just donate it to us. That would be even better."

"You are, Miss Smith, the most vexing woman I've ever met. I shall not be gifting you the building, now or ever, I can promise you that. I'd also like to ensure that your little scamps do not harass me again." He came around the front desk and stood not an inch from her person.

"I've also noted you're very apt at throwing out the insults to my sphere of Society. Are you jealous, by chance?" Lord Aaron asked.

"Of you and your friends? Well of course, my lord. I long for the days that a woman of a lower class will save my pitiful self on the street because I'm too drunk to see vehicles that are barrelling toward me."

He scoffed, a little muscle in his jaw flexed. "It is only expected that you would find my Society a little daunting since your rank is well beneath mine, and nights of enjoyment such as I endure would not suit you, I think. You're too clouded by your judgements, and would undoubtedly find such entertainments silly and beneath your moral notice. Why I'm surprised you lower yourself to speak to the Duchess of Athelby. However do you manage to do that?"

A peculiar and quite unfamiliar ache pierced her heart. "The duchess is a good woman, and helps those in need, unlike so many of your ilk, including yourself. As for your comment regarding your social sphere, are you saying that I could not hold my own if I attended one of your higher Society's balls?" How dare he imply such a thing. He was baiting her, she knew it, but it didn't change the fact that his words pricked her pride. She'd once longed to be able to attend such dinners and parties. Her own Society was lovely, and she'd grown rather fond of it, but a ball in the *ton*, where jewels and gowns were of the latest fashion, and everyone was free from working restraints, well, she couldn't help but want to see it. If only once.

He leaned closer still, and she caught the scent of mint on his breath. Annoyingly her gaze took in his mouth, his lips appeared soft and well looked after, not chafed or cracked from lack of good food and living. His hand reached out and slid along the desk, trapping her partly within his hold.

"If the slipper fits, Miss Smith."

She met his gaze and glared all the while her body fought for control. He was so close, so large and everything a gentleman of his ilk should be. Strong, intelligent, cutting and witty. A gentleman who seemed to have the uncanny knack to get under her skin. Not many did, but the marquess seemed to be apt at it.

She stepped back. "Since you're here my lord, and you have been most generous with your donations this past week, maybe you'd care for a tour. I can show you the classrooms and where the children sleep if you like. Maybe you'll find the organ that's within your chest wall, and sell to me after all."

He glanced about the foyer, his eyes flicking to the staircase where two little girls chuckled and ran off when spied.

"Lead the way, Miss Smith," he said, holding out his arm for her to take.

Well, she hadn't wished to link her arm with his, and she realized her mistake as soon as she did it. A jolt of awareness shot through her, and she took a calming breath to quiet her racing heart. Cecilia made the tour as short as possible, showing him the varied classrooms which they had in order of age, not gender. The less time she had to be touching him the better. They headed upstairs to where the children slept, their beds, rows after rows, showcasing just how many were in need of help.

"There are so many beds." The marquess frowned, halting at the sleeping quarter doors. "How many schools such as this one do you run, Miss Smith?"

"I have three in London, and one in the country. Of course, the number would grow should I purchase a property in Ludgate as planned."

He nodded but did not venture to enter the room. "I did not know there were so many in need."

Cecilia met his gaze, hearing the surprise in his voice that rang with truth. "A lot of people do not, but it is as you see. A growing problem, and one that I fear I shall never see fixed." They stood there for a couple of minutes, before heading back downstairs.

The duchess bustled into the room, carrying a box, no doubt the missing chalkboards they'd been searching for the past several hours. "I have decided to invite Miss Smith to the ball the duke and I are hosting Saturday next."

Cecilia moved to stand behind the reception desk, her chest tightening at the thought. "I cannot possibly attend your ball, your grace. It wouldn't be correct."

"Correct? La, half of those in attendance have less class than you, my dear and I do not care what anyone of my sphere thinks. You're my friend, we do charity work together, and I wish for you to be there with me. I will not accept any answer from you, but yes."

Cecilia's stomach roiled at the idea of all those people, women who could cut her dead in Society, people looking at her as a second-class citizen simply due to the fact her father worked for a living, didn't inherit it like all those who would be around her. But then, she was friends with the duchess and never felt belittled or looked down upon when with her, so maybe she was a little prejudiced against his lordship's social sphere. And she would not allow the marquess to think she could not attend because she was scared of how she would be treated by his kind. She had nothing to prove to them, if anything, they were the ones lacking in morals.

"Well then, it's a yes." She met his lordship's eye. "You see, Lord Aaron, since you viewed a little of my life, I will now get to view a little of yours. I look forward to seeing you at the ball."

He bowed and started for the door. "Alas, Miss Smith, I do believe I'm otherwise engaged that evening."

Cecilia glared at his back as he walked out the door. She didn't bother to reply, merely ripped open the box that held the chalkboards and pretended it was his lordship's head.

CHAPTER 5

S till smarting from the rude and inappropriate remark from Lord Aaron the week before, Cecilia had thrown herself into her charities and helping her father prepare for court. It left little time for her to dwell on his parting words. How was she to convince him to sell the property if he wasn't in attendance at the ball?

The duchess had said he would be, but until Cecilia saw him with her own eyes, the doubt he would not attend festered.

The young woman she'd hired to help her with her hair placed the last pin in the fashionable and pretty design. Tonight her hair was completely up, but the curls were large and soft looking. A strand of her mother's pearls threaded throughout the design. They may not be rubies or diamonds as so many of the women of the social sphere she was about to enter wore, but they did well enough and at least gave her an air of wealth, even if she did have the stench of trade floating about her silk slippers.

"You look beautiful, my dear. Stand and let me look at

you." Her mother bustled into the room and took her hands, making her stand.

Cecilia twirled for good measure and laughed when her mother dabbed at her eyes.

"It's only a ball, mother. I'm not getting married." She walked over to her bed and slid the soft pink slippers on that matched the dress she'd been lucky enough to find only a few days ago on Cannon Street. The gown had been made for a woman of means, but then when she'd gone to collect the garment, she'd disliked the colour against her skin and refused to take it. The modiste, Madame Perrin was only too happy to give her a small discount if Cecilia would take the dress, and lucky for her, the gown had suited her complexion perfectly, and was suitable without being too fancy.

"Even so, you look so lovely. How wonderful for the Duchess of Athelby to invite you as her special guest. I do hope you'll remember to be polite and try and not let anyone vex you."

Cecilia pulled on her white silk gloves. "I won't pretend to not understand what you're saying, because I do perfectly well. But I promise I shall behave myself, and not allow my mouth to run away from me and tell off all the rich nobs or at least tell them what I truly think of their shallowness. Will that suffice, mama?"

"Now now, you cannot tarnish everyone the same. Some of those in attendance will be just like you, not full of airs and graces, just attending for the enjoyment of fine food, music and dancing. Oh, I do hope I can stay up to hear all about it, but alas no doubt you will not return until the wee hours of the morning."

"I should think so, but do not wait up mama. I'll tell you everything tomorrow at breakfast." Cecilia pulled on her cloak and started for the door. "Now, I must be off. I think I just heard our carriage pull up."

"Have fun, my dear!"

Cecilia chuckled as she made her way outside to the carriage. Well, if she didn't have fun, at least it was a memory that she could keep for the rest of her life. She could say to her children that she once danced and was merry with the haute *ton*. Not everyone could boast such a triumph.

HUNTER NURSED A GLASS OF WHISKY, the amber liquid quenched his thirst, but only for a short time. He needed many more of these tonight if he were to survive it. His nemesis, Miss Smith, stood next to the Duke and Duchess of Athelby and was talking to a fellow Hunter hadn't seen in town for two years or more. The gentleman's name eluded him at present. Who was the blasted flirt?

He took another good sip and blinked to clear his eyes. He'd not intended to attend this evening, certainly not after hearing Miss Smith was invited, but the allure of a pair of very pretty blue eyes changed his plans. Miss Smith was certainly looking very well this evening, the rose pink of her gown suited her fair complexion and long blonde locks, that were arranged atop her head. He had to admit, the hell cat almost looked like one of them, but every now and then something would catch her eye, and the disdain she carried for his lot in life was visible to his inspection.

Hunter sighed and started toward the card room, but his feet, a little more unsteady than he'd believed only got as far as some empty chairs and he sat down, gesturing to a footman to bring him more of that delightful amber liquid.

How long he sat there, lost in his own thoughts was anyone's guess, so when a vision in pink sat beside him, he was startled when she spoke.

"You're foxed, Lord Aaron. Please tell me I'm not going to have to rescue you tonight as well. I don't think these silk slippers would survive the London streets."

He harrumphed. "I need no rescuing, and least of all from you." He frowned at his cutting words that he didn't mean to be so abrupt. But Miss Smith had a way of annoying him greatly, and the fact that tonight she looked more becoming than anyone he'd ever met before only made the situation worse. She was common for crying out loud. No better than the maids who worked in his homes. Well, maybe a little above his employees, but not by much. She took care of everyone, always sought to make people's lives better, whereas he thought of little other than himself, how to enjoy life as much as he could. His parents had certainly lived in such a way, and no harm ever came of it.

A little voice reminded Hunter that no good came from it either.

"Do you get so very drunk all the time, my lord?"

The footman delivered his drink and he took a sip. "Being from the Society that you are, I'll forgive your crass behaviour and give you a little lesson in manners. You never, ever ask a gentleman if he is foxed at any event he attends. You never ask at all. It is no one's concern but mine, and as I'm unwed, and nor am I engaged, I shall do whatever the bloody hell I want."

If he'd expected his words to send her packing, he was greatly disappointed. Miss vexing Smith simply narrowed her eyes at him and wrenched the whisky glass from his hand.

"You are making a spectacle of yourself. Twice now

I've had the unfortunate pleasure of seeing you in such a state. Do you never attend a ball where you're sober? You know if you tried it, you might actually enjoy it."

"I doubt it very much," he said, taking back the glass and finishing it. His eyes watered and he rubbed them, blinking a little to try and clear his vision. Miss Smith was starting to look like a blurry mound of pink.

"You do realize that if you sold me the building, I will leave you alone. I promise never to enter your Society again and will never seek you out as I have done so this evening. So, what say you? Are you willing to reconsider my proposal?"

He blinked again, wanting to see her clearly. Hell, she was pretty, ethereal almost, her features soft, delicate and perfectly structured. Until her eyes that was. They were intelligent, calculating and right at this moment, judgemental. It stung when it shouldn't have, for he did not care about her opinion. Or did he? Hunter frowned, not understanding the unknown disquiet stirring inside.

"No matter what you think of me, Miss Smith, let this be known. I may be a lord, but I do enjoy business, such as buying and selling horse stock, estates that I've inherited but do not use, the building on Pilgrim Street being one of them. But in this instance, as I have explained, I wish to develop it into a gentleman's club, not ruin an area that is improving as a location which should increase in value. It will decrease in value if that site is turned into an orphanage. That would never equate to good business."

She shifted on the chair beside him and met his gaze, her angelic features hard with loathing. Loathing for him. Damn, he didn't like that look on her. He wanted her to look at him with anything but that. Sweetness, heat, passion, anything but contempt.

"You're an embarrassment to Society, *my lord*. At least I'm trying to better the world for those who are less fortunate. What do you do?"

"You're so intelligent, why don't you tell me?" he said, wanting to mock her words as, damn it, they stung. The images of the needy children who'd begged him for money bombarded his mind, and he frowned. Was he an embarrassment? An uncaring, toff. Surely not, it was simply his way of life. He did not deny those who begged him, and over the years he'd instructed his man of affairs to donate to charities when his patronage had been sought.

"You do nothing other than drink yourself into a stupor and make money with your ventures, and yet all around you people live in poverty. At least I can sleep at night knowing I've done my best. You, my esteemed lord, are a parasite."

She stood, and he watched her go. His jaw ached, and he summoned another glass of whisky to dispel his annoyance. What did she know anyway? Who was she to criticise him for how he lived his life.

Hunter stood and started for the card room. He would dispel his frustrations in a game of cards. Better that than strangling the little middle class, righteous heathen in front of all the *ton*.

The card room was full of men, like him no doubt trying to escape the fairer sex or looking for a diversion from them. He spied the Duke of Athelby who had joined a game, and sat himself down at his table, willing to wait for him to be able to join in.

The duke, Cameron to his friends, threw him an amused glance. "What's got you all flustered? You look like you've danced every reel since the beginning of the ball."

Did he look like he'd been dancing like a popinjay? He

shook his head and summoned a glass of brandy from a passing footman. "The vexing woman that your wife brought if you must know. Right now, I have no doubt she's telling your wife that I'm greedy and have no heart, just as she implied to my face five minutes ago."

The duke choked on his wine, and Lord Nash seated across from Hunter bellowed out a God almighty laugh, bringing to attention their table.

"She did what?" Cameron asked, putting his card playing aside for a moment.

"Told me I'm a parasite because I do not help charities like the one she runs, with the help of your wife I might add."

Cameron smirked. "Darcy likes her. She thinks she's intelligent and kind, more than a lot of those in attendance this evening. No offence to you, Lord Nash, of course," the duke said, smiling.

Lord Nash nodded but didn't comment, merely studied his cards. Hunter took a long pull of his drink. "Even so, she does not suit this environment. She is not one of us. Does not fit in. Admit it, Cameron, even you wouldn't lower yourself to talk to her had your wife not made you."

The duke frowned, this time placing his cards down and levelled his gaze on Hunter. "I've known Miss Smith for some years, longer than I've known you, in fact. I use her father's firm for all my legal matters. They may have ink stains on their fingers, but they're very respectable people. And Cecilia is beyond intelligent, even Darcy admitted the other day that she thought Cecilia was more intelligent than her, and that's a rarity." The duke laughed, picking up his cards. "By the way, how sober are you at the moment? I don't want an unjust advantage against you in cards. I always find winning under such circumstances tedious."

Hunter looked down at the empty glass in his hand and waved to the footman for another. "Not foxed enough if anything. Not if I have to put up with middle class hell cats who call me a parasite."

"You are not a parasite, merely misunderstood perhaps or even, not aware so much of what goes on about us outside of Mayfair. I know from Darcy's charity work that I've become more in tune to the poverty people live with. Miss Smith wants you to sell her your building, I think she's showing you her strong opinions regarding the poor, merely to change your mind. I don't believe she means to be cutting or judgemental."

Hunter fought not to scoff. Miss Smith was the most judgemental woman he knew, no matter what Cameron said about the fact. "I am not blind to the poor, I just choose to live without it dictating my every move." The thought sounded uncaring even to Hunter's own ears, and he cringed.

"You're acting as I used to, dear fellow. Like the world should pander to your every wish and desire. Be pretty and correct, not ugly and poor, rough about the edges. Not everyone in London are as fortunate as us. As human beings, we accept this and remain polite, help when we can. I hope you've remained polite to Miss Smith. She does not deserve your cutting words."

Hunter took the drink from the footman and revelled in the sharp scent of brandy. "I was honest with her."

"You were rude, admit it. And now I shall have Darcy onto me about how my friend was rude to hers."

"Darcy is my friend too."

"She won't be after tonight if she finds out you were a prig."

Hunter downed his drink, and the room spun for a

moment. "There was a time when you were a very good prig."

"Just sell her the building, and your troubles with Miss Smith will disappear."

Hunter ran a hand through his hair and leaned back in the chair, no longer looking to play a game of cards. Not here at least. Maybe he'd go to Whites later tonight, and anywhere else the night may take him.

"I have plans afoot on the location for a gentleman's club for bankers and lawyers, men of that calibre. Miss Smith thinks my idea foolish, but I digress, I think it's an untapped money-making venture I want to get started as soon as may be." A flash of pink caught his eye, and he turned to see Darcy and the very woman who vexed him greatly come to stand before them.

Miss Smith curtsied as the duke, and regretfully, Hunter stood to greet them. The duke took Darcy's hand and placed it on his arm, covering it with his as they glanced at each other. A year after their marriage and the pair were still madly in love. As much as Hunter was happy for them, it was also too, a little confronting. He'd grown up in a household where love was folly, fun and games, and not always with your spouse was the tone, not all this affection and fidelity. Hunter wasn't sure what to make of them, or the fact that the duke and duchess made a mockery of his parents' marriage every day. Made a mockery of what he'd always thought as normal in a marriage.

"I've come to steal my husband away for a dance."

Hunter glanced at Miss Smith and smarted at the look of horror that crossed the woman's face. No doubt being left alone with him and his Society left her horrified.

"Lord Aaron, will you do the honour of dancing with our guest, Miss Smith. We would be very pleased if you would," the duchess said, smiling at them both.

"Do not feel that because I accompanied her grace here that I was looking for a dance partner, Lord Aaron." She turned to the duke and duchess. "I shall return to the ballroom and meet up with you after the waltz."

Before the duchess had a chance of reply, Miss Smith turned on her heel and headed back toward the ballroom. Darcy turned her steely gaze on him, and he groaned.

"Hunter, follow Miss Smith and ask her to dance," the duchess said, glaring at him.

"It's obvious she does not care to dance with me." He snatched another glass of whisky from a passing footman. "I do not wish to force her hand."

Just as quick as he'd claimed the drink, Darcy snatched it out of his hands. "I think you've had enough liquor tonight. Now go, and ask her, and be kind or you shall have me to deal with."

He raised his brow at the duchess and instead of arguing the point, which damn it, she probably had an argument for, he headed into the ballroom to seek out Miss Smith.

He saw her nestled in one of the corners, her height making her easy to find. Some rather large and boisterous matrons stood before her and gave him a sharp look when he asked to move past them.

Cecilia too looked at him with contempt, and he tampered down his annoyance and held out his hand.

"Would you care to dance, Miss Smith? I do believe the next song is to be a waltz."

"I do not," she said, crossing her arms and looking over his shoulder.

He took her hand anyway and pulled her toward the dance floor. Hunter cringed as she tightened her hold, stabbing him with her fingernails. What did she have in her gloves, little knives?

"That hurts, Miss Smith."

She swung into his arms, fitting him like a glove. He liked that, and what's more, he liked the feel of her in his hold. Her silk gown slid against his palms, her hand fit perfectly within his, her waist was small and yet still held delectable womanly curves he adored.

"I never do anything without a purpose, Lord Aaron."

He chuckled and steered them down the ballroom floor. "I think we shall enjoy the dance more if we suffer our time together in silence. Are you in agreement, Miss Smith?"

Her crystal clear eyes, unlike his which had a tendency to see things a little blurry most nights narrowed slightly. "I fail to care if we converse or not, but I will tell you this, your breath reeks of whisky, and if you step on my feet again I will retaliate in kind."

Pox on her for insinuating he was foxed. "Maybe you ought to stop breathing then?" He smiled at her shock and then swore when her slippered foot, something that had looked delicate slammed down on his toes.

CECILIA STOOD in the middle of the ballroom and waited for Lord Aaron to regain his composure. Gentleman had their feet stepped on often and so too did women, why he had wrenched her out of his arms while he inspected his injured toe was simply embarrassing. And not for her.

"Is your toe well, my lord. I do apologise. I certainly didn't mean to be so clumsy on purpose." Cecilia smiled at the haute *ton* who looked on, some down their pointed noses, but Cecilia simply allowed their censure to roll off her back. What did it matter what these people thought? Outside of these walls, the majority of them didn't worry about anyone else except their own person or families. Cecilia could count on one hand how many she knew here who worked for her charity or those that worked for other charities like hers.

It was a pitiful few, and the dandy who kneeled before her, inspecting his toe, which she was surprised he could feel at all since he was so drunk, was simply absurd. This was the fourth time she'd been in his lordship's company and the second time she'd seen his glassy, unfocused eyes, not to mention his unsteady gait, although he seemed quite apt at hiding that a lot of the time.

But she didn't miss the slowing of steps to regain one's balance, or the shaking of his hands when he drank, or that the trembling ceased a little once he'd imbibed himself of that liquor. The man was a drunk. Unfortunately, Cecilia had seen many like him, fathers, mothers, carers of the children she dealt with daily. Most of the time the children chose to stay at her institutions on their own accord simply to stay alive.

He stood and pulled her into his arms, twirling them once again into the fray of dancers as if nothing was amiss. Did no one see this man? Did no one know the troubles he fought within his outer visage?

"All is well again, my lord?"

"Yes, it shall be," he said, flicking her a glance that spoke of annoyance more than anything else.

"While I have your ear, tell me, have you thought more on my offer? I do hope you've realised by now that the amount we're willing to pay is reasonable and my idea for the location is more suited for that part of London."

"The property is not for sale, Miss Smith."

His stoic and no-nonsense tone said more than anything that he was at an end with her trying to make him sell. "It doesn't matter anymore anyway. We've found another building for sale, right next door to yours. So even if you refurbish your building to a be a gentleman's club, I'll ensure no one will want to go there simply because of who your neighbours are."

He didn't look at her, merely continued to look bored. "Gentleman will still come, no matter how much you try and sabotage me."

He was the most vexing man she'd ever met.

The dance continued on for a few more minutes, but by the time it came to an end, Cecilia had well and truly had enough being around Lord Aaron and his friends. Cecilia thanked him for the dance, curtsied and sought out the Duchess of Athelby. It was time she returned home in any case. She had an appointment at lunch to look over the paperwork for their new location, and she needed to have her wits about her.

She found the duke and duchess speaking privately, but Darcy as she knew her by when alone, smiled as she came closer and didn't reject her company. "Did you enjoy your dance, Cecilia?" the duchess asked, looking past her, no doubt trying to locate Lord Aaron who was nowhere to be found. Thankfully.

"I did, thank you, but I must return home. As you know I'm looking at the new building we've found tomorrow, and I want to be refreshed and ready for my meeting."

"Did you wish for me to attend? I admit I do not know much about contracts and what is legal, but having a duchess there could be beneficial if the vendor starts to increase his price or some such nonsense."

"No, that shall not be necessary. My father's business partner, Mr. White will be in attendance with me and will ensure all runs smoothly."

The duchess' lips flattened. "Mr. White is going to be there? In that case, I shall be in attendance."

"Why so, my dear?" the duke asked, looking down at his wife, a small frown line between his otherwise perfect brows.

"Mr. White wishes to marry Miss Smith, my dear. Has so for some time. A chaperone is necessary I think."

"Who wishes to marry Miss Smith?" Lord Aaron asked, coming to join them, with two glasses of whisky in hand. He caught her looking at them, and she didn't miss the reluctance when he handed one over to the duke. Like that was what he wanted to do. Ha. He didn't want to part with any of his fine wine or hard liquor if he didn't have to.

"Mr. White, Hunter. Not that we should be discussing such things, here and so openly. I do apologise, Miss Smith."

Cecilia could feel the heat start up her neck and tried to think of anything else other than the fact they were discussing her life and who wanted to be a part of it, if only she'd say yes.

"You're to be married, Miss Smith. Well, aren't you a sly fox. You didn't tell me the wonderful news."

"No, my lord, I did not. And the only thing around here resembling that animal is you. Now, if you'll excuse me." She turned to the duke and duchess. "Good night, your graces."

They bid her farewell, and she ignored the burning between her shoulders. Lord Aaron could try and intimidate her as much as he liked, but she wouldn't allow him to get the better of her. Unfortunately, she would have to make allowances to his lordship since he had a vice that seemed well and truly solidified in him. A man, who, unfortunately, was in his cups most of the time and did not and could not have his wits about him. A man who had learned to not care about anything other than his own self-worth.

Cecilia waited for the footman to collect her shawl and send for her carriage. She sighed in relief. At least that should be the final time she would have to deal with Lord Aaron.

CHAPTER 6

The offices of J Smith and Sons were busy today with in chambers work for upcoming court cases. Cecilia walked into the office her father had gifted her, not only to help him with matters pertaining to law but to have someplace other than their home to work on her charities.

The office had a delightful view of the footpath outside, and she sat behind her desk a moment to enjoy her solitude and her own little space. She'd always loved the room and most of all that her father had given her wall to wall bookshelves for anything she wanted to fill them with.

A light knock on the door sounded, and Mr. White peeked around the threshold, smiling in welcome.

Cecilia pasted on a polite visage and bade him enter, not that she wanted to go over the paperwork for the new location they'd found, and certainly not with him. There was a time when she had liked Mr. White, counted him as a friend, but not anymore. His advances since her father had given him leave to court her had sometimes gone beyond acceptable, and he seemed to think he had the right to touch her person, even clasping her hand to place on his arm or to touch the small of her back. Neither of which she wanted him to do, now or ever. Her objections did not seem to deter the man, and that lowered her estimation of him even further.

"Mr. White, thank you for helping me with these contracts. Please, do be seated. We'll go over them before we head down to Pilgrim Street to look through the building with the vendor."

He sat, his oiled hair slicked severely back made him look like a raven. Pity he wasn't as smart as one of those birds, certainly not when it came to women at least.

"My pleasure, Cecilia, and let me say how fetching you look today. Is that a new gown?"

Cecilia looked down at her drab, brown dress that had no feminine features on it other than the fact it was a dress. She didn't like to wear her best gowns when she came into the office, preferring to be comfortable over fashionable. "Thank you for the compliment, but as this is work, we should probably forget about our clothing and discuss the matter at hand. The purchase, remember?"

"Ah yes, now, I have been thinking over the matter. Your father gave me the contract to look over on the weekend, and while everything within it looks fine, I do not believe it would be a sound investment for your charity." He leaned back in his chair, pulling out a cheroot from his coat pocket and proceeded to light it using the candle that sat burning on her desk.

"Please enlighten me as to why you've come to that conclusion?" The building was solid, not damaged or needing major repairs. The interior, of course, needed full refurbishment and upgrading to house the school and dorms for the children, but that wasn't anything they'd not attempted and completed before in other areas of London.

"A woman of your age should be looking to other things to occupy her time. Like marrying, starting a family, looking after the offspring of her own, not worrying about the poor of London. Who, I might add, will take advantage of your charity and then proceed to do nothing at all with the education you give them. I see such expenditure as a waste of time."

Cecilia stood and made her way to the door, picking up her shawl. "Pick up the papers on the desk and follow me. I don't wish to be late for my appointment." She walked from the room, her teeth clenched tightly closed lest she turnabout and tell this buffoon exactly what she thought of him. How dare he even suggest helping others was a waste of time. The pompous fool had not an ounce of empathy in his body.

What was with the gentlemen of her acquaintance who all seemed to think charity was a waste of time. Was she the only one who cared, who had sympathy?

Cecilia ripped open the carriage door and jumped up into the firm's coach and waited for Mr. White. He soon followed her out and into the vehicle, seating himself next to her instead of taking the seat across. A welcome reprieve from having to occasionally look at him during the journey.

"I did not mean to offend you, Cecilia, but I was talking to your father, and he agrees. This kind of lifestyle you're leading is not becoming of a lady." He paused, pulling at his neckcloth before he met her gaze. "Have you thought any more on the prospect of us marrying? If you agreed, we could be married within a month or so. I know I for one would wish for this very much."

Cecilia held his gaze and for what felt like the hundredth time, picked her words wisely lest she offended the silly man who did not understand the word no.

"Mr. White while you're an honourable gentleman I must repeat what I've said already to you. We would not suit and as sorry as I am to hurt you, my answer regarding your proposal is no. Please do not make our acquaintance any more awkward than it already is by asking again."

He clasped her hand, kissing it with an absurd amount of embellishment. Cecilia stilled and tried to pry her hand free without success. "Mr. White let go of my hand."

"Marry me, Cecilia. I want nothing but to pleasure you in all ways. Let me love you as a husband should love a wife. Perhaps if you allowed yourself to kiss me, you may see I am the man for you, that we would suit."

She tried to wrench free, and it was like trying to pull her hand from *stone*. "I apologise, but I do not see you in a romantic way, sir."

He lunged, an ominous sound if ever there was one, before he pushed her up against the squabs, trapping her there. His disgusting, sloppy mouth took hers, and she gasped. The action was the worst thing she could have done, as he took advantage of the fact and kissed her deeply, more deeply than she'd ever been kissed before.

Vaguely she felt the carriage rock to a halt, all the while she fought to get him off her person. She couldn't breathe, and panic started to rise in her stomach. What if he didn't stop. What if he...

Cecilia heard the carriage door open and watched as the Marquess of Aaron ripped Mr. White from her, pulled the man through the door and throw him most unceremoniously onto the footpath.

For a moment she sat there, trying to regain her composure. Her blood pounded in her ears, her breathing erratic and sitting up, she clutched her hands together to stop them from shaking.

"Miss Smith, are you well?"

The voice, deep, cultured and one filled with concern lulled her from her shock.

"Miss Smith?" he asked again.

Cecilia turned toward Lord Aaron who studied her in a way she'd never seen before. He actually appeared genuinely concerned. She nodded, and a curl dropped beside her cheek. Reaching up she tried to amend her hair which had been terribly dishevelled during her scuffle with Mr. White. Oh dear lord, what would the marquess think of her?

"I am well." She turned to his lordship and spied Mr. White standing aside from the duchess, his cheeks flushed red. "Thank you for removing, for helping me to remove…"

"You're welcome, come," he said, holding out his hand. "I accompanied the duchess today as she insisted she be here for the inspection and the duke was unable to escort her. I would say after what I just witnessed that it was a good thing we did come."

Cecilia nodded, giving his lordship her hand as he helped her step down. "Are you not angry that we're inspecting the building right next to yours, my lord? I hope you're not here to outbid me on the property."

"I am not here for that, I do have an alternate reason for coming."

"And that is?" she asked, not sure she was fully comfortable with the caring, sober marquess. When he was like this, he was likeable and more handsome than she liked to admit.

"To apologise for my treatment of you the other evening. I was harsh and unkind, and I'm sorry for that."

Lost for words, his lordship placed her hand on his

arm, gesturing for the duchess to start toward their intended location. "But before we go any further there is a matter I need to address." He came up to where Mr. White was standing and stopped. "Go ahead, Miss Smith. I will join you and the duchess shortly." Cecilia did as he bade and came up to Darcy, who took her hand in support.

From where they stood Cecilia couldn't hear what the marquess was saying to Mr. White, but whatever it was the man's cheeks turned a darker crimson with every word. The marquess made Mr. White appear small, and he was a tall man himself. Cecilia couldn't help but take in the marquess's appearance and revel in it a little. For all his vices and opinions, he was dastardly good looking. A hell-raising rake.

Mr. White looked over at her, glaring, and she refused to back down to his bullying and look away. How dare he try and make her feel like she'd done something wrong? When she returned home, she would inform her father of his inappropriate conduct in the carriage and have the leech fired.

The Marquess stood back gesturing to the carriage, and Mr. White stepped inside, and before long the carriage was gone, and Cecilia and the duchess were left with his lordship. A gentleman came toward them on the footpath and waved as he came closer.

"Miss Smith, how very sorry I am for being late. I was held up at the office." He held out his hand, and Cecilia shook it.

"This is the Marquess of Aaron and the Duchess of Athelby, Mr. Conners." Cecilia made the introductions, and comically the older gentleman's mouth popped open and couldn't form words for a moment. She supposed it wasn't every day that the lawyer would meet such people of high rank.

Their tour of the building was brief as most of the interior was the same, run down and dark. It did have potential, but would cost more to repair than Cecilia's first choice. There was plenty of room for sleeping quarters and large enough that the school could be kept separate from those areas. Cecilia clasped her hands before her, trying to stem their shaking. She would not let her altercation with Mr. White dampen her inspection of this site.

The duchess had moved into another area of the building with Mr. Conners, and Cecilia found herself alone with the marquess. Quite alone and in quite a dark little room, maybe a storeroom at one time. Unlike when she was trapped in the carriage with Mr. White, her stomach didn't have a ball of uneasiness lodged within it, if anything, she felt protected and safe. How strange, but also perplexingly wonderful.

"I still think my building is a much better option," the marques said, taking out a silver flask and having a small sip.

"Have you changed your mind? I would purchase that one if only you weren't such a greedy little lord," she said, grinning a little to temper her words.

He chuckled, and a devilish light flickered in his cobalt coloured eyes. "There is nothing little about me, Miss Smith."

She rolled her eyes and fought not to blush. The man had no shame. "Self- praise is never a virtue, my lord." Cecilia chuckled and walked to a nearby window, looking over the street below.

His footsteps sounded behind her, coming to a halt near her back. "Did he hurt you?"

Although he didn't ask who had hurt her, she understood who he meant. "He forcibly kissed me, wouldn't let me go. I shall speak to my father about his conduct. Mr.

White wishes to marry me, you see. I should amend, that is to say, he believes we will marry, it's just a matter of time."

"Will your father allow the gentleman to get away with such insult to your person. Do you wish for me to speak to him?"

Cecilia turned and met his gaze. "No, it'll be fine, I'm sure my father will deal with Mr. White severely and immediately upon my return."

"Has he tried to kiss you before?"

His lordship's gaze dropped to her mouth, and the most delicious shiver rolled about in her belly. Did the marquess wish to kiss her too? Was that what he was thinking? *Oh, yes please.* He might vex her at every turn, but she'd rather have any other memory than that of Mr. White.

"He's shown little signs of ownership of me in front of his work colleagues and my father, but he's never tried to kiss me before. But then, we'd never been alone before."

"Like we are now."

Cecilia nodded. "Exactly, but I don't think I have anything to worry about with you, Lord Aaron. We are not what you would call friends or anything near lovers."

"Are we not?" he stepped closer still, and Cecilia caught the scent of sandalwood.

Oh dear, not only was he one of the most handsome men of her acquaintance, but he also smelt divine. Their eyes met and held. A shiver of expectation ran through her as he leaned toward her. Cecilia followed his lead, and at the last moment, before their lips touched, she closed her eyes.

The chatter of the duchess' voice sounded in the corridor outside and as slow as a cat, Lord Aaron stepped away as if nothing, in particular, had almost occurred between them. Cecilia took a calming breath, her blood thumping loud in her ears.

What was she thinking even contemplating allowing his lordship to kiss her? Especially here where they were not entirely alone. She watched him, and he cast a quick glance her way, and her stomach flipped at the unsated need that burned within his cobalt gaze.

"I think the charity should put in an offer, Cecilia. This will be the perfect location, and it's large enough with little structural things fixed on it, if I'm reading the report correctly that is. Of course, we'll have your father's law firm look over the contract, but I think it's quite perfect. What do you say?"

Cecilia couldn't agree more. "If father approves the contract we'll place an offer Mr. Conners. We'll be in contact again next week to let you know."

With their appointment completed, they made their way back outside. Cecilia cursed Mr. White as the fiend hadn't bothered to send the company carriage back for her. The carriage sporting the Marquess's emblem on its door sat parked beside the curb, the driver seated atop with a large whip in hand. "Allow us to escort you back home or to the offices, Miss Smith."

"Thank you, that is very kind," she said, taking his lordship's hand, and climbing up into the equipage.

Once seated, they pulled away and the duchess glanced at her. "I have an appointment with the duke that I cannot be late to. Do you think you could drop me off first, Lord Aaron? I know it isn't ideal, but we've spent longer than I thought we would at the building, and I'm now in danger of missing it."

"That is no trouble, I assure you." Lord Aaron turned toward where the driver sat and opened a little window inside the carriage and notified the driver of the change of direction. Closing it again he caught Cecilia's eye and her stomach clenched in that odd little way that only he seemed to bring forth.

"Are you comfortable with me taking you back home or to your office, Miss Smith? We shall be unchaperoned for a few minutes at least. I do not wish to injure your reputation."

"That will be fine, my lord." Within a few minutes, the carriage rocked to a halt outside the duchess' London home, and Cecilia couldn't help but look up at the massive, impressive Georgian structure and marvel at its size and the opulent wealth and power it portrayed to those looking in.

And yet, the duchess was a kind, honest woman who didn't see people for what material things they had. No, she had a solid moral code and surrounded herself with people who helped others before themselves. Cecilia supposed somewhere within the marquess he must have a heart beating and more common sense than what she'd been privy to if the duchess called him her friend.

Bidding the duchess goodbye the carriage pulled back out into the busy London traffic. "Did you wish to return to your father's offices or home, Miss Smith?"

"Actually, I'd prefer to return home. It's in Cheapside I'm afraid, so you'll be doubling back. I'll talk to papa about what happened today in privacy and without the possible interruption of Mr. White."

The marquess called out the change of direction and settled back in the squabs. He took out his flask and had a small sip before placing it back in his coat pocket. "The gentleman your father has as his successor is no gentleman at all. If you only ask, I shall ensure he's removed from your father's employ where he can never touch you again."

Cecilia sighed, if only it were that easy. "Father wishes

for me to marry him, and I suppose if he gets his way, Mr. White will be able to touch me whenever he wishes."

"Never say such words. The thought of him touching you makes my blood run cold."

The blood in her veins did the exact opposite. "I think you've been imbibing too much on that silver flask in your pocket, Lord Aaron," she said it with a tinge of amusement, but his statement was anything but funny. His lordship would never look to her as a possible wife, she was too bossy, too opinionated and most of all, too common. A man like Lord Aaron would expect her to become a lady of leisure, sew, paint and be at home so other ladies of similar standing could call and they could all discuss the mundane news of tonnish life.

But then, the duchess didn't live such an existence, she was involved with many charities and Cecilia had never heard her mention that she must be at home for appointments of that kind. So maybe life could be different... If he stopped drinking which by the looks of it would not stop anytime soon.

"No such thing. I may like my liquor, Miss Smith, but I still have my faculties, most of the time at least and I can assure you, seeing you married to Mr. White would not please me."

"Really," she said, raising one brow. "What would please you, my lord?" Did she really wish to know? His gaze met hers and the intent she read in his blue steely eyes would have made her weak in the knees had she been standing.

HUNTER WATCHED AS MISS SMITH, Cecilia bit her bottom lip. He wanted to reach for his flask, soothe the hunger he had for the liquor almost every moment of every day, but he didn't. Another hunger rumbled within, one where he kissed the woman who sat across from him with abandon. Crush her lips against his and taste her sweet self that had haunted his dreams for days.

He leaned back against the squabs. "What an interesting question Miss Smith. What would please me? Do you really wish to know? You may not like what I say in return."

"I think I shall be able to handle your reply."

He shifted over to the seat beside her. Miss Smith merely raised her chin at his forward manner but didn't move away. "Last chance to deny me."

She shook her head. "No, I want to know. Please tell me," she said, breathlessly.

"I want...I want to kiss you, remove all trace of that god-awful thing that was molesting you when I opened your carriage door." His hand reached up, and he traced her bottom lip with his thumb. "So soft."

Her attention snapped to his lips. He had her now, and she was thinking possibly even imagining what it would be like to kiss him back.

"Do you think that would be a good idea? We're in the middle of London, anyone could see us and what we were doing in here."

Hunter quickly untied the carriage blinds and let them drop. Ensconced in privacy, he raised his brows, grinning. "Better, Miss Smith? Or are you too scared to kiss me."

"I'm not scared of anything, least of all you," she said, shuffling closer, clasping his jaw and kissing him just as he'd hoped.

For a moment he was stunned that she'd been the one to initiate the kiss, chaste as it was, but when she went to pull away, he put paid to that and wrenched her back. He'd wanted to kiss her for days now, and no way in hell would he leave today without tasting her. Her lips were soft, supple and kissing him with the expertise of a courtesan. For a moment he wondered where she'd learnt such skills before the light graze of her breasts against his chest made him lose all train of thought.

He ached with want of her, something he'd not experienced before, not even with his past mistresses. Her hand slid into his hair, tugged him closer still, and he didn't deny her. His tongue touched hers, tentative at first and within a moment she was kissing him with as much need, as much enthusiasm as he was. He would never get enough of her.

Her hairpins gave way, and her long golden locks fell about her shoulders. He wanted to wrench away, see what she looked like in such disarray, but he couldn't, no matter how much he tried.

The carriage rocked to a halt, and she drew away, her cheeks a pretty shade of pink, her eyes wide and full of revelation.

"I hope that hasn't scared you off, Miss Smith," he managed to say, clearing his throat when it sounded too heavy with need, too deep with want.

"On the contrary Lord Aaron, it's merely made me more curious."

Although her words rang with truth, Miss Smith did in fact bolt from the carriage and toward her front door which opened when she started up the stairs. Hunter watched her go, even if he wanted to follow her and see where that kiss could lead. He took out his flask and the scent of the whisky smelt less tempting. There was something much more delicious and damn it, it had disappeared into the house without even a backward glance.

He tapped his cane on the roof, and the carriage pulled away. Where would he see her again? Or better yet, how could he manage to get them together again without being obvious. He would write to the duchess on his return home and see if she had any plans of inviting Miss Smith to any more events.

And if not, well, he would just have to ensure he ran into her somewhere. And somewhere soon.

CHAPTER 7

Cecilia sat in her father's office at home, staring in disbelief as he chastised her for the atrocious behaviour she'd partaken in within the carriage the day before. For a moment, Cecilia had thought he'd learnt of her forwardness with Lord Aaron but was only slightly relieved to hear he was, in fact, talking about Mr. White.

"I was not at all in the wrong, papa. He forced me to kiss him. Something that has not, nor ever will interest me."

Her father leaned forward on his desk, clasping his hands together atop the parchment that lay before him. "He is a good match for you, my dear. He's also going to take over the business when I pass on. I would prefer that he marries someone in the family if only to keep the business in our hands. I would so hate for it to be lost."

Cecilia stood and paced in front of the windows. "Father, I do not love him, nor do I find him at all attractive and even less so now that he took the liberty to insult me when he had no right. I'll not put up with that from him or anyone else, and I'll not do as you ask. If you want the company to stay in the family hands, I suggest you have another child with mother and try for a boy, or you leave it to me."

"Cecilia, that isn't fair," her mother said. "You know we tried for other children, alas unsuccessfully."

Her father's face mottled in anger and for a moment Cecilia wondered if she'd pushed him too far with her words.

"How dare you, child. How dare you speak to us in such a way! I'm the head of this household, and under no circumstances shall you address me or your mother with so little regard or forethought."

Cecilia took a calming breath. How dare she? How dare they try and make her marry a man that made her skin crawl. "I may be your daughter, I may be female and looked upon as a lesser person in our Society, but I know I'm smarter than Mr. White and more than capable of keeping the men who work under you in control, motivated and in employment under my authority. You do not need to give it away to Mr. White simply because he's a man. You know, deep down what I'm saying is true, you simply have to trust me enough, love me enough to see that I'm worthy."

"You are worthy dear, never think that we believe anything other than that," her mother said, wringing her hands.

Her father shook his head, a deep frown line between his brows. "A woman would not be suitable, and it would only be a matter of time before people stopped seeking our services. I cannot risk the family's livelihood, a company I've taken twenty years to build up, to lose it simply to make my daughter happy. No," he said, standing and pouring himself a tumbler of brandy. "You shall marry Mr.

White and inherit the firm through him. It is more proper and suitable."

"Are you saying you're going to force me to marry him?" The horror of such a thought made her reach out and clasp the wall for support. To imagine Mr. White touching her again, not just kissing her, but sleeping next to her in bed, laying with her over and over. Her stomach recoiled, and she covered her mouth fearing she'd vomit.

Her mother came over and took her hand. "Mr. White isn't so bad, my dear. He's from a respectable family and is not unkind. You could do worse."

"While I do not want to force your hand, my dear, I will if you keep fighting me on this. I'll give you this season to become accustomed to Mr. White and his ways. Get to know him a little better. He isn't as bad as you may think, Cecilia."

He was worse. Cecilia looked out the window and watched as a coal cart rumbled by. She would ruin herself before she allowed herself to be married to such a prig. A slimy one at that.

She walked from the room and didn't reply. There was nothing left to say. Her parents' mind seemed made up and unless she found someone more suitable than Mr. White, better connected and willing to take on her father's firm, she would end up married to the man.

She paused at the bottom of the stairs. How could she bear such a life? She could not. She would not.

"Miss Smith, a letter from the Duchess of Athelby for you."

Cecilia took the parchment and broke the ducal seal. Scanning the letter quickly it stated that she was invited to a masquerade ball to be held at their good friends London estate, his lordship Hamish Doherty, Earl Leighton. The letter also said she could bring a guest.

She would take Katherine with her. She'd love to attend such a high Society event, and it would be one night that her future with Mr. White would be out of her mind. She had the season to convince her father. Otherwise, she would have to take matters and her life into her own hands and walk away from the family. She would not marry simply to ensure her father's company remained in their family. Such a bargain was neither fair nor right. She could become a teacher at one of the schools she'd opened. They raised their own funds, and other wealthy benefactors, such as the Duchess of Athelby might be willing to donate more to substitute the loss of her father's patronage, which she'd no doubt lose.

Even living on limited means as such a change in circumstance would ensue, was better than marrying a man she did not love. She would do anything but that.

৩৩৩

A WEEK PASSED, and finally, it was the night of the ball. The masquerade was a crush. The array of gowns, jewels, laughter and candlelight made the room seem like a glittering dream and Cecilia, and Katherine stood at the doors as the Duke and Duchess of Athelby walked ahead of them into the throng.

"Oh my, Cecilia. What a magnificent spectacle!"

Cecilia smiled and entwined her arm with Katherine's, pulling her forward. "It is truly a sight and one we shall never see again most likely. Promise me one thing tonight, my dear."

"Anything," Katherine said, her attention snapping from one costume to another.

There were many. The guests had outdone themselves with an array of characters present, jokers, pirates, mythical creatures and those who were less risqué, simply chose evening attire, silk gowns adorned with masks that sparked with jewels or feathers.

"That we forget where we're from, we take the opportunity to have fun, dance and laugh and forget all else."

"That sounds heavenly," Katherine said, smiling when a gentleman bowed before her in a flourishing, very much over the top manner, and asked her to dance. The man's costume was almost entirely black, foreboding even, and his mask covered his face entirely giving him an air of mystery.

Cecilia watched them disappear into the throng of dancers already on the ballroom floor and continued behind the duke and duchess.

They came to stand at the end of the long room beside the terrace doors which were open. Many of the guests were taking the opportunity to step out to take the air. The gardens were well lit, and outside looked just as pretty as the interior of the house.

Cecilia checked her attire. This evening she'd worn a white satin short sleeved gown with a green cape fastened on one of her shoulders that folded over her front, almost concealing her waist, but not quite. It was pinned to her hip by a pretty diamond paste broach her mother had loaned her for the evening. A single green plume was incorporated into her hair, and a plain silver mask concealing her eyes completed the outfit.

"Lord Leighton has gone to a lot of trouble for this ball. Does he hold it yearly?"

"He does," the duchess said, taking the glass of champagne her husband passed to her, before giving it to Cecilia. "I remember last year when I attended, my husband who wasn't my husband at the time didn't approve."

The duke looked down his nose at Darcy before he grinned. "I approve now, my dear."

Cecilia looked away as it seemed a private, husband and wife conversation was happening between the pair and she didn't want to intrude.

"I believe Lord Aaron will be here this evening."

"As to that, my dear." The duke scanned the crowd, frowning a little. "Hunter may be late. I believe he's bringing a guest."

"Really," the duchess said, casting a glance in Cecilia's direction. "Who?"

Cecilia picked out Lord Aaron well before the duke said anything else, and she watched as his lordship made his way over to them. Tonight Lord Aaron seemed bedraggled, his hair hardly tamed and the stubble growth of his beard barely covered by the mask that he wore. The woman holding his arm oozed breeding and rank, and she looked stunning in her red empire style gown with gold embroidered flowers about its hem.

Cecilia turned her attention back to the dancers and tried to ignore the ringing in her ears. The room spun, and distantly she heard the duke of Athelby curse. Unable to stop herself, her attention snapped back to the pair coming toward them while she tried not to die of humiliation. Did he make sport of kissing many women in carriages and then attend balls with new lovers? Not that he owed her anything. He'd surely not promised her courtship, or that their kiss was the beginning of an understanding, but really, what was he about. As it stood, he certainly looked like the ass he'd painted himself the first day she'd met him.

Lord Aaron bowed before them, hardly glancing in her direction when he bade her a good evening.

The duchess smiled at the woman and gestured her

toward Cecilia. "Miss Smith, may I introduce you to Lady Henrietta Morton, recently from Bath if memory serves me correctly."

Lady Morton curtsied. The woman's eyes were glassy and a little bloodshot, similar to Lord Aaron's. "Your grace, it's lovely to be back in town. Bath, as you understand, is only very small, and when Lord Aaron begged me to come to town, well, how could I refuse him?"

How indeed… "You live in Bath most of the time, your ladyship?" Cecilia asked, not wanting to seem rude and uninterested in Lord Aaron's partner. She took a calming breath and smiled tentatively even though her hands shook in her silk gloves. What a fool she'd been. A silly little game to his lordship and now his new little game was smirking at her in return.

"I'm sorry, who are you?" Lady Morton asked, inspecting her as if she were a bug.

Cecilia fought not to fidget. "I'm Miss Cecilia Smith, your ladyship." Cecilia took a glass of ratafia from a passing footman, anything to help keep her hands from giving her unease away.

"Are you related to the Smiths of Hampshire? They reside at Woodrest Abbey."

"Ah, no," Cecilia said, taking a sip of her drink. "My father's a barrister and runs J Smith and Sons law firm in Cheapside."

Her ladyship laughed, and the duchess glared at the woman, but Lady Morton took no heed of the silent warning from her better, merely continued to chuckle. "And you're here, why? I didn't think these events allowed people of your ilk to attend."

Cecilia bobbed a small curtsy. "The same could be said of you, Lady Morton for you have no manners and therefore no class. Please excuse me," she said, heading toward the retirement room, hating the fact her ladyship's cutting remarks had gotten the better of her. She needed to get away from the woman before she said anything else as rude as what her ladyship said.

Entering the foyer, she followed a small group of women who were talking and walking toward their mutual destination. How dare Lady Morton speak to her in such a way and how dare Lord Aaron allow it. She might be of a lower class, but she was friends with a duchess, that at least should afford her some meagre amount of respect.

An arm came about her waist and pulled her into a small sitting room opposite the retirement room that she was about to enter. Before she turned, Cecilia knew who was behind her, and she masked her features before facing Lord Aaron. He had played his cards and shown their value, and she would not be fooled again.

"What are you doing here? The duchess never informed me that she was inviting you this evening."

Cecilia raised her brows, nonplussed. "And she has to inform you of everything she does? I think not. Excuse me," she said, making for the door.

He pulled her back, and she caught the stench of whisky on his breath. "Already in your cups, my lord. How very original of you."

Lord Aaron swallowed, running a hand over his face and pulling off his mask. "I was going to call on you."

She narrowed her eyes, staunchly ignoring the butterflies taking flight in her stomach. "And why would you do that? We are not friends nor do we circulate in the same Society. I'm only here by invitation by the duchess. And I can promise you, after tonight, I will not be attending another ball near any of you people." She would exclude the duchess of course from this, but everyone else could go hang.

"Lady Morton is an old friend of my family, a woman who's been brought down financially by her late husband. Being the younger son of a penniless duke, they were never flush with cash. She merely asked me for assistance in helping her re-establish herself in London. There is nothing romantically happening between us if your prickly attitude toward me has any explanation."

She sucked in a very audible breath. "Excuse me, Lord Aaron I am not prickly in any way. And if I was rude about your friend, it was merely because she was very impolite. I'll not be talked down to from anyone, least of all a woman who smells as strongly of liquor as you do."

A muscle on his jaw clenched. "May I remind you that your continual reminders and sly remarks about my intake of alcohol are not acceptable. Not by anyone."

She shrugged. "I care not what is or isn't acceptable. You, Lord Aaron, are always foxed, slurring your words, and bringing women of questionable morals to balls. Do you not see how unacceptable that is? If your friends will not try and help you see a better way forward than being in your cups all the time, caring for nothing but folly and how you can spend your precious money on unimportant things, then I shall. There is nothing lost if we are not friends."

His lordship stepped in front of her when she went to make another escape. What was the man's problem! She glared up at him. "Move out of my way."

"Nothing lost? Do you mean that?"

"You continue to prove my point. No man who was not drunk would ever ask a woman so forward a question. You are practically asking if I like you, and you should not and would not if you weren't so drunk."

"I'm not that drunk," he said, swaying a little toward her.

Cecilia crossed her arms. His gaze veered to her bosom, slightly pushed up because of her stance, so she dropped her arms at her side.

"I think there would be a great opportunity lost if you walked out of my life."

"You made me feel like a fool. I kissed you and then you arrive at a ball with another woman. I know you've made no promises to me, and I have no expectations, but you should at least, as a gentleman, act with some sensitivity. Now if you'll excuse me, Lord Aaron, I wish to leave."

❦

HUNTER SWALLOWED the panic that coursed through him at Cecilia's words. He'd not thought she would be at Lord Leighton's masked ball. He'd only brought Lady Morton this evening to reintroduce her to a Society she'd been absent from for some years. No harm in that.

Stupid mistake seeing Miss Smith was in attendance, and it made him look like he had women at his beck and call. Brought them to balls and parties without thought to women, or to at least one woman whom he'd kissed with abandon only last week.

"You may be right, I may drink more than I ought, but know this. There is nothing between Lady Morton and myself. I will admit to having relations with her during her marriage, which is not my proudest moment I grant you, but I have not, and I am not looking to renew those relations anytime soon."

Hunter clasped her chin and brought her crystal blue eyes back to look at him. Hell, she was pretty, with a mouth that begged to be kissed, and damn it, he wanted to kiss her again. Had thought of little else since last week.

"If you must know the truth, I think of you. Of your

opinionated self, of your intelligent conversations and witty repertoire. Of your beauty both in and out. Your charitable personality that leaves me to shame. You are the only woman who's not throwing themselves at my feet, and it is literally driving me to distraction."

She did look at him then, her perfectly straight teeth clasping her bottom lip and driving him even more obsessed with her person.

"I think about you all the time. I think about kissing you all the time," he murmured.

"You wish to kiss me again, Lord Aaron?"

He nodded before caution could halt his reply. "Yes, I do," he said, not willing to hide anymore his feelings toward the woman before him. Not wanting to, if he were honest. She would be the perfect mistress, keep him interested and never bored. Blast it all, he wanted to taste her again if she'd allow.

"If you ever wish to kiss me again, my lord the price you need to pay is the liquor you're so fond of. Do not touch a drink at any event up until you see me again, and I shall grant you such a boon."

His gut clenched at the thought of not having brandy in front of his fire at home, or a lovely, well-aged whisky at events such as this. "Am I allowed wine?"

"No, tea and coffee are acceptable, along with fruit punch, so long as it's alcohol-free. And if you are then, my lord, still interested in kissing a woman half your rank, a bluestocking well on the shelf, sober of course, then I shall allow you to kiss me," she said, with a stubborn lift of her chin.

"You think I only want you because I'm in my cups? Which by the way, I'd like to point out I'm not that drunk." He hated that she was thinking such things. It couldn't be more from the truth. There had been many times he'd thought of her, wanted her and had not taken one ounce of drink.

"I do think that."

He frowned. "Well don't, because when I win this war, and I'm standing before you sober, you will experience and see just how much I want you for you, not because of any liquid courage." And then he would ask her to consider being his mistress, allow him to pamper and care for her in a mutually satisfying manner.

His life up to the point when he'd met her was filled with nothing but self-gratification. Cecilia was a pure soul, made him want to be a better man. Due to her rank, he could never look at her as anything other than a lover, but that didn't mean he couldn't make her life sweeter, make his own life worth more than how it currently stood. With such a lifestyle she could continue her charity work and never have to worry about marrying anyone to keep a roof over the children's head that she cared for.

She gazed up at him, innocent and yet there was a strength, and intelligence that lurked in her cerulean orbs and he wanted that for himself. He wanted her in his life. Hunter straightened his back and bowed. "I will ensure you're invited to the next event the duke and duchess attend, and there, Miss Smith, you shall lose this wager."

She reached up and clasped his jaw, and he stilled at the feel of her touch. At some point, she'd removed her gloves, and her soft hand was warm and comforting, making his gut clench. "No, Lord Aaron, don't you see, I shall win either way and so too will you."

"Will you dance with me?"

CECILIA NODDED. "YES."

They made their way back to the ballroom to the orchestra playing a waltz. Cecilia spied Katherine dancing with another masked stranger, and the duke and duchess too were partaking in the risqué dance.

"Do you like to dance, Miss Smith?" the marquess asked, twirling her quickly and making her laugh.

"I do, although we do not go out as much as we used to during my debut. If it hasn't passed your notice, I'm quite on the shelf."

"You never wished to marry?" he asked her, watching her so closely that heat spread through her veins. Did he like what he saw? Did his questioning of her mean he wanted to get to know her better?

"I was courted, but I never found any gentleman whom I cared for enough to give myself to. And so I threw myself into charity work, found a new love, that of the children who rely on me. I'm not concerned if I never marry, no matter what my father may think. I'm quite content with my situation in life."

He shook his head at her words. "You're so confident in your direction. I fear I have little. I suppose I truly do look like a fop who does nothing with his life, other than spend it unwisely."

His hand tightened about her waist during a turn, and her heart thumped in her chest. She swallowed. "You do not have to live in such a way. You're a powerful lord, think of all the wonderful things you could do if only you wished to."

"Give to charity, you mean? Not build my gentleman's club," he asked grinning.

She chuckled. "Not just that, you could pursue other venues to help others, like enter the house of Lords and seek change for the poor. Stop children from having to work and instead send them to school. Better housing for the poor, better water supply, drainage, and heating for their homes."

He shook his head. "I'm in awe of you, Miss Smith. I do believe you're born before your time. Never have I ever met someone with such determined, good opinions. A steadfastness to try and make others' lives better. You shame me."

"No," she said, not wanting him to think in such a way. "I'm far from perfect, like you I have my flaws. I'm opinionated and judgemental, as you've seen. Not everyone has the stomach for the work I do, and I should be more understanding of that, not condone and condemn."

"Sometimes, as with me, it's appropriate, but I know, with your help I can change, possibly make changes in my life and others."

Cecilia smiled, having not thought she'd ever hear his lordship state such. He'd been so impossibly blind to others that she'd placed him in the box of no hope. "I know you can."

CHAPTER 8

T he following week Cecilia sat in her father's library, crafting letters to his clients on their updates and progress as per her father's notes. It was an occupation she enjoyed and since her hand was more legible than her father's it was something he allowed her to do for him.

A loud, knock sounded at the door, and Cecilia placed her quill down as the voice, speaking quickly to their butler was familiar. The library door swung wide, and the Duchess of Athelby strolled into the room, her usually serene countenance, reddened by exertion and marred by worry.

Cecilia stood. "Your grace, is everything well?"

The duchess came to stand before the desk, shaking her head. "You must come with me. The Marquess of Aaron is in a terrible state. Now, before you say anything, hear me out."

The duchess paused, and Cecilia nodded her approval.

"He mentioned to the duke that you'd made a wager with him, one that he has taken very seriously over the last seven days. So much so, that he's become very unwell."

A warmth flowed through her veins that the marquess had gone through with his promise. Did it mean he cared for her, maybe saw her as someone to spend the rest of his life with, have a family of their own? Is he someone she would want to spend the rest of her life with? Cecilia gestured for the duchess to sit and took a seat herself, dismissing the thought. Never had the marquess stated anything of the kind, other than wanting to kiss her he'd made no promises to her. She shouldn't get ahead of herself. "May I speak, your grace? Plainly, if you will allow."

"Of course, but this is not all I have to tell you."

"I think I know what the rest of your words will be, but may I tell you what I know?"

The duchess nodded, wringing her hands in her lap. "Of course."

"Working in the charities that I do, we see similarities with people who suffer from different afflictions. I don't know if you're aware, but I fear the Marquess of Aaron cannot control himself when it comes to wine or whisky, drinks of that nature. To brutally say it, he is a drunk, your grace. A very well spoken and dressed one at that, but even so, he has barrel fever. Our wager was for him to cease drinking, and he is now having repercussions due to his choice. It is not pleasant, and it will take time, but he will get through this."

The Duchess stared at her a moment before she said, "While I admit to being aware somewhat of this affliction, what is happening to him now is not at all good. He's very unwell, and he's asking for you. Will not allow anyone else to see him. Cameron is worried sick, and even though what I'm asking you to do is beyond proper, will you come with me. Help me, help him."

Cecilia stood, not needing to be asked twice. The thought of Hunter suffering made her stomach recoil. "Of course, I'll help. Let me pack a small valise. When I go to visit the orphanage in the country, I always sleep over. I'll leave a message for papa stating that is where I've gone. He'll not assume I've gone to the marquess's home instead."

The duchess clasped her hand. "You're very good, and we will keep your name and your visitation to the marquess's home secret, I promise you that. We'll not allow anyone to know that you were there."

It wasn't long before the duchess' unmarked carriage pulled into the mews at the back of the marquess's home on Berkeley Square. A stable hand came out and helped them down, before going through the back garden to ensure they weren't seen arriving and headed indoors.

The home was not what Cecilia had expected. For some reason, she'd assumed the house would be dark, mysterious just like its owner, but instead, it was brightly lit, wax candles burning in every room and hallway. There were well-kept carpet rugs and highly polished floorboards. The staircase that sat centre in the entrance hall too was well lit, and from the base of the stairs, Cecilia could see that the first-floor landing housed many portraits, possibly of past family members.

"Shall we go up?" the duchess asked, stepping toward the stairs.

"Of course. I'll follow you." They went upstairs, and the duke met them on the landing.

"He still will not allow me to enter." The duke bowed.

"Good afternoon, Miss Smith. I do apologize for our intrusion into your day, but we would not have done so had we not thought it the most important."

Cecilia curtsied. "Do not tax yourself, your grace. It was my silly bet with the marquess which has brought on his current symptoms, it is only right that I try and alleviate them in some way."

"You're too kind," the duchess said. "Hunter's room is the third door on the left. We shall go downstairs and order some tea. Please have a servant fetch us if there is anything we can do to help. There is one outside his door at all times. Unfortunately, it is not us the marquess was asking for."

"I shall," Cecilia said, making her way to the room and placing her bag beside the door. She stood there without making a sound while she watched the duke and duchess head downstairs. Taking a deep breath, she knocked hard twice.

"Lord Aaron, will you let me in? It's Miss Smith."

No sound came from the room, and just before she was about to knock again, the lock turned, and the door swung wide. He was worse than Cecilia had imagined, and without saying a word, she entered the room, leaving the door ajar just the slightest.

Taking his lordship's hand, she walked him over to the fire, which was nothing but coals and sat him down. Turning to the hearth, she added some more coal, then wood, and blew on the embers that still glowed red, but no longer formed any heat. She concentrated on her task, creating a draft with the fire, and thankfully a few spots of the wood took light, and the fire started to burn.

"You are the most accomplished woman I know. You can even create fire."

She laughed, standing and taking a seat across from him. "Growing up we didn't have a lot of servants, and even though we are able to afford them now, it was not always the case. And so yes, I learned how to do many things. I can wash clothes, cook food, dust and clean, even make fires. Not what your Society would call accomplished, but I think they're excellent life skills that everyone should have."

He stared at her, his eyes glassy, and dark-ringed with tiredness. His hair was matted and looked in need of a good wash. He was a right state, and she frowned, guilt pricking her soul. "You know why I'm here don't you, my lord?"

The marquess cringed, turning his attention to the fire. "Call me Hunter, please. You're seeing me at my worst, I do not deserve the name of a gentleman in this condition."

"I shall call you Hunter, but you are worthy of the title, my lord. Your condition does not make you who you are. It is simply a symptom of what you've been doing to yourself."

If broken had a face, the marquess would be a portrait of it. "I feel like horse dung, and I do beg your pardon on the use of such a word, but I never felt so ill in my life. But even so, my desire to be worthy of your kiss overrides my misery."

Cecilia's heart did a little flip, and she fought not to go to him, to wrap him in her arms and give him what he wanted. What she wanted. But not yet, first they had to vanquish this inner demon he fought against and beat it. The pain she read in his eyes made her question her decision, not that to help, but to keep at a distance. Maybe she would be a better addiction for him than the one he now fought.

Against her better judgement, she kneeled at his feet. Clasping his stubble roughened cheeks she pulled him toward her, kissing him gently on the mouth. The feel of him so close, the touch of his breath against her lips left her longing for more. Even in his state, both physically and mentally, she wanted to kiss him. Allow him to lose himself in her, anything but allow the need for more of what he'd been imbibing himself in for however many years he'd been drinking.

"You are worthy, never think otherwise," she said softly.

Even as uneducated in the art of love that she was, she was able to distinguish the burning desire he had for her when she saw it. And she saw it now, in the depths of his eyes, a yearning to be free, to forget what ailed him and lose himself in her.

Cecilia kissed him again, leaning up and taking his mouth in much the same way as he'd kissed her in the carriage. Unhindered, without restraint and with a need that pulled at her own wants and desires she'd long buried.

Hunter as he now wanted her to call him roused all her buried wants, her dreams of a life with a man. Not just any man, like the one her father wished her to marry, but a man who excited her, stimulated her mind and soul, vexed and maddened in all the most wonderful ways.

A life with Lord Aaron…

"I've longed for you. You make me forget who I've been, and see what I can become." His voice, roughened and deep sent her pulse to skip a beat. She fought not to kiss him again until they were both lost in their own world. "Let me love you. Let me have you."

Cecilia leaned back and captured his gaze. "I will stay with you, help you as best as I know how, but I cannot allow you the liberties that you ask. But I will give you as much as I can."

"Your soul is so pure. Mine is as dark as the devil himself."

She caressed his stubble roughened cheek. "Then it is lucky that I do not have idle hands, for there is no place in this room for the devil's work and you will be well again. I promise you that."

CHAPTER 9

By late that evening Lord Aaron was wrenching about in his bed, his skin clammy and dripping with sweat. His lordship constantly begged for a dram of whisky, anything, anyone to help him. Cecilia ordered the butler to pour all the remaining alcohol in the home down the drain, and she also ordered the cook to hide any beverages of the kind that she used in her cooking. Nothing was to remain in the house that his lordship could drink if any one of them turned their back on him for even a moment.

Cecilia sat beside his bed, holding his hand. "Please, Lia, just a little drink," he said, making the nickname he'd bestowed on her sound endearing, even if he only seemed to have used it in the last few hours. It was the name her mother had called her as a child, and she adored it, even more, coming from the lips of Lord Aaron.

She shouldn't, of course, he was so far above her in station, had demons that even she didn't know if they could remove, not to mention to marry such a man could limit her charities or at least the amount she was involved in them. He may have previously stated he wished to change, to help others, but what if that lifestyle bored him. What if he grew weary of her.

Cecilia was terrible at needlework or idly walking in parks merely to be seen, she had always felt out of place in such situations. Not to mention, her father relied upon her too, to help out with his cases and do his bookwork. Not that Mr. White thought she was useful, but Cecilia had always harboured the idea that if she could prove to her father she was capable, he would allow her to inherit.

Would the marquess in time expect her to be a pretty ornament on his arm, behave and hold her tongue. The life of one of the upper ten-thousand was not for her, no matter how much his lordship beckoned her soul to try. The risk was great, and she wasn't sure she was capable of such a gamble.

But she would assist him like she helped so many people in need. Help him regain who he once was so he may marry wisely and hopefully with love and affection. Make more of his life than the silly folly he'd partaken in to date.

"I cannot give you what you want, Hunter." She bathed his forehead with a damp cloth and tried to soothe him with talk of her charities, of idle gossip, anything to take his mind off what his body craved. The hours ticked by and as dawn broke the night sky into a golden haze, Lord Aaron was worse.

She stood beside the duke, biting her bottom lip as she thought of how to keep his lordship safe, from himself and others. "We need to tie him to the bed. He's too large to control, and if he took flight, it would take a lot of us to overpower him. His need for alcohol will make his strength double."

"How do you know all this, Miss Smith?" the duke asked, looking down at her.

She frowned, staring at the marquess who lay crunched up on the bed, clutching at his stomach. "As you know, I work and run charities for children mostly, but I do have a small charity that I run for the parents of the children I help. These parents have never had a good life, never had opportunities and at every turn, seemed to be kicked and trodden on by life and those who should be there to guide and help them make the right choices. A lot of these parents have drinking problems or other medicinal addictions. The troubles Lord Aaron now faces means it'll be a month before he's feeling himself again. But he'll never be truly free. This fight will be a life-long one I'm afraid."

"God help him. And God bless you for doing such charity. I know my duchess speaks quite highly of you, and now I know why."

Cecilia nodded, but the fear and concern she had for the marquess did diminish the kernel of pride that the duke awoke in her. He was so very ill, perhaps more addicted than she had imagined. "The duchess has been a pillar of strength and friendship for me these past twelve months. I cannot tell you how much I appreciate her help. We need more of it if we're to change the boroughs of London and their outcomes for those less fortunate."

"I'm sure you will always have it."

The marquess yelled out, groaning and Cecilia walked to his tall chest of drawers and rummaged through his clothing until she found what she was looking for. "Take these cravats and tie his arms to the bedhead. The marquess will have to be contained for the next few days possibly."

The staff who stood in the room looked horrified by her words, but with a nod from the duke, they did as she asked. Seeing the marquess in his current state left a hollow void in her chest. How she loathed that he fought such demons, had well and truly lost against them, but no more. She would help him through this, she and his friends would not let him fail this test.

The day wore on, and the duchess came to sit with her for a few hours, gave Cecilia time to bathe and allow Hunter's manservant to wash his master. Evening approached, and Cecilia stood at the marquess's windows that overlooked his back garden and stared at the silver light from the moon that bathed the garden.

"Cecilia, come sit with me."

She turned to see the marquess staring at her from under hooded lids, eyes that were slowly clearing and becoming clearer as the alcohol left his body. Walking over to him, she sat on the edge of the bed, taking the opportunity to bathe his forehead and face. He was so very handsome, even in his state and dishevelment she had to admit that she liked him, was attracted to him from the very first moment she'd met him. She wiped the cloth down his neck to the vee of his shirt.

Heat prickled her skin as her imagination ran away from her. What was she doing thinking about what lay under his shirt with his lordship as sick as he was?

"I'm going to be sick, Cecilia. Please, untie me and fetch me the bowl. Quickly," he said.

She did as he asked, and only just managed to get the bowl over to the bed before he cast up his accounts. He heaved, over and over before flopping back onto the bed, spent.

Cecilia rang for a servant, ordering tea and ginger biscuits if the cook had any. She then went about removing Hunter's shirt, wiping his clammy body down, all the while trying not to blush or gawk at the toned muscles that had a fine dusting of hair. Over the next few days, his lordship's progress ebbed and flowed in an array of stages. Anger, contrite, begging to railing at them all. Having been away from home for a few days, she returned to Cheapside, only to find her father waiting for her in his library.

"I wish to speak with you, Cecilia. Now."

His tone didn't bode well, and a small stab of concern pierced her gut. She entered the room, features masked, only to find Mr. White seated before her father, his slimy features smirking in her direction.

"Good morning, father. Mr., White."

"You're back from your orphanage in Hampshire I see."

She did as he bade and clasped her hands in her lap. "As you see. My work there took a few days longer than I expected, and later today I'm to attend a charity meeting at Old Bell Tavern."

Her father stared at her with indifference and the concern she had before doubled. Why was he so out of sorts? And why was Mr. White here? Her father knew she hated the man, especially after he took liberties in the carriage that were not returned. The vile piece of flesh had no shame and her father either did not believe her or did not care.

Cecilia pushed down the hurt that thought conjured, and steeled herself for what she feared was to come.

"I had some time the last two days, and so I took the opportunity to visit you in Hampshire, but you can imagine my surprise when I arrived at your country school and orphanage only to hear the headmistress tell me she had not seen or heard from you in relation to your supposed visit. I returned home but found you were not here or at any of the London orphanages and schools you run. So," her father said, steepling his hands beneath his chin, the frown line between his eyes as deep as the Thames river. "Where were you, Cecilia?"

She swallowed and refused to look at the smirking Mr. White who for the first time in his life had no opinion it would seem on her disappearance. "A father of one of the children was in need of help. I along with the people who assist me often with these types of troubles, helped me nurse him, and he's now recovering at home."

"Really, then please do explain why Mr. White saw you enter Lord Aaron's home. A place you have been ensconced the past few days?"

Cecilia did look at the little vermin then. How she loathed the man, his greed and uncharitable nature. "You followed me? How dare you?"

He merely chuckled before the slamming of her father's fist on the table broke her fury directed at the bastard.

"How dare Mr. White? How dare you, Cecilia. Are you mad, child? To be entering an unmarried gentleman's home in the dead of night? What were you doing there? No, please, don't answer that," he said standing and rounding the table toward her. He pulled her to stand, and for the first time in her life he manhandled her, squeezing her arms. "How dare you place your reputation in jeopardy in such a way. I ought to throw you out of my home."

Cecilia wrenched free and took a step away from her father. Never had she seen him so angry before. His voice was calm, yet there was a steel tone of loathing she'd never heard before and panic lodged in her throat that maybe she'd overstepped his bounds.

"I apologize for helping Lord Aaron, but it was at the behest of the duke and duchess of Athelby. They were there the entire time, you may ask them yourself. And if you're worried that Lord Aaron abused me in some way you're mistaken. We are simply trying to get him better."

"Well, I shall ask the duke and duchess what they think

they're doing taking my unmarried, maiden daughter into the home of a renowned rake. I shall ask them to explain their high and mighty decision to put your reputation in jeopardy. You, Cecilia, shall heed this warning, and you shall do as I say from this moment on."

Her gaze flicked to Mr. White who again looked too pleased for himself by far. "What do you mean by that? And as for my reputation, I can assure you it is quite sound and not in any jeopardy unless this information is leaked to Society and what I've been doing the last few days becomes public knowledge."

Her father stiffened. "Are you insinuating that Mr. White would go to the press with such rumours?"

"If it made it impossible for you to refuse his designs of me becoming his wife, then yes, I think him capable of such underhanded ways."

Mr. White feigned shock, clasping his chest for added dramatics. "I would never do such a thing, Mr. Smith. I assure you."

Cecilia scoffed. "You are no gentleman, Sir. No man of any moral value assaults women in carriages. And if you think I'm going to marry this swine because I have helped Lord Aaron you're sadly mistaken. I shall walk away from my life here with you if you try and force my hand and make me marry Mr. White."

Her father's face mottled in anger. "You have no choice but to marry Mr. White as without doing so I shall stop all funding toward the charities you're so very fond of. It is about time that you settled, had children that will inherit the firm. Mr. White is willing to take your hand, even if this latest news becomes public knowledge and your repu-tation is ruined. He is smart, from a respectable family and loves you. You will obey, Cecilia. That is my final word."

Cecilia stormed from the room, slamming the door

closed behind her. Tears blurred her vision as she climbed the stairs. How dare either of them speak and demand such things of her? She would not do it, she could not give herself to such a man.

She made it to her room and snipping the lock went to stand at the window. Hundreds of children relied on her. Many, many families needed her to give them a chance, to keep the orphanages and schools going so their children might have some future. She had no doubt her father would be as vindictive as he threatened and take away the funds, therefore unless she had a large investor who was willing to take the expense on, there was nothing she could do. The Duchess of Athelby already donated a significant amount, she couldn't ask for more, it wouldn't be fair.

Would it?

Cecilia worked her bottom lip, before sitting at her desk and pulling out a piece of parchment. She could never marry a man she did not love so she would have to beg the duchess for help. Her pride would need to take a seat so she could secure her other greatest love, the children. That was all that mattered now.

Hunter squinted as the bright sunlight streamed into his room. He stared at the blue sky beyond and did a mental check of how he felt. *Good.* Better than he'd felt for a long time. Weeks in fact and he knew who he had to thank for such nursing. The same woman who sat beside the fire, mending a button on one of his shirts if he weren't mistaken.

The image was so reminiscent of a married, family life that he smiled. He liked having her here, talking to him, calming him, being in his room as if it was a common and ordinary thing for her to do.

Which it was not.

Even he knew in his state of delirium that Miss Smith, Lia as he'd come to call her, should not be here, chaperoned by the Duke and Duchess of Athelby or not.

"Lia, can you ring for tea, please. I'm in need of sustenance."

She looked up, her bright blue eyes twisting an emotion in his chest he didn't want to think about at the moment, although when better, he would have to admit for what he'd come to feel toward her. Miss Smith was quite literally the woman who saved his life.

He adored her.

"How are you feeling this morning," she said, coming over and sitting on his bed as if it were the most normal thing to do. They were on dangerous ground, Lia and him. Should she have sat on his bed when he was in his cups, there was no doubt he would've leaned forward and kissed those, perfectly rosy lips and try and seduce her.

"For the first time in as long as I can remember I feel clear headed." His stomach rumbled and Cecilia chuckled. "And I'm hungry by the sounds of that," he said, smiling.

"I'll have breakfast brought up to you as soon as they arrive with your tea." She rose from the bed and sat in the chair beside it, seemingly rethinking her location. "I thought we'd go outside for a little while today. You've been indoors for almost a month, and it would do you good to have fresh air and a little sun."

The idea, as menial and boring as it sounded lifted his spirits. It would be delightful to be out of this room, as long as he had Cecilia's company. "You will join me?"

"I will. I'm here until lunch, and then the duchess and duke will take over for me. We have a little schedule going, you see." She smiled, a sincere gesture he didn't see too often in the *ton*. Hunter studied her, she was a marvellous girl, and she would make a perfect mistress. He would lavish her with gifts and freedom she'd never known, so long as she shared his bed, and only his bed.

THREE WEEKS later Hunter was well enough to attend his first evening out about town. The duke and duchess sat across from him in the landau. They hadn't said the words, but Hunter understood why they were with him. To watch and ensure he did not lapse into the life of drunkenness and folly that he'd partaken in before.

Miss Smith sat beside him, her pensive gaze staring out at the busy streets beyond. Over the last week, she'd been distant, pulling away from him whenever she came to keep him company and ensure again he didn't seek out his whisky.

Although the staff had poured out every ounce they found, Hunter had his own little bottle hidden in his room, and yet he'd not sought it out. It was almost a test against himself, a wager to see if he had the willpower not to touch it.

Not that it hadn't been hard ignoring it, it was torture. He longed to feel the burn of the golden liquid sliding down his throat, leaving him warm and comforted. Losing the ability to handle his drink, not being able to have such repast in the future was a longing he fought every day to ignore. If it weren't for his friends, Lia included, he would not have made it as far as he had.

The light headed beauty beside him met his gaze as if she was privy to his thoughts. He would kiss her tonight, sneak her away and do what he'd wanted to for weeks.

The carriage rolled to a stop before Sir Colten's London home, and they waited for a footman to become available to open their door. Once inside, they greeted their hosts and made their way through the throng of guests.

Some cast odd glances at the appearance of Miss Smith, a woman not of their sphere, who in some of their eyes should not be attending. But with the Duke and Duchess of Athelby supporting her, they dare not speak a word about it.

Cecilia shone like a diamond in a sea of paste, and the

temptation to dance with her grew. Hunter looked over to where the musicians sat, playing music that was congenial for conversation. Other guests gathered on the floor, and it wouldn't be long before the dancing began.

They stopped before one of three fireplaces in the room, and Hunter held out his hand to Miss Smith. "Will you dance with me?"

She took his hand, nodding slightly. "Thank you, yes."

The strains of a waltz started to play, and Hunter could've dropped to his knees in thankfulness. The perfect dance for seduction, for talking intimately.

"You're very beautiful this evening, Lia," he said, drinking in every nuance of her right down to the little freckle that sat above her lip.

"You're very handsome."

She blushed, and he laughed, pulling her a little closer than he ought.

"You also smell divine. What is that scent?"

"Jasmine." She tipped her head to the side, eyeing him. "You're flirting with me, Lord Aaron."

"Can I not flirt with the prettiest woman in attendance?" The slide of her silk gown against his palm sent desire coiling through him. He wanted her, all of her, to be his, now and forever. He would not survive without her he was sure.

"And now that I'm better and being watched day and night by my valet due to the duke's strict instructions, you'll not be able to visit me anymore. Come up to my room and nurse me back to health," he said wiggling his eyebrows.

Cecilia laughed. It was about time she did so, she'd been reserved and troubled, a constant frown had formed between her eyes whenever she didn't think anyone was watching, but he was. "Is everything well, Lia. You seem unsettled about something."

She bit her bottom lip, and he pulled her close as they manoeuvred a turn. "Tell me what it is. I want to help you if I can, just as you helped me."

⚜

CECILIA FOUGHT to keep her attention on the guests that lined the dance floor and not at Lord Aaron, Hunter as he wished to be called. If she looked at him, she would be lost. She sighed. Who was she kidding, she was already lost. "My father found out about me helping you. He knows I was in your bedroom, unchaperoned at times. He does not know what ailed you, but he's aware only that you had an illness that the Duke and Duchess of Athelby asked me to help with."

"Why has he not called on me and demanded that I ask for your hand?"

"What?" Cecilia lowered her tone and met the marquess's gaze. "Because he doesn't want me to marry you."

"What! What do you mean he doesn't want me to marry you? I'm a marquess, a rich lord, I could give you everything and more. Why has he not come to me, that is the most preposterous notion I've ever heard."

Cecilia couldn't help but chuckle at Hunter's self-praise, and she patted his shoulder to ease his tension. "There are two reasons, one that is my own doing I'm afraid."

"And what is that?"

"I've always been critical of those who are more fortunate than so many. As much as I have enjoyed the duke and duchess' company, and your own, especially now as you're more yourself, after your illness, this is not my world. I do not fit in here. I'm too rough about the edges, too willing to get down on my hands and knees and scrub floors if it's required. Too often I take sick children home and nurse them back to health. I could do none of those things as a Society wife. My father understands this about me, and does not think I would suit the life of a lord's wife."

"And the second reason?"

"Father will be announcing my betrothal to Mr. White Friday next. He has threatened to remove his patronage to my orphanages and schools I worked so hard to build. He has threatened to give the firm to Mr. White and leave me nothing if I do not do as I'm told, especially now that my reputation is sullied, or would be sullied if my visiting of you was to be made public knowledge."

"Like hell he did." A muscle ticked on Hunter's jaw, and looking about he pulled her from the dance and escorted her onto the terrace. Seeing an array of couples, he turned away from them all and started toward the stairs at one end that led to the gardens.

Nerves fluttered in Cecilia's stomach, and the strong, determined line of Hunter's jaw left her mouth dry. What was he thinking? What he was about to do was anyone's guess, but if she could wish for one thing, it would be to kiss him again. To take one last memory of him before she lowered herself, even more, out of his sphere and became a teacher at her schools. With the duchess having confirmed that she would become the charity's principal sponsor, it was safe no matter what her father decided.

He walked along the side of the house, and seeing a stone chair against the wall, pulled her down to sit. "I will not allow you to marry Mr. White. He is vile for one, and you do not care for him."

"I have no intention of marrying Mr. White. I have secured the safety of my charities for the years to come, but by doing so, by denying my father his wishes, I shall suffer the consequences."

"How do you mean you'll suffer the consequences," he asked, beseeching her to tell him the truth.

"When I tell my father that I no longer require his help with my schools, and when I tell him that I will not marry his heir, I have no doubt he will banish me. Maybe even throw me out. I'm to become a teacher, and have already prepared lodgings at Spitalfields orphanage."

He frowned, leaning away. "A teacher, a tutor, but that is beneath you, Cecilia. I'm sure you've not thought of all your options."

She sighed, having searched her mind for days trying to think of other options, but she was tired of it. Cecilia would by far prefer to be a tutor than have Mr. Smith as her husband. The only thing that tinged her choice with regret was that the marquess would never look to her as his wife. She would well and truly be beneath his gaze now. "It is done, my lord. And that is that."

Cecilia met his gaze hoping it was disappointment she read within his stormy blue orbs. "I will not deny that even with your troubles and that we did not start out as friends, I find you the most interesting, and vexing man I've ever met. A man that after one kiss left me questioning my own rules, my own opinions of what I wished for in life. But I'm happy with my choice, and although my forays into your Society will come to an end, I do not regret our time or our friendship. I hope I shall always have it."

He cupped her face, and as if in a trance Cecilia watched as Hunter closed the distance between them and kissed her. In relative darkness, she slid her arms around his neck and kissed him back, wanting to take this one moment and capture the memory forever.

Cecilia gasped when his tongue slid against hers, an

odd but enjoyable sensation that pooled heat at her core. Her breasts strained against her gown, and without knowing why, she pushed against him, his firm, warm body relieving a little of the need that coursed through her blood.

"You cannot kiss me like this Lia," he said, his lips feathering kisses down her throat, "and become a tutor, leave me alone in all this pomp and ceremony. We may be opposites, but in this we are equal."

She clasped his hair, a gasp escaped as his tongue ran against the top of her breasts where her gown began. "Just kiss me, Hunter, and let me forget everything else."

He did as she bade, this time it was no slow seduction, but a hot, maddening conquering that left her reeling. She'd never thought kisses could be so wicked, so tempting into the world he dangled before her, one of passion and pleasure.

Cecilia wanted so much to have a marriage with such emotion as Lord Aaron brought forth in her, and tonight, if only this night she would take whatever he was willing. She would not enter her future of reduced circumstances without knowing the touch of a man. And not just any man, but Lord Aaron.

A curl of hair tickled her back, and she pulled back, reaching up to fix her coiffure. "We should return to the ball before we're noticed missing."

Hunter rubbed his thumb across her bottom lip. She clasped his hand and kissed the digit.

"I'm mad for you, Lia. Be my—"

The sound of someone clearing their throat sounded a little distance away, and Cecilia wrenched back looking up to see who had caught them, only to see the Duchess of Athelby.

"I've come to fetch Miss Smith. Her father has arrived

to collect her, and Cecilia I should warn you, he's made a spectacle of himself."

Dread pooled in her stomach. "He knows I was attending Sir Colten's ball this evening, why would he arrive like this." She stood, and cast another glance at Hunter who met her gaze, hunger raw and unsated even at the news of her father's arrival. "I best go. I will see you again Lord Aaron. Good night."

He stood and bowed, and taking the duchess' arm, she headed indoors. They didn't go back through the ballroom. Instead, the duchess brought her around to the foyer through a servants door that led out near vegetable gardens.

"While I cannot pretend not to know what you were doing outside with Lord Aaron, as your friend I feel I must caution you, Cecilia."

Cecilia slowed her steps, frowning. "It was only a kiss, your grace. Nothing more." Cecilia knew it to be a lie as soon as she uttered the words. It had not been just a kiss. For her, it had been everything, meant everything. Somewhere along her crazy few weeks with his lordship, she'd fallen in love with the man.

"Lord Aaron is a rake. And as much as I adore him, love him as a friend, I worry that your attachment to him is more than his lordships. I do not wish to see you hurt."

The duchess was too kind to care for her, even if she were the marquess's friend also. Cecilia shook her head. "Please do not worry. I'm more than aware that I have no future with the marquess."

The duchess nodded, continuing toward the foyer. "Your father is not pleased. He's stated that he was not aware that Lord Aaron would be present this evening and that the duke and I are trying to sully your reputation by playing your friends. Not actually being one."

She sighed. Hating that her father could do such a thing to her and the two people in the *ton* she trusted with her whole life, not excluding Lord Aaron of course. "I'm so very sorry, your grace. The man my father wishes me to marry no doubt has been watching Lord Aaron's movements and notified my father. I hope we can still be friends after my father has acted so atrociously."

The duchess took her hand, squeezing it a little. "We shall always be friends, and nothing your father says or does will change that. But I think considering our current location, you should go with him without a word. Words between you two can happen when you're in the privacy of your own home."

Cecilia nodded and walked into the foyer spotted her father pacing the space like a caged lion. "Father." She curtsied, taking her shawl from a waiting footman who held it. "Shall we go?"

He slapped on his hat, and without uttering a word of goodbye to the duchess, followed her from the ball. It wasn't until they were in the carriage that his temper frayed.

"How dare you daughter, go to a ball with a man I have expressed my dislike for. Did you know he's a gambler, a man with a string of mistresses about town? The rumours that came across my desk this evening stated that the reason you've been nursing this man back to health is because he cannot hold his liquor?"

"Who divulged this to you. Mr. White? Not the most reliable source, father."

Her parent squirmed on his seat the little muscle in his jaw flexing. "It is little consequence who told me. The truth of the matter is that it is true. And why were you not with the duchess upon my arrival. Where were you, child? Were you with him? Alone?"

"And so what if I was? I'm sick and tired of men like you telling women what to do. You may threaten me with your money and threaten to hurt my charities, but I no longer need to bend to your rules. I have found another sponsor for my charities, and have secured myself employment, so I shall not have you speak to me in such a way. If I were a boy, you would not be sitting here, lecturing me, you would be slapping me on the back, congratulating me on my folly."

"You sullied yourself with Lord Aaron!" her father flopped back into the squabs, clasping his chest. "Oh, the shame."

Cecilia swallowed, wondering how truthful she should be. She erred on the side of caution. "Of course not. I was simply at a ball where my father arrived and dragged me home like a naughty little child. Not a woman who was simply at a ball."

"There is no need for you to even attend such events and there will be no talk of you leaving home and finding employment. You're marrying Mr. White. The contracts have been drawn up, both the marriage contract and that of the contract regarding the inheriting of my firm. The banns will be called and in one month you shall be Mrs White."

"Are you listening to me, father. I said I will not marry Mr. White. Ever."

Her father leaned forward, pointing a finger at her face. "You've said that for years, Lord Aaron and his set is not a life that you would look for. That you loathed the *ton* and their foppish ways, their gossiping and inane lifestyle. Mr. White suits you, and he loves you I'm sure. Given time I'm positive you'll make a happy marriage and give me grandchildren."

The carriage rocked to a halt before their home, and

without waiting for a footman Cecilia jumped down, hurrying into the house. She could hear her father behind her, and even when he called out to her as she made for the stairs, she ignored him. Just as he ignored her, in all that she was and everything that she did.

CHAPTER 11

H unter lay on the daybed in his library and smoked a cheroot. He watched the flames lick the wood in the grate while his mind fought with the notion of Cecilia being ostracised by her family, becoming a tutor and removing herself even more from his social sphere. It would never do and to imagine her living in such reduced circumstances, well, it wasn't to be borne.

The library door opened and he sighed, closing his eyes. "I'll not be needing you any further tonight, Thomas. You may retire." The patter of footsteps didn't halt, and he sat up, throwing his cheroot into the fire. "Miss Smith," he said, not believing she was standing beside him, here, in his library and alone. Quite alone. "What are you doing here?"

"May I join you?"

A blush bloomed on her cheeks, and he climbed off the daybed, going to her before she could run away. "What are you saying?" Before he touched one inch of her, he wanted to hear exactly what she meant. Not just assume. As a man who had slept with too many women when under the cloudy haze of drink, tonight he wanted to remember every little ounce of detail. Know when the day dawned tomorrow that the memory of her, the smell of jasmine that would touch his bedding, would bring forth all the delicious details of him making Lia *his*.

Cecilia boldly met his gaze. "I'm saying, I want to be with you in every way a man and woman can be together."

A fierce blast of need burned through his veins. He wanted to haul her into his arms so badly. He clenched his hands to his side to stop their shaking. Though he wanted her as his mistress, if he could have this one moment, this beautiful memory of being with her he would take it, and treasure it for this lifetime and the next. With her fierce independence and bluestocking ideals there was no certainty that she would agree to his terms.

Hunter took in her attire, a heavy dark cloak covered her gown, and a bonnet tied tightly beneath her chin helped conceal her identity should anyone have seen her enter his home. He walked to the windows and pulled the drapes closed, then told the footman near the front door to bolt it and go to bed.

Coming back into the library, he shut and locked the door. Cecilia had removed her bonnet and gloves, but the cloak remained. Hunter was fine with that, it would enable him to strip it from her body, like opening a present.

He strode over to her and clasping her face, kissed her soundly. She didn't shy away from the onslaught of his desire for her, if anything she met him, stepped into his hold and kissed him back. Her innocence pulled at him, and he consciously slowed his desire, reigned back his need to take it slow. She was a virgin after all, not used to a man's touch.

"You're so beautiful," he said, pulling the ribbon that held her cloak closed at the neck. Slowly, the tie pulled free, and he slipped the cloak over her shoulders, it hit the floor with a heavy thump.

His breath hitched when he saw what she wore beneath, or better yet, what she hardly wore. A fine, silk chemise did little to hide Lia's figure, thanks in part to the fire that burned behind her, making the material almost translucent. Reaching out, he followed the delicate embroidered pattern across her chest to where he could see her pinkened nipple puckered beneath.

He watched her, as slowly, he traced the circular flesh, loving how it beaded harder beneath his touch.

"You said at Earl Leighton's ball that you were mad for me," she gasped, half moaned.

How he loved that sound and wanted to hear more of the same. "I did," he breathed, leaning down to kiss where he was teasing her flesh, needed to feel that little bud in his mouth, wanting all of her and at once if he could.

"I'm mad for you too," she whispered into his hair. "Please keep doing what you're doing."

Oh, he would and more so before the night was out.

Her breast was heavy, and soon the silk chemise merely became a barrier he was no longer so patient to work with. Standing before her, he slowly untied the ribbons that ran between her breasts, her breathing laboured, her skin flushed with desire.

He'd dreamed of such a vision. Had wanted this for both of them for so long, maybe even from the day she'd saved his life on the street, had pulled him out of the way of the carriage.

There were not many people, least of all a delicate woman who'd put themselves into peril as Miss Smith had. But her generosity of character, her unfailing support and determination to help others was a character he'd come to admire in her and of course saving a drunken fop, as he was, was merely another thing thrown before her that she had to deal with.

Thank the good lord that she had.

The chemise gaped at her front and meeting her gaze he slid the shift from her shoulders, leaving her as bare as the day she was born. His need for her made his body ache and pulling his own shirt from his breeches, he dragged it off and threw it away into the shadowed room.

Not willing to stand idle, she reached out and touched his chest. The feel of her fingers on his body sent heat coiling through his blood, and he took a calming breath to steady himself. He was not a green lad on his first experience with a woman, he'd done this a few times now, but tonight, before this woman, he was like a ship, plummeting at sea.

"I've never felt a man before. You're harder than I imagined you to be."

He nodded, unable to form words as her hand ran down his chest and across his stomach to stop at the front of his breeches. Hunter didn't need to look down to know his member strained against his frontfalls.

And yet she did not halt her inspection of him. Her fingers slid across his breeches before her hand cupped him fully. There was no masking his groan, nor was there any chance that he could deny himself her a minute longer.

He scooped her up, taking her lips in a fierce kiss before throwing her onto the daybed, laughing as she bounced once, her breasts rocking with the action.

Hunter fumbled with his breeches, ripping open his frontfalls, pushing them down and off. He kneeled on the bed and crawled up her body so as not to frighten her away with the size of him. The less she saw of him down there the better. He'd not missed the uneasy flare of her eyes that told him of her unease at the decision she made, but he would not hurt her, tonight she would feel passion, ecstasy and care. Nothing else.

Her fingers slid over his shoulders and pulled him down for a kiss. Willingly he went, the taste of her on his lips an elixir he'd never tire of. The hint of jasmine came from her hair, and her skin shone in the firelight like a beacon of what he could have, of what he wanted for himself from tonight and this day forward.

He kissed her with all that he felt for her but couldn't voice into words. Reaching down he pulled her leg to sit up on his hip and the hair on her mons pressed against his engorged cock. Unable to deny himself, he rubbed against her heated flesh and could've died with the pleasure of it when she pushed up against him, instinctively and wantonly seeking her own release.

"Please, Hunter. I cannot—"

He could no more deny her as he could deny himself, and taking himself in hand, guided his cock against her wet, hot core.

Damn, she was tight as he pushed slowly within her. Lia bit her lip and watched him, only the slightest flicker of pain passed her visage as he breached her maidenhead. He pulled out before guiding himself in again, relief pouring through him when he had no resistance, only sweet acceptance. Delight pierced him when she wrapped her other leg about his hips, holding him firmly against her body.

"This is so wonderful," she mewled, arching her back as he took her.

Hunter forced himself not to release before she'd found hers. He wasn't a selfish lover, ever and he wasn't about to start now.

Their joining became frantic and clasping one ass cheek he ground himself hard against her, relentlessly taking her. He shouldn't, of course, treat her in such a way, a maiden, a woman with no prior idea of what was before her, and yet she did not balk at his lovemaking. Did not ask him to stop, if anything the sounds that came from her urged him on, begged him to do more of the same.

And so he did.

"Hunter," she gasped her fingers pressing hard against his shoulders. "Don't stop, don't stop."

"Never." He thrust once, twice and she shattered in his arms, her sex clamping his own and with a cry, he found his release. He didn't stop until they were both spent, every last ounce of pleasure pulled from their loins.

Hunter flopped beside her, pulling her into the crook of his arm. Both their breathing laboured and he smiled, unable to wipe the grin off his face.

"Was it what you imagined?"

He felt her smile against his chest as she kissed him there before running her hand up to cup his face. "It was more than I could ever imagine."

⚶

THE FOLLOWING afternoon Cecilia took a sip of tea in her mother's parlor and tried and failed to censure her tone towards Mr. White. "I'm sorry, but can you repeat what you just said?"

He sat on the chaise beside her, his eyes bright with expectation. "I said, Miss Smith, that today the first of four banns will be called, marking our betrothal as official. The documents are now all in order, and your father has confirmed that you're to be my wife and so now you may show your gratitude."

Cecilia clenched her teeth. "My gratitude? I will admit to believing you capable of anything, especially after mauling me in the carriage, but to hear that my father has gone through with securing my hand to your own, after all that I told him is not going to bring forth gratitude from me, sir. It'll bring pain and misery. I will not marry you."

His expression hardened. "It is done, my dear. If you cry off, you'll look like a flirt, a woman of loose morals and character. The shame on your father will be too much for him to bear and may injure his constitution."

As much as she loved her parents, had hoped they had the best only in mind when it came to her, this decision of theirs proved they did not. "I'm not a virgin, Mr. White. I have slept with another man and may be right now carrying his child."

If she had hoped he would stand, bow and make a hasty exit she was mistaken.

"Being of the age that you are, and that we are not high Society, I had wondered if you would remain chaste until your marriage, if you ever married that is. But if you told me such things with the mind that I would break the contracts, then you are greatly mistaken. With you comes your father's law firm. Years of clients, families and money that I have worked so hard to keep, only to lose it at the last hurdle. You, my dear, are that hurdle, and I care not that you are chaste. It will merely mean you may be free with my body prior to the wedding. We do not have to wait until the wedding night."

Horror ran down her spine, and she shuddered. "I will never sleep with you, Mr. White. How dare you say such a thing to me?"

His lips twisted in a mockery of a smile. "You're no lady, your actions have shown that this is so, and so what does it matter if you're fast with me too. You'll soon be my wife."

"I'll never be your wife." Cecilia stood and walked away, the thump of her heart loud in her ears.

He followed, clasped her arms in such a tight grip that tears bristled. "Let me go."

"While our conversation today has been most enlightening, I came here to tell you, on your father's behalf that you're to attend the Opera with me tonight. There is a new client your father wants to gain favour with, and so you'll attend as my betrothed. Which of course, you are."

Cecilia wrenched herself free and walked over to the fire, rubbing her arms. "Father has not mentioned this to me before."

"The family have only just arrived in town from their country estate, and he's managed to gain a box beside theirs. And so," he said, leaning down on the chair and picking up his black gloves. "You will do the pretty, smile and be most congenial. You shall pretend to be happy and happy with me, or I shall notify your father of your disobedience. I very much doubt he'd appreciate hearing his daughter has whored herself out."

"You black-hearted blaggard. Get out." Cecilia raised her chin a chill slicing through her veins.

He stormed over to her, clasping her chin in a punishing grip. "Do as you're told Miss Smith, or you'll find when we're husband and wife, the money for your charities will also stop. Be an obliging, faithful and dutiful wife and all will stay well."

Cecilia clasped the mantle for support when the door closed behind him. She would attend tonight, for her father's sake, but then this would be the last time she would be obliging. The funding for her charities was secured as was her own employment. She did not need Mr. White, her father or even Lord Aaron to rescue her. After tonight, Cecilia would commence the future that she'd chosen and revel in her decision. No man would threaten her into a life of misery. Not now or ever.

CHAPTER 12

The Opera at Theatre Royal, Covent Garden, was full to the brim with Society out to enjoy the famous Sarah Siddons who was in town to play Lady Macbeth. Their box did, in fact, sit alongside the esteemed and wealthy family new to town and recently returned from abroad due to the elder Mr. Grant passing away and the massive inheritance now bestowed on his namesake.

Mr. White's entire conversation was directed to the Grants. In fact, he'd spoken of little else. And the more Cecilia learned about the man her father had betrothed her to, the more she realised the man was a scheming, heartless rogue looking for nothing but how to fill his pockets with coin.

"I think my discussion with Mr. Grant went well, what do you think Cecilia?" Mr. White asked, casting another glance in the direction of Mr. Grant's box and receiving a nod in return from the gentleman.

"Yes, it went very well. Father will be happy." Cecilia kept her smile pasted on her mouth, and yet it took every effort to keep it from falling. She wanted nothing more than to leave.

Mr. White droned on, and she kept her eye on the stage as the main attraction for this evening's opera stepped onto the stage to a round of applause. It wasn't until Mr. White's hand slid atop her own in her lap that she was pulled from her own musings.

With her smile firmly in place, she said, "Remove your hand, Sir. I neither seek nor like you touching me in this way."

Anger lit in his eyes briefly, then his expression smoothed to icy civility. "We are engaged, there is nothing wrong with me holding my betrothed's hand."

She pulled free, chuckling as if he'd said something funny when Mr. Grant in the box beside them caught her action. Thinking of her father's firm, she hooked their arms instead, leaning into him as if to whisper a secret. "If you keep being familiar with me, Mr. White I shall walk from the box, whether the gentleman you wish to do business with sees my escape or not. Is that understood?"

Mr. White glared, but sat up, returning his attention to the opera singer. "You have no power in this, Cecilia. Do not threaten me or I shall marry another, and you'll never inherit your father's precious business."

Cecilia listened to the beautiful Sarah play out her role and ignored Mr. White for the remainder of the first half. She glanced about the theatre, but couldn't see anyone she knew. Footmen came about the stalls and started to light the sconces and notified everyone supper and drinks were served in the foyer.

They made their way downstairs, Mr. White taking the opportunity to continue to hold her hand firmly atop his arm. "You do not have to walk so close to me, sir."

"I wish for all to see that we are happy and betrothed. What is wrong with that?"

"Nothing would be wrong with such a thing, had the woman involved not been forced into the situation. A situation that is not of her choosing or liking."

"Miss Smith, good evening."

Cecilia jerked and turned to see the Duke and Duchess of Athelby smiling before her, although their gazes were a little guarded. She curtsied. "May I present Mr. White? He is a solicitor at my father's practice. Mr. White may I present the Duke and Duchess of Athelby."

He bowed. "Your graces, a pleasure to meet you." Mr. White caught the location of Mr. Grant. "If you'll excuse me, there is someone that I need to speak to."

Cecilia bit her lip, not at all liking the duchess' frown. Was she upset with her? Had something happened to Hunter that she wasn't aware?

"Cecilia, what is going on?" the duchess whispered, leaning toward her to ensure privacy.

"A question that we're all in want of being answered."

She gasped, turned to see Lord Aaron towering over her. The pain she read in his gaze tore at her soul, and Cecilia wanted nothing more than to reach out and assure him all was well. That her being here tonight meant nothing to her, only her parent.

"I read the oddest thing in the paper this morning. It was about an upcoming marriage of a Miss Cecilia Smith to a Mr. White. I read it twice in fact, maybe even more than that for I thought it must be wrong. Was I wrong?" he asked, flicking a glance at Mr. White.

The duke and duchess moved away without a word, and Cecilia pulled Lord Aaron to the side of the room, a little distance from the other guests. It afforded them some privacy, but not a lot.

"You did read that right, but—"

"That is all I needed to know." His lordship went to move off, and she clasped his arm, pulling forth some interested stares from those about them.

"Let me explain. Please."

"You're betrothed, and to be married in four weeks. What is there left to know that isn't written in black and white."

"I do not love him, Hunter."

"So you would throw yourself at him without affection." He stood back, his face stoic and hard, but his eyes, they were pools of hurt and she'd put that pain there. At least, her father and Mr. White had, and she'd been too cowardly to do anything about it. Until now.

"My father wanted me to attend here tonight with Mr. White because of a potential client."

"That does not explain the fact that you're to be married." He rubbed a hand over his jaw. "I thought that we may have a future. It seems I read you wrong entirely."

"You did?" she asked, a slither of hope arrowing through her. "You never stated such a thing before."

He glanced about the room, breaking eye contact with her. "I had hoped to set you up as my mistress. To be with me always, where we could be together whenever we wished. I wanted you to be able to have the independence you craved without being beholden to me by law."

Heat bloomed across her face, and Cecilia took a calming breath as the room spun. *Mistress.* The hope she had for them crumbled at her feet and no matter how she tried, she could not stem the tears that fell unheeded down her cheeks.

Hunter reached out, before checking himself and clasping his hands behind his back. "Please, do not cry. I cannot comfort you here."

"No, I suppose you cannot. You only wish to comfort me in the home you'd no doubt set up for me. A little place where you could use me as your whore, whenever the urge struck."

His eyes flared before his mouth tightened into a thin line. "It would not be like that."

"Really? Being your mistress wouldn't be like being your mistress. I'm sorry Lord Aaron, but I'll never be your personal whore."

"What do you want? Marriage?" he asked, frowning.

Cecilia shook her head, not comprehending where this conversation had gone. "Of course marriage. I thought you were different from the peers around us. I thought you cared for me to see past my breeding. It seems I've been a fool."

He checked the whereabouts of other guests, but everyone seemed occupied with their supper and conversations. "I'm the Marquess of Aaron. I'm expected to marry a woman of rank and property. But that does not mean we cannot be together. I do not wish to lose you, Lia."

"Don't ever call me that again," she said, glaring at him. "Your actions tonight are not that of a gentleman, nor are you worthy of me or my love. I reject your offer, my lord. Find someone else to lie on their back for you."

His eyes searched hers a moment before he bowed and walked from the room. Cecilia watched as the duke and duchess followed his lordship. Disappointment swamped her, and she took a fortifying breath. She would not crumble here, show the *ton* that the man she loved had killed all that she'd hoped and dreamed for when she had been wrapped in his arms. Deep inside she'd known their position in Society would make a marriage unlikely, but how she had hoped, especially after the sweet, yet fiercely passionate way he'd made love with her. Swallowing back the tears of pain and piercing disappointment, she hurried away, not wanting anyone here to see her hurt.

Stumbling outside, Cecilia hailed a hackney cab, wanting to return home as soon as she could. Giving the driver the direction, she jumped up into the equipage, hugging herself to stem off the flood of tears that burned her eyes. What a fool she'd been. A silly, naïve nincompoop.

She should've known his lordship would never look to her as his wife and she'd been silly to have ever entertained the idea. Tears slid over her cheeks and she gasped, trying to calm herself. All to no avail, as the hurt won out and she sobbed, quite uncontrollably all the way home, and most of the remainder of the night.

CHAPTER 13

The following week Hunter sat in his library at Yardley Hall, his country estate and battled with his will. Will to do as he should, and will to do what he wanted, craved, longed for.

His mouth salivated at the amber liquid that sat in a crystal tumbler before him. The decanter full to the brim and the scent, strong and cutting called, beckoned him to taste. Just once, a little sip. It wouldn't hurt. He would only have one.

Hunter licked his lips, reaching for the cup before throwing himself back in his chair, rubbing a hand over his face. The last week he'd run a kaleidoscope of emotions. Those of anger, hurt, resentment. Right now he'd do anything to apologise to her, tell her he was sorry for insulting her in such a way. Never did he ever wish to hurt her.

He stood, paced before the decanter of whisky, willing it to be in his mouth. How he wanted to feel the burn as it slid down his throat, to throw him into oblivion where he'd not have to think about Lia and what his proposition meant. That she now hated him. Knew him to be the cad the *ton* knew him as. A man who practically stated she was not worthy of him, not good enough. He sat and picked up the glass, breathing in deep the woody scent.

The drink held the temptation of numbness, a place where he'd no longer hurt. For the pain of losing Cecilia was enough to rip him in two. With a bellowing shout, he threw the glass into the fire, shattering it into a million pieces before swiping the decanter off the table and removing the temptation to fall back into that pit of hell.

He'd fought hard to step away from losing himself in that way, and the loss of Cecilia, while it hurt now, and would hurt for many months to come, their hard work to get him well would not be in vain.

He would not fail in that as well, nor would he allow her to think she was only good enough to be his mistress. The last week had been torture, he'd missed her, dreadfully so and would not allow his error, his rank to determine whom he wanted to be his wife.

There was only one real choice as to who that should be. Hunter stood, starting for the door. No time like the present in winning back the woman he loved and would only ever love.

CECILIA SAT on her bed in the small room at the Spital-fields orphanage and thumbed through papers regarding the charity's latest pupil who'd only arrived yesterday after being dropped off by her mother, a very sickly woman who stated she could no longer look after her four year old child.

Cecilia had ensured she'd been placed near her room and with some of the older girls who promised to take care of her when she wasn't about. The past week had been horrible, her mind muddled and hurt over Lord Aaron's proposal to her.

Not that she would ever consider being his mistress, but the fact that all the time she had been falling in love with his lordship, he'd been merely thinking of a way to make her his mistress. Never had she been so mortified, not even now when all of London found out she'd called off the understanding with Mr. White or that she was now living in reduced circumstances. None of that seemed important when the man one loved found you wanting and unworthy.

A light knock sounded on the door and placing her papers on the small wooden desk that sat before a window, a chair, fireplace and bed the only furnishings the room beheld. It was a small space, but it suited her well enough.

"Come in," she said, picking up her shawl and placing it about her shoulders as her visitor stood within the threshold.

"May I really come in?" Lord Aaron asked, working the gloves in his hand, so they twisted back and forth.

Her body tingled at the sound of his voice. How she'd longed to hear it again, foolish as that thought was. "No, you may leave." Cecilia sat at her desk, fussing with her papers. She had nothing to say to him, nothing she wished to import. His lordship had made his opinions and stance very clear last week, and they did not need to repeat the conversation.

She heard him step into the room, the door closing behind him. "I'm sorry, Cecilia."

Cecilia stared out the window, the anger and pain that she'd been pushing down deep into her soul erupting like a volcano. "You're sorry? I think not. Had you ever cared for me at all, even in the slightest way, you could never have asked me to be your mistress. I may not have your rank, but I have a family, my reputation. How could you ask such a thing from me?"

He took the three steps that separated them and kneeled at her feet, clasping her hands. His piercing blue gaze earnest. "Because I'm a fool who didn't know that the feelings I had for you were not merely lust, but so much more than that. This past week, knowing that I hurt you, insulted you in such a way has broken me. I don't pretend to be a perfect man, by God you know more than anyone that I'm not, but I kneel before you, this very day saying that I do not wish for you to be my mistress, but my wife. Nothing less will do."

Cecilia blinked away her tears and fought to control her emotions. "I'm penniless and as you can see, a woman who no longer has a family. How would the marquess stomach such a woman as your wife? You'll come to regret your choice, and I do not want such a marriage. I will not be anyone's disappointment."

He shook his head, clasping her hands tighter. "I cannot prove to you today that what I say is the absolute truth, that I shall love, care and worship the ground you walk on for the rest of our lives. All I ask is you allow me to prove it in time. I promise I shall not fail you again. I shall never insult your person ever again. You saved me from myself, and for that alone, I owe you my life, but that is not the only reason I love you. Your compassion, care, unfailing determination to make others' lives better shames me. I've been the most selfish being all my life, a family trait I think and one I no longer wish to be. I cannot live without you, and I do not wish to. Please accept my proposal and marry me. You are the love of my life, Miss Smith. My one and only love."

Cecilia sniffed her body shaking with happiness. Could this be true? Did he really mean all that he said?

Hunter reached into his pocket and pulled out a piece of parchment, handing it to her. "What is this," she asked, opening it slowly.

"Read it." He smiled, waiting.

Cecilia quickly scanned the document, refolding it once she'd read it entirely. "Are you trying to buy my love, my lord?"

"I will do anything, will try anything to hear you say yes to my proposal."

"I thought you said you'd never give me the building on Pilgrim Street."

Hunter stood, and picking her up and depositing her on his lap. "It seems I was wrong. Consider it an early wedding gift, if I may be so bold."

She couldn't hide the grin that tweaked her lips. "I'm open to these types of gifts. And I'm in mind to accept your proposal. If you truly mean it."

"Yes, I mean it more than anything."

She clasped his cheek, catching his gaze. "Then yes, so do I."

❧❦❧

HUNTER KISSED HER GENTLY, wanting to linger, but there was more to be said. "I shall purchase and remodel any and all the buildings you want. I shall throw all the money I have, which is more than we'll ever spend on the children you so love if only you'll forgive me for hurting you so."

She kissed him back, and for a moment Hunter lost all thought as she wrapped her arms about his neck, kissing him with as much passion as he'd ever felt.

The touch of her hands against his chest, clasping his shoulders, the little mewling gasps and moans shot heat to his core, and his cock hardened. He'd denied himself everything the last week, drink, food, personal grooming, but right now none of that mattered, he would feed off her.

Clasping under her legs, he lifted her and sat her on the small desk, never breaking their kiss. Her gown was heavy and made for manual labour, and reaching down, he slid the garment slowly up her leg, taking the opportunity to feel her stockinged soft flesh on her legs.

"Here, Lord Aaron? Is that wise?" she asked, grinning up at him, her eyes sparkling with mischief.

"No, but we're going to in any case." He fumbled with his breeches, just freeing himself enough to have her. He needed to be with her again, to know that she was his and he was hers.

The soft, tentative touch of Lia's made him groan, and as much as he wanted to claim her, he allowed her to stroke him, feel and learn his body. Damn, it felt good. Too damn good and when her thumb wiped over the top of his cock he groaned.

"I need you, my love," he whispered, aching for her.

She shuffled closer to him on the desk, guiding him within her all the while keeping her eyes locked on his. To see her close the window to her soul at the pleasure of their joining ignited a fire Hunter doubted would ever be doused.

He wanted nothing but to make the woman in his arms happy, loved and cherished and from tonight onwards that's exactly what he would do.

❦

CECILIA WRAPPED her legs about Hunter's back and held him close. She clutched to him as he took her, a feral edge to their lovemaking. His hands gripped her hips and bottom hard, holding her in place, relentlessly taking her hard and fast on the desk. It was the most exhilarating, and naughty thing she'd ever done in her life.

And she loved it.

Her whole centre zeroed in on the place of their joining, the growing pleasure, the tension that increased with every stroke, every gasped breath against her ear, each wet and desperate kiss.

"Hunter," she moaned, clasping his face to kiss him. "I'm-"

"So am I," he gasped.

His strokes became frantic, deeper before unable to deny herself the release she craved, the tension coiled to a point of no return and she tumbled into waves of pleasure, endless delectable loveliness that she'd never tire of.

Hunter groaned her name, sending shivers down her spine as he too found his release, seizing her tight against him as they both regained their breaths.

"I know it has been seven days, but those seven days were the worst of my life. I thought I'd lost you by my own stupidity, my own pretentiousness."

Cecilia laughed, kissing him. "I am not blameless in this. I judged your Society without really knowing them. I too have faults that I shall work on redeeming."

He tilted her chin up to catch her gaze. "I'm going to spoil you and all the children who enter your charities, and God willing our own. I love you," he said, wiping away her tears that would not stop, no matter how wonderful his words. She was a veritable watering pot.

"And I love you, Hunter Always." And forever...

EPILOGUE

Six months later...

CECILIA SAT on the floor in a circle of children at the new orphanage and school on Pilgrim Street. With Hunter having gifted her the building that had thrown them together all those months ago, and her purchase of the second one before their marriage, the buildings had been joined, renovated and now was one of the cleanest, structured learning and loving environments that these children had ever known.

Today she was teaching the youngest in their school geography and what wonderful natural things in the world one could see and explore. The bell rang, and all the children looked at her expectantly as it was time for their midmorning break. "Remember to clean your hands before you eat and play safely and fairly. I shall see you tomorrow."

They waved her goodbye and Cecilia made her way down to the foyer where she was to meet Hunter. They were going out for lunch today, but he wouldn't tell her where the vexing rogue. Not that she minded, she'd allow him anything, especially after all that he'd given her, lavished her charity with money and anything and everything to make the school and orphanage functional.

The bell on the door chimed and in walked her husband. They had been married for six months now, and even after all this time, her parents refused to meet with her. It was the only shadow on their love, but Hunter had been caring and understanding of her pain, and so that made up for a lot of the hurt she hid from the world.

"Coming darling?" he held out his hand, helping her toward the carriage.

"Have I told you today how much I love you?"

He chuckled, holding her hand as she stepped up the carriage steps. "You may love me more after the surprise I have in store for you."

Excitement bubbled up within her, and she could hardly sit still as they made their way through the London streets before stopping at the front of Gunther's Ice Cream parlor. "Is this where you're taking me?"

"This is the first stop, I have another for you, but that journey will take some hours."

He was mysterious and wonderful and the past six months had been the happiest of her life. Exiting the carriage, she took his arm, and they walked into the store. Other women sat about the store eating ices with their friends, and most cast warm smiles of welcome their way, but Cecilia's gaze was locked on who sat at a table near the back of the shop on his own.

They came to stand before the couple, and they stood, a small smile playing about her mother's lips. "Daughter, you look lovely today."

A rush of emotion swamped her, a common occurrence the doctor had said would happen to women in her condition, not because both her parents were here. Parents she'd thought lost forever.

"What are you doing here, mama, papa? I didn't think you wished to see me any longer." They'd been so terribly hurt and angry after she'd married Hunter, marquess or not, the scandal that broke across London that she'd had the banns read regarding one man, and then turned about and married another did cause some salacious talk and no doubt hurt her father's firm, but she would not apologize for the trouble. For that would mean she regretted Hunter and marrying him, which she did not nor ever would.

"We were wrong, Cecilia dear and with your husband's support, he promised us a fair hearing with you to try and make amends. We're sorry for hurting you so, my dear. I truly do not think we were thinking right, nor clear in the least. We wronged you, and I cannot tell you how happy I am that you followed your heart, remained strong under a great deal of pressure that we had no right to bestow on you in the first place. We love you, and want you back in our lives if you'll have us."

Cecilia walked into her father's embrace and hugged him fiercely, swiping at the tears that fell unheeded. "Of course I forgive you both. All I wish from this day on is to forget about our past troubles and start afresh. What say you?"

"We say yes," her father said, kissing her on the cheek and helping her to sit.

"I suppose now is a good time to tell your parents our news, Lia," Hunter said, ordering ices for the four of them.

"What news is this?" her mother asked.

Lia smiled at Hunter, before turning to her parents. "I'm going to have a baby. You're going to be grandparents."

Her father laughed, shaking Hunter's hand and leaning

over to kiss Lia again on the cheek. Her mother wiped at tears and clasped her hand across the small table. "I am very happy for you both. You will be the best mother in the world. With your kind nature and nurturing ways the child will want for nothing," her father said, smiling.

"I do hope so," Lia said, dipping into her ices with a spoon. "But I believe we shall be."

Their outing soon came to an end, and her parents departed, but not willing to leave, Hunter ordered tea for them instead. "I was going to wait until tomorrow when we travelled to my other surprise, but I find I wish to tell you now."

"Really?" she said, taking his hand. "Tell me. What is it, I cannot wait."

"I was listening to your conversation the other week with the duchess and the trouble that's been taking place in Bath and the surrounding district with children and inadequate facilities to deal with the issues that face that town. And so tomorrow you shall inspect a large warehouse that we can convert to help amend this shortfall."

"In Bath?" Cecilia asked, unsure if it were possible to be as happy as she was right at this moment. She'd thought her wedding day had been the best day of her life, but Hunter with his gifts to those in need over the last few months, he kept surprising her, helping her that she was no longer sure what her favourite gift was. "You are too good, darling. I do not deserve you."

"You do deserve me, never say that. I love you, and I adore how you helped me and so many more who have not had the privilege of such an upbringing that we both had by pure chance. I was such a selfish fop for so many years, turned my back not only on myself but the suffering around me. I will not be that person any longer. I do not want that to be my legacy. You inspire me every day, and it is I who hopes to deserve you."

Cecilia moved and sat on Hunter's lap, ignoring the gasped shocks that sounded about them. "You do deserve me, never doubt that my love," she said, kissing him. "Shall we go home, my lord. I wish to be alone with you."

"It seems that I have corrupted my beautiful, honorable wife as well. Whatever shall I do with you."

Cecilia leaned down against his ear and whispered, "Whatever you like."

TO TEMPT AN EARL

Lords of London, Book 3

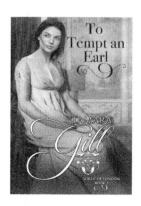

Hamish Doherty, Earl Leighton is having a terrible Season. A portion of his home burned to the ground, he was attacked outside a gaming hell, and a debutante he cannot stomach is determined they'll wed. It's enough to make any lord head for the hills, but his luck turns worse in the country. A large unpaid bill at an inn and a missing purse later, he's ready to concede defeat to the fickle Fates — until rescue unexpectedly comes from an intoxicatingly beautiful stranger.

. . .

As the daughter of a successful tradesman, Miss Katherine Martin has no time for peers and their problems. However there is something about this handsome and yet unlucky earl, and when their paths cross again, Lord Leighton offers to repay his debt to her in any way she pleases. Katherine decides one night in his arms will be just right, and yet as two kindred souls find passion together, it seems one night won't be enough. But can a woman of no rank and trade in her blood be enough to Tempt an Earl?

CHAPTER 1

It was, without question, the worst week of Lord Hamish Doherty, Earl Leighton's life. He lay sprawled on the main floor of the Two Toads Inn, near the Berkshire border. His eyes watered as pain ricocheted through his face, blood pouring from his nose, that no amount of dabbing with his handkerchief would halt. So much for his unblemished profile, the ladies of the *ton* would be most upset to see that his nose was now a little crooked.

"I told ye, no matter who ye think ye are, if ye can't pay ye debt, I'll belt the money out of ye," the proprietor growled, his bulky frame distinctly menacing.

Hamish swiped at his nose, searching his pockets again for his purse, which was regretfully missing. Where the hell was it? He had it when he arrived three days past, had tipped the busty barmaid a gold coin after a very thorough servicing of his room, but after that his memory was hazy.

He'd gone for a ride yesterday to visit his good friend the Duke of Athelby at Ruxdon house, but with no need of funds there, he'd left his purse in the room. A stupid error of judgement considering the state his nose was now in.

Pushing away a surge of anger, he replied calmly, "This is merely a misunderstanding. I have funds. I left them in my room."

"Are ye saying that they've been stolen? That my inn is an establishment that allows such theft from those who stay under its roof?"

The publican wacked the wooden baton against his hand, a sure sign that would replace the fist that smacked into his nose a moment ago. Hamish looked about the room and cringed that he was now the centre of attention of other guests who were privy to his humiliation. No doubt he'd be the on dit all over town next week once they knew who he was. "Not necessarily...only that I had it when I left yesterday only to find it gone today. And I'm not saying that it was stolen, but only that it's missing, and *I* have not misplaced it."

The barmaid who he'd tupped huffed out an aggrieved breath. "Sounds like ye are trying to pin the stealing on one of us."

Hamish held up his hand when the publican took a step toward him. "I'm not, but I don't have the funds to pay for my debt. Let me send word to my friend, the Duke of Athelby and he'll pay the bill. I assure you." The publican narrowed his eyes and seemed a little less sure of his abuse at the mention of the duke, but it was only short-lived as he seemed to disregard Hamish's lofty contacts and took a threatening step toward him.

"Ye are a liar as well as a lout who cannot pay," the publican accused.

Damn, if there was anything Hamish disliked it was conflict, and he didn't wish to cause trouble so close to the Duke of Athelby's estate, but nor would he allow being treated so poorly. He was a peer, being beaten like a low life criminal. If the publican did not watch his future actions, he would find himself before the local magistrate for battery and theft.

"I'm the Earl Leighton. Do not confuse me for a lout without money or influence. If you come any closer to me with that bat, you'll find out quick enough just how true my words are."

The publican's eyes widened, and his advance stopped. Clearly the man was rethinking better of splitting Hamish's head open. "How do I know ye not lying about being a toff?"

A pair of sturdy boots came up to stand beside his head and he noticed they were well worn and a little dusty, probably from the inn yard. The gown that followed the boots was a dull, grey color, good for traveling. The face that glanced down at him was nothing short of angelic.

"How much does his lordship owe?" this mystery woman asked the publican, stepping between him and the man who'd already given him a bloody nose, which by the way, refused to stop bleeding. He pinched his nose harder.

"Four pounds will cover it, Miss Martin, and may I say how glad we are that ye are here to stay with us again."

She rummaged into her reticule and pulled out the correct amount, placing it into the publican's hand. "Have our luggage moved up to our rooms and have his lordship's carriage packed straight away. As for the gentleman's claims of being Lord Leighton, I can assure you he is who he says. I can vouch for him as we have mutual friends." She glanced at him quickly, her voice no-nonsense and calm. "I'm assuming since he was wanting to pay his account that his intentions were to leave."

"Of course, Miss Martin," the publican said, bowing and yelling out to the surrounding staff to do as she bade. "Apologies, my lord for any confusion. I hope you'll understand not knowing who ye were made me actions necessary."

Hamish glared at the bastard. "Let it be known I shall not shadow your establishment again, and nor will I ever recommend it."

Miss Martin kneeled beside him, holding out her gloved hand for him to take. He did, and she helped him to stand.

For a moment Hamish stared at the angel who'd saved his poor ass without his purse before she raised one, dark eyebrow.

"Lord Leighton, Miss Katherine Martin at your service. We've met before, at a ball I attended with my good friend Miss Cecilia Smith, now the Marchioness of Aaron."

Hamish frowned, racking his brain to place the beauty before him and came up blank. How could he forget such a woman? She appeared a lady who commanded authority and also had a backbone of steel. Even the hefty, large-boned publican didn't seem to faze her.

He met her piercing, intelligent brown orbs that were as dark as a rich coffee and his gut clenched. Upon standing one thing became perfectly clear, she was tall, almost as tall as him. She would never be regarded as a diamond of the first water, but Miss Martin was attractive. Her long, russet brown locks sat about her shoulders, neither tied back or accessorized with a bonnet. She stared at him with unwavering frankness, and as for her mouth, well, sensual and plump were two terms that came to mind…

"I'm embarrassed to say that I do not remember, but I'm very pleased to meet you and I thank you for your help today. I'm unabashedly ashamed of myself. I should have looked after my belongings better."

"I have no doubt that you've been stolen from, and yes, please when staying in such locales in the future, take better heed of your things. I may not always be about to save you." She threw him a grin and turned about on her heel, heading for the stairs.

"Wait!" he said, clasping her arm, gently urging her to face him once again, then releasing her. An inexplicable need to see her again welled inside him. A pretty blush had heated her cheeks possibly because of his familiarity, and he suppressed the urge to pull at his cravat like a schoolboy. "I must repay your kindness. We have mutual friends, shall I see you in town? How can I get in contact with you?" Hamish stopped saying anymore before he sounded like a desperate fool.

She rummaged in her reticule again, pulling out a small card. "We move in quite different social circles, even though my friend has married into the aristocracy. But perhaps we shall see each other again. As for repayment, should you or someone you know ever need a builder, please recommend my father's company. You'll not find more quality or better prices."

Hamish looked down at the card, it read: Mr. Montgomery Martin, Master Builder. "I hope we meet again, Miss Martin." No truer words had he said. She'd saved his hide, stepped in like an Amazonian warrior and fought off the evil publican. The need to meet again, not when he was bleeding like a stuck pig and dishevelled from being assaulted, burned though him. He wanted to see her again within his own sphere, his own terms. He would send a note to the Marchioness of Aaron on his return to London and see what she could arrange.

Miss Martin laughed, heading for the stairs. "Safe travels back to London, my lord. And please, remember my advice for the sake of that pretty nose of yours. I would hate for your bone structure to suffer any more ill effects from a fist."

A warm sensation tugged inside his chest. "So, you think I'm pretty, Miss Martin?"

"I believe I remarked only on your nose, my lord. Is it possible you are fishing for a compliment?"

Hamish chuckled and watched as the impudent, delightful miss walked up the stairs, the last image he had of her the little black boots as they stepped out of sight.

CHAPTER 2

T hree months later…

Hamish hadn't thought life could get much worse after his sister's death. Her loss had cracked his heart open, and though echoes of grief still tormented him, a blessed numbness had wrapped his heart in a protective layer. A series of unfortunate incidents seemed determined to compound his misery and he truly hadn't thought anything could again stir his emotions which had been cauterized by pain. However, looking at the charred remains on what was left of a good portion of his London home, a home which had rung with happy memories of her joyous laughter, well, he had to amend such thoughts.

The year could bugger off for all he cared. First, he'd been assaulted at the Inn, the very Inn where his purse had been stolen. Upon arriving back in town he'd attended his favourite gaming hell, only to have been set upon by footpads where his winnings for the night, totalling almost a hundred pounds had been fleeced from him. He'd also suffered another bloody nose for his troubles.

Why he had been so unfortunate he could not fathom, unless the almighty was annoyed at him for not doing his duty and marrying a suitable young debutante. He was not looking to marry anytime soon if at all. His beloved sister's child would inherit his fortune and property, there was really no need for him to marry and reproduce at all. Even so, the amount of misfortune that had plagued him was starting to cause talk among his servants, and he no longer knew what to do to turn the tide back to being lucky instead of unlucky.

And now this. He shook his head, stepping back from the building when a large beam gave way, taking a portion of the floor with it. Servants and neighbors milled about him, looking up at what had once been part of his home. The part where he held his annual ball, and his sitting room on the first floor. All gone, nothing but ash and charred wood.

Damn it.

"I just heard, Hamish. I'm so sorry."

Hunter, the Marquess of Aaron, clapped him on the shoulder, holding him. "We'll have it rebuilt in no time. Do not despair."

Hamish wondered the time as the marquess was still dressed for his evening out, but there was no sign of Cecilia in the carriage. He sighed, not sure if he had it in him to take on such a task. He'd had so much bad luck of late, he'd likely have the job completed only to have it burnt down again. "Do you ever feel as though your life is wrong? That you must've done something so heinous, that the world is out to get you?"

Hunter looked at him. "No, but is that how you feel?"

Hamish grimaced. "I cannot help but feel that I need

to right some wrong or I'll continue to be somewhat cursed. No one I know has had as much misfortune as I have this year."

"You're talking about being attacked by footpads down in Vauxhall."

"Yes, but there have been other things as well." Maybe he'd not told Hunter all of what had happened to him since the death of his sister. Even so, it didn't change the fact that bad things continued to happen to him and he didn't know why. He was a rogue and a well sought-after gentleman yes, but he was not evil. He donated to the Duchess of Athelby and the Marchioness' of Aaron's London Relief Society every year. Paid his employees a fair wage and tried to be courteous to all, no matter their station. So, what was he doing wrong? Why did the fates of the world seem determined to have him crumble to his knees? It made no sense.

"You'd best be going. Cecilia will be wondering where you are, and I do not need to share my misfortune with others. It's probably best that you stayed away permanently."

"Do not take any heed of what the rumor mongers are saying about you."

Hamish rubbed a hand over his unshaven jaw. When the fire took hold last evening, he'd been abed and heard the cracking, popping sound coming from outside his door. Thank god he'd gone to investigate for he could've lost his whole home had he not alerted the servants and had two of them run and fetch the water engine while they fought with buckets of sand, water and sodden hessian bags.

"People are talking about me, and after this they will be even more so."

"Let us not worry about what has happened to you, but

what our next steps are in moving forward. You have to rebuild."

Which means he'll have to hire a master builder. The thought left him weary.

"You can stay with us until your home is repaired."

Hamish called over his steward who was inspecting the charred remains of his home. "Mr. Oakes, contact J Smith & Son lawyers and have them do an assessment for the insurance. We'll need to get this rebuild completed as soon as may be. We'll also need to hire two strong men to keep watch on the home until it is secure once again. I don't wish to lose anything else in this conundrum."

His agent bowed. "Yes, Sir. I'll get onto it right away."

"Henderson," Lord Aaron called out, gaining the attention of Hamish's valet who also stood on the street, his visage one of shock. "Pack up what you can of his lordship's clothing and have it sent around to my townhouse as soon as may be. Have Stubbs pack up whatever valuables he can manage. That'll have to do I'm afraid."

Hamish followed the marquess into the home to view the destruction more clearly, and although a lot of the building was smoke damaged, at least it was standing. How the remainder of the house hadn't caught alight was anyone's guess, but the thunder storm that came through, dousing the building with rain had helped. A little silver lining had been there at least. It was the reason the flames had been subdued and eventually put out. The charred walls, peeling, blackened wallpaper, family paintings that were smouldering was too much to take in, and within a few minutes Hamish strode toward the door. He couldn't look anymore. Tomorrow would be soon enough to deal with the mess.

"Sir, if you please before you depart," his steward said,

coming out of the room that had suffered serious damage due to the fire on the floor above.

"Yes, Mr. Oakes what is it?"

"I have sent for the insurance brokers and your lawyers. Stubbs and Henderson will bring everything that you asked for to the Marquess of Aaron's London home before luncheon tomorrow."

"Very good. I thank you," he said, eager to be away.

Their carriage waited down the lane a little way, due to the men who were already working on his home to secure it as best they could and to ensure the fire was definitely out. Hamish shook his head at the chaos this disaster had caused his neighbors and himself. To think only yesterday all was as it should be in Berkley Square and today, well, it was not what anyone would wish for.

KATHERINE SAT at her desk in her father's library and read the missive from a Mr. Oakes, steward for the Earl of Leighton. She'd heard about the fire in Mayfair but hadn't know it was Lord Leighton who'd suffered the consequences.

She took out a piece of parchment and wrote Mr. Oakes, notifying him she would attend his lordship's home to commence a quote on the rebuilding of the wing that was damaged and that he could expect her by two in the afternoon.

"Everything well, my dear? I saw there were a few missives this morning."

Katherine glanced up to see her father poking his head about her door, his clothing was worn and dusty from the morning's job down at the south west dock on the Thames. His grey beard and bushy eyebrows also sported a little dust and she chuckled. No matter where he was, if he were in London he always ensured he came home to dine with her, especially after the loss of her mother only two years before. Whether he did it because he thought she was lonely, or he was, Katherine wasn't certain, but she enjoyed his company either way.

"We've been asked to quote up Lord Leighton's rebuild on his home on Berkeley Square. He was the gentleman who suffered from the fire last week. From what his man of business states, he lost a whole wing of his home. The entertaining part of his abode, so they're set on having it fixed as soon as may be."

"Entertaining part, hey?" her father said, grinning. "Did you not attend a ball there a year or so ago? With Cecilia?"

"I did," she said, standing and joining her father, taking his arm and leading him toward their dining room. "It was a lovely ballroom too. A great shame that it has been lost. They need a master builder and since you're by far the best in London, they've asked for you and no other."

"Well," her father said, standing a little taller by such praise. "I am honoured. Make sure when you go out on site that you are fair but honest, reasonable, but understanding. I should like to do another such project of such import, we have not had one for a year or so."

"No, we have not." They sat at the table, the smell of vegetable soup, warm and inviting filled the room as the first course was placed before them. This time of night, when it was just the two of them was Katherine's favourite. Since her mother's death the time they spent together talking about the events of their day had become religious.

They sat and started to eat, her father making complimentary noises with each spoonful of soup.

"What other rooms were damaged do you know?"

"The ballroom of course, part of an upstairs sitting room, the passage leading to these rooms has smoke damage and the roof in the ballroom has since collapsed, so it's all a rightful mess. But I'll take Thomas with me, and he'll measure up, make a detailed drawing of the rooms, such as they were, and we'll quote up after that.

"Do we know who'll be refurbishing the rooms?"

Katherine took her last sip of soup, laying down her spoon. "No, I have not been informed of that as yet, but I should imagine it'll be Mr. Hope who works with all those of Earl Leighton's calibre."

"Of course. I should've remembered."

The door to the dining room opened and in walked Katherine's cousin, her late mother's niece, Jane Digby. Katherine inwardly groaned. Since Jane had arrived a week past to enjoy the season with them, it had been seven days that Katherine was looking forward to putting behind her.

Jane, a pretty woman of nineteen had long blonde locks with just enough curl to add volume and enable styles to hold correctly. She wasn't too tall, like Katherine was, and her figure was pleasing. Worse was Jane knew she turned heads wherever she went with her bright blue eyes and flawless skin. Her only fault, her very bold, knowing speech. Maybe due to the fact that living in the small country parish near Nottingham didn't allow for her to learn what one should and should not discuss. It was no error of the girl, her mother obviously lavished attention with little restraint, but now the result of such laxity in her upbringing meant Katherine made every effort to avoid her since Jane and her lofty opinions now included all of Katherine's faults. What she could wear that would bring out the color of her eyes better, or help in hiding her almighty height that was not favourable to men of their class. Or what she could do with her hair to help conceal the dull brown she'd been born with.

"Oh, I'm so sorry I'm late. I wanted your maid, Mary to do my hair. She's so very clever, but it took an age to complete." Jane sat at the table, and placing a napkin on her lap, gestured for the footman to serve her the soup course.

"It looks lovely, my dear," her father said, catching Katherine's eyes, a twinkle of mirth in his.

"Where did you find the feather?" Katherine took a sip of wine, anything to stop her lips from grinning at the girl's exuberant hair style.

Jane ate her soup, nodding eagerly. "Oh yes, I wanted a peacock's feather, but I could only find one from an old hat in the attic. I think it may be a chicken feather."

Her father coughed, and Katherine took pity on her cousin. "We shall go down to the haberdashers tomorrow and we'll see if we can find you more suitable feathers for your hats. What do you think of that?"

Jane literally bounced in her chair, her eyes bright with excitement. "Oh, how I should love to do that. And maybe while we're there they may have a hat for you to replace the one you use on our walks in the park each day. Your hair is such a bland, dull colour of brown and your bonnet being of the same color does nothing for you. If you're to catch a husband, you really ought to put more effort into your appearance."

Katherine smiled, thanking the footman as he served her the second course. "Thank you, Jane. I shall take your advice into consideration," she said with forced politeness, not wanting to snap at Jane's inconsiderate remarks and cause an argument that would distress her father.

"Oh, you should," Jane continued, pushing away her soup and asking for the second course. "All my friends in

Gotham tell me I'm an expert on these things and they do everything that I tell them. You should. I would lay a wager that should you take all my advice you'll gain a husband sooner rather than later."

"If Katherine gains a husband, I lose a daughter. Do not rush into anything my dear. I should miss you."

Katherine smiled at her father, having no intention of gaining a husband, not unless they were ideal ones like her two good friends, Marchioness of Aaron or the Duchess of Athelby. The Marquess and Duke were the best of men, possessing qualities she wanted in her own union. They were loving and caring toward their wives, and Cecilia coming from the same stock as Katherine, so much lower in society than his lordship only made him worthier of her friend's love. To put what Society expects of him aside and marry for love ensured Katherine adored him almost as much as Cecilia did.

"Are you attending Cecilia's card night tonight, my dear? Unless I'm mistaken and it's a different day altogether."

Katherine pulled her mind away from her musings of her friends' happy marriages or the fact that she'd once longed for something similar. To have a family and children, but now at six and twenty, those dreams seemed ever more distant with each day. "I am, papa. I'll be leaving after dinner."

"In that gown?" Jane asked, assessing the gown , distaste clouding her inspection.

She looked down at her light pink muslin dress. Although not the height of fashion, it was pretty and not damaged or marked. After all, it was only a card night with close friends, not like a ball where Katherine would be expected to dress in the heights of fashion.

"What is wrong with this dress? I thought it suited me very well."

"You look beautiful, my dear," her father stated, pushing away his second course.

"It's so plain and boring. Why, you positively look drab."

"Jane, that is unkind," her father put in with a frown.

At her father's response, Jane turned her attention to her meal. Their quiet repast didn't last long.

"I didn't mean to be mean, uncle. I merely wish for Katherine to do well when she's out at parties and events. Should my cousin gain a good marriage, it would improve my own prospects. I would loathe having to marry a country clergyman. How awful that should be. I'm sure I should die of boredom within the first month."

If only they were so lucky... "Tonight's event is merely a friendly get together and I can assure you, my gown, as plain and dull as it is, will do very well. My friends do not care what I wear, so long as I attend." Katherine stood, coming around and kissing her father's cheek. "I shall leave you now. I asked for the carriage to be out front by seven and it's almost time."

Her father patted her arm. "Very good my dear. I shall see you when you return home."

"I may be late. Do not wait up."

Katherine headed out into the foyer, slipping on her bonnet before picking up her cloak and gloves where she'd left them near the front door. As expected her carriage sat waiting for her. Leaning against the cushioned squabs, she sighed in relief being away from her cousin. As much as she cared for the girl, she was best served in little doses. Her constant criticism of her person was wearing. Katherine didn't need anyone to tell her of her faults. She knew them very well.

She was a woman who worked for her father, managed most things other than the manual labor her father's building company was known for. A tall woman, she was too thin, too lanky to be attractive. A Long Meg as some called her. Not to mention small breasts made her look like a stick. Katherine looked down at her bodice and tried to adjust her gown to give her the appearance of more cleavage. She sighed, giving up when her efforts accomplished nothing. There was no hope, she was what she was and there was nothing she could do about it.

The carriage pulled up before Cecilia's home, and Katherine jumped down without help. The front door opened, and Cecilia's butler smiled in welcome.

"Miss Martin, please come inside. The marchioness is waiting for you in the drawing room."

"Thank you, Thomas." Katherine handed him her cloak and started toward the hall beside the stairs. The home was bright with light and smelt of flowers. Since Cecilia had married the Marquess last spring, she'd taken to having floral arrangements in every room no matter the season, and the home smelt divine always.

Katherine smiled as a footman opened the door for her into the drawing room and she entered to a room full of people, laughing and playing cards. A woman sat playing at the piano-forte, there was more in attendance than she had thought to be, and Jane's reminder of her gown made her stomach drop. Perhaps she should have changed into something more fitting.

"You're here," Cecilia said, making her way through the guests, and reaching Katherine, pulled her into a fierce hug. "I'm so glad you came. I need someone I can really talk to." Cecilia wore a striking cerulean blue silk gown that flowed over her like water. Her friend had such beautiful clothes these days that she couldn't help but feel a little jealous over her remarkable sense of style.

"You can talk to me," the marquess said, coming to stand beside them.

Katherine laughed, and Cecilia smirked. "You know what I mean," she said.

"Luckily I do," the marquess said. He turned to Katherine and leaning down, kissed her cheek. "We have not seen enough of you, Kat. You need to visit us more often. Thank you for coming tonight."

Cecilia took Katherine's arm, pulling her into the room. "Come and sit by me and Darcy. We're discussing what we're going to do this Season and we want you to be involved as well. As much as your father can spare you, of course. We know you're very busy."

The thought of working each day, and now with the possibility of Lord Leighton's home rebuild, didn't leave much room for socializing. Though if she was to find a husband as loving and sweet as the duchess and marchioness did, well, then she'd have to put her need for sleep aside and do what she must. Dance until dawn. She loved her papa and loved working with him, but she still yearned for the fulfilment of a husband and children someday.

Her parents' marriage had been such a happy one, full of love and respect. Growing up she'd been supported and unconditionally loved, and wanted the same for her own children if she were so fortunate.

"What did you have in mind?"

The Duchess welcomed her with a warm hug also, and before long it had been an hour of nothing but chatter about gowns, balls and parties. The duchess was looking forward to holding a country visit mid-season at their estate in Berkshire. All of which Katherine was invited to should she wish to attend.

A slight tittering from the ladies who stood about the room caught Katherine's attention and she turned to see Lord Leighton enter, standing in the threshold and surveying them all like a sitting god looking over his mere mortals. Katherine had seen him before, a few times in fact considering they had mutual friends, but tonight dressed in light colored satin knee-breeches and a long-tailed blue superfine coat he was beyond perfect. He appeared like he was attending the grandest ball in London.

Not cards and drinks with friends.

"I am here!" he declared, laughing and walking over to the Duke of Athelby and the Marquess who stood aside of the guests talking. The men shook hands and Katherine watched them, unable to tear her eyes away from Lord Leighton and his lovely, extraordinary male form.

Not that she should be looking at men in this society, certainly not in the way she was regarding Lord Leighton, but it was hard to not admire their dashing elegance. No men should be born with such beauty and his lordship had that in droves. Unlike most men of his set, Lord Leighton had long hair, or at least, shoulder length. His locks were tied back in a black ribbon tonight, and the design brought out his cutting cheekbones and generous lips. As for his eyes, they were his finest feature if she had to pick one, and in all honestly there were many to choose from. But his eyes were almond in shape and were such a dark shade of onyx that they were almost black. She inwardly sighed at his beauty, marvelling how anyone could be born with not only wealth and stature but also looks. How lucky he was.

"Have you met, Lord Leighton?" the duchess asked, sitting back in the chair and flicking a glance in the direction of her husband.

"I have. And tomorrow I'm to meet with him in relation to supplying his man of business with a quote for the rebuild of his home. What a terrible situation for him to be in. Do you know where he's staying while his home is repaired?"

"He's staying here," Cecilia said, matter of fact. "Will be here for some time from what I understand. The damage was substantial and will take some months to repair."

"It is very bad, but it could've been a lot worse. It was lucky he woke up and was able to sound the alarm, or he could've been killed," Katherine added.

"Very true." The duchess smiled, as her husband came to stand beside her.

"Miss Martin, have you met Lord Hamish Doherty, Earl Leighton," the duke said, gesturing to his friend as he came to join them. The Marquess of Aaron following close and went to stand behind Cecilia.

Katherine met the Earls eyes and saw the moment he recognized her.

"Well, what chance is this? The lady who saved my life. How do you do, Miss Martin. I hope you're enjoying your evening?"

"I am, thank you, my lord. And I must say I'm glad to see that you made it back to London after all, although I am sad to hear about the fire you've suffered this past week."

"Thank you, yes. As you can see I'm back in town, thanks to you."

"Why do I get the feeling you two have a little story that we're not aware of." The duchess said, glancing back and forth between them.

"Because we do," the Earl said, matter of fact, before taking a sip of his champagne. "Miss Martin saved my hide at an inn on my way home from your estate in fact. And I have not forgot your kindness, my dear. I still owe you."

"And you shall owe her more after tomorrow," Cecilia added, grinning.

The Earl frowned. "Why is that?" he asked.

Katherine took pity on the man. "You may have forgotten, but I believe I mentioned that my father is a master builder, my lord. I'm to meet with your man of business tomorrow to quote for the structural repairs to your home here in London."

"You?" the Earl said, his brow raised in obvious shock.

"Careful, Hamish, remember you're surrounded by three very strong women right at this moment," the duke said, smiling.

"I meant no offence, Miss Martin, I'm just shocked that is all. I did not think women partook in such employment."

"Normally they do not, but I'm the exception," she said with a small smile, pride warming her chest. And tomorrow she would prove to him exactly how much of an exception she was. Her mind was quick, and her mathematical skills better than most, as was her ability to barter for the best wood prices one could get in London and beyond. It was why her father trusted and relied on her so much in the business. Between them they checked, and double checked their calculations and sums and they were yet to make a mistake, hence why they were so very busy.

The Earl's direct gaze caressed over her length and a peculiar shiver stole over her. Did he like what he saw or was he merely curious that the woman across from him wasn't the standard so many of his ilk married?

She didn't need her cousin Jane to remind her of her lack of charm and elegance. Around the duchess and

Cecilia, it was no secret she lacked their beauty and social confidence. Katherine was from trade, quite literally, a builder's daughter and one who worked in the company. And although Cecilia, a woman from her social sphere had married a marquess, she was at least considered not as rough about the edges as Katherine since she hailed from a barrister's family.

Katherine took in her gown and compared it to her friends. Their elegant silk, the cut and design of their dresses were the height of fashion, made her own modest dress look as cheap as it was compared to theirs.

Lifting her chin, she took a sip of her wine and fought to push the self-doubt aside. Darcy and Cecilia were her friends and would never ostracize her, no matter what Society might like to do.

Life was passing her by, her friends were starting families and marrying, while she seemed to be stuck, never moving forward, except towards old age.

"I look forward to viewing your quote, Miss Martin. Pleasure to meet you again," Lord Leighton said, bowing before going off to join another set of guests. They welcomed him with laughter and perfect curtsies and his absence was missed.

Katherine watched him for a moment before turning her attentions back to her friends. Men like Lord Leighton didn't see women like her as equals. Not wealthy or connected enough, and now at six and twenty her prospects of actually marrying at all, even in her own social sphere seemed a lost dream. As she grew older, Katherine had to admit that she didn't seem to belong anywhere, except at her work. She was doomed to die an old maid. A woman who'd never experienced a stolen kiss or a wicked embrace from men of Lord Leighton's ilk. Or anyone's for that matter.

As the night wore on, as the card games and music started with impromptu dancing, and no gentleman asked her to dance, the little demoralizing sound of Jane's voice wouldn't abate. It's constant reminding that she didn't belong, wasn't wanted and was not refined enough for her friends wouldn't quieten.

No matter how much she told herself it was not so.

CHAPTER 3

Katherine stood with Mr. Andrew Perry, their foreman outside Earl Leighton's home and tapped her pencil against her notepad. The lord was over an hour late and still there was no sign of an arriving carriage or gentleman heading toward his home on foot.

"Maybe we ought to come back another time, Miss Katherine. His lordship seems to have forgotten."

Katherine looked up and down the street again and frowned. "It is odd that his man of business hasn't even arrived. I see there are men inside cleaning up, maybe if we start the measuring up and do the inspection his lordship will arrive afterwards. There may have been some kind of time mix up."

Andrew harrumphed, but followed as she walked up the townhouse steps, entered the entrance hall where a flurry of workers stood, some upstairs and others working on the room beneath where the fire took hold.

"We'll start upstairs and work our way down."

Just then the front door opened and in walked a hurried Mr. Oakes, a sheen of sweat covering his face, his hair sticking up on end as if he'd been running. "Mr. Perry, Miss Martin, I presume."

Katherine held out her hand and the man shook it, before shaking Mr. Perry's as well.

"I do apologize. His lordship had stated he wished to attend today but sent me a note that arrived only half an hour past that he'd changed his mind. I was not prepared and knew you would already be waiting, and so I'm terribly late. I am most sorry."

Katherine smiled, trying to put the harried man at ease. "No need to concern yourself. Shall we begin?" It did not surprise her that Lord Leighton didn't wish to see her again or discuss his repairs with a woman. After their initial conversation last evening, he'd gone off and practically twirled about the room, talking to any and all female guests Cecilia had invited, gushing over them, and making all of them blush and giggle like little nincompoops.

It only proved yet again that she was plain and unbecoming and not a woman that would ever turn Lord Leighton's head. He was a man who oozed charm and spectacular looks, while she oozed trade and little appeal at all.

A pity, she had anticipated seeing him. Perhaps it was for the best, for what good could come of any interaction outside of business matters?

"This way, if you please," Mr. Oakes said, starting up the stairs.

Katherine followed and over the next hour they measured, discussed wood, took samples of what was there, and Katherine drew the layout of the room, the structure of the ceiling, or at least what was left of it.

Katherine felt for his lordship having lost one of the grandest ballrooms in London, but at least one of its greatest features being the marble fireplace had survived, even if it was a little discoloured by smoke.

Mr. Oakes explained what the Earl expected with regard to the rebuild and what changes he wished to make, the largest being a terrace that came off the ballroom and considering the ballroom was on the first floor of this home, it would take a little design and consideration to have this put in place. But it was no hardship for her father to do, and when all the building work was completed, Lord Leighton would be satisfied, just as all their customers were.

With their business complete, she turned to Mr. Oakes and held out her hand. "Good day, sir. Thank you for your assistance and input. We'll have a quote ready for his lord-ship by Monday next week."

He took her hand, shaking it. "Thank you, Miss Martin. You've been very professional. Give my regards to your father."

They left and climbed up in their waiting carriage, telling the driver to return to the office.

A pleased smile crossed Mr. Perry's lips. "I think that went well. Your thoughts, Miss Martin?"

"I agree, and I think after seeing the damage, that should his lordship choose us for the rebuild we should have him back in his home within six months, if the weather is favourable."

"Has his lordship decided on who'll refurbish the home, we should probably consult with them before we commence."

"I will send word to his man of business, I don't know why I forgot to ask him today. But even so, should he not know, I shall ask Lord Leighton directly. He is staying at my good friend's home, the Marchioness of Aaron." And she was to dine with them the following Saturday, just a select few of friends, which Katherine assumed to be the duke and duchess of Athelby. If Lord Leighton attended she would ask him then. Settling back on the squabs, Katherine pushed away the little flutter that took flight in her stomach at the thought of seeing his lordship again.

There was no point in her dreaming about him, he would never look to her for a wife or a dalliance even. Too plain, too common to turn anyone of his sets' eyes, but even so, it didn't mean she couldn't look at him, take her fill and enjoy daydreaming about what his soft looking lips would feel like against hers.

She sighed. *I bet they would feel wickedly good…*

"Did you say something, Miss Martin?"

Katherine shook her head. "I was just mumbling to myself. Please ignore me." Just dreaming of things she'd love to have, even if for a moment, but might never experience. The fact that Lord Leighton didn't even bother to show up for their appointment today told her all she needed to know where he ranked her importance in his life. Why she was so invisible to people other than her friends baffled her. She had a good dowry, wasn't beautiful she would admit, but nor was she unattractive, so it had to be due to her uninspiring figure. And the fact she worked for a living. Perhaps Jane was right and she needed to upgrade her wardrobe and purchase a new hat. Anything to mix it up a little, make her appear to have all the appearance of a lady who knew how to dress, how to attract men, when really, she had no idea at all.

HAMISH GLANCED across the dining table at the marquess of Aaron's home and slowly chewed the roasted chicken he was eating while trying to figure out Miss Martin who sat across from him. Her mind was as quick as any man's he'd ever known, her intelligence and knowledge on news and current affairs was better than his own he also admitted. By all appearances she was a modern, educated woman. But her gown, it was at least two seasons old, and although her hair was tidy, it did little to bring out her dark, alluring eyes.

Did she dress with so little care to hide the becoming, charming visage, or maybe she simply did not care for the fripperies that so many women of his class lived to purchase.

For him, he loved seeing women dressed in the latest fashions, their hair bejewelled and a little rouge on the lips made one long to smudge it across their mouth in a passionate kiss. When Miss Martin had saved his nose from further damage at the inn some months past, he'd not thought to see her again, but he also hadn't forgotten that he owed her a small debt of gratitude.

And now after seeing her father's building company's quote, a very reasonable one considering they were the best in London, he would be seeing a lot more of her in the coming months since he'd decided to use them. For reasons even he didn't know, he would like to see her again. Talk to her more. Find out what her passions and pursuits were and see if this wallflower before him would blossom into a rose.

Hamish cleared his throat. "I wished to tell you, Miss Martin that I've decided to hire your father to rebuild my home. I know it is crass to talk business at events such as these, but my man of business spoke highly of you and Mr. Perry's professionalism and the quote was very reasonable. When do you think you shall be able to start?"

The duchess clapped, smiling. "Oh, I'm so glad you've chosen to go with Mr. Martin, Hamish. You shall not be disappointed. He's helped us with all our building works we've taken part in with the Orphanages and schools. Katherine and her father are simply the best."

A light blush stole over Katherine's cheeks making her even a little more handsome than Hamish thought possible. She was not the type of woman he would normally ever glance at, not because of her rank or clothing, he wasn't an idiot, but simply she was so very lithe and tall. He loved nothing more than a woman with a little curve to her, a woman who held the shape of the female form. He was, to put it bluntly, a man who adored breasts and bottom of equal size.

Miss Martin, although not completely unfortunate in relation to her breasts, had a good handful at most, but not much more.

He took a sip of wine when her gaze met his. "Thank you, Lord Leighton. I'm very happy to hear this and shall tell papa the good news on my return home tonight."

He grinned, amused by her proper speech to him. With everyone else she was carefree, laughing and involving herself without second thought, but with him, she was a little guarded, careful with her words and it made him wonder.

"Katherine, I forgot to ask you last week, but we've all been invited to the O'Callaghan's ball and we hoped you would attend with us. I shall have the carriage sent around to pick you up and then we shall all travel together from there. It is Thursday next," Cecilia interjected.

Again, she confounded Hamish. At the mention of a ball her eyes brightened and without qualm he could term Katherine a beauty. When she wished to be and wasn't hiding under dowdy clothes.

"Thursday next? I shall have to check with papa that

we have no outstanding engagements, but I'm sure it'll be fine."

"There is supposed to be good gaming, Hamish. Are you attending?" the duke asked, pushing his dessert away. Lord Aaron called for the port, and the ladies stood, signalling the end of the meal.

"I will be. I promised Lady O'Callaghan that I would dance the first waltz with her and I should hate to disappoint her ladyship."

"Be careful, Hamish or you'll find yourself betrothed to her ladyship right smart. You know as well as all of us, that she's after a new husband after her last one died under unfortunate circumstances." The duchess said, chuckling.

"I would think dying under any circumstance would be unfortunate," Katherine said, matter of factly.

Cecilia placed her napkin on the table, nodding. "The duchess meant Kat that her ladyship's husband died under her ladyship when they were within their private apartment."

"Well, poor man, or maybe, lucky man depending on which way you look at it," Katherine said, chuckling.

Hamish shut his mouth with a snap having never heard a woman speak so openly and about that particular subject in polite Society. His past mistresses had sometimes spoken with such candor and little regard to those about them, but never had he seen it take place within his own Society. Men, yes, very often spoke in such ways, but women, never. The duke and marquess laughed and Hamish too found himself amused and not a little intrigued by her.

The ladies stood, and Hamish's gaze followed Miss Martin...*Kat* out the door before a footman closed it, leaving just himself, the duke and marquess alone.

"Do the ladies always talk in such ways? I say, I've never heard Cecilia ever say such things in polite Society."

Hunter chuckled. "Those three women are the best of friends and I shudder to think what they discuss when we're not around. I'm sure Katherine knows all about married life, and what happens between a man and woman in the marriage bed. To hear them speak so at table, around friends, is nothing to them."

"A quite common occurrence I should say," the marquess added. "Why the other day I heard Cecilia telling Kat about the rumors circulating the *ton* regarding Lord Leslie and his valet."

"What rumors? I've not even heard this one." Hamish looked from both men, wondering when they had become so, so *married*! He leaned back in his chair, taking a cigar when the duke offered him one. "What do you think of Miss Martin?"

Both men turned steely gazes on him and Hamish took a long pull of his smoke, wondering what exactly was going through their minds right at this moment. His mind was filled with thoughts of a woman he had no right to be thinking of at all. He didn't even want a wife.

"She is lovely, and we care for her as much as Darcy and Cecilia would care for a sister should they have one, and so, when you ask what we think of her, we wonder what you mean by such a query, Hamish," the duke said, raising one brow and looking quite severe.

It reminded Hamish of what the duke looked like before he married Darcy, stern and ill-tempered. Hamish paused, wondering himself what he meant. He rubbed his jaw, contemplating his words. "Miss Martin is polite, and well mannered, but she lacks refinement that the duchess and marchioness both exhibit. I know Cecilia and Katherine grew up beside one another in Cheapside and look at each other like sisters, but it is odd now that Cecilia is a marchioness that their friendship is still as strong."

Hunter leaned forward in his chair, putting out his cigar in the tray provided. "Why would their friendship not continue? Kat is wonderful, and I would never suggest to Cecilia to cease such a friendship."

"You must admit, she is getting on in years, and is yet to be married. Not to mention her clothes, her hair. And she's to attend lord and lady Keppel's ball with you all next week. What will she wear! I fear to find out. It is a little peculiar, you must admit." Hamish leaned back in his chair, picturing Miss Martin in an embroidered silk gown in a deep, rich color. She would be as beautiful as any woman he'd known. He frowned. Where the hell did that thought come from.

The duke shrugged. "I like Miss Martin and would never wish to exclude her in any way. I grant you her clothes are not the most fashionable, nor her hair the most styled, but she is loyal, honest and kind. And Darcy loves her, and then, so too do I. I hope this is not going to be a problem for you, Hamish. She is our friend, and I do not want you to injure her pure soul just because she's not as fashionable and rich as so many of your friends are."

At his silence Hunter glanced at him. "Hamish? Do we have a problem?"

Hamish threw his cigar into the fire, standing. "Of course not. I merely thought it odd, is all. But if you wish her to be part of your set in our society, who am I to naysay that. Even if she is the builder of my home I shall be obliged to dance with her at balls."

Hunter laughed. "I shall hold you to that, and you never know, you may enjoy your dance with Miss Martin. She may charm you as much as she's charmed all of us."

"Perhaps," he said, heading for the door that a footman opened for them. "But for now, I shall bid you all goodnight. I have a card game to attend and a buxom lady friend who wishes for her own private dance with me."

The duke shook his head as Hamish took his cloak and hat from the footman in the hall. "See you at the ball, Hamish. And remember to bring your best manners with you."

He clasped his chest in mock insult. "Of course. When have I ever been otherwise?"

Hamish was soon settled into his carriage and looking out the window he thought of his friends, their love match marriages and how lucky they were. He'd once thought such a life was what he'd wanted, but after the death of his sister, the pain it caused his family and that of her husband he was no longer so sure. To lose someone again he loved seemed an idiotic thing to do. To put one's feelings on the line, be vulnerable wasn't what he wanted for himself.

His nephew would inherit his title, he didn't need to marry if he didn't wish to settle with a lady. His life was full, he wasn't short of bed partners, and the entertainments of his set kept him busy. The image of Katherine Martin floated through his mind, of being greeted at home by a woman of her lively intelligence and prettiness, having her warm his bed and no one else, and he wondered at his course in life.

Wondered if his life of idleness was what he really wanted.

CHAPTER 4

"I t is too much, your grace. I couldn't possibly wear such a masterpiece." Katherine slid her hand along the golden silk gown with an abundance of silver silk embroidery and decorated with hundreds of glass beads and silk cording. Never had she seen such a beautiful dress and picking it up she held it before her in the looking glass, surprised the color suited her.

"You will look beautiful, and since you're staying here this evening, I shall not take no for an answer. I'll have my maid do your hair, and you'll be the prettiest lady at the Leeders' annual ball." Darcy rang the bell for a servant in the pretty little room she'd allocated her. A single bed covered in a blue floral design complimented the blue velvet drapes across the bank of windows. A small chaise sat at the end of the bed and considering the size of the room it allowed one to warm themselves before the well stoked fire.

"You're being too nice, but truly, I'll feel odd wearing something that suits people of your sphere more than mine. Won't people look at me as a fraud?"

Darcy sent the footman who she was talking to at the door away with orders to bring up a hip bath and turned to her with a small frown across her brow.

"I don't ever wish to hear you say such a thing again. You're the duchess of Athelby and marchioness of Aaron's closest friend. No one would dare look down on you in any other way other than pure adoration. And if they do not, they will have me to face."

Darcy came over and clasped her hand, squeezing it a little. "Some people are not born into privilege such as I was, and some marry into this life, such as Cecilia has, but it does not make anyone anywhere else any less worthy of respect or cordiality. We are all humans after all. I do not want you to feel like you're lesser than us for you are not." Darcy took the gown from her and laid it on the bed. "If I have made you feel like you would be uncomfortable in this gown, you are of course free to wear whatever you like, and I shall stand beside you, just as proud as I would should you be wearing nothing at all."

Katherine chuckled, and went to stand before the dress. Oh, it was so very pretty, so very heavy and would've had hundreds of sewing hours in the creation of it. "I merely worry that people will think I'm trying to be someone I'm not. But," she said, sighing, admiring the gown yet again.

"You're right. What should I care what people think or believe, it is only a gown." Katherine turned to Darcy. "I shall wear it, and I shall enjoy every moment I'm in such a beautiful masterpiece. Thank you for allowing me this little luxury."

Darcy clapped her hands just as a light knock sounded on the door. "Kat, the night will be so much fun, and you will look utterly stunning." Darcy bade the servants enter and a footman carried in a hip bath along with a bevy of other servants who brought up steaming buckets of hot water. A maid left her linens and lavender soap on a chair beside the bath.

"I shall leave you now, my dear, and will see you after you're dressed. Ring the bell when you're ready for your hair to be dressed and my maid will attend you. I shall see you in the entrance hall by eight."

❦

THE LEEDERS' ball was a crush and Katherine followed the duke and duchess into the ballroom after they were introduced at the door. If it felt as though hundreds of eyes had turned her way she was not far off. Looking about the room, a lot of the *haute ton* glanced in her direction, some curious no doubt on whom the duke and duchess had brought while others, those that had seen her at other events looked down their nose at her even being in their presence.

Katherine raised her chin and came to stand beside Darcy as a footman carrying a tray of champagne stopped before them. Katherine picked up a flute and took a well needed sip. "There are so many people here this evening. How will we find Cecilia in this crush?"

The duchess craned her neck, looking about and nodding in acknowledgment to those who tried to gain her attention. "Cecilia and Hunter will be along soon, and I told her I would be in this situation in the ballroom, so she should find us well enough."

Lady Oliver, who had been traveling abroad with her husband Viscount Oliver waved to the duchess and made a direct line toward them. The duchess smiled, clearly pleased that her friend who'd been away from town for the past eighteen months was back among them.

"Fran," the duchess said, kissing her friend on both cheeks before they embraced quickly. "I'm so happy to see you again." She kissed the viscount and then turned them to where Katherine and the duke were waiting.

"Athelby you know, but let me introduce you to my new friend, Miss Katherine Martin. She grew up with Lady Aaron, as you may remember me telling you in my letters."

Lady Oliver smiled at Kat and she had the impression she was genuinely happy to meet her finally. She let the few nervous knots dissipate in her stomach that had lodged there wondering if the duchesses' friend wouldn't approve of her.

Katherine bobbed a curtsy. "It's lovely to meet you, Lady Oliver. I understand you've been traveling abroad and have seen even the pyramids of Egypt."

Her ladyship smiled, clearly remembering the wonderful sights she'd visited. "We did, and they were the most wonderful of places. And I almost forgot to tell you Darcy, but I found the most amazing woman while traveling there. Her name is Lady Georgina Savile, a widow of great fortune, and she'll be arriving in London by month's end. Lord Oliver and myself are going to be holding a ball in her honor and you must simply come, you too, Miss Martin, if you wish to."

"I should be honoured to attend," Katherine said, delighted to be included. The conversation turned to the other sites the viscountess' had seen over her many months abroad and Katherine took the opportunity to watch the dancers and other guests.

On the dance floor a flash of scarlet caught her eye and looking, spotted Earl Leighton dancing with a blonde woman in a deep red silk gauze gown and silk trim that sat over a white muslin gown. The gown was so becoming on the woman, and her figure highlighted every pretty little feature and silk design that sat across the bodice.

Katherine's enjoyment of the ball dimmed a little at seeing Lord Leighton so entranced by the woman who had curves that perfectly accentuated the woman's form. It shouldn't surprise Katherine that she would not turn his head. One needed to be a siren to capture the beautiful and popular Lord Leighton.

The night passed and soon it was after midnight and still no one other than the duke and the marquess of Aaron had asked her to dance. Not even the pretty gown her friend had given her to use could persuade men to ask her to step out with them.

Katherine tried to include herself into her friends' conversations as much as she could, but as the night crept further into the early hours of the morning, it became harder and harder. She'd been up early the day of the ball to check the delivery of the hardwoods that were to be used at Lord Leighton's home, and she'd had a meeting with Mr. Perry and his lordship's man of business Mr. Oakes to discuss the week's progress and what was to go forward the next. Her presence at a ball, when it was well past her retiring time, left her eyes heavy and her feet aching, even in slippers that felt like she was walking on air.

The mention of Lord Leighton's name caught her attention and she looked up from inspecting her champagne glass to see his lordship walking over to them. This time a different woman from the one in scarlet she'd seen him dancing with earlier in the night. This woman had striking auburn hair, tied up in in a motif of curls and a delicate strand of diamonds threaded throughout. Her gown was almost ebony in colour with gold thread in decorative flowers around the hem, bodice and sleeves.

Katherine gritted her teeth, not wanting to believe his

lordship was so obsessed with beauty as he seemed to be. She was a fool to have even thought of him in any other way more than as a mutual acquaintance.

"Lord Leighton, how good of you to drag yourself away from your entertainments to come speak with us," the duchess of Athelby said, giving him her hand to kiss.

He bowed and introduced his guest to them all. A Lady Scottle, wife of the late Baron Scottle.

His lordship's gaze moved over them all but stopped on her, his eyes widening as he took in her appearance. She raised her chin, readying herself for whatever he was about to say. The last thing she wanted him to think was she was dressing up to impress his set. It was the last thing she was doing, no matter what she wore, she would never succumb to changing who she was.

"Miss Martin?" he asked, stepping toward her and dropping Lady Scottle's arm who merely went to stand beside Darcy and Cecilia and started to chat.

Katherine bobbed a curtsy. "Lord Leighton, I hope you're enjoying the ball."

His attention flicked over her again and warmth speared through her stomach as his eyes heated appreciatively. She'd seen disappointment often reflected in others, and duty by gentlemen when they'd done the right thing and danced with her. But in this case, the reaction on Lord Leighton's face wasn't anything she'd ever seen before. Certainly not at her. She'd seen appreciation and desire bestowed on others, but she'd never been pretty enough to warrant such sincere admiration.

It would seem a beautiful gown and a little rouge on one's lips could do wonders.

"Is that really you?" he said, picking up her hand and bowing over it. "How beautiful you look this evening."

Katherine took back her hand when he forgot to let it

go and smiled to quell the butterflies taking flight in her stomach. "It is me, merely dressed a little more appropriately for the occasion."

"Gold suits you," he said, staring at her with what Katherine hoped was awe.

The lady he'd walked over to their group with came up to him and slid her arm through his lordship's. A very familiar gesture if Katherine had ever seen one. "Dance with me, Hamish. It's to be a waltz."

Katherine stepped back to give them privacy and started when Lord Leighton clasped her hand, placing it onto the crook of his arm. "Forgive me, Lady Scottle but I'd already promised this dance to Miss Martin."

The duchess stepped in and pulled her ladyship over toward where she was speaking with Cecilia. Katherine walked out onto the floor with his lordship, masking her shock that his lordship had just lied to a woman. Fibbed most believably and worse she'd allowed him to, just so she could dance with him.

He swung her into his arms and she met his gaze, trying not to get lost in the beautiful vision that was Lord Leighton. "You just fibbed, my lord. To a woman who did not expect you to ask another woman right in front of her to dance. Are you always so flippant?"

His lordship grinned, his gloved hand warm about hers. His touch upon her hip made her conscious of the fact that she wasn't as rounded and womanly as the lady he'd left with their friends. Her figure although thin, and pleasant enough, wasn't soft womanly curves, or as bountiful in some regions as all men liked. Or so she'd heard...

"I think that is the wrong word and unless you tell Lady Scottle she will never know the truth of the matter. And anyway, I wished to dance with you."

"Why?" she asked, truly baffled by being in his arms.

Katherine couldn't help but wonder if he was playing with her, gifting her with crumbs before moving on to more substantial delicacies. She dearly hoped her admiration wasn't evident to him, especially if he felt no regard or admiration or something of the sort.

"Well, we have mutual friends, and it's only expected of me to dance with you at least once. Why, I'm sure Athelby and Aaron have both already stepped out with you, have they not?"

"Yes, they have," she grudgingly admitted, but still, that was no excuse to dance surely. Katherine shook the idea away that he actually wanted to dance with her because he liked her. Such notions helped no one, especially herself. She was a wallflower, well and truly, and no matter what her friends did to try and enable men to court her, that didn't always happen.

Who was she fooling. It never happened.

"And if you think I have forgotten the service you paid me regarding my bill at the Inn some weeks ago you're mistaken. I have not forgot that I promised I owed you for your generous service. This is merely me trying to right the wrong I placed you in that night."

Katherine couldn't meet his eye as a thought so wicked landed and flowered in her mind. The idea was tempting and at six and twenty was she brave enough to actually ask his lordship what she desired. Him, mostly. For one night at least... "While it is pleasant dancing with you, my lord, I do perhaps have something to ask, but here is not the place or time."

He pulled her close as they made a turn in the waltz. "You have me curious, Miss Martin. Please, let us talk now. Tell me what you wish."

Nerves pitted in her stomach. Could she be so bold? The words stuck in her throat, but having been privy to the affectionate nature of her friends' marriage, of their discussions of married life, it made Katherine curious. What was it like to be with a man. Did all men make a woman's toes curl in their slippers when they were kissed, like the duchess said the duke makes her? Taking a deep breath, she met his gaze with more determination than she thought possible. "Meet me on the terrace in half an hour and I shall tell you, but here is too public, too many eyes watching. Will you do that for me?"

Lord Leighton frowned, but nodded. "Of course. I shall meet you, just as you asked."

❦

HAMISH DANCED with Lady Scottle after leaving Miss Martin with the duke and duchess of Athelby. The late Baron's wife was a beautiful woman, lush, loving and widowed, and if he played his cards right this evening, the night might end pleasurable for them both.

He stepped out of the card room, whisky in hand and watched as the woman who'd knocked him off his feet with her raw beauty an hour before slid away from her party and headed for the terrace. He didn't move, merely waited a few more minutes before he too, headed outside.

The night was warm, and there were a few couples outdoors, enjoying the balmy night air that was refreshing after being indoors with a room that smelt of wax, perfumes and human odour no one enjoyed sniffing.

Hamish strolled along the terrace, stopping to talk to those he knew, all the while sipping his whisky and looking for Miss Martin who seemed to have disappeared. He came to the end of the terrace and all that lay before him was the shadowed manicured garden.

The sound of 'psst' came from the balustrade. Looking

over he couldn't help the chuckle that escaped at seeing Miss Martin step out from a small alcove along the terrace that sat at ground level. Hamish strode down the stairs and joined Miss Martin in the secluded spot that wasn't visible to those strolling the terrace and sat on the cold stone seat.

"You're being very mysterious, and may I add a little scandalous Miss Martin. Should you be caught here with me…me especially, your reputation will be ruined."

She shook her head, dismissing his words before sitting straight and clasping her hands firmly in her lap. "You said before, you wished to help me, that you owed me after I came to your aid in Berkshire. And if you're sure your hiring of my father does not dispel your debt, then there is something I wish to ask. Before I succumb to logical thought and run away."

He chuckled, liking the fact that Miss Martin had a sense of humor. "Now I'm even more curious. Please ask, and I shall see what I can do."

"Please ensure you're sure, for once I've spoken the words there is no turning back." Her eyes were wide, and there was an edge of vulnerability to her words that he adored. He clasped his hands tight in his lap lest he reached out to touch her, any part of her, just because.

"It came to me tonight what I would like you to do for me."

"Really?" he asked, a little unsettled by the fact that he was quite alone in the garden with a woman who the more time he spent with, grew more becoming with every moment. He pulled himself up on the thought. Her father was the builder, a tradesman he'd hired to rebuild his home. He did not need to start seeing potential where there was none. Miss Martin would no sooner look at him for a husband, than he would look at her for a wife. Not that he was looking for marriage he reminded himself.

Hamish tried to remember how many drinks he'd imbibed this evening, and lost count after four. "What is it?"

She bit her bottom lip and he fought not to growl. The woman was making this bloody dreadfully hard not to kiss her.

"It is a well-known fact in my usual social sphere that I'm a wallflower. I do not delude myself with the thought of great marriage now. Did you know that I'm the oldest of all my friends? Even Cecilia, who I'm two years her senior."

His lips twitched. "I hardly believe that calls for you to be termed a matron, Miss Martin. You are still younger than myself, and I do not consider myself ancient." Although it was unfortunately and maybe even unfairly true what she was saying. By Jove, he'd even said such a thing to the duke and marquess. Not that he would admit to such things. He wasn't a complete imbecile.

"How old are you, my lord?"

"I'm six and twenty."

She half smiled, shrugging. "Then yes, we are the same age, but I fear you're forgetting what that means for a woman to what that means for a man. You're still young, perhaps even too young to even consider marriage, whereas for myself, I'm considered on the shelf and practically decrepit."

He couldn't help himself, he chuckled. "You do not look decrepit tonight, my dear." And she did not. Not at all. If anything, she was becoming one of the most beautiful and intelligent women he'd ever met. His steward couldn't speak highly enough of Miss Martin, her ideas and no-nonsense approach to tradesmen and those who worked for her father. Perhaps if she believed herself not marriageable quality he should push her toward his steward. The man wasn't attached from what he knew, and Miss Martin was from the same social set as Mr. Oakes.

Hamish went to mention such facts but held his words when he caught her eye. They were so wide, and a little conniving that he wondered and wanted to know how she wished for him to pay her back.

"Thank you for the compliment, even though I believe you hand them out like Gunther's hands out ices. Even so, this is what I propose." She took a fortifying breath and said, "I wish for you, Lord Leighton to sleep with me. Sleep with me as a man sleeps with a woman he desires, how a husband ought to sleep with his wife. How a man sleeps with his mistress."

Hamish swallowed, his body roaring to life, his mind answering yes, while his mouth seemed barren of words. He cleared his throat. "You cannot mean such things, Miss Martin. You will be ruined." Damn it, this idea was wrong. Immoral even. Miss Martin was a gently bred young lady who could still make a suitable, happy match in life. "It would not be right. I will not do it." Blast it though, the idea, now that it was in his head was not a bad one...

The image of her long legs wrapped about his hips. *Blast it.* This was not at all proper.

"I'm becoming an old maid, my lord. Let me experience what it is like for a woman to lay in the arms of a man just once. I do not want to die, whenever that shall be and wonder what I missed out on. For I'm sure after being around the duke and marquess and their wives I'm missing out on something."

He stood, needing to distance himself, although he kept himself hidden within the small alcove. Hamish understood very well what she was missing out on, and as much as his heart went out to her, this was not something he could help with. No matter how alluring the thought may be. "Our friends, should they find out would never speak to me again. They would demand that we marry, and I do not wish to marry—"

"Me?" she finished for him, hurt crossing her features before she masked the emotion.

The single word brought him up quick. "No, not you, not anyone. Not yet at least, or at all." Hamish ran a hand through his hair, his mind conjuring up all thoughts of images of what Miss Martin would look like naked on his bed, beguiling and begging for more. Her long legs, and slim waist, her dark, chocolate rich hair, laying softly against her perfect creamy shoulders.

Bloody hell...

"I will make no demands on you other than one night in your bed. Forgive me but I must speak plainly. I have a substantial dowry, more than most in my circle, but I'm passable pretty and marriage does not look forthcoming to me. I have tried to gain the attention of gentlemen when they'd bothered to court me, but it has always failed and come to nothing. I will make no demands on you. My future, even if an unmarried maid, will be a future of comfort where I would not have to work if I do not wish. I merely want to experience the marriage bed and nothing more. You said you were in my debt. This would clear that debt. It is what I wish."

He came and sat beside her again, hating the fact that she damn well smelt as alluring as her words. "What if you become pregnant? What then, Miss Martin?" That would be the worst of disasters. The memory of his sister haemorrhaging, writhing in pain shot through his mind.

He looked at her, her large brown eyes wide in hope and vulnerability.

"I'm not so green that I do not know there are means, things women and men can do to stop such things. Why," she said, gesturing, "there are many mistresses in this city that are not mothers, so I know some methods are successful."

Hamish wasn't sure if he wished to strangle the woman for offering herself to him like a sacrificial lamb or damn well kiss her senseless, right here and now. His attention snapped to her lips. Damn she had a delectable mouth, lips that begged kissing, and plenty of it. How had she not been married by the gentlemen in her social set. Were they dunderheads!

"There are ways, but nothing that a well-bred young woman such as yourself should know about or even mention." And even with such ways, women still ended up pregnant. His sister for one who was very similar in frame to Katherine had been warned not to have children. The doctor termed her body as unsuitable to enable birth, something about her narrow hips, and Miss Martin's were very similar. Should she become pregnant, the thought of her dying due to his irresponsibleness was enough to turn his stomach.

She laughed, covering her mouth with her gloved hand. "I'm as old as you, Lord Leighton, not a green country miss. Have you forgotten I work at the London Relief Society with Cecilia? There is not much I have not seen or been told in some way or another. We are both adults. I'm proposing to you what I want and offering solutions to problems you're throwing at me. The way I see it is we're having a reasonable and grown up conversation. Something more women should do with the men in their lives if you must know."

No, he didn't know, and nor did he wish to be having this conversation at all. He would not sleep with a virgin simply because she did not wish to die an old maid. Why, even tomorrow a young man could bow before her at an event where they could fall madly in love, and then where would she be. Ruined.

"I will not do it. I'm sorry." He stood. "Please, since we're to work with each other on the rebuild of my home do not bring up this suggestion again. I shall repay you in any way I can, in any other way I can, but I will not take you to my bed." He would not risk her life or her honour.

Hamish swallowed when she stood, a tall woman he could almost look her straight in the eye. "Is there any way I can change your mind, my lord?"

He swallowed, fisting his hands at his side less he wrench her into his arms and kiss the hell out of her. Scare her away. Damn it all to hell. He wasn't a debaucher of virgins. And what the hell was a woman doing tempting him so? Even now, the deepening allure of her voice, her slight but determined lean toward him as she waited for a reply told him all he needed to know as to what game she played. She was playing him, but she would not win. This would not do.

"There is not. Goodnight." Hamish strode back toward the terrace steps and sought the safety of the ballroom, anything but the enticement that remained in the garden. He knew what it was to feel sorry for Adam now, but he would not bite the forbidden fruit. Not even for one night.

CHAPTER 5

Two days later, Katherine stood before Lord Leighton's home on Berkley Square and watched as the heavy beams were loaded off the cart and laid along the footpath. The roof was scheduled to go on this week, and by her calculations the home would be water tight within three weeks. All was progressing well, and she made a note in her diary to check that the slates for the roof were on schedule for delivery.

"Miss Martin, how are you this afternoon?"

The familiar voice caused a shiver to run down her spine and gathering herself, she turned and smiled in welcome to Lord Leighton. "I'm very well, my lord. It is fortunate that you have arrived today. As you can see," she said, gesturing to the piles of beams, "your roof has just arrived and looks very well indeed if I must say so myself."

Another carriage arrived on the street and the Earl mumbled something under his breath before going to open the door to the carriage himself when it came to a stop before the home.

A woman in a black gown, heavy set with lace stepped

from the carriage. She was an older woman, and across the eyes was similar to his lordship. Katherine checked her gown and hoped she'd not wiped any dust across her cheek when she'd been inside looking over the construction.

Lord Leighton kissed the woman's cheek and brought her toward Katherine. "Miss Martin, may I present my mother, the dowager countess of Leighton. Mother, this is Miss Martin. Her father owns the company that is rebuilding my townhouse."

The lady's severe frown needed no explanation of exactly what she thought of Katherine and her presence on a worksite that was normally reserved for men.

"Miss Martin, singular that your father isn't present. Are you here, unchaperoned?" The slight Scottish burr went some way in explaining Lord Leighton's non-English name.

Katherine bobbed a small curtsy, holding her diary and clipboard before her breast. A means of protection perhaps, quite possibly. Lord Leighton was so very easy going, a free and happy type of man, where as his mother seemed quite severe and cross.

"My father is inside the home, your ladyship. Over-seeing the builders. We shall be on site more often over the next few weeks as we finish up this construction and make it ready for the internal decorators to begin."

"You're a woman."

Katherine raised her chin, having been subject to such conversations before, but for some reason the dowager Leighton made her being here seem more wrong than she'd ever experienced. Knowing that the woman before her was Lord Leighton's mother, did she want to impress her? Did it matter what her ladyship thought and what her opinions would make Lord Leighton think? Never before had Katherine ever responded to a man as she did with

Lord Leighton. Never before had she wanted to feel the glide of lips as much as she wished to feel his against hers.

Even so, she would not feel shame and embarrassment over her position in life. Her employment was the one source in her day where she was proud of what she achieved, for she achieved it very well.

"I am, your ladyship, but lucky for you and your son, I'm an intelligent one, just as my father is, and I can assure you once the rebuilding of your home is complete, you'll be well pleased, just as all our other clients are."

She sniffed at Katherine and looked up at the townhouse. "Oh, I so loathe having tradesmen trample through our beautiful home. I hope you have all the valuables removed, one cannot trust the men not to steal whatever is not nailed down. They are poor after all, Hamish."

Katherine bit her tongue less she cost her father a very profitable, and very connected customer. "I can vouch for our employees and state with full confidence that nothing will be damaged or stolen."

"You cannot know that for sure, why look at them," her ladyship said, her lip turning up in disdain as she watched the men unload the cart of beams. "Dirty, filthy commoners."

His lordship balked at his parent's words. "Mother, that is rude and unkind. Apologize to Miss Martin. These men are under her employment and guarantee. You cannot make such claims of them."

"I shall do whatever I wish." Her ladyship turned back toward the carriage, waiting at the door for her son to help her up the steps. "Do not forget that you're to accompany me and Lizzie to Everys' ball. We'll expect you at eight."

Katherine moved over closer to the cart, not wanting to be anywhere near Lord Leighton's mother. Never in her life had she ever met a woman with such ill manners. The carriage moved away, and the clip of his lordship's steps sounded before he came to stand beside her.

"I do apologize, Miss Martin. My mother is…well, she's stuck in her ways and there's no shifting her ideas I'm afraid."

The last of the beams was unloaded and Katherine thanked the men delivering the goods, asking them to send around their invoice as soon as they could. She turned back to Lord Leighton who stood beside her, staring at the building. "I'm here to do a job, and we shall complete the job well, on budget and in time. And I can promise you, my lord, nothing will be stolen or damaged as we do so."

"Even so, I am sorry she insinuated otherwise."

With the beams now unloaded at the building site, Katherine's day at his lordship's home was complete. Her father would take care of anything else that needed attending. Calling out her goodbye to her foreman Mr. Perry, she made her way over to her gig leaving Lord Leighton staring at his townhouse. He hurried over to her, frowning.

"You're driving yourself back to your office in London traffic?"

Katherine settled her skirts, picked up her reins and unhooked the brake. "I often drive myself about town, my lord. We have other building works happening around the city, and I cannot rely on people driving me about like some queen who cannot handle a horse."

"And you're going to another work site now, Miss Martin?"

She nodded, amused he was a little shocked by her ability. "I am. Not all of us have the luxury of lazing about all day at our clubs, or our friends' home. Some of us must work for a living, so we may pay for lords who turn up at Inns in the country and require their bills to be paid."

"Touché, I shall allow that remark, but if you think I'm

going to change my mind about what you asked of me the other night you're mistaken. I shall not change my mind, no matter how fetching you look in your drab, grey working gown."

His lordship started at his own words. Had he not meant to say such a thing? She studied him, wondering for the first time if he actually meant what he said regarding their one night of sin. "However," he continued, "I will offer a large donation in lieu of your request to the London Relief Society as recompense."

Katherine ignored the pang of hurt his words brought forth. Not that she would begrudge money to the orphanages and schools, but here was another gentleman who would offer anything other than be with her. It wasn't like she was asking for much, simply one night. She would settle for a kiss at this stage in her life, and she couldn't even gain that. She steeled her back and refused to feel sorry for herself. At least she tried to find out what married life would be like, which was better than not trying at all. "The donation would be welcome, thank you. You wish to have a working relationship and I'm quite resolved to accept your decision. But remember this Lord Leighton," she said, flicking the reins and walking on, "it does not mean I cannot ask someone else."

HAMISH SAT UP IN BED, his body soaked in sweat and the bedding damp to touch. His heart beating a million times too fast in his chest. He leaned over toward the bedside cabinet and picked up the glass of water he had there, downing it quickly. After accompanying his mother and Lizzie to the Everys' ball this evening, he'd decided to stay at his mother's townhouse instead of the marquess of

Aaron's. If only to give his friends a little time away from him. He would hate to become a nuisance while he enjoyed their hospitality.

He ran a hand through his hair, his body hard, his mind awash with images of Miss Martin. Images that he knew he should not be thinking since he'd determined never to sleep with the woman, not even after her parting comment that she'd simply find someone else to do it for her. Even though the very idea of another man kissing her, touching her…. he couldn't even think it. *Bloody hell!*

He threw off the bedsheets and walked to the window, throwing up the sash and breathing in deep the cool night air. His door opened, and a slither of light flooded the room.

"Are you well, Lord Leighton? I heard the commotion in your room."

Hamish inwardly groaned. His distant cousin, Miss Lizzie Doherty was in town for the season and being fully sponsored by his parent. Worse was the fact the young girl had taken it into her head that he would make her the perfect husband.

"I'm quite well, thank you Lizzie. Please shut the door on your way out. You should not be in here."

She threw him a tentative smile, and he frowned, loathing the idea that he could be caught in the middle of the night, alone in a room with an unmarried miss. His mother would demand he marry her, and that would be disastrous for both of them. He would not be pressured into marriage, not by his mother and her desires to see him settled with someone she approved of. Marriage on such terms would only lead to heartache and resentment and would ultimately end in disaster.

"Very well. Good night, my lord."

He nodded. "Goodnight." He sighed in relief when the

door closed behind her. Whatever next! Hamish made a mental note not to stay at his mother's townhouse again, not unless Miss Doherty was back safely stowed in the country and her home or married off to a man who was at least interested in the chit.

Wanting to make sure he wasn't checked on again, Hamish locked the door and went back to bed. The dream he'd had regarding Miss Martin was an anomaly, he was sure of it. It was simply her words from the other day playing tricks in his mind. She wouldn't sleep with another man simply to throw her maidenhead out the window.

The thought of her making love with another gentleman; perhaps even enjoying the act and wishing to do it again left a pit in his gut. He wouldn't' allow it. Perhaps he should talk to her friends the duchess and marchioness to stop it. Surely, they would not condone such an absurd idea.

❧

THREE NIGHTS later Hamish stood in the Duncannon's ballroom and groaned. Damn it, the vexing Miss Martin would turn his hair grey before the season was over. She was dancing with Lord Thomas, a gentleman with a title, but little else. His pockets were well known to be for let. And the coy, fluttering eyelashes that Miss Martin kept flashing at the gentleman told Hamish exactly what he needed to know. She'd picked another man to deal with her introduction to sensual delights and was trying, right at this moment to seduce him.

He wouldn't have it, nor would he be lured in by her charm. But he would warn her of the licentious reputation of the man she danced with, hopefully sparking some sense into her.

His mother waved to him from a little way up the room, Lizzie beside her smiling in hope that he'd greet them. Unable to escape, he headed their way. "Good evening, mother, Lizzie. I did not think you were attending Duncannon's ball this evening. I thought you were for Sir Colton's musical loo."

The dowager gestured to the guests milling about them. "We're here because I wanted to see you before we quit this ball and headed over to Sir Colton's. You know Lady Colton is one of my closet friends, and she's just returned from her country estate and I so dearly wish to catch up."

"Well then," Hamish said, not wanting to postpone their departure. "Would you like me to walk you to your carriage?"

"Oh, no, we do not need assistance, Hamish, but I come with news. Your late sister's husband, Lord Russell is returning from Bath. He'll be in town for the season if you wished to see little Oscar at all."

Hamish smiled. This was good news. He always enjoyed Lord Russell's company, and adored Oscar. "I look forward to seeing them. It has been several months since we last spoke."

"I thought you would be pleased. He's staying with me at my townhouse, since he has no fixed address in London at present. You may call on him there after Friday next."

Hamish took his mother's hand and placed it on his arm. "Allow me to walk you to the carriage. You'll miss your friend if you do not leave soon."

"Oh, you're right. We must go," his mother said, allowing him to maneuverer her toward the entrance of the home.

After seeing his parent off, and Lizzie, though she begged to remain with him, Hamish strolled back into the ballroom and headed for the first footman he could see who held a tray of champagne. Taking a glass, he mingled with guests about him, promised a dance to Miss Grey, a young woman he'd often admired. The ball was a crush and standing back from the dancefloor he watched Miss Martin from afar. She was talking with Cecilia, gesturing with her hands and both of them laughing.

Miss Martin looked up and their gazes locked across the ballroom floor. A peculiar sensation thrummed through him and he took another sip of his champagne. Tonight, she was dressed in a silver muslin gown with a deep blue trim that accentuated her figure. She looked simply stunning. He didn't want to feel desire for the woman, that would never do. He did not toy with virgins, no matter how old or on the shelf they were, neither interaction was fair.

But nor did he want to miss out on sampling her sweet lips. He could imagine being the first and only man to know her intimately. To give her what she wanted. How she tempted him, more so than any other woman he'd ever known. The woman was fairly bewitching him.

Something Cecilia said caught her attention and Miss Martin looked away.

"I heard the most peculiar thing from Darcy yesterday," the duke said, coming to stand beside him but not venturing to say any more.

Hamish fought not to roll his eyes at the duke's vague disclosure, but when nothing further was stated, Hamish had to ask. "Well, are you going to tell me, or do I have to guess."

The duke chuckled and as Miss Martin was pulled out on the dancefloor for another turn about the room he ground his teeth. How much dancing could a woman do in a night. Surely, she must be getting fatigued.

He was surprised she'd not sought him out to renew her scandalous idea. The fact that she had not left a sour taste in his mouth. He adjusted his cravat, keeping his attention on anything but the woman clouding his thoughts.

Damn it all to hell.

"Very well, I shall tell you since your name was mentioned, I thought you better have your wits about you when it came to Miss Martin," the duke drawled, censure in his tone.

Hamish groaned. *They knew…*

"I already know, your grace. Miss Martin asked me for the favour after all. I have refused her of course," he added quickly when the duke's gaze turned thunderous.

His grace sighed in relief. "I am glad to hear it, although I was shocked that Miss Martin would even venture such a notion. Not that I have any say in her future or what she does, but I would not like to see her ruined since she is a particular friend to my wife."

"Are you warning me not to change my mind?" The veiled hint was not hard to miss, but the duke needn't worry, Hamish had no intention of seducing the delectable Miss Martin.

Not at all, he promised himself.

The very woman if by design crossed in front of them while dancing a reel with Sir Fraser. Her mischievous gaze met his and he scowled. Never had he ever met such a vexing woman in all his days. Was she laughing at him now? Did she suspect what they were talking about.

"By Society's standard there is no doubt Miss Martin is on the shelf, a matron in the making, even though I find her very pretty. She is from a social sphere so much beneath our own. Even so, I think it would be a mistake to trifle with her, even if she wishes. We're all friends and there will be situations in the future when we're thrown together. I do not want there to be any awkwardness or ill feelings."

"Or the fact that she could get with a child." Hamish shuddered at the thought.

The duke nodded once. "There is that as well."

Miss Martin continued to weave and dance before them, her silver gown, making her look ethereal and showcasing her long legs when the forgiving material flowed about her. Hamish swallowed. He needed to get himself together. "I promise you," he said, unable to tear his gaze away from her. "It will not be me who ruins her."

Darcy came up to them and dragged the duke out on to the dancefloor, and Hamish made his way over to Cecilia and Hunter. His reprieve was short lived when Miss Martin was brought back to her friends by her dance partner. The gentleman didn't stay long, going off and dancing again with another woman minutes later.

None of which seemed to annoy Miss Martin in the slightest, her cheeks flushed with exertion only threw images into Hamish's head he didn't need there. Of them, together, of kissing her senseless and bringing forth such a shade of pink across her cheeks and other delectable parts of her body.

There was something seriously wrong with him, and if he didn't get hold of himself soon, he'd whack himself about the ears.

KATHERINE SIPPED her ratafia and fought not to giggle, maybe there was a positive to dressing more fashionably. This ball had been quite a triumph with the amount of dance requests she'd had, and for the first time in a long time, she was enjoying herself immensely.

Poor Lord Leighton though, he did look very conflicted, and it was all her doing. And yet, she couldn't find the desire within her to stop her teasing. For the first time in her life , a wealthy, powerful lord was regarding her, his gaze all but burning admiration threatened to light her up in flames. She could get used to such inspections. A heady feeling indeed.

She had no hopes that he would take her up on her quest to lose her virginity, and nor would she look to anyone else, no matter what she told the silly man, but he did owe her, and this is what she wanted. So, if he only said the word yes, she'd meet him anywhere and at any time to spend just one night in his arms.

The thought of him above her, doing whatever it was that gentleman did above their ladies left her flustered and a peculiar flutter deep in her belly.

If she were honest with herself, she was desperate for him to kiss her. To ruin her, as scandalous as that was. Explore and take part in all the things that would normally be denied her and be damned what Society said or her friends for that matter. She would do as she wished, and deal with any consequences later if there were any.

The Marchioness and Marquess stepped out onto the ballroom floor to dance a waltz and Hamish turned to her. "Stop looking at me like that."

"Like what?" she asked, gazing at him from under her lashes, a little trick she'd seen the duchess do to the duke when she wanted to get away with something.

He leaned toward her to ensure privacy. "I will not sleep with you."

She sighed, having expected as much. "Are you sure? You do owe me, my lord, and you promised me anything that I wished. I think it very unfair you will not give me what I want." Katherine stepped closer still. "I've heard it can be quite pleasurable, my lord. Would you deny a spinster her only chance of experiencing a man in such a way?" she whispered against his ear.

She was being overly bold, but she was sick of missing out while others did not. She was forthright, opinionated and sometimes loud in her employment, and it seemed if she used similar traits in trying to gain the attentions of the opposite sex it also worked to her advantage. It certainly had this night at least.

He stilled.

"Do not play with fire, Miss Martin."

His words were low and thrummed with warning. "I hired your father's company, surely that is payment enough after your assistance at Two Toad's Inn."

She raised her brow, having not expected him to seek out that excuse. "You hired my father's company to rebuild your home because he's the best. My wishes for us are unchanged, but I will seek another if you refuse to honor your debt."

A muscle worked in his jaw and he pulled at his cravat. "The duke has warned me away from you, so you see, even if I wished to have you, I cannot."

Did he wish to have her? How delicious if he did. "The duke has nothing to do with it." Katherine cursed that Darcy had been able to swindle out of her what she desired of Lord Leighton. How the woman had accomplished such a feat, Katherine was still trying to figure out. That the duke knew of her idea was part mortifying and vexing. Did these married couples have to share everything between them?

"I will honor my debt to you, Miss Martin in any other way than this. I have already sent a donation to your charity and I will enclose the four pounds you paid for me when I settle your building fee. Please, anything but what you ask."

He ran a hand through his hair, his words torn and with a pleading edge to them. Her insecurities threatened. Was she so horrid, so tall and thin that he was worried she would not inspire him enough when they were alone for him to lay with her? Of course, she was, and she was a fool to hope otherwise.

Katherine swallowed the lump that formed in her throat at the mortifying thought. She would put a stop to the duchess and marchioness giving her beautiful gowns to wear, having their maids do up her hair in fashionable, intricate styles. The false bravado they were giving her was giving her airs that she did not need, nor what others saw. She was at her core, still the plain, lanky woman from trade who was only here due to who she knew, not because of what she was.

Shame washed through her and she blinked, horrified that tears threatened to spill over her cheeks. "Lord Leighton your words have made me realize what a terrible and shameful thing I've been asking you. Please forgive me and know that I shall not ask again, nor will I state your debt as unpaid. I never sought repayment in any case, it is not in my nature to do so. I think these past months have made me see what I shall never have, and I saw an opportunity to gain it and in doing so I've embarrassed both you and myself. I'm so very sorry."

Katherine managed a quick curtsy before she walked from the room, needing to get away from everyone less they see her upset. She would return home and send a missive apologizing to her friends for leaving early. Better that than to make a spectacle of herself in public.

THE FOLLOWING morning Katherine walked out of the breakfast room, having come down early after a restless night. It suited her plans in any case as she had to oversee more of the roof construction at Lord Leighton's townhouse.

"You're not wearing those, I hope," Jane said, all but floating down the staircase in a light blue muslin gown, her blonde hair perfect and coiled to perfection. The vision of her cousin only amplified her own shortcomings and she snatched up her riding gloves from the small table beside the front door. Gentlemen wanted women who were beautiful and full figured, they did not care for wit or intelligence, such as she possessed.

"As you see. I often wear breeches and father is aware of the fact." Katherine placed the grey felt cap on her head which all but covered her hair, and glancing in the looking mirror, she would easily pass as a man. Certainly, her figure was not the most feminine and not desired at all by Lord Leighton. He'd certainly made that plain enough last night, and she had been dressed as well as any woman there.

"I suppose with your long legs and body that doesn't have one ounce of womanly curves, you'll pass as a gentleman easily enough."

Katherine stopped at the front door, debating whether she'll let her vexing relative get away with such an insult or simply ignore it. She chose to ignore it, and pulling the door open, strolled from her home.

The day was young, the air fresh and crisp and hailing a hackney cab, she headed over to Mayfair. Their workers would have arrived by now, and just as she presumed, upon arrival she was happy to see the men busy up on the roof.

"Can I help you?" A man asked when she walked through the front doors and into the entrance hall of the home.

Katherine stifled a scream, having not seen the gentleman standing by the library doors.

"Lord Leighton, you frightened me. I did not see you standing there," she said, coming over to him.

His eyes widened, his attention snapping to her legs. "You're in breeches."

It wasn't a question and Katherine raised her brow. "As you see. I often wear breeches in such a way for this employment, it enables me to move about more freely and help the men here when required. It also saves my gowns from being unnecessarily ruined."

His lordship swallowed, but didn't reply straight away, just continued to stare. "You cannot," he said, regaining his voice at last, "go upstairs, with a group of men in those breeches."

Katherine turned on her heel and headed for the staircase. "Oh, don't worry, my lord. The men are quite used to seeing me dressed like this. As for you, I do apologize for startling you so, but I assure you, once I have completed my inspection here I shall leave you to yourself, where there will be no chance of me embarrassing you."

HAMISH TOOK a calming breath as he watched Miss Martin climb the stairs, the men's breeches showcasing every long, sculptured line of her legs, her small buttocks that were only minimally covered by her bottle green jacket.

He'd never seen a woman dressed in such attire, and as ridiculous as it would seem, he damn well liked it. More women should wear such clothing if they looked as well in it as Miss Martin.

He followed her up the stairs, unable to tear his gaze away from her ass. She never turned to look back at him or engage him in further conversation. He stewed, worried that their conversation last night had insulted her in some way.

Who was he deluding, of course she'd been hurt. He hadn't missed her tears after his denial of her. But what Miss Martin didn't know was his denial of her was not because he did not want to have her, run his hand along every line of her body, find out if she was as smooth and sweet as he imagined, but because his want of her went against his better judgement. He may be one of the rogues of London, but even he had rules.

They had a working relationship and that is where it would end. Should they sleep together and she fell pregnant, he would be honor bound to marry her, a situation that he did not look for in his future. And then for Miss Martin to thicken with child, the idea made him break out in a cold sweat and his heart trembled.

His sister May's atrocious labour with her son was something he never wanted to see again. May, like Miss Martin was delicate and small boned. Neither of them even looked suitable to having children. The doctor who'd looked after his sister had even stated that women who were small across the hips, delicate boned and thin were not suited to go through the trauma of birthing a child.

Miss Martin might go on to marry and have children, take such a risk, but it would not be by him.

They made the first floor landing and headed toward the ballroom which was a hive of activity. Hamish could see the foreman in conversation with two of his workers, all of them looking up at the beams going up in the new roof.

The room, with the structure coming together was starting to take shape into what it had once been, except for the newly designed balcony that opened to allow guests to congregate outdoors, even if up on the first floor of the home.

"Do you like the design, my lord?" Miss Martin asked, coming to stand beside him out on the balcony that looked over his large, manicured back garden.

The air smelt of oak and some of the workers had set up saws on the newly constructed balcony and used it to cut wood to suit their needs. Hamish walked out to where the balustrade was taking shape. A stonemason had been brought in to create one that matched the terrace below, and large stone pillars were already beneath them taking some of the weight the new structure placed on the home.

"I trust it'll not collapse," he said half joking. It was a very long way down after all.

"Most certainly it will not. We've built support beams into the home itself that run beneath the ballroom floor. As you know, most of it was damaged, and has been replaced. Before we did that, and because you stipulated you wished to have a balcony terrace, we laid the support beams. Of course, the balcony is also supported from beneath, but once the stone pillars are in, this balcony is not going anywhere."

"Is it safe for us now?" he asked, not quite convinced of her words yet.

"Yes, for the few of us who're on it. Obviously, you're not holding a ball where as many as twenty people could be standing out here at any one time. Until the pillars are finished I wouldn't suggest such a thing, but just us and the couple of workers at a time is perfectly safe."

Hamish nodded and glanced back through the terrace doors, those too were new and still in their natural form, not painted or with any handles. "You've done a marvellous job so far. Give my thanks to your father."

She smiled, and pride filled her face, making her look even prettier than he thought possible. And he'd turned her down. Refused her one wish...

"Thank you, Lord Leighton. Father will be pleased to hear you say so."

"I'm not blind to your own input and hard work on my home, and I do thank you too. I will recommend your company to anybody I know who's looking for a master craftsman."

She started to walk off and he followed.

"We're only doing our job, and soon enough we'll be out of your way and your life can return to normal."

Normal...boring. He enjoyed having her here, talking about things other than gossip or the latest fashions. Miss Martin was an interesting woman, a very smart and educated one at that. "Are you heading somewhere else?" he asked, as she waved goodbye to the foreman and continued toward the staircase. Maybe they could extend this tête-à-tête with an impromptu lunch.

"I am. I have to inspect a building out at Richmond we've just finished building. We build homes as well as repair them you see. Always busy."

Hamish caught her hand and pulled her to a stop as she made the footpath. It wasn't until Miss Martin pulled her hand away that he realized he still held it. "Miss Martin, will you do the honor of allowing me to call you by your first name? Calling each other Miss and Lord seems overly formal, and we're friends are we not? If you feel more comfortable only calling me by my given name when we're here or alone that would work too."

She met his gaze, a small teasing grin lifting her lips.

"Alone, Lord Leighton, you didn't wish to be alone with me, so perhaps it's best we stay formal and aloof."

"And if I said I do not wish to remain formal and aloof." Why he suggested it Hamish couldn't fathom, nor did he regret his words, which was something that he couldn't fathom either.

Miss Martin climbed up in her carriage and leaned a little out the window. She contemplated him for a moment, a small frown line marring her usually perfect brow. "My name is Katherine, but Kat to my friends. You may call me either one, in private or public, in either locale does not bother me."

Katherine. He liked her name, and the shortened version Kat had a vixen ring to it. It suited her. He picked up her hand that lay atop the carriage door and kissed it. "Until we meet again, Katherine," he said, liking the fact that her cheeks coloured with the lightest shade of rose.

"You didn't tell me your name, Lord Leighton?" she said, grinning.

"You can call me Hamish." He stepped back and watched as the carriage pulled away and made its way around Berkley Square. *Kat...*His gut clenched at what such a name brought forth in his imagination and he couldn't help but wonder if she'd be like a wildcat, untamed and feral or sweet and affectionate. Or perhaps she was both, and that thought brought a flush to his own body.

He shouldn't want her like he did, but there was something infinitely different about her. Perhaps it was the fierce independence and self-assurance that attracted him so. When in his Society he had seen moments of her where she'd looked fearful, but walking within the *ton's* viper nest that was to be expected. Hamish turned and started back toward the house, his man of business had asked him to go through some letters he'd left in his library, and deal with the business of two of his country estates. Normally he would shirk most of this work off to his steward, but not today. Katherine's unwavering dedication to her employment made his own lacklustre approach shameful. He ought to do better for his tenants and those who worked for him.

He ought to spend less time socializing and more time looking after the things that actually mattered. Since seeing Katherine again, he had to admit that his bad luck had waned, in fact, had disappeared.

Miss Martin, was out making a difference in the world and so too would he. A self-deprecating laugh escaped. She was already a good influence on him and his pampered ways.

CHAPTER 6

The duchess hosted an afternoon tea party for some of the upper echelons of the *ton* two days after Katherine's run in with Lord Leighton, and unfortunately, or fortunately depending on Katherine's disposition on any given day, she was invited.

The never-ending tittle-tattle of gossip, of gowns and who was recently returned to town and those that had scuttled back to their country estates was all that she'd heard, nodded to and gasped at the past two hours. If she did not escape soon she'd simply expire of boredom.

Excusing herself from three recently married women who were fixated on finding the proper children's nurse for their impending children, Katherine moved away and started toward Cecilia who looked as bored as she did.

Upon joining Cecilia, the lady Cecilia was talking to made her excuses and moved away, thankfully leaving them alone. "Save me, or I shall tell you everything I know about nannies, for I have just had a very lengthy and involved discussion on the topic."

Cecilia chuckled, handing her a plate with a sugar biscuit on it. "Eat one of these, it'll make you feel better."

Katherine took a bite, and almost choked when Lord Leighton's mother entered the room with her young charge whom she was sponsoring this year. The woman looked almost friendly when she greeted the duchess and looking about the room she nodded and waved to women she knew, but her ladyship's ease and enjoyment slipped somewhat when she spotted Katherine.

Instead of simply moving her gaze along and joining in with her friends' conversations, she came over to them instead, her visage one of displeasure and ire.

"Lady Aaron, so lovely to see you again and I must thank you for housing my son for the next few weeks after the dreadful fire. You're the best of people to open your home so."

Cecilia dropped a curtsy and Katherine quickly followed, having forgotten to show her respect to the matriarch of Society. "Lord Leighton is always welcome, as well you know. It is a pleasure to have him as a guest." Cecilia turned to Katherine.

"Lady Leighton, may I present my friend, Miss Katherine Martin. She is a good friend of mine and the duchess of Athelby and is a founding member of the London Relief Society that I run."

Katherine bobbed a quick curtsy again, and then remembered she'd already done so. Heat spread across her cheeks and she took a calming breath. What did it matter if her ladyship was glaring at her, her displeasure obvious to any who looked their way. The woman was nothing to her, only the mother of the man whose face kept her up at night. Awake with a longing she didn't understand, but desperately wanted to know.

"Lady Leighton and I have already met, although it was very brief."

The woman's eyes narrowed, but she feigned surprise. "Oh, of course, at my son's home. You are the builder's daughter are you not?" She smiled to temper her barb. "How is the family business going my dear? From seeing your harried appearance, the other day, I can only assume that you have little time for frivolities like outings such as these. You looked quite tired if I must say so myself. Perhaps in future you will consider your health and whether attending such events as these would be in your best interests."

Katherine swallowed the heated retort that formed on her tongue, and instead bit into her little cake, all but halting any thoughts of replying.

Not that she had to worry about such things, as Cecilia wound her arm within hers and lifted her chin. "Did you know, Lady Leighton that Katherine and I grew up together, in Cheapside. We were neighbors from a very early age. As you're aware, my father is a barrister."

Lady Leighton's appearance did not change, but the warmth in her eyes for Cecilia diminished a little. "I did not know that, Lady Aaron. How interesting."

"Isn't it," Cecilia said, smiling quickly at Katherine. "But enough about us, tell us about the young woman you've brought today. She seems very sweet."

To her credit, Lady Leighton took the opportunity to change the subject away from Cecilia and Katherine's upbringing in trade. "She is my niece, Lizzie Doherty. I'm sponsoring her this season and hoping to have her married and settled by next season. Our family is in need of an uplifting event, such as a wedding."

"Are there any suitors that have made their intention

known, your ladyship," Katherine asked, simply not to be standing beside them like a mute.

"There have been a couple, but she's refused their offers. I do believe she holds fond feelings for my son, Hamish, and what a good match they would make, but alas, he does not seem to return her feelings and so she's quite downcast."

"But they are cousins. Is marriage between them even desired?" Katherine blurted before she thought better of it.

Her ladyship's eyes widened, and her mouth worked but no words came out for a few moments. Katherine inwardly cursed for asking, for her ladyship did not appreciate her question.

"Let me assure you, Miss Martin, cousins have married and are allowed to marry, so your question that reeked of disgust can be kept to yourself, if you don't mind. Hamish would be lucky to marry such a lady, for that is what Miss Lizzie Doherty is, unlike some of those who walk among us."

Cecilia gasped, and Katherine studied her ladyship a moment, what she found there was very lacking indeed. She was born to privilege, was a Countess, but she was unkind and that's all she had to be for Katherine to take her measure. "Do you mean me, your ladyship?"

The woman glanced at her with disdain. "How dare you ask me such a thing? I would never be so rude."

"I beg to differ," Katherine said, placing down her now empty plate on a small table beside them. She turned toward her friend. "I must go, Cecilia darling, but we're still on for De Vere's ball Friday?"

"You needn't leave, Katherine. Come ladies, let us not quarrel."

Katherine threw one more scathing glance at Lady Leighton and walked from the room. Conversation swam about her, and thankfully those in attendance hadn't seemed to notice that she'd disagreed with the countess. But what a disagreeable woman she was. So high and mighty and thinking she was not worthy of having friends in this sphere of Society.

And perhaps she was not, she was a builder's daughter after all, but by happenstance and simple luck she'd become friends with a duchess and her best friend had married a marquess and so like it or not, she now had a foot in both levels of Society.

A waiting footman handed her cloak and called a hackney cab for her. Katherine sighed, laying her head back against the squabs. Lady Leighton was an unpleasant harridan. But why did she dislike her so much? It is not as if she knew her, would've heard any rumors as there weren't any. Katherine wasn't a woman who courted scandal, and if she removed the one time she'd asked Lord Leighton to sleep with her, she'd done nothing at all.

She thought back to when she'd met her ladyship at the building site. Was there something she saw in Lord Leighton's eyes that had worried her. Had she sensed her son was attracted to Katherine, an attraction that all but hummed between them whenever they were near?

Katherine certainly did, and that very allure had been the reason she'd asked him to lie with her. Even if he was adamant he wouldn't grant her wish, it could not stop her from dreaming about being with him so. She'd seen often enough the glances and small affection touches Darcy and Cecilia made and received in turn. Over the time she'd been friends with them, seeing them married and happy left an ache in her chest. If she could not find a gentleman to marry, not to say she hadn't tried, for she had, for years, she at least wanted to know the touch of a man, to know if she were missing out and ought to look again.

The carriage rolled to a stop before her home and thanking the footman who raced down the house's stairs to open the carriage door, she went inside, only to come to a halt in the hall at the sight of Jane, standing before Lord Leighton, a blushing, gushing mess.

"Dearest Katherine, look who has paid us a call. You know Lord Leighton of course."

Katherine had just about had enough of spiteful women and seeing Jane all flustered and preening over Lord Leighton in her home left her teeth to ache. Katherine ripped off her gloves and unpinned her hat, handing them to a waiting footman before turning to face them both.

"Good afternoon, my lord. Can I help you with anything?"

Jane chuckled. "You must forgive my cousin, my lord. It seems her social niceties were lost along with her youth." The brazen little hussy reached up and plucked an invisible piece of lint from his lordship's jacket, and Lord Leighton stepped away, uncertainty clouding his eyes.

"On the contrary, Miss Digby. I have never known Miss Martin to be other than a pillar of manners and kindness. Something that you may wish to aspire to."

Jane paled at being chastised and Katherine fought not to crow at his kindness toward her.

"I was hoping to have a private word with you, Miss Martin. If you're free," he asked, catching her gaze.

"I suppose you shall not need a chaperone since you're well past that necessity," Jane said, clearly out to make her point now that Lord Leighton had told her off. "Although, you really ought to start wearing a cap, dearest cousin, it would cause less scandal if you're to attend gentleman callers in private."

"Thank you, Jane, you may go," she said, her words

blunt and to the point. Katherine moved past her with little regard, having had enough of people judging her simply because she didn't fit into their mould of what they expected women to be.

Lord Leighton followed her into the library and she gestured him to take a seat before the fire that was alight, ready for her father when he would return home later in the day. Katherine sat beside him and tried to shake off her annoyance and damn it, the hurt her cousin caused by her words.

"How can I help you, Lord Leighton?" she asked, settling her skirts about her legs.

He was quiet for a moment, fiddled with his cravat before he seemed to gather himself. "I wanted to discuss what you asked of me."

Katherine inwardly groaned, not wanting nor in the mood to discuss such matters. Not today at least. After her run in with his mother at the duchess of Athelby's afternoon tea and now her cousin, her disposition to remain nice after hearing why he couldn't sleep with her waned.

"There is no need to explain anything, my lord. I understand perfectly well."

"Do you?" he asked, watching her intensely.

What did he see when he looked at her, beauty, desperation, she was certainly the latter, but the former she'd never claimed to be. Passable was what she heard one gentleman state, rich but not biddable another, too much work if one was willing to take her on.

"You've already explained your reasons, my lord. You do not need to do so again." She went to stand, and he clasped her hand, pulling her back down.

"I wasn't entirely truthful when we spoke last. I used the excuse of rank, of our mutual friends and their reactions should our interlude become known, especially when

I'd promised never to darken your bedroom's door. I used your potential fall from grace, the ruination of your reputation should you get with child."

Her heart squeezed at the recitation. Katherine pulled her hand away, folding them into her lap. "I think they are worthy enough excuses, you do not need to come up with any more."

"I do, because I fear you think it's because I do not desire you."

Heat rose on Katherines cheeks and she bit her lip, unsure as to what to say to such honesty. "Then what is it?" she asked, unable to stop herself.

"I know you have not asked for anything but one night in my bed, but I wonder if you've thought of the consequences of such actions. I do not hide from the fact that I have had lovers, many of them but they are seasoned lovers, players of this game and they know how to play the game without consequences. If you understand what I'm saying."

She understood perfectly well. "You mean children, and that our one night may result in me carrying your child. Something you do not wish for any more than I, my lord." Not that the idea of having Lord Leighton's child didn't make her weak at the knees. Whoever persuaded him into marriage, into love would be very well pleased. Under his charm and beauty, he was kind, not vicious. Was there not a saying that rakes made the best husbands...

"I've seen you around the duchess and marchioness. I've seen your wistful looks at their happiness. If we were to be together, I fear you'll want more of me than I'm willing to commit. And that is no reflection on you," he said, reaching out to clasp her hand. "It's me. I do not wish for marriage, not now at least and perhaps never."

His thumb glided over the top of her hand and

Katherine realized he still had hold of her. "Do not think for one moment Katherine that I do not desire you. From the very first moment we met I've had a peculiar craving to kiss you. To speak plainly, the hunger you rouse in me isn't something I'm familiar with and I do not trust myself with you. And that, can lead to folly and consequences," he declared his voice thick with emotion.

She met his gaze and a shiver stole over her. "I'm not asking for marriage or children. Nor will I hide from life. I refuse to do so any longer. I wish to experience everything I can before I die, and while I understand your fears, it does not mean I cannot seek out what I want to know. What I want to feel."

HAMISH STARED at Katherine as her declaration brought a flush to her cheeks and a sparkle in her dark brown eyes. Were his fears unreasonable? Perhaps, but it did not change the fact that women died during childbirth, thin, delicate women like Miss Martin. Never before in his life had he been asked for a night of sin with a woman of respectable standing. His liaisons had always been over before they started, he'd never tried to deepen connections, grow to care for the women he bedded. It was not what he wanted.

"My coming here was to explain my reasons behind denying you. I did not want you imagining anything other than what I've stated here this evening."

"Thank you for being so honest with me and because you have, I shall be in return."

"Really," he said, curious. "Do tell me."

Katherine chuckled, pulling him back toward the chaise lounge to sit. "I had believed you turned me down because I'm not what you find attractive. I've seen you at balls and parties too, the curvy, bountiful women with blonde golden locks that you seek out." She gestured toward herself. "I'm obviously none of those things. So, in an odd way, it's a relief to know your reasons."

HIS GAZE SLID over her form, from her face down to her toes, and heat spiralled in her stomach. She bit her lip, wanting him with a desperation that she'd never felt before. It was the oddest thing, and yet she could not help herself. Was it because he'd denied her that she wanted him so, or simply because he was the only man who'd ever brought the feelings that were rioting inside of her to life.

"But now you know the reasons behind my choice, do not think it's because I do not find you attractive. Why even now all I can think about is what you want from me. What I'd love to do to you."

Katherine gasped, unable to help it. What he'd love to do to her? What did that even mean? Her heart thumped hard in her chest and her light muslin gown felt tight about the breasts. What was he doing to her? Raw hunger crossed his features and she shivered.

"Damn it," he growled, moving quickly and taking her lips in a searing kiss, his hands against her jaw tipped up her chin so he could deepen the embrace.

The world spiralled out of control and one word went around and around in her head. *Yes…*

So, this is what made her friends all dreamy eyed when talking of their husbands… Hamish moaned when she mimicked what he was doing with his tongue and a beautiful ache thrummed between her legs. She squirmed, needing to be closer to him. He pulled her hard against his chest, the thump of her heart loud in her ears.

Katherine kissed him back with eagerness, willingness to know more, to experience this side of life. She'd never been kissed before and being kissed now by a veritable rogue of the *ton*, a man who was famous for his beautiful women and quick liaisons made her even more desperate to do as much as he'd allow.

For there was no doubt that this wicked embrace he was bestowing on her was simply a chink in his armor. She was going to kiss him until he stopped and be damned what happened after the event.

Her breasts raked across his chest as she wrapped her arms about his neck. His kiss was ardent, deep and claiming. The glide of his hand on her thigh made her shiver, and it was only when the cool air kissed her ankles that she wondered at his loss of control. Had he changed his mind? Was he willing to sleep with her now that he'd kissed her?

Oh, please say that you are.

Hamish wrenched out of her arms, setting her back to her side of the chaise and rose, running a hand through his hair and leaving it on end. "God's blood." He took a couple of steps back, colliding with the chair behind him and almost falling over. Righting himself, he watched her, his eyes wide, his lips reddened by their activity.

She'd done that. She'd rattled one of the most sought-after gentleman in the *ton*. It was a heady feeling and she stood, wanting more of the same.

He held out his hand to halt her steps. "No. We cannot. I cannot. I'm sorry," he said, bolting out of the room like a startled horse.

Katherine watched the empty doorway until she heard the front door slam closed behind him. She flopped down on the leather wingback chair, finally, after six and twenty years she'd had her first kiss. And not a chaste, peck on the lips, but a true, toe curling, heart pounding kiss. One that made everything else pale in comparison. If being in Lord Leighton's arms was as enjoyable as she'd just experienced, there was no wonder women married men or indulged in scandalous affairs.

Who would not want that every day?

And now all she had to do was figure out how to get him to kiss her again. She stared at the flames licking the wood in the hearth. There was the Curzon ball coming up that she was to attend with Darcy and Cecilia. Maybe she would put off her idea of wearing one of her own gowns and borrow one from Darcy instead. Darcy had loved nothing more than to shock the *ton* of their sensibilities prior to marrying the Duke of Athelby, and that's exactly what Katherine needed to do with Lord Leighton. Seduce him in to having her or at the very least, kissing her again. Either option would be enjoyable.

CHAPTER 7

Hamish arrived late to the Curzons' ball and there was a very special reason for doing so. He wasn't normally a coward, didn't shy away from events that could prove trying, but tonight he wasn't so sure he was up for battle.

This would be a very particular battle with the very charming, very good at kissing, Miss Martin. It had been four days since he'd kissed her in her library, an event that should never have happened. He'd no sooner told her why he wouldn't sleep with her, to then maul her on the settee.

One touch of her soft lips, the soft little gasps as he took her mouth with his, made him hard. He greeted his hostesses, stopping to chat with them for a time, though his mind was elsewhere. Was she still here? It was after midnight, and their group of friends often attended more than one event when out in Society.

"Lord Leighton."

He heard his name and inwardly swore when he recognized the voice. His cousin Lizzie Doherty waved and walked toward him. Excusing himself from Lord Curzon he met her, away from prying ears as one never knew what was going to come out of the chits mouth at any one time.

"Lizzie, how lovely you look this evening."

She dipped into a quick curtsy, grinning up at him. He tempered his annoyance, the young woman was sweet, if a little naïve and annoying at times. She was still family and he would not be short with her, no matter how much he longed to seek out Miss Martin if only to apologize for his ungentlemanly behaviour the other day.

"Thank you, cousin, that is very kind of you. Your mama said that blue was your favourite color and so I thought this would please you most especially."

Hamish made a mental note to tell his mother to mind her own business in future. "Did she, well, the color suits you very well."

She took his arm, and although forward, Hamish used the opportunity to deliver her to his mother whom he spied over near the supper room doors. Her pleased expression at seeing him with Lizzie warned Hamish, and he knew exactly what she was about.

His parent beamed, leaning up to kiss his cheek as he came to stand before her. With well-practised expertise he extracted Lizzie's arm without causing offence.

"You're very late, Hamish. We've been waiting for you to arrive, you owe your cousin a dance before we take our leave."

He inwardly groaned while nodding in agreement. "Of course, I'll dance with my cousin. When there is another set I shall come and collect you."

"There is to be a waltz next, just before supper. I think now is as good a time as any."

Hamish held out his arm to his cousin, and she all but bounced while taking it. Leading her onto the floor a flash of red caught his eye and looking he stumbled as he recognized Miss Martin, settling into the arms of Lord Lacelles, an Earl of impeccable character and unlimited funds. He could marry whomever he pleased, whenever he pleased being the only child and without family after the death of his parents at an early age.

If the content grin and sparkling eyes that she all but batted toward the Earl were any indication, Miss Martin was well pleased.

"Shall we, Lord Leighton?" his cousin asked.

Hamish wrenched his gaze from Miss Martin, and instead pulled Lizzie into his. He allowed the flow of the music to soothe his ire, but it was dastardly hard when Miss Martin kept floating by, the sound of her joyful laughter like a punch to the gut.

He didn't say a lot to Lizzie for fear of being sharp, but somehow he managed one or two questions, although he could not for the life of him recall if she even answered or what those answers were. As soon as the dance was over, he marched her back to his mother, settled them at the supper room table and left to seek out his friends where most decidedly Miss Martin would be.

Their table was full when he came over to them, the Earl of Lacelles sitting with them where he would normally reside. The duke stood as he came up to them, smiling in welcome.

"Leighton, let me have a chair fetched for you," he said, calling over a footman to attend him.

Soon enough Hamish was seated alongside them all, and yet the annoyance that flowed through his veins would not abate. He'd hoped to speak to Katherine alone, but the likelihood of that at present seemed slim. Darcy, Cecilia and Miss Martin sat at the table, eating lobster patties and drinking wine. They were laughing and chuckling about all kinds of things that eluded him.

And what baffled him when he didn't wish it to, was Miss Martin avoiding any sort of eye contact with him. When he'd spoken she'd simply turned to the Earl of Lacelles beside her and chatted quietly. When he commented on topics their friends raised she busied herself with her meal or wine.

What game was she playing…?

The good conversation flowed, and determined to have her look at him, Hamish simply waited, stared at her and sought patience.

The moment she did it was like a physical blow to his gut. In her dark orbs, there was no masking the burning desire for him. Where had she learnt such a thing? A woman he was certain had never been kissed before his slip the other day. But she had learned the art of flirting, and his body reacted accordingly.

The duke cleared his throat, and Hamish looked to his friend seated to his left, the duke's raised brow told Hamish he'd seen their silent communication.

"I hope you know what you're doing, Hamish. I do not want to see Miss Martin hurt under any circumstances. She does not have a brother to fight for her honor, so be mindful of it."

Hamish took a long pull of his wine. "I do not intend to hurt her, and nothing will occur in any case. I've told her I shall not do what she asks and that's the end of it."

"Really," the duke scoffed. "That look that just passed between the two of you already tells me something has occurred."

He refused to squirm under the duke's commanding presence or knowing eyes. Hamish lowered his voice. "I kissed her, that is all and all it ever will be."

The guests started to make their way to the ballroom, and Hamish stood, not wanting to continue his current conversation. To prove his point, he walked from the supper room and sought out Lady Grey, a widow and a woman whom he was very fond of, a woman who'd more than once warmed his bed. He needed a distraction, a reminder that Miss Martin wasn't anyone special. She was simply a mutual friend he'd kissed.

A footman passed with a silver tray full of champagne glasses and he swiped one and drank it down placing it back on the tray before the footman had gone two steps. Lady Grey threw him an amused glance as he bowed before her, before taking her hand and all but dragging her onto the dance floor.

He moved with her through the intricate steps of the reel, reminding himself that she was the type of woman he enjoyed taking to his bed. She was a woman of medium height, with rich golden blonde locks that accentuated her striking face and equally striking bosom. Her rounded figure and hips that had a little flesh on them, were just enough to hold on to when riding a wave of pleasure. And she was well versed in avoiding consequences that such bed sport often produced.

"I hope I'm being helpful in distracting you Lord Leighton from whatever vexes you so."

He looked down at her, surprised by such a question. "How do you mean?"

She laughed, a sultry, condemning sound that went straight to his conscience. "Who is she?" she asked, meeting his gaze, her features serious of a sudden.

He twirled her, before moving down the line of dancers. "No one." The lie tasted bitter on his tongue and glanced up to see Katherine watching him, her attention on him but a second before moving onto his dance partner then away.

If he wished to see hurt on her features, he was disappointed. No such reaction occurred, merely boredom and curiosity. Did she not care? Did she truly only wish for him to take her to his bed, one night and then they would part. Was he being too emotional over the whole concept, when she was looking at it as merely an enlightening experience she would enjoy before moving on into spinsterhood well and truly.

"She's very pretty, not beautiful, but passable."

Passable? The word sent his ire to soar. Katherine was more than passable. Damn it, she was growing to be one of the most beautiful women of his acquaintance. The women he usually dallied his days away with were nothing but painted up doxy's. Their fortune the only difference between them and the Covent Garden whores.

Shame washed over him at the thought. It was men like him that enabled such sport against walls in alleyways, in rowdy houses of ill repute. It was men like him who slept with women, where the slightest interest was sometimes enough for one to lift a gown in a vacant room at a ball, or deserted passageway. If the women of his acquaintance were whores, then so too was he.

"She is lovely, but she is not up for conversation. Nor should I be dancing with you simply to spite her."

Lady Grey grinned up at him, mischief in her eyes. "Is that what I am right now? Am I a woman to cause jealousy in another simply so you can gain what you want?"

If only it was as simple. There was no doubt he wanted Katherine, but it was she who sought him out, wanted him just as much. A heady, alluring concept he'd never experienced before in his life.

Thankfully the dance came to an end, and returning Lady Grey to her friends, Hamish made a hasty exit and started toward Miss Martin. She watched his approach, the lift of one brow, challenging and vexing at the same time, made his desire for her twofold.

He walked past her, clasping her hand and pulling her around to follow him. She did without a word, and they exited into a passageway that led into a conservatory. The room smelt of exotic plants and fruits. Without waiting, and with no words spoken between them, he pushed her up against the wall beside the door and took her mouth in a searing, punishing kiss.

She moaned the instant their lips met, her hands wrapping about his neck and holding him close. Hamish pinned her there, wanting to keep her just as she was forever. His mind was a cluster of unfathomable, confused thoughts, of what was right and wrong. What he wanted to do versus what he should do.

The feel of her hand sliding down his back, coming to rest on his rump sent heat to his cock and he hardened further. And damn it, he was so hard already it physically hurt.

He kissed his way down her neck, the scent of apples that sprung from her gown intoxicating him. He clasped her bottom, holding her against him and rocked, reveled in her gasp of surprise, before that little gasp turned into a siren's call and she undulated against him, seeking her own pleasure.

Hamish was certain she didn't know what she sought, but the body, when aroused didn't need past experiences to know what it craved. Here, at the Curzons' ball wasn't the place for them, and he would not deflower her here amongst the *ton*, but he would have her.

That he had no doubt of, not any longer. When they were apart he thought of little else, other than to be with her again, even if simply to talk. And when near her, the urge to be tactile, take her gloved hand and dance, was overwhelming. He would no longer deny either of them what they wanted.

"We cannot here, Katherine." His words were breathless, his heart pumping loud in his ears.

"Where then?" she asked, meeting his gaze. "Surely we can come together sometime soon. It is for only one night after all." She glided her thumb across his lips and he playfully bit it.

"Sometime soon, I promise, but not here, not now. I will not be such a blaggard and take you in a conservatory up against a wall."

"And yet," she said, a playful tilt to her head. "The thought of such a way has me curious. Is it even possible?"

Oh, dear god. He hardened further at the image that roused in his mind. "It's possible, believe me, a lot is possible when one wants it enough."

A small frown formed between her perfect brows. "You'll think me silly, but how is it possible. We both need to stand and so I thought…"

Hamish reached down, and hoisted her gown up, lifting her legs at the same time and wrapping them about his hips. Instinctively she wrapped her arms about his neck, her eyes wide with surprise and enlightenment.

It was the worst mistake of his life, for having her like this, his cock hard up against her heat almost doubled him over with need. "Do you understand now?" he rasped, unable to help but to rub himself against her core.

She all but thrummed in his arms, helping him with his undulation. "Don't move, Katherine." He kissed her hard and the little minx moved again. He moaned, but somewhere in the lustful recess of his mind, he set her on her feet, quickly righting her gown before stepping back fighting to control his emotions.

"You should return to the ball before you're missed. Go

back through the main entrance hall, the guests will simply think you've returned from the retiring room."

Hamish didn't move, needing to stay exactly where he was lest he drag her down onto the marble bench and take her here and now, and bedamned who caught them.

Katherine, her eyes cloudy with unsated need, a feeling he was well and truly feeling himself right at the moment, stood before him, leaning close before kissing him softly. She met his gaze as she stopped the chaste embrace, holding his gaze.

"I'll await your summons, Lord Leighton."

His gut tightened at the thought of having her beneath him. Without distractions or the possibility of interruption. "Hamish, please," he reminded her.

She turned and headed for the door, stopping to glance over her shoulder. "Don't take too long, Hamish. After what you showed me tonight, I may seek you out if you do."

Body roaring with need, he grabbed hold of the small cabinet beside him and didn't let go until she was out of sight. When he'd pulled her away from the ball he'd not planned to engage in such antics.

All lies when he cared to admit it to himself. He'd been so distracted seeing her dancing with someone else, that all his thoughts had centered on claiming her, letting her know in uncertain terms that it was he who would deflower her, not some other man.

Blast it all to hell. What was he going to do? After tasting her, having her sweet, willing body hard up against his, tempting him like sin, there was no way in hell he wasn't going to give her what she wanted. But then what? One night only in her arms?

Something told him that would never do. To fully gauge and experience all that could be between them they should at least have two. He would put the proposition to her when he saw her next, which would be sooner rather than later.

THE CARRIAGE RATTLED over the roads on their way to Yardley Hall, Surrey where the Marquess of Aaron and Cecilia had invited a select group of guests to a fortnight long house party. The invitation had come the day after Katherine had experienced the most eye-opening kiss within the conservatory with Lord Leighton.

He wished to see her again, had promised to show her more, so would he act on that at Cecilia's country home. Trepidation and excitement thrummed through her at the thought and she shifted on the seat, enjoying the delicious ache it aroused at her core.

It was a novel experience being wanted, and she knew by his ardent response to her kiss he desired her. For heavens knew, she wanted him.

The carriage turned through the gates of Yardley Hall and Katherine looked down into the gully and saw the sprawling mansion, its glass windows twinkling in the afternoon sun. She'd been the last to leave London due to her work, as she'd needed to oversee the roof slates that were now going up on Lord Leighton's townhouse. The structural work was coming along very well, and soon their side of the building would be complete and her association with his lordship on a business side would be finished. She could only hope it wasn't the end of their personal one.

Before the house party invitation arriving she'd not been summoned by Lord Leighton and she consoled herself that it was simply because he'd see her here. They were not courting, he'd explained his reasonings behind that, and she had accepted them. He owed her, and he would pay that debt back in the most pleasurable way possible. After that, there was nothing more he expected.

The carriage moved down on the gravel road, weaving toward the estate and she lost sight of it for a moment. She'd started to hope for something else. Something more. Unmarried and six and twenty, how could she not? This was likely her last chance of securing a gentleman who'd take her on. She pushed away the negative thoughts that wanted to mock her idea of landing the earl as a husband. Born into a family of builders, she might be from Cheapside, but she was a lady and had grown up with the best tutors and etiquette coaches. She might not have a title or be the daughter of a titled gentleman, but she was worthy and equal to them. In her own mind at least.

But would Lord Leighton see such things, or merely just wish to bed her and be done with it?

The carriage rocked to a halt and she startled so lost in thought. She waited for a footman to open the door and took his arm as she alighted. The afternoon sun bore down on this side of the home, and even though the slight wind was a little chilling, it was refreshing and invigorating being out of the carriage and out of the city.

The front door opened, and Cecilia came out, climbing down the couple of steps to hug her quickly before leading her indoors. "I'm so glad you were able to make it. You have been missed the last five days. I hope you were able to arrange it to return with us Wednesday next?"

"It's all arranged, and I have the time off, but I would so desperately love a bath. I had some last-minute paperwork to do this morning and so have come straight from the office."

"Of course, whatever you wish. I shall take you to your room immediately and send up some tea while they prepare you a bath. Dinner is served at eight sharp, and so once you are rested, we shall catch up more then."

"Thank you, Cecilia," she said, starting up the stairway. Making the first floor, they turned left along the extensive corridor and behind her Katherine could hear a multitude of voices and laughter. Was Lord Leighton in there, waiting for her?

"Maybe I ought to say hello first and then freshen up. I don't wish to be rude."

Cecilia ordered the servants to prepare a bath and refreshments and then took her arm, pulling her back toward the room the guests were gathered.

As much as she wanted to rest and refresh herself, the need to see Lord Leighton, to ensure he was in attendance was too much to deny, and as they made their way toward the room, Cecilia talking about the tidbits of gossip she'd heard the past five days, the entertaining nights and fun they'd had, caused nerves to settle in the pit of Katherine's belly.

They entered the room, and Darcy stood, coming over and kissing her cheek in welcome.

"We're so glad you've arrived. We almost expired of despair when you never came yesterday as planned. We thought you hadn't been able to get away."

Katherine smiled at some of the guests who acknowledged her and taking stock of the room quickly she noted one guest in particular who was missing. Her disappointment must have shown, for Cecilia tightened her grip on her arm, squeezing it a little.

"There are other guests of course. Lord Leighton is out riding with Lady Georgina Savile. They've become fast friends these past days, much in common with their mutual love of travel. I believe Lady Oliver mentioned her in London some weeks past. She's recently returned from abroad, Egypt in fact. She's particularly funny and smart.

And at that precise moment she entered the room, clasped tightly upon Lord Leighton's arm, both of them chuckling on some unknown amusing discussion the rest of the room was not privy to. The woman was everything Katherine was not, and if the world had opened at that moment and swallowed her whole, she would've been thankful.

Lady Savile had rich auburn hair, and skin as soft and pure as milk. If she had travelled abroad, Egypt in fact, she'd certainly taken care not to freckle or brown. Her breasts filled out her green riding gown to perfection, and her cheeks held the slightest shade of rose after their exertions on the horses. She wasn't as tall as Katherine, but not many women were, and she was also not as thin. In one word, the woman was beyond beautiful and it was no wonder Lord Leighton had enjoyed himself these past five days. Who would not with such company?

Katherine was dowdy, her traveling gown was well worn and brown and did nothing for her lifeless coloured hair. Her breasts didn't come up half to snuff of those of Lady Savile's and she could've cried regretting her decision to come and say hello to everyone before making herself more presentable.

What would most of these guests care that she was here? She was nothing but serving class to them. "Do you think my bath would be ready by now," she asked, Cecilia quietly. "I think I shall return to my room."

Darcy's gaze slid to Lord Leighton's and Katherine didn't miss the exchange. Lord Leighton made past them and nodded slightly in her direction, wishing her welcome before he sat down on a settee, a servant handing him and Lady Savile a glass of wine.

Katherine excused herself and left, Cecilia following close on her heels. "Is everything well, Kat. You seem upset?"

"I'm merely tired. I'm going to go rest a while, have my bath and put myself to rights. I shall see you at dinner." And then, once she was recovered, she would figure out a way to tell her friends that she would return to London. She didn't belong here, and she could never compete with a woman of Lady Savile's beauty and poise. And she didn't want to.

Lord Leighton hadn't seemed the least interested in her. It should not surprise her since he was famous about town for being a rake, easily bored and distracted. Perhaps it was best that she didn't follow through with her plan to lay with him. If the jealousy she now felt was any indication, she didn't need that to be one-hundred fold after knowing him intimately. The thought of his losing interest in her, maybe even finding a woman he wished to marry left a hollow sensation in the location her heart should sit. Such a notion would be unbearable.

CHAPTER 8

Hamish sat at table that evening, his attention snapping to Katherine with any opportunity. How beautiful she'd looked this afternoon after her arrival. Her hair had fallen down a little during her carriage ride to Yardley Hall, and her eyes were alight with possibility when talking to Cecilia and the duchess. That was, until she'd seen him with Lady Savile and all enjoyment, pleasure of being at the country house had vanished from her features. She'd looked devastated, if one could look such a way, and he'd cursed himself as a fool for being the one who'd put that look of disappointment in her rich brown eyes.

Lady Savile was a very beautiful woman, and certainly had he not known Katherine the way he did now, he might have tried his luck with the lady, but that wasn't the case now. He wasn't interested at all in the woman, only that of a friend, and before the night was out he'd make sure Katherine knew that fact too. He would not allow her to spend even one night fretting over something that didn't exist.

To make matters worse, he was seated beside Lady Savile who unknowingly with her amusing countenance, and their new friendship had no idea that the small touches she placed on his arm, her chuckling banter during dinner was causing the woman he cared for, more than he'd known up until he'd seen the hurt in her eyes this afternoon, more pain than he ever wished to imbue on her.

Damn it, he inwardly swore. As the dinner progressed, he didn't fail to miss that Katherine grew more and more quiet, refused to meet his gaze or converse in any conversation he was part of.

"Shall we play a game after dinner. I know of one that I think will be such fun," Lady Savile said, beaming at everyone, her jovial charm making the gentlemen present enthusiastic and the women more so. All except Katherine who sipped her wine without comment.

"What a wonderful idea," Cecilia said, more than happy to get in on the act.

"The house is large, with numerous rooms and corridors, attics and cellars. And tonight, you'll get to explore some of it, but there's a catch," Lady Savile said, standing now and meeting everyone's eye to gain their attention.

"Oh, do tell." Katherine's words dripped with sarcasm and the worried glance Cecilia threw her didn't seem to temper Miss Martin's growing annoyance.

Hamish knew the root cause for her ire, and it was him and his bad handling of her arrival. He'd hoped she would arrive today after missing her own arrival date the day before. Still, he'd hankered to get outdoors and had gone out on a horse ride, only at the stables running into Lady Savile who asked if she could join him since she wasn't familiar with the grounds. He'd not been able to refuse, and when he'd seen Katherine's carriage roll down the hill he'd turned back to the estate, eager to see her again.

Yet, the moment he'd walked into the room, he couldn't allow anyone to see just how impatient he'd been and so he'd nodded in welcome, and that was all. And now, it would seem, Katherine was annoyed.

"Tonight," her ladyship continued, "we're going to play a game of hide and seek. After dinner, you will find in the entrance hall a footman who has a pack of cards in a hat. They are all black, bar two. You will each be required to pull out a card. The black card will mean you hide, the white card will mean you are the seekers. For those who pick white cards, you must find as many people as you can within one hour. Whoever remains hidden and is not found, wins," she said, beaming with excitement.

Lady Savile resumed her seat, seemingly pleased with her instructions for the evening and Cecilia stood to speak. "You may continue with your dinner and we'll get onto our little game in a short while."

From there, dinner passed pleasantly, and as expected, the discussion turned to the game they were to play afterwards, each of them discussing what was in bounds and out about the house. By the time dinner had passed, Hamish was desperate to speak to Katherine. After her hasty departure to her room this afternoon, she'd not returned, and she'd been one of the last guests to arrive for dinner. That she was avoiding him was obvious, but he wouldn't allow it to continue. He hated the fact she'd been hurt by his actions. And he hated the fact that he'd tempered his reaction to seeing her all because it was what was expected.

With the dinner at an end, and the guests coming to stand in the entrance hall, as promised, a footman waited for them all, holding a black beaver hat. A few of the women tittered in excitement. Was it because they were to explore the home, full of hidden passageways and secret compartments, or merely the possibility of finding oneself alone with a gentleman admirer.

Hamish waited back, wanting to see if Katherine would play at all, and because of the good humor from her friends the duchess and marchioness, she pulled out a card. It was a black card meaning she was to hide.

Hamish too took a card, it was white, before sliding up to Katherine, leaning close to ensure privacy. "Do not hide too hard, Miss Martin. I'll not be able to find you."

This close, he felt the shiver that ran down her body, it gave him hope that she wasn't through with him, had cast him out as a swine and rogue.

"You forget, I've been here before, twice in fact, and I know this house well. You'll never find me." She met his challenging gaze with one of her own and heat shot through him. He wanted her. He wanted all of her and no one else.

Hamish grinned. "We will see, shall we not." He left her, knowing full well as he made his way back into the library she watched his every move.

KATHERINE KNEW EXACTLY where she was going to hide where no one would find her. The marquess and Cecilia's home was a rabbit warren of rooms, corridors and hidden passageways, one of which ran along the gallery wall. Cecilia had shown her only the last time she was here. One simply had to hold back the tapestry of knights in battle, and a wooden door sat behind it. In fact, it wasn't even a door, simply a door disguised as the wall panelling.

As she made her way up to the first floor, people ran past her, men and women both, laughing, squealing in delight. One or two even disappeared into rooms that were not part of the game. Katherine shrugged it off, and continued on to the gallery, happy to find that no one had followed her into this part of the house, which was sparsely lit and devoid of servants.

She found the tapestry and pulling it out a little, pushed on the panel behind. It opened with only the slightest creak and picking up a candelabra she slipped into the passage and closed the door. For a hidden passage it was reasonably clean, and someone had even placed a chair in the corridor. She would have to ask Cecilia if she'd done such a thing and why.

The sound of running footsteps outside and more laughter passed, and Katherine smiled. No one, not even Lord Leighton would find her in here. She supposed she might miss out on all the fun of being found being so well hidden, but it was too late now to change her mind. Not that she wished to be found by his lordship in any case. Today, he'd proven to her really what a silly numbskull she'd been to think he might possibly care for her more than he did. That he might actually like her for who and what she was, not simply because she asked him to deflower her.

Katherine shook her head, what a stupid fool she'd been. And it was not something she could take back. Even her friends knew of her idea regrettably. For the rest of her spinsterhood days, she would be thrown into his sphere simply because they had the same friends, and she would feel mortified each and every time. If only she had never asked him.

Footsteps sounded and stopped on the other side from where she sat. Katherine stilled, her heart surging in alarm. Surely no one knew where she was... The panelling pushed open and the dark head and teasing grin of Lord Leighton came into view. He shut the panel behind him before he spoke, leaving them alone. Quite alone.

"How did you find me here?" Not sure if she was affronted by being found so easily or that the nerves coursing through her veins were due to them being solitary and in a darkened space to boot.

"The tapestry in the gallery was kinked. I walked through here earlier today, and it wasn't, and so I took a guess. And what a lucky guess it was."

He came to stand before her, for the first time in forever, he made her feel a little small. After all, he was taller than her by a good two inches, not many men could boast such a thing in either her social sphere or his. "You were lucky, and one would say I was unlucky. I suppose we'll have to return downstairs and you may boast that you found me."

His gaze dropped to her lips and stayed there. "Or, you could grant me a winner's boon."

"Such as?" Katherine had the overwhelming urge to pull out her fischu and use it as a fan. For a hidden corridor that ran in either direction and was long and winding, it was awfully hot and crowded in the space.

"Maybe you will grant me," he stepped even closer. "A ki—"

"I shall not kiss you, my lord. I find I'm not at liberty this evening."

He grinned and damn it, her heart fluttered. "*Not at liberty*. May I ask as to why you scorn me? I have not seen you this afternoon, nor before dinner. I had hoped to talk to you before we dined."

Katherine shrugged, and Hamish stepped back, the separation making her chest hurt.

"You're angry at me. Why?"

Something in his tone told her he already suspected,

but if she were to admit to her annoyance, her hurt, it would pave the way to him knowing that she'd hoped for more. That she cared. And she would not have that. She would not be made a fool of twice.

"I made a mistake when I asked you to make love with me. I apologize, and I no longer wish to act on my curiosity. I'm sorry to have thrown myself at your head." Katherine went to move past him and he blocked her way.

"I'm not sorry that you asked me. Although I know you're aware I'm not seeking a wife, it does not mean with care that we cannot enjoy each other. No matter what you believe, Kat, for some weeks now you've become an important part of my life. You inspire me with your independence and your employment. You do not need a man to guide you through life, as you're your own woman. I admire you and I desire you." He stepped closer still and Katherine instinctively stepped back, only to come up hard against the wall. "I want you, no one else, no matter what you think you saw today, it was all a show. It is you that my heart beats hard for, that my body reacts to. It is you and only you that I want to warm my bed."

She swallowed, heat blooming on her cheeks, and she was thankful for the shadows about them. His words, thick and husky pulled at the part of her that was lonely, longing for a future that she thought lost. A moan rent the air, and Katherine jumped against him, clasping his lapels. "That sounded like what one would think was a ghost."

He chuckled, wrapping one arm about the curve of her back and a delicious shiver stole down her spine.

"I think it came from up here." He pulled her along. "Come, we will investigate further."

"I'm not sure that is wise. I don't want to see any of Lord Aaron's ancestors floating past me, thank you very much."

To her astonishment, he stopped and lifting her chin, kissed her. A gentle, feathered touch that shot straight to her heart. *Oh dear, she was on dangerous ground, and not because of the dark...*

"Do not fret, darling Kat. I shall save you."

Katherine leaned close to his side as they started down the corridor, the single candelabra their only light. The corridor remained straight for some time, following the portrait gallery outside before it made a sharp left.

. There was no warning other than a curse that echoed off the walls as his lordship tripped over, their only form of light guttered in the process. She froze, not wanting to trip over too. "Are you alright, my lord."

"Hamish, please. No titles, it's too formal."

"Are you really worried about that now? Simply answer the question." She spoke into the darkness, not able to see anything at all.

More scratching and another curse. "Where the hell?"

Katherine gasped as one, large, male hand landed directly on her breast. Her body shot to life, and she hoped, even craved that his hand would curve about her aching flesh and squeeze it a little. Anything to save her from this throbbing need she had for him. "Hamish..."

His rapid breathing told her without sight that he reacted in kind and he took an awfully long time to remove his hand. "I should apologize. It's certainly what a gentleman should do."

Her breast ached with the lack of his touch when he pulled away, and she wasn't ready for him to stop touching her. But here and now wasn't the time for a rendezvous. The whole company at the home were playing a game, and should they go missing, especially Hamish as he was supposed to be finding other guests, it would cause a huge scandal.

"It was an accident, brought on by the fact we're stuck in a hidden passageway in pitch black. How on earth are we going to find our way back?" she said, hoping to change the subject. Around Lord Leighton she did not trust herself. Impulses he'd awoken refused to settle and demanded she do as she wanted, not what she ought.

"There, ahead of us," he said, his voice close. "There is a small light." His hand fluttered down her arm before he took her hand. "Let us take it slowly, less we both fall over next time."

She chuckled and let him lead the way. They walked slowly, more cautious now that their vision was impaired by the darkness, but the small light that they had spied wasn't a door at all, a small hole gave them view into the corridor, or what Katherine thought was the corridor at least.

The groan that they'd heard earlier sounded again and she clutched at his arm. Lord Leighton paused to look through the hole and cursed. "Do not look, Katherine. Come, we'll continue this way."

"What is it? What have you found?" She pushed him aside and standing on tiptoe she looked through the hole. It was something that Katherine had never seen before in her life and loathed to think that such a thing may be located in her room, as it was in this one.

"Oh my," she gasped, unable to look away from the vision before her. That of two of the guests, who came without partners following the death of their spouses were enjoying each other very much in private.

"Come, Kat."

His voice was strained, deeper than she'd heard it before and she cursed not being able to see him, see what the vision they'd just viewed was doing to him. "I'm glad they're enjoying themselves," she said, grinning at her own words.

"Are you not enjoying yourself?"

She reached out for his hand and her palm landed directly on his chest. He was all muscle, a virile healthy man. The only man who'd ever made her weak at the knees. "I would enjoy our time here more if we were doing what was happening right now in the room beside us."

In the dark, everything seemed magnified, his breathing, her shivers as his hand came up to cover hers sitting on his chest. After seeing him today with Lady Savile she'd not thought she would ever feel jealousy, hurt even inflicted by someone else, but thinking of Hamish in the arms of another woman, loving her as she wanted left a hollow in her heart.

She bit her lip. Would he do as she asked, as they'd agreed, or since being here, meeting a woman who suited his tastes more, both in looks and social standing, did he simply not want her?

He pulled her into his arms, and a small flutter went off in her stomach. "If you will have me, Katherine, I will come to your room tonight. I've already found out which one it is. And then my dearest," he said, his hands bracketing her face and kissing her. "We shall do everything you want."

Heat pooled between her legs and she moaned when he kissed her again. The thought of them doing what she'd seen the couple undertaking through the peep hole left her longing for the night to end so theirs could begin.

"Anything?" Katherine hadn't been shy about reading up on what lovers partook during a sexual act, and there were some very interesting ideas that she longed to try. But would he let her? Excitement thrummed through her veins. She supposed she was to soon find out. If this was her one and only night with Lord Leighton, then she would make the most of it.

He chuckled, pulling her back along the passage. "I'm yours to do with as you wish, but first, we have to find a way out of this infernal passage. If I don't return you soon to company, I cannot be held responsible for my actions. Not even in this black hole."

CHAPTER 9

Hamish paced back and forth in his room, waiting for the house to quieten after the night's activities. The game had continued after Katherine and he had found their way out of the secret passageway, and with her help, he'd found most of the guests. After that, the party gathered in the music room downstairs for cards, some dancing and good conversations.

Yet, the entire time, all Hamish could think about was what was to come. He wanted to make Katherine's first time a pleasurable one and he'd gone over in his mind again and again what he could do to ensure that.

It was not the best course of action since he was in company at the time, and would not, under any circumstances stand to converse. Katherine had mingled for the remainder of the night, and after their talk upstairs, she seemed to have mellowed a little around Lady Savile and yet, every now and then he caught sight of her admiring the woman and a little alarm went off in his mind.

Did she think she was not as attractive, not as beautiful as the other women that were present? To him, Katherine was the most beautiful woman he'd ever met, and after tonight she would know that.

He checked the time, it was past one and still he could hear people out in the corridor, guests heading for bed. Finally. Some minutes later, his door opened, and he turned to see Katherine slip inside and close it quickly. She turned to him, a silk dressing robe over her shift. He let out a pained breath. Damn it, she was beautiful, and his. His to adore and to cherish for the night.

"You took too long, Lord Leighton. I hope you've not changed your mind," she said, coming toward him and sliding off her robe, only to throw it on a nearby chair.

Hamish found his voice, although even to himself he sounded breathless. When had she become an expert siren? He met her half way and pulling her into his arms he kissed her, like he'd wanted to kiss her when he'd entered the parlor this afternoon after his ride.

She melted against him, all soft womanly flesh that sent his wits spiralling. He ran his hands over her back, over her buttocks to pull her hard against his bulging cock that strained against his breeches. That she was here, in his room, and they were alone, wouldn't be disturbed all night, sent his pulse to gallop.

He nibbled her lips, explored her mouth with his tongue, groaned when she matched him, stroke for stroke, touch for touch.

"Katherine," he whispered against her neck, nipping on the little vein that protruded there. Her skin smelt of soap, and jasmine, her hair of fruits. He had no doubt she'd taste just as good.

Hamish couldn't wait much longer to see her, he wanted to gaze down upon her full glory and revel in it.

She broke the kiss and stepped back, holding his gaze, hers heavy with desire that shot blood straight to his groin.

Katherine stood before him, her shift almost translucent and pulled the small ties at the front of her gown apart. He could not pull his attention away from her hands, or what they were doing for anything, and then, with a lift of her shoulder and little shimmy the shift dropped and pooled about her feet.

Underneath she was gloriously naked. Hamish reached out and traced her collarbone, her audible gasp almost put an end to his resolve to look, to admire and learn every ounce of her. Her breasts, which were larger than he'd thought rose with every breath, her nipples the sweetest pink he'd ever beheld, and puckered into tight buds.

He wanted to lick them, suckle and kiss them until she was writhing and begging for him. He licked his lips, imaging it, all the while knowing that within a few moments he'd be doing what he'd wanted to for weeks. His gaze moved downwards to her perfect waist, and hips that flared. She was so beautiful his breath caught in his lungs.

"You do me such an honor, Katherine." He grazed his hand over her navel and meeting her gaze, moved it down to cup between her legs. She was gloriously wet, ready for him.

Her hands came about his neck and she cried out, the sound breaking the little control he held. Swinging her up in his arms, he walked them to the bed, laying her down and coming to lie over her. She shook beneath him, and he kissed her, wanting to dispel any nerves. If he could help it he would never hurt her, but if there were the slightest pain during their joining it would be minimal and soon replaced with pleasure.

KATHERINE POSITIVELY TREMBLED with want of Hamish. His strong, lean, muscular body over hers, the wisp of hair that tickled her breasts, the slight grazing of his stubbled jaw as he kissed her, conquered her mouth in a punishing kiss. Katherine promised herself then and there should she never have another such kiss her life would be content. For to have such a kiss from Hamish, one that told her without words that she was wanted, desired, longed for, was more than anything she'd ever expected.

His hands clasped her thigh and he lifted her leg to sit against his hip. The position allowed him to press himself against her fully, and all her thoughts centered on the one place that begged, throbbed for more.

"What is this madness you're doing to me," she gasped, watching him as he kissed his way down her chest to only stop at her breasts and look at them. Katherine fought not to hide herself, conscious of the fact that she wasn't as full in the breast area as his usual lovers, but his exquisite unbidden delight when looking at them seemed to say he didn't mind. One hand cupped her breast and pleasure rocked through her. He leaned down, licking first her nipple before giving it a teasing nip.

She moaned, a sound that mingled with his own groan. Katherine pushed up against him, his hard member solid against her core and she ached so very much to have it inside her. Although she'd never experienced such things before, surely it would feel as good as his mouth on her now.

He moved to lavish attention to the other breast, and she speared her fingers through his hair, holding him against her so he might never stop his attentions. His hand slid down her stomach, clasping her there before delving between her wet folds.

Katherine shut her eyes as he slid his fingers against

346

her most private of places, using his thumb to roll against a part of her that made her want nothing but him. "Hamish," was all she could manage to say while her mind whirred. Was it like this always between married couples? To know this kind of pleasure would be unbearably hard to only experience once.

He groaned and kissed his way down her stomach. So, lost in her own enjoyment she didn't realize what he was doing before his heated breath caressed her mons. She attempted to sit up, but he merely met her gaze, a feral edge to it that made her flustered and warm, before pushing on her stomach, warning her to stay.

"Lay back and relax. If we're to only have one night, we're going to have a long and very varied one." He bent his head and Katherine sighed, biting her lip as his mouth, his tongue…What his tongue was doing was beyond anything she'd ever thought. When she'd seen such drawings in the books she'd borrowed from the Duke of Athelby's library, she never imagined how wonderful it would feel.

He slid a finger across the spot that thrilled with every touch and then slid it inside.

"Damn Kat, you're so tight."

Katherine was beyond thought or words, she simply clung onto his head, holding him, undulating against his face like a woman gone wild. How had she not known it could be like this with a man. How could she ever move forward in life and only have this once.

Only make love with Hamish once…

His ministrations continued, with every thrust of his hand, his tongue matched its purpose and with agonising delight, her body coiled, thrived on his touch and sought something she'd never known.

"That's it darling, let go. Come for me," he said, kissing

her again without restraint. His teasing lightened to a slow torment and her body hitched, her hips pushing up to find release. Without any care as to how wanton she might seem, pleasure like none she'd ever known rocked through her body. Tremor after tremor of delicious spasm ran across her skin and she giggled, her limbs weak, her body slackened and sated.

Hamish kissed his way up her body, hitching her leg over his hip. "My turn," he said, kissing her deeply.

She tasted herself on him, and it sent the beginnings of pleasure to build once again. This is what she wanted after all. To have Hamish just like this, her lover, a man who for one night at least would worship her body, make her feel just as beautiful as anyone else.

He positioned himself at her opening. "I'm sorry, my darling, this may be uncomfortable." He thrust forward and Katherine gasped at the sting of pain, clutching at his shoulders. He stopped moving, and simply stayed fully lodged within her. It allowed her to get used to the feeling of him being there, inside her.

It was odd, there was no doubt about that, but when he moved again, instead of pain there was only the residual delight of her own release, doubly so, now that Hamish was going to experience the same.

He pushed into her, groaning against her neck when she lifted her legs higher.

"You're so beautiful, Katherine," he rasped against her lips, watching her as he took her. His arms strained as he held himself atop her, his corded muscles straining with the effort and never had she seen anything so desirous in all her life.

His strokes became faster, harder and she found the more he took her like this, the more her body craved release. She was becoming a woman who couldn't get enough of him, and one night seemed such a waste. Surely, they could have two.

"Katherine," he moaned, taking her lips, his hips flexing. Warmth spread through her, and at the last minute he pulled out, spilling his seed across her stomach. Hamish collapsed beside her, and reaching into the bedside cabinet drawer, he pulled out a cloth and wiped her clean before drawing her up against his chest. "We shall rest for a time, and then my dear, I will show you what else we can do."

His teasing grin mimicked her own. "There's more we can do?" The idea never occurred to her, not really. She'd seen images in books, but she'd always assumed those positions were exotic, not performed by well-bred English lords. Excitement thrummed through her as one image she wanted to try came to mind.

"You look positively naughty. What is going on in your mind?" he asked, kissing her so gently on the lips that her heart gave a flip.

She leaned up and whispered her thought in his ear, unable to voice it out loud, even though they were quite alone. His eyes went wide, before they darkened in hunger. He rolled her over onto her back, pinning her to the bed.

"Are you sure?" he asked, his body tight and his manhood hard again against her leg.

She nodded, her body wiggling in renewed need. "Oh yes, I'm sure. Show me everything."

He growled. "With pleasure."

CHAPTER 10

Katherine sat in the morning room alone. Before her was an untouched pot of tea and an assortment of cakes. She stared at the little flowery design on the side of the teapot and thought about what had transpired between her and Lord Leighton last night. Actually, even this morning if she were honest about their interlude. It had been quite vigorous and lengthy and very much enlightening. She grinned. How different she felt now that she'd slept with a man. Wiser in her wisdom, certainly wiser as to what she'd been missing all these years. Silly dolt.

She kicked her legs out from beneath her and poured herself a cup. Limiting her milk so the tea wasn't too cold, she took a small sip, relaxing back in her chair. When they'd parted this morning, a quick chaste kiss in the corridor there had been no mention of any more nights. Would he stick to their agreement of only one night together? They seemed to get along very well in private, and it would be a shame to stop it since it really had only just begun.

"Oh, here you are, my dear. I've been looking all over

for you." Katherine smiled as Cecilia bustled into the room, her morning gown of white embroidered cotton making her look like a summer's dream. Marriage seemed to suit her friend very well, and if the glow on her cheeks was any indication, she got along quite well with Lord Aaron in private too.

"I'm just having a cup of tea, before I'm to head outdoors to join in the game of croquet you have set up outside. Do you care to join me?"

"I'd love to. After all the running about this morning I'm in need of substance." Cecilia sat, her golden locks were pulled up high on her head, and yet a few wisps framed her pretty face.

"You do look like you've been busy. Can I help you with anything?" Katherine asked, sitting back in her chair and taking another sip.

Cecilia busied herself pouring a cup of tea and picking up a small biscuit. "No, everything is under control, but I would like to know what happened last evening with Lord Leighton."

Katherine coughed, choking on her tea. "I'm sorry. What?" How did she know? When she'd snuck into his room she was very discreet and had made sure the last of the guests had gone to their rooms before she scuttled down the passageway to his suite.

Cecilia raised a knowing brow. "He's outside partaking in the games and seems quite jovial this morning. In fact, the poor fellow keeps looking back at the house as if he's expecting someone and it made me wonder. Especially when everyone who's here for the fortnight is outside on the lawns. All but one."

Pleasure ran through her veins. Was Hamish looking for her? Waiting for her? "These cakes are delicious,

Cecilia. You must give my regards to your cook when you see her next."

Cecilia wagged her finger, grinning. "Oh, no you don't. You're going to tell me Kat what you've done under this roof, if only so I can be there for you. Support you in your choice."

Katherine stood and walked to the window to look out onto the back grounds. Sure enough, in buckskin breeches and a day coat of bottle green stood Lord Leighton, deep in conversation with his friend Lord Bridgman. The game made him take a couple of steps, and it was only then that Katherine was reminded of his lean form, his strong arms and very darling bottom.

She turned and faced her oldest friend. "I slept with Lord Leighton and worse," she said pausing. "I want to do it again."

Cecilia's eyes went wide, and she placed her tea cup down. "Come and sit. This we need to discuss at length."

Katherine did as she was asked, folding her hands in her lap as she waited for Cecilia to either condone or condemn her. She hoped it would the former.

"I did not think that Lord Leighton wished to have such intimate relations with you. What changed his mind?" Cecilia asked, her gaze trained on her with unwavering focus and concern.

She shrugged. "I suppose it has something to do with the fact that whenever we're together the feelings, the desire that we both feel overrides what our decisions should be. I will never marry, at my age it's too late for me, and I know I'm also not the kind of woman that Lord Leighton has normally chased. Not that he chased me, but I do not fit his ideal mould." Tears pricked her eyes, and she sniffed, unsure where all this overwhelming emotion was coming from. Did all women cry after a night of bliss? Surely not.

"We parted on good terms, but no mention was made on continuing our liaison. And so, it seems that perhaps he has held up to his end of the bargain by giving me the one thing that I wished and that is that. But I hope it's not the case. I like him," she stated. It was the truth after all. "I like him a lot."

"Oh, Katherine," Cecilia said, coming to sit beside her. "Do not despair, not yet at least. Today is a new day, and such liaisons between two unmarried people is highly scandalous, so he will not be forward in his regard with you, not in public. You may find today when you do speak to him, that he feels the same way and wishes a courtship with you. I can have Hunter have a word with him if you like. Remind Lord Leighton of his honor as a gentleman to not dally with unmarried women only to kick them aside when he's had his fill."

Katherine shook her head, hating even the thought of others telling Lord Leighton what he ought to do simply because of what they'd done. After all, it was her idea to have him sleep with her. "Please don't. I'm sure no matter what transpires today, Lord Leighton and myself will remain friends. I was the one who instigated all of this in the first place, you cannot have someone chastise him simply because I teased him until he did as I wished." What a conundrum she was in. And one of her own making.

"Let us join the others outside. I'm merely being foolish hiding away indoors." Katherine stood. "Shall we?"

Cecilia expelled a resigned sigh but stood. "Very well, but please confide in me if anything troubles you. I want you to be happy above anything else."

Katherine hugged Cecilia to her as they walked out onto the terrace and made their way down the stairs and onto the large expanse of lawn. "I will come to you should anything upsetting occur, but until then, please don't fret over me. I'm older than you remember. I'm perfectly well and capable of handling my life."

"I know you are."

Darcy waved and came over to join them, and for a moment the three simply stood and watched some of the guests play croquet. The players' laughter during the game brought a smile to Katherine's lips and she found herself forgetting her troubles over what to do with Hamish and simply enjoyed the house party.

Lord Leighton took a shot and the small white ball went through the hoop, giving him the lead. He whooped, laughing and smiling at his good fortune. She sighed at how good looking he was, especially compared to her. She wasn't foolish enough that she believed herself a great beauty, not when Lady Savile walked up to Hamish, placing her hand on his arm as they laughed about something going on in the game.

"It is harmless, Kat. Lady Savile is simply flirtatious by nature. She's not interested in Lord Leighton. I promise you that."

Katherine looked back toward the pair, and caught Hamish watching her, leaning casually against his croquet stick, his dark hooded eyes raking over her in a way that her skin prickled in heat.

"And from that look," Darcy said, chuckling a little. "He's not interested in Lady Savile either, but in fact, another woman altogether."

Her stomach twisted in knots and she smiled a little.

The game ended and as Hamish started in her direction, Darcy and Cecilia joined their husbands who were seated at an outdoor table, fully engaged in what looked to be a very loud and engaging debate over Tattersalls' upcoming sale.

"Are you not going to congratulate me, Miss Martin? I won."

Katherine raised her brow, nerves fluttering in her belly knowing this was the first time they'd spoken since last night. A night where he'd shown her a great many things a woman and man could do, that even now made her ache. Would he be willing to continue their liaison? Could trust that what she suspected of him, his liking of her, and his need were real, and not just because she'd been desperate and begged him to make love to her?

"Congratulations," she said, "you must be very proud." Katherine smiled, ignoring the fact that all she wanted to do right now was fling herself into his arms and kiss him.

He checked the whereabouts of the other guests before he said, "Is that all I'm to receive from you? Nothing else you're willing to give to the winner?"

"I do not understand your meaning, my lord," she said, trying not to look at his full lips that again reminded her of where they had been last night on her person, and the pleasure they'd wrought. She failed utterly. His hair was tied back, but in the outdoors little wisps floated about his face. Last night she'd clasped his hair, holding him as she'd kissed him to distraction. She wanted to see him in such a way again.

"Tell me, Miss Martin, what do you think would be a fitting prize for a gentleman such as myself. A bottle of the finest whisky? A few sovereigns to line my pocket." He leaned toward her. "A kiss from the woman who keeps me up all night for want of her?"

She shivered, knowing that if they were to kiss, the embrace would lead to so much more. The duke of Athelby and the Marquess called out to Hamish to come and join their new croquet game. Hamish waved to them over his shoulder, yelling out, "Just a minute."

"You want to kiss me again, my lord. I thought after last night our agreement has been completed and you're free from any obligation to me." Her stomach roiled at voicing her fears, that what she actually said was true. Would he agree, turn from her and move on to his next lover? Someone more positioned in Society, more to his tastes and desires.

"I want to do a lot more than kiss you, Kat. I know our interlude was only meant to be one night, but it's not enough. Not enough for me and I hope for you too." He walked them along the lawn, giving the illusion that they were simply strolling and enjoying the day. "There is a hot spring here on the Marquess's lands. I will come to you tonight, and we shall go there."

"I don't know if you've noticed, Hamish, but it isn't very warm. We shall freeze."

He chuckled, his free hand coming to rest atop hers that sat on his arm. "I'll keep you warm," and with those words he threw her a devilish grin and joined the duke and marquess.

Katherine could do little but stare after him. He wasn't finished with her. He wanted to spend more time with her, just as she'd hoped.

She'd never been desired by a man before, and it was a mix of trepidation and exhilaration that Lord Leighton did. Katherine held no illusions that this liaison would go anywhere, but she'd asked to know what life would be like with a man, and he was going to show her, and no matter the risks she would jump into the void and revel in it.

CHAPTER 11

Later that night they crept out of the house and stole across the lawns down toward the river that ran through the Marquess of Aaron's estate. The night was bright thanks to the full moon and very little clouds, although in the distance Hamish could see the flash of lightning and hear the low rumble of thunder.

The hot spring was a fortunate addition to the estate, and many years ago, the Marquess's grandfather had the spring transformed into a location family and guests could use. Today the spring was lined with stone, and housed paving about the edges, so people could get in and out without making their feet dirty. Inside the spring there was a ledge that ran along the outer edges of the circular bath, giving those enjoying the warm water a seat to sit on while partially submerged.

"Oh my, this is amazing," Katherine said, as the path gave way to the spring.

Steam rose into the night sky, and the closer they came toward it, the warmer the air became.

"If I were Cecilia I would live in this." She let go of his

hand and went over to the water, dipping her hand into it. "It's so hot."

A condition that Hamish was feeling most decidedly as well. Seeing Katherine under a moonlit sky, her skin translucent and flushed after their exertion of running toward the spring, left an odd ache in his chest. He untied his cravat, laying it on a bench that sat beside the spring. "Shall we get in?" he asked, removing his waistcoat.

Katherine joined him. He sucked in an audible breath when she clasped his shirt and pulled it over his head. "Most definitely."

They undressed quickly, both helping the other with buttons and ties. Hamish stood back and watched as she dropped her shift about her legs, her figure more magnificent than he'd ever thought possible. He'd not thought he would ever want a woman as much as he wanted Katherine, and the emotion gave him pause. To feel more for someone other than merely like was dangerous ground. Such emotions led to marriage and then children, and the latter was an affliction that he would never submit his bride to. The woman he married would not want children. He had his heir, and he would not risk the life of his wife simply to have child. He'd already lost a sister, that was well and truly enough.

Her hand clasped his jaw, and he met her gaze, surprised to see concern in her rich brown orbs. "Is everything well, Hamish? You seem a little lost in thought."

He pulled her into his arms, kissing her soundly. She chuckled through the kiss, before her arms came about his neck and she kissed him back with as much passion as she brought forth in him. Scooping her into his arms, he carried her into the spring, stepping down into the water with care. Releasing her, he allowed her to gain her feet, and watched in delight as she waded into the hot water.

"Oh, it's heavenly. Thank you for bringing me here." She kneeled into the water, covering her body and he missed her puckered nipples that had reacted to the cold night air.

Hamish went and sat on the bench, watching her as she floated about in the water, simply enjoying their time there before she joined him on the seat. She slid her hands up his chest and kissed him quickly on the lips.

"Now that you have me here, all alone and...naked, what are we going to do?"

Her grin was infectious, and he chuckled. "What did you have in mind?" Hamish knew what he had in mind, what he'd thought of all day and nothing else. When Katherine had played croquet, she had bent over to hit the little white ball he'd been decidedly conscious of the fact his buckskin breeches and day coat could only cover so much of his desire for her. He'd had to sit himself down and talk about London's latest *on dit* just to distract himself. "Maybe you ought to straddle my lap, and we'll go from there."

Her eyes brightened with interest and she quickly did as he suggested. Her body fit him like a glove, smooth and silky in his hands. Her mons pressed against his cock and she sighed when she purposefully slid against him, her gaze darkening in arousal.

"And now what?" she asked, running her hands into his hair and holding him tight. Her breathing deepened, and he could see that her continual sliding against his rock-hard member was giving her pleasure, teasing her to do more.

"Now," he said, his voice taut. "You'll guide me within you. And then, my darling." He ran his hand along her spine to clasp her nape. "You're going to fuck me."

She half gasped half moaned, and the idea of what

he'd said threatened his sanity. She reached between them, and clasping his cock, moving it toward her cunny.

Katherine bit her lip , and with a torturously slow descent, she took him fully within her. Her eyes widened before hunger crossed her features. "I thought it would hurt."

He shook his head, holding her hips and guiding her into a steady rhythm. "If we're doing it right, it will never hurt again."

Something shifted in her eyes before she blinked, and it was gone. She moved more forcefully and all thoughts of anything else vanished from his mind. He would have her like this for as long as she wished it. He could not give her up. "I knew one night with you would never have been enough."

She shivered in his hold before she kissed him with sensuous heat. He reveled in the arms of a woman who wasn't afraid to take or ask for what she wanted. To give her the control to take their lovemaking at her own pace. While it might drive him to insanity, he would ensure she gained her pleasure before he would take his.

Katherine arced her back, giving him a beautiful view of her breasts that rocked in the water. "You're so beautiful." He clasped one breast and leaning down kissed the rosy pink nipple. She moaned, increasing her pace and he fought for control. Damn it, he wanted to fuck her hard, sit her on the side of the spring, lay her down on the pavement and take her with his mouth. Wring every little amount of joy that he could while they were here, away from London and their normal lives.

Her core tightened about him, her pace increased, deepened and he groaned. "Yes, like that," he said, helping her to keep her rhythm.

Katherine shut her eyes, threw back her head as she

climaxed in his arms. Her satisfied sigh distracted him and at the peak of coming, he pulled out, wrapping his hand about his cock and pulled himself to climax.

She flopped against his chest and he held her close, running his hand along her back while they both regained their breaths.

"London will be so very boring when we return. Now that I've had you, how will I ever continue the life I had before? You've opened my eyes to what I've given up on, what I thought I didn't need," she murmured.

She laid her head against his shoulder and he met her gaze, leaning down to kiss her. He too wasn't unaffected by their joining. Hamish had never had an emotional reaction to having a woman before, he'd never had an over-whelming need to protect, to worry and care about her thoughts, needs and desires. His past liaisons had simply been sterile, non-emotional contacts. But with Katherine, something was different. He was different with her.

He liked her. A lot.

"Tell me something that you've never told another soul," he asked, wanting to know her better.

Her hand idly ran through his hair and she sighed. "I lied to you when I told you I wear breeches to work. I never wear them and had my father found out about my attire I would've been locked in my room until I expired of old age."

Hamish chuckled, not expecting that declaration of honesty. "You were very comfortable in them. What made you do it?"

"I found out you were to be at the house that day and I wanted to shock you, tease you even."

His hands ran down her back, sliding over one globe of her ass and his cock twitched. "Well, it worked. As I watched you walk up the stairs I thought of nothing other than whipping you into a vacant room, and removing those breeches."

"Really," she said, leaning up and kissing him.

Yes, really.

His heart thumped hard in his chest. "Maybe we could continue our affair in London, Katherine." He was a cad, he should never ask her to continue such an affair. The risk was all hers being unmarried and not his social equal. But he could not help himself. There was no doubt their paths would cross in London, their mutual friends ensured that. How could he turn away from her, not want her every time they met.

It would be torture and he couldn't do it. A warning gong sounded in his mind that he was going against his own rules, but at this moment, with the thought of not having Katherine in his arms again, just as she was now wasn't appealing. Hamish shoved the rules aside. They would simply have to be careful, both with not being caught and not getting her with child.

Her hand fluttered against his chest, settling over his heart. "You want that?"

He nodded without hesitation. "I do. You are not rid of me yet, Miss Martin, and until you've had your fill of me, that is how things will stay."

She sat up, squirming against him again. "What else can we do, Lord Leighton. I'm yours."

Her words rang with sincerity and spiked his lust. What was so different about her? What made her so special. "You're playing with fire, Katherine. Are you sure you want to know?"

She chuckled, her breasts grazing his chest and hardening his cock to rock. "Oh yes, I want to know and do everything before our time is up."

The thought of not having her this way, then watching

her walk out of his life and being only an acquaintance left a sour taste in his mouth. He would have her, care for her for as long as she wished him to. He hoisted her onto the side of the spring, sliding his hands against her thighs. "Lay back and open your legs. I want to taste you."

She bit her lip and he inwardly groaned. "If I do as you ask, can you promise me you'll allow me to do the same to you?"

Last evening she'd touched his cock, stroked it with her hand, but he'd not allowed anything else for fear of losing all control. The thought of her having her beautiful lips wrapped about his member, suckling hard, her tongue licking up his member almost made his eyes roll back in his head. "Very well, but first, it's my turn."

Katherine did as he asked. "Teach me," she said, sighing as he kissed her mons.

Oh, he intended to.

CHAPTER 12

H amish sat in the library at his mother's townhouse, a pile of paperwork on his desk, some of which related to the rebuilding of his townhouse in Berkley Square. The letter, scrawled in delicate hand was signed by Katherine's father, but Hamish knew she'd written every word.

Since their return to London a month past, they had been inseparable, stealing away at events, coming together at nights when he'd take her home from balls and parties. He couldn't wait for his home to be completed so he could take her there instead, have her in his own bed and not a bloody carriage or room at a ball or party.

Hamish hadn't delved too much into what Katherine had come to mean to him, but what he did know was that he cared for her more than he'd cared for anyone else. Her happiness was paramount in his life, and that she still met his desire with as much eagerness as she did told him more than words ever could that they suited.

A knock sounded on his door, and he placed down Katherine's letter telling him that the construction part of his property was now complete, and the interior would commence, handled by Mr. Thomas Hope. It was a letter stating that her father's part in the reconstruction of his home was at an end and that payment would be due.

"Enter," he said, not liking the thought of going back to Berkley Square and not seeing Katherine there, dressed in breeches, the small grey cap perched jauntily atop her hair and looking so delectable that he'd had to steal her away one day and have her. He'd managed to lock them in his dining room where he'd taken her on the table. Never would he ever look at the mahogany set with anything but fondness.

"May I come in, Lord Leighton?" Lizzie stood at the door. He gestured her to come in.

"Have a seat, Lizzie." She did as he bade, and he gave her his full attention. "How can I help you?"

She clasped her hands tight in her lap, and her wringing of them gave her anxiety away.

"What troubles you?" he asked, placing down his quill.

Tears sprang into her eyes and he balked, not used to such feminine theatrics. Katherine never lost her countenance, she was calm and collected with everything. All except their lovemaking. He shook the thoughts aside and concentrated on Lizzie and her problem.

"Your mother wishes for us to marry my lord and I didn't know who else to turn to. For weeks she has been pushing me to gain your favour, but this time she's gone too far, and I cannot do it."

Hamish clenched his jaw not surprised Lizzie's upset was caused by his meddling parent. "What has she asked of you?" He hated to know, but if he was going to deal with the situation, and his mother in particular, he needed to know everything.

"She wanted me to be caught in your arms, near ruin

me so you would, as a gentleman, have to offer for me. I cannot do it, my lord. As much as I respect you and thank you for your service during the season, I do only feel brotherly affections for you."

After her impassioned speech, Hamish had to admit for a new-found respect for Miss Doherty. He'd thought her his mother's pawn and creature, but the girl had spunk, a little independent will and he liked that. She would need her backbone when his mother learned of her treachery.

"I thank you for being honest and notifying me of my mother's less than proper proposition. I shall speak to her and I can assure you, you will finish out the season without any influence from her or what her wishes are."

The girl pulled out a handkerchief and dabbed at her cheeks. "She'll send me back to the country where I shall die an old maid and never have what so many of my friends do."

The notion made him think of Katherine and the fact that at six and twenty she was termed old maid already and well on the shelf. The idea didn't sit well with him, never had. A woman of such independence of mind, a beautiful soul inside and out should never sit on a shelf and die an old maid, never loved or cherished.

"I promise you, that will never happen. And surely, there are men closer to you in age that have caught your attention. You will not pass away an old maid."

"I have no dowry, my lord. My father has settled everything on my brother and all that's left for me is a measly two-hundred pounds per year gifted to my husband upon my marriage. I may have admirers already, but I do not have the money to tempt them to propose. I seem to be only worth monetary value within our Society, not the value placed on myself."

She met his gaze, her words striking him as an unfortunate truth in their lives.

"I therefore shall never marry, for I cannot buy my husband," she said with a bitterness normally not seen in one so young.

Hamish stood, coming around the desk to lean on it before her. "I'll not allow that. Because you're under our protection, I shall ensure that such a thing will never happen. I will give you a dowry Miss Doherty. Ten thousand pounds in fact, a measly sum to my family, but, there is a condition."

"But my lord, I couldn't possibly. That's too much," she stammered, eyes flaring with shock.

"It is done. I shall have the papers drawn up by month's end, but as I said, there is a condition."

"And that is?" She'd paled, but she seemed to be listening.

"That we keep it a secret. And then, Lizzie, when you find the right gentleman, who'll love you as poor as you supposedly are, you'll know its love. You'll know that he is the right man for you."

She sat there for a moment, her mouth agape with no sound, before she jumped up, throwing her arms about him and hugging him tight. "Oh, thank you so much, Lord Leighton. Thank you so much. I shall be forever grateful and if you ever need anything, just say the word and I shall stand beside you always."

He set her back, shaking his head. "There is no need to thank me, you've paid penance enough for the dowry having to spend the season with my mother. Now," he said, pushing her toward the door, the paperwork on his desk waiting for no one. "Be on your way and enjoy what's left of the season, and don't be too quick to choose a husband.

Sometimes the one for you will arrive when you least expect it."

She nodded and quietly closed the door behind him. Hamish stared at it a moment, thinking of Katherine and how she had arrived in his life not at eighteen, and new to town, but at six and twenty, a woman, one who knew her mind, and wanted to know all that her body was capable of. A woman who worked for her living, and ran a very successful business.

Lizzie reminded him in many ways of his sister. Of her trepidation at having a London Season and trying to make a grand match. Luckily for May she'd married for love, a consolation considering she passed away giving birth to her other greatest love. He'd given his sister very similar advice that he'd given to Lizzie. To marry the man of her choosing, not that of their parent. After all, it was they who had to live with their choice when it was all said and done.

He smiled, thinking of Katherine. He would see her tonight at Lord and Lady Oliver's ball, the event of the season by all accounts. He would be returning to Hollyvale in a few weeks and the idea of leaving Katherine in town left a sour taste in his mouth. Would she come with him? If he invited their friends, perhaps she would, and then he could have her there, in his home, spend time with just her and no one else.

The word marriage flittered through his mind and he paused. Could he marry her, have a life with her? Panic tore through him at the thought of her getting with a child and dying. He could no longer deny what he felt for Katherine, for it was love, absolute, uncensored love, but he'd loved his sister too, and she had still died. Nothing could save her, other than the choice of not having children.

He doubted he'd be able to stop Katherine from wanting children and she deserved to be a mother, she didn't deserve to have his fears, his nightmares become her future. No, she deserved so much more than that.

CHAPTER 13

The ball was well under way, and Katherine had danced and laughed the night away with Cecilia and Darcy, along with Lord Leighton who hadn't left her side. He'd danced a waltz with her, stepped out with his mother's ward Miss Lizzie Doherty who seemed a lovely young woman, beside the fact she had to deal with Hamish's mother most days. Hamish had then danced with her again but seemed quite content not to move from his current position and dance with any others.

It suited Katherine perfectly well. She adored having him dote on her, and that's exactly what he'd been doing since their return from Surrey. Within their friendship group it was no longer a secret of their liaison. The duke had warned her of the scandal that would break should such a liaison become public knowledge. They'd been very discreet and careful and there was no reason why their relationship could not continue. At least in her mind.

Lord Leighton reached down between them and slid his finger over her pinkie. "Meet me in the music room. No one will be in there."

Need coursed through her veins and she met his gaze, reveling in the desire and heat that she saw there. He looked exactly how she felt. "Where is it?"

"Head toward the withdrawing room upstairs, but on the landing, turn right instead of left. It's the only door on the right-hand side of the corridor. I'll leave it ajar," he whispered, moving away through the throng.

Katherine made a point of taking little heed of his leaving and turned to Cecilia who was discussing the invitation Lord Leighton had bestowed on them all for a month-long house party at his country estate after the Season. Upon receiving the invite she'd thrilled at the idea of seeing his home, and yet, the thought gave her pause. They had been having an affair for almost two months and he had not once suggested as to when they would end, when he'd wish to leave.

And even though she'd asked him to sleep with her, show and teach her everything, it now felt like an arrangement, almost as if she'd become his mistress. Not that he wasn't caring, or loyal to her, for she never doubted that, only that she wanted more. Being loved by Hamish had showed her that she was valued as a woman, not just a Long Meg with plain hair that people passed over. But a woman, one who now knew how to love, not just Lord Leighton but herself. She did not dress to please anyone but herself, and she certainly carried herself as an equal with her friends. Never would she allow anyone to cast her out as if she was nothing but trade. But as time progressed, each liaison she had with Hamish had started to make her feel as if she wasn't worth more than a tumble. And it was no longer enough.

"I'm going to the retiring room. I shall be back shortly," she said, bobbing a small curtsy to her grace and the marquess and marchioness.

The room was easy to find and entering she quickly looked to ensure no one had seen her and shut the door. Hamish stood by the windows, looking out over the gardens. Her heart did a little flip and she took her fill of him before walking over to where he stood.

"You look so beautiful tonight," he said, kissing her. It had been almost two weeks since they'd seen each other, and the embrace quickly turned from sedate, and sweet to incendiary. Somehow, each time they were together they just worked. They knew where each other liked to be touched, what kisses drove the other mad, and Katherine clung to him, meeting his demand with her own to match.

"I have to have you," he murmured.

Katherine acquiesced his request, wanting him too, and forgetting her own misgivings of earlier let him push her over toward a settee. There was time to discuss what they were, whatever that may be. They could do that tomorrow, away from the ball and any eavesdropping matrons of the *ton*. Tonight, right now, she wanted to have him all to herself, love him as much as she adored him and show him that she was his, if only he'd ask.

The settee hit the back of her legs and she sat. Hamish didn't waste any time before bearing her down, hitching her skirts up about her waist, his hand sliding against her core in tantalising strokes.

"I cannot get enough of you," he said, his voice roughened with desire. He kneeled between her legs and ripped at his frontfalls, coming back over her and thrusting into her hard. They both moaned at the sheer delight of being together in this way. He kissed her hard, and she gasped as he pushed her toward a fast climax. They fit so perfectly well, and she shut her eyes as tears pricked behind her lids. She wouldn't become emotional over their joining, even if it was so very good. All that she'd hoped to have with a husband one day, back when she'd thought to marry.

His strokes deepened and with it the pleasure of their joining teased with exquisite torture. "Hamish, just there. Don't stop."

The whispered word 'never' tickled her ear and ecstasy rocked through her, hard and fast and she muffled her moan into the shoulder of his jacket. He took her without restraint then and with a muffled groan found his own pleasure within her.

The moment he did he stilled.

"What's wrong?" she asked, pulling her head back from his shoulder to look at him.

"I didn't pull out," he said, frowning. "Damn it, Katherine. I'm sorry."

She shook her head, dismissing the idea that the one time he'd made such an error would ever result in a baby. "I'm sure it'll be fine. Let us not needlessly worry unless we need to."

The fact that he hadn't mentioned that he'd marry her should the mistake result in a child, hurt. Hamish had come to mean so much to her. Did he feel the same? By his reaction she could only assume he hadn't come to feel for her as she did for him. For it had been many weeks since Katherine, without any doubt came to realize she loved him. With all her heart and would give anything for him to feel the same.

He moved off her, righting his clothes and she stood, doing the same, going over to a nearby mirror and fixing her hair. "I had better return to the ball. I shall see you again soon." Moving toward the door, he grabbed her arm, pulling her to stop.

Leaning down, Hamish kissed her with such tenderness that she pulled away and left without another word. Why she was so emotional made no sense, she was not normally a woman who succumbed to hysterics. She just needed some time, to think about what she would say to Hamish when she saw him again, but no matter what, if they were not going to have a future, then the liaison had to come to an end. The thought made her double over and she leaned against the wall, not wanting to even imagine a future without him. Why did she have to proposition him? Why did she have to know what lying with a man would be like? If only it wasn't going to be her heart that broke in two when he agreed to her fears and they parted as friends.

THE FOLLOWING day Katherine had been summoned to the Duchess of Athelby's for afternoon tea, but upon arrival found only Darcy and Cecilia present. Pleasure at having her friends to herself was soon replaced by the tempered looks they cast her upon arrival.

Katherine sat in the available wing back chair, folding her hands in her lap and wondered what was amiss. "You two are very glum this afternoon. Is there something wrong?"

Darcy poured the tea, throwing her a tentative smile before sitting down. Cecilia was quiet, contemplative and taking a sip of her tea then placed the cup on the linen covered table and met her eyes. "You were seen last night, in the music room, and not by us. Should it have been any one of us, as your friends we would've hidden any infraction you may have taken part in, but we cannot hide what is in today's gossip rag."

Thankfully Katherine was seated, for had she been standing her legs would've surely given out. She'd been seen? Oh, dear lord, which part had they seen? The kiss or the second act where Lord Leighton had pinned her upon the sofa and…Oh no…

She cringed, and picking up the paper, read the words that seemed to scream out at her, mocking and ripping her reputation to shreds. Harlot!

"Father reads this paper." Her heart skidded to a stop, her gown too tight, the room spun and distantly she heard Darcy call out for salts. Within a moment she was cast back to reality, but no sooner had that occurred the thought of what all of London knew, what they were thinking ricocheted through her mind.

She read the article a second time, not wanting to believe what was written in black and white.

A certain woman, with the initials of KM, from a social sphere several steps below that of the ton was seen frittering with a certain gentleman Lord L. The lady seen, in a most compromising position will not reconstruct her reputation from here, no matter how well her family have the ability since its their specialized trade.

"I'M RUINED. I should probably leave." Katherine stood, and Darcy reached out a hand, stopping her.

"You're not going anywhere. What happened last night, Katherine, we need to know. The duke has gone to fetch Lord Leighton as we speak, there are things we must do to try and salvage your reputation."

Katherine stood and walked to the decanter of whisky, pouring herself a glass, drinking it down before repeating it all again. Her father would be crushed to know she'd fallen. He would be livid, which was not a state that Katherine ever saw him in. And she'd done that to him. She'd embarrassed everyone including herself.

She met her friends' concerned eyes and sighed. "You know I wanted an affair with Lord Leighton, to experience a little of what you both have. I had resigned myself to never marry, never finding the man whom I loved and respected."

"That is not true, Kat. You're a beautiful woman and anyone would be honoured to marry you. If only you would let us seek you potential suitors," Cecilia said, taking her hand.

Katherine squeezed it a little before letting it go. Either way, her friend's words did not change what she knew to be true. Had she been desirable, attractive she would've married years ago. Her dowry was large, more than a lot of people imagined, but even that had not been tempting enough. Or too tempting and her only courtiers were fortune hunters. "Lord Leighton is famous for his blonde, goddess like women who have curves in all the right places. Beautiful skin, and sparkling eyes. I may have pretty eyes, I will admit to that, but my hair is the colour of rats' fur."

"Katherine, that is absurd. Stop talking about yourself in such a way. I'll not allow it," the duchess declared, crossing her arms about her front.

"But you will allow it because it's the truth. The only reason why Lord Leighton and I were together was because he owed me a favour. Nothing more. I've come to realize that now."

The front door slammed and within a moment the front parlor door opened and in walked Lord Leighton and the Duke of Athelby. Hamish looked wretched, his hair askew and cravat laying untied about his neck.

The duke went to stand over beside a window, looking

out onto the street, and Hamish came over to her, kneeling beside her.

"Kat, I'm so sorry. I should never have allowed all that I have to happen between us, and now I've ruined you."

"You must fix this, Leighton. Make this right," the duke said, not looking at them.

"Right?" Hamish asked, frowning at the duke. "And how do you suppose I'd manage that?"

Heat bloomed on Katherine's cheeks and she stood, walking over to stand before the fire, suddenly chilled. "He means make it right by marrying me, Lord Leighton."

His lordship met her eyes, the horror on his features all that she needed to see to know her place. The little piece of her heart that hoped he may care for her, would wish to maybe marry her instead of continuing his bachelor ways shrivelled and died.

The shock and disappointment in Darcy and Cecilia's gaze made her understand more than ever before that he was only ever having fun. And it was her own fault, she'd offered herself as a prize, too ugly and thin to be worthy of love, too tarnished by trade, housed too far away from Mayfair to be suitable. She should've let Lord Leighton have his skull cracked open that night at the Inn. She should've walked away, but she hadn't. Because she'd known who he was and knew they had mutual friends, even if he wasn't aware.

"I must go," she said, walking to the door.

Lord Leighton crossed in front of her, blocking her way.

"Katherine, we will make this right. I shall not allow your reputation to be tarnished over something that cannot be proved."

She shook her head, not knowing that someone who had given her so much ecstasy only hours before could cause so much pain that she physically hurt. "Go to hell, Hamish. I want nothing from you."

"You will marry my friend, or I'll call you out," Cecilia said, standing and throwing her hands on her hips.

Katherine smiled in thanks, but she could never marry a man who did not want her.

"Thank you, Lia, but I wouldn't marry Lord Leighton now even if he asked?"

"Why not?" Hamish and Darcy demanded in unison.

"I don't intend to marry at all and I can promise you that I would never marry a man who hesitated, promised all sorts of ways to fix the ruination of my reputation, all but the one way in which to fix it. Marriage. I knew when we were together from the first that it was a risk, but I was willing to take it for one night with you. I will not throw myself at your mercy, for a union with a man who does not care for me." Katherine dipped into a small curtsy and left, only making the front steps before tears broke free and her shoulders shook in despair.

He had not been falling in love with her as she had been with him. She'd been alone in that emotion. The stone pavement shivered before her and without warning, she ran for the small hedged garden that sat on either side of the door and cast up her accounts.

A woman she'd seen at a ball stopped and looked down her nose at Katherine. She pulled out her handkerchief. If her ruination hadn't been sealed by todays paper, vomiting in front of Lady Cavendish certainly put paid to that.

CHAPTER 14

Hamish returned home to his country estate, disinviting his friends to join him, friends that had rallied about Miss Martin, consoling her in her upset, her despair of being ruined. He'd left for his estate, the draw of the city no longer what it once was, and nor would it ever be again.

Katherine was lost to him, despised him, just as Marchioness of Aaron and the Duchess of Athelby did as well. With their scorn, their husbands also saw less of him, withholding their invitations to dinners at their homes.

He sat alone in his dining room and stared at the long, deserted table before him. After seeing Katherine leave him at the duke and duchess of Athelby's home, he'd been in such a blind state of panic that he'd not chased her. Instead, he'd listened to the duke rile at him over his atrocious behaviour.

It was all he could do not to scream back. He'd been honest from the start with Katherine, had tried to make her see that he could not promise anything, that he didn't wish for a wife or children. Other than that one time, he'd been so careful with her, not wanting her to have consequences from their times together.

All a cold comfort for the pain at not having seen her, of having no contact or knowing if she was well tore him in two. He picked up his wine and poured himself another glass. He'd thought that his time away from town, of having space and not seeing her would help him move on from their liaison.

He was a fool. If anything, his time away from Katherine only made him yearn more for her. Night after night he woke up in a cold sweat, not from want or desire, but simply concern, the knowledge that he was no longer privy to her whereabouts or if she was well. He should have chased after her. By doing nothing that day he may have severed any possibility of gaining back her affections.

Damn bloody fool! He muttered.

The door to the dining room opened and he glanced up, groaning when he realized who'd come to stay.

"Hello mother," he said, saluting her with his glass.

His mother stormed into the room. "How dare you! How dare you throw our family into such scandal. Having an affair with the woman who ran the rebuild of your home. I'm beyond disappointed." She whacked her gloves down on the table. "What do you have to say for yourself?"

Hamish shut his eyes and counted to ten, anything but to lose his temper. He wanted to lash out, and if his mother kept speaking to him in such a way she would be the recipient of his opinions.

"Miss Martin may not be titled or as well connected as us, but she's a lady and was raised as one. Do not speak ill of her."

"You know that she's ruined, that she is no longer

welcomed at any Society ball. I can expect such base actions from her, she is after all tarnished by trade, but you. You I expected much more from. To have been intimate with someone of such little connections is beyond the pale."

Hamish pushed back his chair and stood, throwing his napkin on the table. "Do not lecture me about how I live my life. And do not talk about Katherine in that way. I ruined her, I walked away from her and let her face the costs of our actions alone. If anyone should be derided, it is me, and the society that saw fit to judge her when it wasn't their damn business."

Shame washed over him that he'd left Katherine alone. He was a disgrace and he'd allowed his fear of losing her to get the better of him when she'd needed him most.

"What do I care what happens to the doxy? You, my son need to marry a woman of respectable birth and untarnished reputation as soon as possible."

Hamish knew his mother was hard, uncaring even, but this. This coldness and the disdain of others was beyond the pale. How could anyone be so heartless? "Do not speak to me of such things. I will not be marrying anyone of your choosing."

Her eyes darkened in temper and she slammed her fist down on the table. "You will do what I say for it is plainly clear that you're incapable of acting as a responsible adult."

He shook his head. "No mother."

She didn't reply, simply glared at him a moment. "Who then? Who are you going to marry, for you had better marry someone to fix this scandalous mess our family now finds themselves in. Society will forgive you your affairs with whores, but to sleep with an unmarried woman who is under the protection of the Duke of Athelby through friendship, they will not."

"I will marry Miss Martin if she'll have me, just as I should have done weeks ago." He would return to town and fight for her forgiveness. Even if he had to lay himself bare on her doorstep and beg for forgiveness. First thing in the morning he would return to town and secure a marriage license. He would also have the housekeeper prepare the countess's room for their new mistress.

He would make this right again. He would beg Katherine's forgiveness and marry her if she'd have him. The thought of how he had not said anything, simply stood in the duchess's parlor that day like a simpleton and allowed her to walk out of his life.

"I will not allow a builder's daughter to be your bride."

Hamish started for the door. "Then I suggest you pack your things and move to the dower house, for I shall try until my last breath is spent to win back her love." For that was exactly what it was. Love. He loved her, and he would make it right again. In this, he could not fail. He would not fail Katherine again.

KATHERINE HEAVED into the bowl on her nightstand over and over again, the sickness had come on suddenly and every day now she had the nausea as a good morning present. But no mornings would ever be good again. Tomorrow she was traveling to a cottage on the duchess of Athelby's country estate where she would stay for the duration of her pregnancy and then after that...well, she wasn't even sure what would happen after that.

Her father had surprisingly supported her, listened to

her when she'd gone to him with her shame. He'd been a pillar of strength for her, and she would miss him when away.

A knock sounded on the door and she walked back to the bed, sitting on its side. "Enter," she said, taking the glass of water from the nightstand and having a sip.

"It's me, dearest. I'm sorry to disturb you, but you have a visitor." Darcy said.

"I cannot see anyone. Send them away." Katherine lay back on the bed, pulling the blankets up to her chin. If only she could hide away here forever.

She heard the door creak open further and then a voice she'd not expected or wished to hear again sounded at the threshold. "May I come in, Katherine?"

She bolted upright. "No," she gasped, "Get out of my room and my life."

The door closed, and she sighed, half in relief, half despair. In the moment when she'd needed him most three weeks ago he'd not chased after her, not tried to right his wrong the following day. Instead he'd hightailed it back to the country and left her to the wolves.

Bastard.

The bed dipped on the other side, and anger coursed through her veins when the door clicked shut. Obviously, Darcy approved of Lord Leighton coming to see her. Well, she did not so he could go the hell away.

"Katherine, while I know whatever I say will never be enough, I want you to know that I'm so sorry. I panicked. Marriage always leads to children and I could not bear that for you. Childbirth is such a risk, and I've already lost a sister to the vile undertaking that I could not risk your life in the same way."

She cringed, knowing what a useless apology this was.

When he found out that she was carrying his child she would watch him again hightail it out of London and this time she doubted she'd ever see him again.

"I love you. You're everything to me, since the moment we met you've drawn me into your goodness, your laughter and independence." The bed wobbled as he stood and came about to kneel at her side of the bed. He took her hands, kissing them quickly. "Marry me, please. Forgive me my sins and tell me that you're mine and I'm yours. Please, I cannot live without you a moment longer."

Tears prickled behind her lids and she sniffed. "You left me. You left me defenceless and alone. You turned away without a backward glance. I will never forgive you for that."

His pallor changed to a sickly grey at her words and she shuffled off the bed, the nausea back with a vengeance. Katherine heaved and the silence behind her was deafening in the room.

"You're pregnant, aren't you?"

Had the situation not been so dire, she would've laughed at the horror on his voice.

Katherine picked up a cloth from beside the bowl and wiped her face and mouth. "Aren't you smart to have worked that out. Now off you go, Lord Leighton. There is the door, let me watch you scuttle away like the coward you are."

He ran a hand through his hair, not moving.

Damn it, he needed to leave. The despair on his visage at her cutting words pulled at her emotions and she didn't want to feel anything for him anymore. Least of all feel sorry for him! He'd played *her* the fool, and she wouldn't have it, no matter that she still loved him. Loved him more than anything ever in her life, save for the babe now growing inside her.

"Please Katherine, hear me out. I couldn't marry you for I knew I couldn't deny you anything, even the wish to have children. I wanted to keep you safe, to spare you such a fate. It was wrong of me, I know that now. I allowed my fear, my grief to guide my reactions and I will never forgive myself for it. Please, don't send me away."

"Why are you here, my lord? I am not the type of woman you're famous for having a taste for. What does it matter that a woman from Cheapside does not accept your hand in marriage? If we marry, you will soon tire of me and seek comfort elsewhere. I'm not willing to risk my heart in such a way. If I ever marry it shall be for love, and above all else loyalty and respect. You, Lord Leighton are lacking on the last two virtues."

"Did you just admit to loving me?" he said, stepping toward her. "For if it is love that you feel for me, and love that I feel for you, then surely that is as good a place as any to rebuild our trust and respect?"

She turned away from him, hating that her body yearned for the man while her mind railed at his treachery. "No, it's not."

He came about and stood before her. "Yes, it is. It is exactly the right base on which to start a life together, the very best, for with love, there is nothing that can break such a bond." He kneeled before her, looking up to meet her gaze. "Marry me, Kat. Be my wife and countess. Allow me to give you children. I cannot promise not to fuss over you, to worry and ensure you have the best doctors around at all times, but I shall try and tamper my anxiety over the condition if only you'll be the next countess of Leighton."

He held up a small velvet box and opened it. Inside sat a ring with the roundest, largest diamond Katherine had ever seen. Her heart skipped a beat.

"Your trinkets will not win me, my lord," she said,

wanting to look away from him and his gift, and yet, she couldn't do it. Both were magnificent really. His lordship begging for her was something she simply would not allow to stop. Not yet at least.

"I am the complete opposite to what you desire. I'm not blonde, full figured with birthing hips. You'll tire of me, leave me to rot in the country like so many noble women while you go about Covent Garden and spread your seed about like farmers feeding chickens."

He grinned, and she had to admit, the analogy wasn't the best one she'd ever thought of.

"You're everything that I want I just didn't know it. To me, there is no one more beautiful, of mind, body and soul. Make me a better man and say yes. Say yes to me, please."

She raised her brow, wanting to let him stew a little, while she thought about it.

"Katherine, your answer?" he said after a time. "What will it be, Miss Martin?"

She pursed her lips, coming to kneel with him. She took the ring and pulled it out, inspecting it while her stomach did somersaults. Could she forgive him. Could she marry an Earl?

"Yes," she said, slipping the ring on her finger and admiring it. Yes, she could.

He pulled her into a fierce hug and she laughed as he kissed every inch of her cheeks, her nose, her lips. "I love you. So much. I love you so much it hurts to think I could've lost you."

She nodded, running her hand through his hair and realizing she'd missed this, missed them. "I love you too." Katherine swallowed not wanting to cry and yet, she found Hamish wiping away a stray tear off her cheek.

"We will marry tomorrow. I have a special license and

then by tomorrow night you will be safely ensconced at my estate Hollyvale in Kent. And there, my dear, we will start our life together, raise our children and enjoy our existence."

"That sounds simply perfect."

EPILOGUE

T he day of their daughter's second birthday started
with a thunderstorm and by afternoon the sun had
come out. Much like the day of her birth. On that day,
Lord Leighton had stormed about the house, yelling at
everything, cursing God and anyone who came within
visual contact of him, and then by afternoon, when Rose
had been born, he was all calm again. The happiest and
most relieved lord in all of England.

Katherine had forgiven him his outbursts that day. She
knew what it had cost him emotionally to see her go
through with the birth, the worry, the fear. He was not
alone, giving birth to a child was not an easy thing to do,
and at times she hadn't thought she was capable of
following through. But a woman's body is a strong and
powerful thing, and she had managed through it. And in a
few short months she would manage it again.

She hoped it was a boy, if only so Hamish would have
a daughter and son. Two perfect little cherubs that they
would love and adore until their dying breath.

Katherine finished reading the little nursery book to

Rose, and set her on her feet, just as her papa entered the bedchamber.

"How is my little princess," he said, picking her up and kissing her cheek. "Happy birthday beautiful girl."

"Present," their daughter said, clapping her hands.

Katherine laughed, how quickly children learned what birthdays and Christmas meant.

"Present," Hamish said in mock surprise. "You wish for a present?"

Rose nodded, her eyes bright with expectation.

Hamish set her down and tapped her bottom, pushing her toward the window. "Look outside princess and you'll see your gift."

Katherine stood and walked Rose to the window, pulling back the curtain she grinned at what she saw being led about on the lawns. A little white pony, with a great big pink bow tied about its neck.

Rose squealed and turned about, running for the door as fast as her little, unbalanced legs would take her.

"I think she likes it," Katherine said, taking Hamish's hand and following Rose. Her nursemaid picked Rose up before she reached the stairs and together they all walked outside to see the new addition to the family.

"She's beautiful, Hamish. Rose already loves her."

"It's a filly, and is very placid, I made sure of that. I think it will make a suitable first horse for our daughter."

Katherine leaned up and kissed him, not caring that their staff were about, not that she ever did, not from the first day she'd become mistress of this great estate, and the many others he owned.

"Thank you, Katherine."

She frowned up at him. "Whatever do you mean? Why are you thanking me?"

He met her gaze, his serious of a sudden. "For this life.

Had I not met you, had I not been having the worst start of any season I'd ever partaken in, I would not have met you or been given the greatest gift of all, our child."

She clasped his jaw, rubbing her thumb across his cheek. "You too have given me more than I could ever wish for, so thank you too. We're equal in this, Hamish. Always have been."

He nodded and turned his attention back to their daughter. Katherine stayed where she was as Hamish lifted Rose onto the saddle and holding her, allowed the groom to walk them about the yard.

This, Katherine mused was what life was meant for, meant to be like. Total bliss with abundance of love. How wonderful that a woman of little beauty, social value and dirt beneath her gloved fingernails had been perfect for one of London's most revered rogues. Had been enough to tempt an Earl.

Dear Reader,

Thank you for taking the time to read my Lords of London box set! I hope you enjoyed the first three books in this series.

I adore my readers, and I'm so thankful for your support. If you're able, I would appreciate an honest review of *Lords of London, Books 1-3*. As they say, feed an author, leave a review!

If you'd like to continue the series, the Lords of London box set, books 4-6 are now available. I have included the prologue of To Vex a Viscount for your reading pleasure.

Tamara Gill

TO VEX A VISCOUNT

Lords of London, Book 4

For the past six years, Miss Lizzie Doherty has had exactly zero proposals. Not because she isn't attractive, or from a good family, or doesn't have well-connected friends, but simply because she is poor. Or so the ton believe. Invited to a country house party on a stormy night, her journey takes an unexpected turn when her driver delivers her to the wrong estate. Upon entering the home, she's soon masked and sworn to

secrecy. Never has Lizzie ever experienced such an odd and intriguing event, so she plays along to see where the night will take her.

Lord Hugo, Viscount Wakely lives for sin, for anything scandalous, and for house parties that involve all of those things. At least he used to. But imagine his surprise when his good friends' ward, Miss Lizzie Doherty, an innocent and a successful debutante six years running, arrives at the last debauchery house party he'll attend. Or when an impromptu, scandalous kiss turns his life upside down.

Lizzie decides to stay for the week-long house party. Masks keep the guests' identities secret, but Lizzie would know Lord Hugo Wakely anywhere. And that one impromptu, scandalous kiss tells her that he is the Viscount for her…he just doesn't know it yet.

PROLOGUE

J. Smith & Sons Solicitors, London, August 1812

Lord Hugo Blythe, fourth Viscount Wakely, stared mutely at his solicitor of many years, Mr. Thompson. He blinked, fighting to comprehend the meaning behind the gentleman's words.

Damn my father to hell. Had he not already been dead, Hugo might have killed him himself for playing such a game.

"I'm sorry, but can you explain to me again what the terms are of my father's will? I'm not sure it's making sense to me. You said I must marry within a year? This part I'm a little muddled about." How he dearly wished there really was some confusion on his part.

Mr. Thompson, a stout older gentleman with a receding hairline but honest features, threw him a pitying glance and then stared down at the paperwork before him again.

"The will explains that as per your birthright, you inherit the title of viscount, and Bolton Abbey, along with

395

the London home and the estate in Cumbria and Ireland. However, the dowry your mother brought to the family upon her marriage to your father will revert to her family should you not marry by your thirtieth birthday. I believe that is less than twelve months away."

Disbelief sat in Hugo's gut like a heavy boulder. "Only just. July twenty-third, to be exact," he said, running a hand over his jaw. How could his father do this to him? Of course, they'd had many discussions—very well, arguments—about his dallying and raking about town without any direction toward marriage, but to do this to him, forcing his hand, was beyond cruel.

His solicitor placed down his papers and met his gaze. "I suggest that you find a wife before the end of the next season. If you fail to satisfy that clause, the money will go to your uncle in New York according to your father's instructions. Your uncle has been notified of this condition and is receptive to claiming the money that went with his sister to your father upon their marriage. The clause is quite watertight and cannot be waived. Of course, looking at the financial statements regarding your inheritance, should you lose this money, there will be very little remaining to keep the estates running. You may have to look to leasing them out indefinitely, as you're unable to sell due to them being entailed properties."

A weight settled on Hugo's shoulders and he slumped back in his chair, not having known it was as bad as all that. "Did Father state exactly who I'm to marry?" He'd certainly spoken loudly enough from beyond the grave with his will, he might as well also state who was acceptable.

"As to that…" Mr. Thompson said, shifting on his seat and looking a little uncomfortable for the first time during their meeting.

The weight on Hugo's shoulders doubled.

"Your father has stipulated that not only are you to marry before your thirtieth birthday, but you are also required to marry a woman of fortune, as he did. No less than thirty thousand pounds must be her dowry. Your father wrote that he asks this of you to ensure that the family name, and all those who rely on your lands for their livelihood, are kept secure. He also wrote that he believes you are more than capable of this task, and he wishes you well and every happiness in your future marriage."

Hugo met his solicitor's gaze, unable to fathom what he was being told. He'd thought he would have more time before he settled down. He very much enjoyed being an eligible bachelor, but the select, very scandalous house parties that he was accustomed to would all have to stop if he were to find a wife. How dull. A wife. His life was over.

Mr. Thompson stood, holding out a rolled-up copy of the will tied with dark pink ribbon. Hugo clasped it, the urge to scrunch it up into a ball of rubbish being his first thought.

"Good luck, Lord Wakely. If you have any further questions, please do not hesitate to call on me. I'm at your disposal whenever you need."

Hugo shook his hand, then, swiping up his hat and gloves, strode for the door. "Thank you, sir. Once I have found the poor victim who will become my wife, I shall be in contact."

And she would be a victim, for a marriage made in haste, and solely due to requiring funds, would never be a good match. He'd always admired the love match marriages of the couples with whom he associated, knowing he too would desire such a connection for himself. Just not yet.

He stopped on the cobbled pavement and slammed his

beaver hat on his head. *Damn.* If what the solicitor said was true, and there was no doubt that it was—he had the will in his hands to prove it—then he had to find a wife.

Eleven months approximately before his time was up. Before his uncle made the trip across the Atlantic and took back what was rightfully Hugo's. His birthright.

Well, he wouldn't have it. He would adhere to the clause, but he would enjoy his final year as an unmarried gentleman as well. There was nothing he disliked more than being told by his father what to do. That his sire had managed this from beyond the grave was not something he'd thought the old curmudgeon capable of, but alas, he was wrong.

He swore. Eleven months and then, and only then would he find a willing heiress wanting a marriage of convenience, and be done with it.

In all the past Seasons he'd failed to find anyone who inspired him with anything other than with lust, so, in the next season, he would marry a biddable heiress to secure his properties. A perfectly convenient plan if ever he had one.

Under no circumstances was he willing to lose his lands, have to lease out his estates, and live off meager funds for the rest of his life. His name would be ruined; he'd be a lord pitied by everyone. The Wakelys had never had to ask for money, and he would not be the first one to do so. He shuddered. Oh no, that would never do.

Heiress hunting he would go. Well, in eleven months in any case.

Want to read more? Purchase, Lords of London, Books 4-6 today!

ALSO BY TAMARA GILL

Royal House of Atharia Series
TO DREAM OF YOU
A ROYAL PROPOSITION
FOREVER MY PRINCESS

League of Unweddable Gentlemen Series
TEMPT ME, YOUR GRACE
HELLION AT HEART
DARE TO BE SCANDALOUS
TO BE WICKED WITH YOU
KISS ME DUKE
THE MARQUESS IS MINE

Kiss the Wallflower series
A MIDSUMMER KISS
A KISS AT MISTLETOE
A KISS IN SPRING
TO FALL FOR A KISS
A DUKE'S WILD KISS
TO KISS A HIGHLAND ROSE
KISS THE WALLFLOWER - BOOKS 1-3 BUNDLE

Lords of London Series
TO BEDEVIL A DUKE
TO MADDEN A MARQUESS

TO TEMPT AN EARL

TO VEX A VISCOUNT

TO DARE A DUCHESS

TO MARRY A MARCHIONESS

LORDS OF LONDON - BOOKS 1-3 BUNDLE

LORDS OF LONDON - BOOKS 4-6 BUNDLE

To Marry a Rogue Series

ONLY AN EARL WILL DO

ONLY A DUKE WILL DO

ONLY A VISCOUNT WILL DO

ONLY A MARQUESS WILL DO

ONLY A LADY WILL DO

A Time Traveler's Highland Love Series

TO CONQUER A SCOT

TO SAVE A SAVAGE SCOT

TO WIN A HIGHLAND SCOT

Time Travel Romance

DEFIANT SURRENDER

A STOLEN SEASON

Scandalous London Series

A GENTLEMAN'S PROMISE

A CAPTAIN'S ORDER

A MARRIAGE MADE IN MAYFAIR

SCANDALOUS LONDON - BOOKS 1-3 BUNDLE

High Seas & High Stakes Series

HIS LADY SMUGGLER

HER GENTLEMAN PIRATE

HIGH SEAS & HIGH STAKES - BOOKS 1-2 BUNDLE

Daughters Of The Gods Series

BANISHED-GUARDIAN-FALLEN

DAUGHTERS OF THE GODS - BOOKS 1-3 BUNDLE

Stand Alone Books

TO SIN WITH SCANDAL

OUTLAWS

ABOUT THE AUTHOR

Tamara Gill is an Australian author who grew up in an old mining town in country South Australia, where her love of history was founded. So much so, she made her darling husband travel to the UK for their honeymoon, where she dragged him from one historical monument and castle to another.

A mother of three, her two little gentlemen in the making, a future lady (she hopes) and a part-time job keep her busy in the real world, but whenever she gets a moment's peace she loves to write romance novels in an array of genres, including regency, medieval and time travel.

www.tamaragill.com
tamaragillauthor@gmail.com

Printed in Great Britain
by Amazon

81617373R00231